each moment, only once

a novel

by David L. Young

Nousemoise Publishing
Baltimore, Maryland

Nousemoise Publishing
627 Anneslie Road
Baltimore, MD 21212
nmpublisher.com

Library of Congress Cataloging-in-Publication Data

Young, David L.
Each moment, only once / by David L. Young
     p. cm.
Includes bibliographical references and index.
     ISBN 978-0-9822866-5-4
Library of Congress Control Number: 2009902040

10 9 8 7 6 5 4 3 2 1

cover artwork by Sarah Dougherty

Rain King
Words by Adam Duritz
Music by Adam Duritz and David Bryson
© 1993 EMI BLACKWOOD MUSIC INC. and JONES FALLS MUSIC

Raining in Baltimore
Words by Adam Duritz
Words and Music by Adam Duritz and David Bryson
© 1993 EMI BLACKWOOD MUSIC INC. and JONES FALLS MUSIC

The Ghost In You
Words and Music by Richard Butler and Tim Butler
© 1984 EMI SONGS LTD.

Monkey
Words by Adam Duritz
Music by Adam Duritz and David Bryson
© 1996 EMI BLACKWOOD MUSIC INC. and JONES FALLS MUSIC

I Miss You
Words and Music by Brandon Boyd, Michael Einziger, Alex Katunich, Jose Pasillas II and
    Chris Kilmore
© 1999 EMI APRIL MUSIC INC. and HUNGLIKEYORA MUSIC

Hard Candy
Words and Music by Adam Duritz, Charles Gillingham, Daniel Vickrey, David Bryson, Mat
    thew Malley, Ben Mize, and David Immergluck
© 2002 EMI BLACKWOOD MUSIC INC. and JONES FALLS MUSIC

Anna Begins
Words by Adam Duritz
Music by David Bryson, Marty Jones, Toby Hawkins, Lydia Holly, and Adam Duritz
© 1993 EMI BLACKWOOD MUSIC INC., JONES FALLS MUSIC, KNUCKLEVISION MUSIC,
    PUPPET HEAD SONGS, and SIREN SAYS MUSIC

For Tiff, Mae, and Scottie B (wherever it is that life has taken them) and for Nick, Curtis, and Katie for having faith.

Acknowledgements

To the ones I love:

I have found that, most of the time, things rarely become what they were intended to be. We start off life, and goals, and projects with these ideal expectations of what they should become. But what we fail to realize is that our lives, goals, projects, and even expectations are evolving, themselves. I have very different hopes for this book now than I once did.

There is simply no way that I could have achieved all that I have without the support of my friends and family. Had my father not inspired me with his love of literature and creativity, I don't believe I would ever have found my voice. Had my mother not continually encouraged me to write my heart out, I may have never put the pencil to these pages. My siblings have always believed that I could do absolutely anything in this world, even when I fought them wholeheartedly to deny it. They got me through what was undoubtedly the most difficult time of my life and there are no words that I could write to express my gratitude for that.

Somehow in my 25 years of aimless wandering, I managed to stumble across the coolest people in the world and gather them into my life. My daily solace is that I am most often surrounded by them. These are the people who saw this project through every stage and transition and supported me every step. If it were not for you, this book would still be a jumbled pile of paper in my desk drawers. Thank you.

The events of this book are my past. In no way do these views affect my love for any of you whatsoever. Please forgive my honesty.

one

To every story, there is one result. There cannot be two. There is only one. Each decision dictates the next, and so the web is woven, and the story is made. I cannot say that I remember exactly how it happened, only that it did. Memory is a funny thing how it reconstructs history to include only those things that seem useful, only those things that are worth telling, only those things that devalue the importance of a present condition—only those things that make you righteous.

Fate is not an unruly master, as He often is described. Instead, He is a clumsy conductor, frantically trying to reconcile the decisions of mankind—decisions made out of anger, sorrow, and love. Made in a hasty instant, without regard for consequence or purpose, these decisions shape the path of the future and determine the outcomes of individuals. I am a product of these decisions, as are you, and all those like us. Even this story is an outcome of these decisions. It is not a fairy tale. Not all stories are fairy tales, and not all fairy tales are happy.

Who I am is a more difficult question to answer. Formalities and introductions will be presented in due and appropriate time. The more important and pressing issue is that of the story. Not all fairy tales end as they should. Not everything is happy. But this story must be told.

It fell. Hurling, spinning through empty time and space, it fell. A ball of energy, of pure, raw, passionate emotion, surging through the air. On course, and full of obstinate determination, it dashed toward Earth. With the force of an ocean wave and the grace of a falling star, it is said to be the most beautiful and horrifying thing at once—such power fused with such inexorable speed. Some of those I have spoken to call it a rift in time, some say a piece of heaven, others believe it's a piece of God Himself. Regardless, we all agree that it is mankind's only hope—an orb of light. Such things do not happen often, but when they do, in those brief moments that they bless the sky, time stops. And then, it happens.

In the grey abyss, the illuminated mass swells and creaks. The intensity increases and the light quivers. The separation starts as a small crack on the face of the orb. The magnitude of speed and throbbing of emotion cause the crack to expand and travel farther across the length of its face, like lightning through a tree. The energy rises and the light flashes brighter as the orb attempts to maintain structure. The exterior begins to collapse as the crack breaks deeper toward the core. Fire roars in pain as the orb expands every fiber, seeking to survive. Red and yellow flames wail blindly in the void. Then all falls silent except the low whistle of the cutting of air. The mass hangs for a moment as the last threads of energy are torn from the weeping orb. Its masterful force is the death of itself. The more powerful the orb, the more glorious and potent its destruction. Some say that in those quiet ominous moments, you can hear the weeping. I believe that's true of this orb. It lingered much longer than most. I believe it bellowed and howled from its very core. I believe that the darkness shook and quivered in fear. I believe that the orb almost won. Almost.

In a magnificent flash, the crack became a chasm and the orb was torn in half. Thunder roared and blinding light spread across the blackness. The two halves slowed for a moment as they spun wildly apart, like two lovers pulling away from a long embrace. Now divided, the two pieces fell lifelessly, their blue flames dwindling as they drifted farther apart. From here, it could take significant time for the halves to reach Earth. Often, one half reaches the ground days, months, or years before the other. These particular halves landed roughly two years apart; the first somewhere in the middle of the mainland, the second on the eastern rim. That is how this story began.

Sitting in the old wooden chair, he ran his fingers through his disheveled hair. He hadn't slept in what felt like days. His pencil scratched frantically across the paper on his desk. He glanced briskly at his watch—4:34 am. He could hear each second passing in the cold dark air of the cabin. Glancing at the fire, which had long since gone out, he stood up and quickly paced around the room. Hands shoved firmly in his pockets, his weary eyes bore the weight of his afflictions. I sat in the corner, only observing, never speaking.

"This has to work. Every detail must be perfect. I need more time." He muttered fragments aloud as he quickened his step.

Stopping in front of the fireplace, he gazed at the cold black coals.

"Envy is not green," he whispered. "It is a coal black obsession."

He poked at the ashes with the toe of his shoe. "That's it!"

He darted back to the desk and into his chair—his prison. It hasn't always been this way. I remember better days.

Striding across the room, I peered over his shoulder at the papers strewn about the desk. Scribbled on the countless sheets were notes, dates, names, and incomplete timelines. I lifted a piece of paper from the desk. It read: "Though it may be trickling down someone else's arm, I'm still patient for your love." He snatched the paper from my hand and shuffled it back into the pile. Slamming his fist down on the desk, he slumped in the chair and began silently weeping. He seemed to have lost his train of thought. Shifting the papers around again on the desk, his eyes searched the pages. I drifted closer, put my hand on his shoulder, and watched him carefully. Within moments, his pencil was working again, pausing only to make quick eraser marks. With his free hand, he waved me off. I chuckled and wandered outside. Leave him to his obsessions.

The sun was not far from the horizon of snowy winter hills. The slopes flowed smoothly down from the cabin like the soft silk arches of a woman. Sporadic trees protruded from the blanket of delicate snow, littering the hills with imperfect twisted branches, knots, and roots. It reminded me of his life. Such a beautiful foundation—a beautiful snowfall—only ruined and interrupted by ugly unpredictable events like naked, barren, gnarled trees reaching upward toward someplace less frozen. Lighting up a cigarette, I thought back to our earlier days together.

When he was young, he spent much of his time alone. His childhood was one full of imaginary friends, make-believe adventures, and solitude. The youngest of five gregarious siblings, he kept most

3

of his thoughts to himself. He was born in the chaotic center of Baltimore, Maryland, but while he was still an infant, his parents had decided that the city was no place to raise children and had moved their family to the rural outskirts of the metropolis. As a result, he found himself secluded from nearly any interaction with his peers.

Down the old country road from his family's house was a weathered barn that belonged to a blind elderly widow who refused to leave the land that her husband had tilled. Many hot summer afternoons were spent lying on his back on the wooden barn floor, staring through the open holes in the roofing. It was flat on that floor that he formulated his first opinions on religion, philosophy, and love. He ran his fingers along the wooden floorboards and contemplated their age, where they had come from, and if they had lived a longer life than he would. He tried to imagine himself as a part of them, part of their history. He imagined a time when someone still cared for them, before they were forgotten and left untended. As his fingers traced the rough grain and imperfections, he wondered if those boards had ever witnessed love. Perhaps in that very spot one hundred years earlier a man had knelt and asked a woman to marry him. He always believed that love must have been quite different back then. In those days, a man toiled for the love of a woman and a woman gave everything entirely to one man, as if she had carefully saved every morsel of her being for that one individual. He wondered if that was how love was supposed to be, if it had gotten warped somewhere along the way like the boards themselves. Maybe it could be that way again.

He tried to imagine the labor of the barn. He envisioned a man building it for his new bride. He tried to imagine each piece of the lumber being nailed to the frame with devotion, not just to survival, but to love—to family. He visualized each nail being pounded in with passion for the task as well as for the woman, each brushstroke of paint an attempt to make the barn a beautiful enough masterpiece for his flawless bride. He imagined that it had rained during the process and that the man had continued to build, his wife watching him affectionately from the window. He imagined that things had gone wrong, that mistakes had been made, but that the man had persevered with determination to provide for his wife. He envisioned the pride the man must have felt as he and his bride finally stood arm-in-arm,

4

in admiration of the barn built for love. He wondered if they had celebrated. Maybe they danced across that very floor. Closing his eyes, he could almost hear the delicate tapping of their feet within the wood.

He wondered if the man ever secretly cried after it was finished. If, in having completed the barn, the man felt sorrow for having exhausted his means of expression. He wondered if the barn was not enough—if the man felt estranged without a purpose. Or perhaps, the barn stood as a permanent flaming red bonfire of their love. Perhaps, after the man had gone, the barn remained as a token of true love—a glorious epitaph. Could the old blind woman have been that bride? Maybe that was why she never spoke and rarely left the house. When he died, maybe she had buried her husband under the barn itself—under the floorboards, as a last act of love.

Breathing deeply, he tried to picture the last moments the man and his bride had spent in the barn together. He envisioned a magnificent storm outside, rain pouring down, lightning ripping through the sky, the two lovers in the barn, safely enveloped in each other's arms, whispering softly to one another. Closing his eyes, he could hear the low rumble of thunder in the distance. He imagined that they kissed as the bright flashes danced across the sky. He wondered if they knew it would be their last kiss in the barn. Through closed lids he could see the sky darkening the holes in the roof. He could smell the wet sad scent of the approaching storm. He used to love that scent. He expected that the raindrops thudding against the roof sounded as if the storm was applauding their life together as they held one another in the darkness. He smiled as the first soft, quick droplets splashed upon his cheeks. Warm, spontaneous storms were his favorite things about summer.

Within seconds, the rain was bucketing down, much as he had imagined. Rising to his feet, he turned his face upward to the holes in the roof and stretched out his arms. To him, that was life. Lightning flashed and the rain poured down harder. Shoving his hands in his dripping pockets, he strolled out of the barn and into the driveway. Glancing back toward the farmhouse at the end of the drive, he stopped short. On the front porch, rocking gently in an old rocking chair, was the blind woman, hands folded neatly in her lap. She was smiling softly, her bottom lip quivering and her face turned toward the tall red barn. He stared at her a moment before turning and walking down her driveway and toward home. Maybe it was still that way.

Other days were spent wandering in the woods, skipping stones, and sleeping in the grass. There was a long empty field just across the street from his house. Sometimes he would sit for hours, just staring out over the acreage, dreaming of companionship. I wish that I could have been there for him then, but he had no need for me yet—no understanding. So, instead, he sat and thought and dreamed. Most would say that he always acted much older than he was. That's because sitting there, he thought about things no young man should think about. He rationalized things in his own mind that took most men years to discover. Sitting there, in those few years, his mind aged.

It was at that point in his life that he started writing. Nothing too complex, just some poetry, a few short stories, but profound. Always profound. It was his only means of expression of all the things he felt, saw, and learned. It was how he first learned to feel. Anyone who read it told him he had talent—a real gift. Through overstated flattery and adamant encouragement, others spurred him to continue to write and craft his skill until he himself was convinced that his gift was unusual. He loved his seemingly natural ability to manipulate words, but still, some days, he sat and stared at that open field. He still felt alone. This solitude consumed the majority of his childhood until, one day, he met his first and only friend. The boy was new to the area, and from the moment they met they became inseparable. They walked to the barn together, but now, rather than listening to the floorboards, they scurried across them sword fighting with sticks. Rather than recreating its construction, they climbed on its ledges and swung from its beams. They raced through the woods together on bicycles, over bumpy roots and through trickling rivers. Rather than skipping stones, they swam. They laughed, they played, they lay on their backs in the grass and made stories out of the clouds. They talked about growing older, about driving, about leaving that town behind.

One summer, as they walked down that old country road together, his friend turned to him and told him that he had something to show him, gesturing toward the old field that the boy had spent so much time examining. The first steps onto the dry crunchy grass were uneasy ones. This field had been the embodiment of his endless search for something more. He had never seen any purpose in traversing its vast plain and even now, as he did, his mind wandered. Squinting against the setting sun ahead of them, he eyed the tree line along the edge of the field. He considered the consequence of their journey. What if there was no purpose to the field? Perhaps it was just a field, leading to nothing more. He imagined the repercussion of exposing his only means of escape as a fraud. How could his imagination be inspired by, and mold, something he had seen? If the mystery was exposed, he could not fashion it into whatever he chose. Stooping, he skimmed his hand along the tips of the dead brown blades of grass. He closed his eyes as a soft breeze blew the sweet scent of summer through his nostrils. He turned and looked back the way they had come. It was a lonely place, but it was familiar. He thought about how long it had been since he had written. It would be a sad thing, he thought, to lose that part of him—that sickeningly sweet feeling of loneliness.

"Come on, it's not that far!" his friend called to him, now a silhouette on the horizon.

He could not imagine life forever; at some point he had to live it. Jumping to his feet, he ran after his friend and didn't look back again.

They were out of breath by the time they reached the tree line, which up close revealed that there were not many trees at all. Panting loudly, his friend motioned for him to follow down the thinning row of saplings and through a patch of bushes. His eyes widened in bewilderment as he stepped through the thicket. Two parallel rows of houses sat facing each other, divided by a wide paved road. He had not seen many in his life, but if he was not mistaken, it was a neighborhood—a small one, to say the least, but that didn't matter. It was a neighborhood—a neighborhood with kids playing in the street. Kids his age. He could have cried. If only they had known how long he had waited for them, how many times he had imagined them.

He stared plainly as he followed his friend across a backyard and up to a large glass sliding door at the rear of one of the houses. His friend explained that he had gone to school with the kid who lived there and that they, too, were friends. Before they even had the chance to knock, a voice called from the side of the house. Rounding the corner, they saw a young girl swinging in a hammock, reading a

7

book. With soft brown hair messily collected at the top of her head and T-shirt sleeves rolled up because of the heat, she lowered her book as the boys approached. His friend knew her also, so he introduced them. She was beautiful. The three quickly became inseparable. He and the boy still played in the barn and walked in the woods, but now the girl accompanied them. Sometimes, when he wasn't watching, the girl would stare at him. Then, when he turned and looked into her deep brown eyes, she would smile. She had such a youthful smile.

Before long, his friend no longer came out to play, leaving just the girl and the boy to lie in the grass. They climbed trees and walked in the woods together. He would skip stones while she sat on a tree stump and watched. At dusk, before the air cooled from the beating sun, they would catch fireflies and talk about music. One night, as they sat on a tree branch watching the sunset, he felt her fingers crawling gently across his. His heart quivered as she slid her hand slowly inside of his. He smiled and squeezed her fingers tightly as she laid her head on his shoulder. He thought back to the days when he was alone, to the things he thought about love. He wondered if this was what love felt like.

For the next several weeks, they spent most of their days together. She would walk with him through the field and he would tell her all the things he had discovered about life. He never spoke of the time before they had met, never of his time alone, only of what he had learned. One night, just after the sun had dwindled over the field, they sat underneath a tall old maple tree together. Nearby honeysuckle vines released their sweet smell. The wind carried it in warm gentle swirls around them. Reaching into his pocket, he fumbled for the metallic heart with his fingers. He turned to her. The orange and pink of the horizon danced across her delicate skin as she stared out over the field. Wrapping his finger around the rugged rope that strung through a hole in the metal heart, he pulled it from his pocket. She turned to him as he pressed the cool alloy piece into her hand. Her eyes widened as her lips stretched into a smile. She flung her arms around his neck and pulled him close to her. He could feel her heart beating softly against his chest. He held her like that for a moment, inhaling every second. She pulled back gradually and looked into his eyes.

"Kiss me," she whispered.

A kiss? He flinched at the word. He couldn't kiss her. They had not even said the word "love"; how could they kiss? He didn't understand. From what he understood, a kiss was a solemn transference of love—an exchange that could not be mocked or taken lightly. To him, a kiss was magical. She stared at him impatiently. He pulled back slowly. The metallic heart symbolized his feelings for her; he saw no urgent need for kissing. What if they were not meant to be together? If they kissed, it would mean that he stole something that belonged to someone else. A kiss? Not yet. He tried explaining these things to her, but she didn't seem to understand. He explained the sacred aspect of a kiss, but she only stared at him blankly. They sat under the tree and he explained how much he cared for her and how he hoped one day sparks would fly each time they kissed—just not yet. He told her how he hoped she would be with him always. She left early that night.

The next day, he went out to the field to meet her. He sat down in the dry grass and waited. The wind carried a mild chill. Soon summer would be over and fall would come. The days would grow shorter and the trees would start to wither. He wondered how they would spend their time together then. More than likely, the two would move inside to talk while the wind shook the trees. Maybe they would sit by the window and drink hot chocolate while the snow fell outside.

He rose slowly as he saw her figure emerge from the tree line. He walked out to the middle of the field to meet her. She didn't smile. She didn't say hello. Instead, she stopped short, a few steps from him, and outstretched her clasped hand. She did not look at him. She stared at the ground. He cautiously reached out his open hand. Uncurling her fingers, she dropped the small metallic heart into his palm. She glanced up at him but only for a second. His throat tightened and breathing became difficult. It seemed like hours that they stood in silence. No breeze blew now, but the air got cooler. She tucked her hair behind her ear and apologized. She said that she would not come to see him anymore. She said that she had met a boy at school that day who liked to kiss. He couldn't speak. She turned quickly and ran back the way she had come. He stood silently, his palm open, holding the cold metal heart. His eyes watered and his throat was dry. His chest constricted. He stood until she disappeared into the trees. His body ached inside. Turning slowly, he walked back home, watery eyes sting-

9

ing as the wind blew roughly into his face.

That evening, he sat up in the tree, this time alone, to watch the sunset. His chest still burned as he contemplated what had happened. Maybe love was not what he thought. Maybe it didn't work that way. It seemed so perfect. He tried to reason what had gone wrong. He wondered if maybe he should have just kissed her. Leaning back against the trunk of the tree, he stared out over the open field and mourned the outcome of his first attempt at love.

Now, it just so happened that I had some business to attend to that particular evening, down that particular country road. It was my footsteps against the old pavement that caused him to stir. As I said before, who I am and where exactly I was going is of no consequence. I heard the branch shaking as he shifted his position to see me. He looked as if he was expecting someone else. Unfortunately, urgent business prohibited me from stopping to talk, but as I strolled past him perched in his tree, we locked eyes. Immediately, I saw great potential in the boy. He was so frail and young then, but I saw it. I saw it buried deep beneath his chest. It had not yet awoken but there is no doubt it was there. It only remained quiet and still inside him then. He waved to me slowly. I only smiled. Even then, I knew we would meet again.

Flicking the cigarette out in the snow, I surveyed the gradual hills again. No one would find us here—up here, away from the world. I don't recall how many days it had been. I wonder if he remembered. Turning, I opened the cabin door to the sound of him wincing softly in pain. He was hunched over the desk, pencil clenched tightly in his fist. Jaw set forcefully in place and eyes squinting firmly, he gripped his chest strongly with his other hand. I raced to his side and caught him in my arms as he slumped out of his chair and onto his back. I hated to see him that way, shivering in pain. I held him close against my chest and placed my hand gently on his cheek. He flinched at the touch of my skin but the shivering simmered to a light tremble. Pulling his arm away from his chest, I rubbed the spot firmly with my fingers. I knew that spot well. It was the spot that I had seen that day when he was in the tree. It was much older now, much more calloused, but nonetheless the same. Underneath my fingertips, I could feel it sizzling. I could feel it fighting. Beneath the skin and flesh and bone, that half of orb crackled as its fire slightly dimmed. It would not be long before it was out. We had to hurry.

two

Hospitals and doctors' offices always made him nervous. He didn't see why. He had never had any reason to be uneasy in the presence of medicine; but sitting there, 15 years old, he was nervous. He sat with his hands tucked under his legs, eyeing the clock on the wall. His mother shifted restlessly in the chair beside him. He could feel her tension. It had been a month since he first told her—two months after it had begun. He could only imagine her anxiety had she known from the start. But that was done now. They had come once, and now they were back to get the results. They were back to learn what was happening inside him.

It had begun as a distant feeling of nausea and dizziness that grew gradually into a constant state of illness. Regular fevers and chills kept him awake at night. His body ached. His skin had grown pale and his appetite dim. Staring at his shoes, he readied himself for the worst. That stagnant, medicinal, latex smell of sickness wafted through the waiting room, making him nauseous. The gentle hum of the vending machine was the only sound in the room. He could feel the apprehension of the entire place—everyone with their eyes scanning the floor. The muted TV hanging in the low ceiling corner seemed to be the only living thing. Its distorted images dancing across the screen contrasted the sallow room. The vibrant colors and fluid motions only made the atmosphere more pale and rigid.

The woman seated diagonal from him moved her mouth silently, rocking gently, a baby wrapped in blankets cradled in her arms. Her troubled eyes were encircled in sagging skin, red and weary—no doubt from crying. Slumped in the chair across from him sat an old man. Shaky legs pressed firmly together, the man held his hand to his face, sad eyes skimming the pages of an old tattered Bible lain across his lap. With his other hand he clasped a cane, which he used in an attempt to steady his quivering frame. He licked his dry, wrinkled fingers before pinching the crinkled corner of the paper leaf and turning the page. The boy could not help but wonder if the man had always read his Bible. Perhaps the old man saw his end nearing and this was a last attempt to find redemption. That was a strange thing he noticed about people—that they only did what needed to be done just before it was too late. He supposed that, oftentimes, it took the looming presence of inevitable consequence for an individual to attempt to rectify his wrong. I know, for a fact, that this is the case. People spend as much time as possible doing what is most beneficial for themselves and renders the least amount of guilt, until ramifications are due. At that point, they frantically try to do the opposite as if to backpedal for the damage done. As if there is some scale, some balance to right and wrong. The boy hoped he would never have the need. Yet, maybe the old man was lucky. Maybe it made him feel justified—acquitted. Some people don't get that chance. Some people cannot rectify their wrong before it is too late.

The boy smirked at the old man, who had shut the Bible now and was resting with his eyes closed. The boy chuckled, realizing his hand was on his neck fingering the small swollen bumps along his spine. That is how he first knew something was wrong. The doctor had called them swollen lymph nodes, indicators of illness. He had tried to ignore them for quite some time, but once the nausea came, he knew it was time to submit himself to the prodding fingers of the family's doctor.

The sudden swinging of the office door startled him as the nurse leaned into the waiting room. Her face was solemn as she turned to him and motioned for him to follow her down the corridor and into the doctor's office. His mother followed silently. Her robotic steps sounded like a death march echoing in the dismal hall.

The white parchment paper crinkled loudly as he squirmed up into the large cushioned chair. Time always passes so slowly when every fiber of your being is hinging on the happening of one event. As the doctor entered the room, he carried a clipboard clasping a stack of papers, which he flipped through methodically. He stopped in the center of the room. It was obvious that he was avoiding eye contact. He moved slowly and gingerly as if attempting not to disturb the solemn stillness of the room, as if in the presence of a dead man. The boy's eyes remained fixated on the doctor's lowered head. The doctor remained frozen. The soft rhythmic gasps of the boy's mother increased the tension.

The notion of death is a difficult thing for young people to cope with. Though he had already aged much beyond his actual years, it was still nearly as difficult for him. At first. The parchment crackled and tore as he slid off the chair. He had heard enough. The doctor need not say a word. As he stepped out into the hallway and closed the door behind him, he could hear his mother's gasps transform into a quiet whisper. The escape from the tension hit him like fresh air. He staggered as his legs buckled slightly. He tried to maintain his composure. The nurse was escorting a young girl down the corridor. At least, she seemed very young to the boy. Realistically, he was probably no older than she was, but he felt much older. An overwhelming feeling of nausea flooded his vision. He stumbled down the hallway toward the exit. The woman, cradling her baby, now paced down the hallway, her infant crying loudly. The weariness on the woman's face had melted into sheer concern as she hushed the baby, bouncing it softly in her arms. He tried to fake a comforting smile as he strode past the woman, through the office door, and spilled into the waiting room. The old man still sat in his chair. This time, his head was propped back against the cement yellow wall. His Bible was no longer in his lap. He looked as if he was sleeping peacefully. The boy stopped for a moment to consider the man. He looked relieved. He looked justified.

"Lollipop?" the woman's voice interrupted his concentration.

Her soft smile broke through his nauseated trance. He looked at her and blinked with confusion. Her outstretched hand extended a slender white stick in his direction. From behind the reception desk, she giggled softly at his puzzlement. She stretched her arm out farther, signaling for him to take the stick. His unsteady steps thudded against the plastic tiles as he walked over to her desk. She smiled again as his fingers pinched the stick and pulled the lollipop from her hand. His face remained unchanged. Turning, he shoved the candy in his pocket and wandered outside.

The drive home seemed much longer than usual. He sat in the passenger seat, leaning against the door and looking at the passing sky through the window glass, while his red-eyed mother drove. He could tell that she'd been crying. He opened his mouth to offer some comfort, but no words came. Instead, the two sat in silence until the car lurched to a stop in the driveway. She turned to him. He kept his eyes glued to the sky. He knew if he rolled them down, tears would pour from their seams.

"It's leukemia." Her voice quivered with weariness.

He didn't react. It didn't matter what they called it; he knew what it meant. Opening the car door, he climbed out and walked quickly into the house and back into his bedroom. His breaths were shallow and shaky as he backed against the closed door and slid down to the floor. Was he going to die? He thought about all the things he would never achieve. He could not restrain the tears any longer. Sitting on his bedroom floor, he wept.

The phone trembled in his hand as he dialed the numbers. He had gained control of the tears, but his eyes still stung. He rubbed them roughly with his free hand. There were few people in the world he felt like he could talk to back then. Ben was one of them. He wasn't quite sure why that was, but he and Ben seemed to believe a lot of the same things. Within their first few weeks of meeting, the two had connected. Ben was a burly, lighthearted jokester with cynical, pessimistic undertones and the boy was a spontaneous, creative schemer with realist, philosophical undertones; they were a perfect match. One name rarely came without the other and was usually followed by some warranted accusation or some comical story. When they weren't causing trouble, the two would sit and attempt to rationalize the social behaviors of life. It was this lengthy spectrum of affinity that made the two so close.

"How bad is it?" Ben's voice asked from the other end.

"The worst," he replied.

For most people, there are distinct events in their past that have molded them into who they are. Whether they remember these events or not, they are still significant. These experiences are the driving forces that cause individuals to make those decisions that shape the path of the future and determine their outcomes. The doctor's visit was the first. The second occurred only two months later.

Growing up in seclusion, there were some things the boy was naïve about. Most of what he believed and understood was based on observation. While that gave him a considerable amount of insight, it also crippled him with an unrealistically optimistic outlook on life—and he applied this outlook to all of the things that were valuable to him, including his family. His older siblings always played a crucial role in his perception of the world. He understood them because they had come from the same places that he had. They had been through the same struggles together, and because of that he felt a profound bond with them.

It was his first time visiting his oldest brother away at college. The day he arrived, his brother welcomed him with a tour of the campus and introduced him to life at college. The two boys ate in the cafeteria and snuck into the backs of classrooms. They bought meals from vending machines, listened to music in the dormitory rooms, and ran through the hallways. He felt so adult. That night, he and his brother sat in the courtyard with a group of fellow college students. It was such a beautiful sense of community and unity. Some played guitars; others beat on old drums from countries the boy had never heard of. No one told them to quiet down; no one sent them to bed. They stayed up as late as they pleased. They laughed and talked about the world and art. They talked about government and religion. They treated him like one of them. Despite his youth, he felt the warmth of their acceptance.

The next morning, some of the students from the previous night decided to go for breakfast. As they paraded down the sidewalk, the boy strode with his head high. His sickness seemed like a distant memory from a previous life. His brother walked a few step ahead of him with a girl from the night before. The campus was alive with commotion. Radios blared from open windows. Students littered the sidewalks. Some played soccer in the courtyard, while others sat under trees reading books. It all seemed so liberated and carefree. They must have loved it there. The boy envied their freedom but, most of all, he envied their endless access to knowledge. Not only did they have the chance to learn about the world and independent life, but they were also learning about art and history. He couldn't wait to be where they were.

Up ahead, he noticed the girl pull a cigarette out of a pack and wedge it between her lips. He had always been taught that smoking was bad, but he had also always believed it. He believed it was a reflection of character. He thought that if you smoked, it showed you had no concern for your own health and thus no real respect for anything. Because if you cared so little about yourself to do something so harmful, how could you care about anything else? He was such a child. It was a good thing that the world broke him. Sometimes, something has to break before you remember that it's even there.

He watched as his brother pointed to the pack, mouthing to the girl. She nodded and handed him the box of cigarettes. As he watched his brother slide the white paper stick out of the pack and place it between his lips, the boy froze.

The night before his oldest brother went away to college, the boy could not sleep. He lay in his bed and imagined life without his brother. Time changed people; he was learning that. Who could know how much would change in the time they were apart? His brother's silhouette in his bedroom door stopped his thoughts. He crept into the room and sat on the edge of the bed and the two talked. The boy explained his fear that things would be different with time.

"Nothing is going to be different," his brother had said. The boy could still hear the words "I promise."

The end sizzled as his brother drew air through the burning shreds of tobacco. He tried to steady the quiver in his throat. You think you know something or someone in life and then the unexpected happens. I don't know why it's unexpected—it happens every time. But for some reason, people are shocked each time things are not the way they perceived them to be. It seems almost arrogant. To think that you—and I use it in the general sense—think that you've discovered and interpreted every aspect of a person. That you have somehow mastered the understanding of how an individual will respond to each presented encounter. It's an unrealistic, impossible notion, and yet people impress it upon themselves. Each day, people stupefy themselves with the

17

realization that they are not omniscient. Life happens unexpectedly. People change erratically, and there's always more than you know. Yet, you—we—are shocked each time we find that out. The boy was shocked when he did. He sat down on the curb and cried—not because he was sad but because he saw how life can change you. He saw how circumstance and decisions can turn something so young and vibrant into something so calloused and destructive. They had come from the same place. They had been through the same things. What could have happened outside of their common environment that had caused such a harmful decision? He wiped his eyes with the backs of his hands. Perhaps he was overreacting. It was only a cigarette. Certainly, it symbolized a diversion from the things they were taught, but people choose worse things. He untied and retied his shoes quickly as his brother's figure shadowed the light behind him.

"You alright, little brother?" his voice asked over his shoulder.

The boy nodded, smiling as he rose. Leaning back, his older brother squinted to look into his eyes. He nodded again and faked another smile. His brother patted him on the back and laughed. He slid his hand around his shoulder and the two boys walked to breakfast. The boy tried to laugh and hide what he'd done, but he was sure it was obvious he had been crying. He knew the sadness had not yet left his eyes.

At that single point when they give in and sincerely believe that they have reached the end of something, people tend to solemnly resign in reminiscent respect for what they have journeyed through. Life is no different. Once you realize the curtains are drawing to a close, you tend to relinquish all affiliation and attachment in a final bow of liberation. Things that once held potent value are now considered secondary, secondary to the looming approach of your inevitable end. Your lack of closure crumbles beneath the realization that everything is flimsy. Your fear of the unknown melts into lustful regard for the present. Your tears and sleepless nights dissipate into solemn resolution and acceptance. The boy pondered these things as he lay flat on his back against the mattress in his dark room. The white paint reflected the moonlight from the window as he stared up at the ceiling. It had been four months since his diagnosis. Four very difficult months.

Life seemed like something very different to him now. At first he had been afraid. All he wanted to do was run away and hide—hide from his sickness, from the world. He prayed every night. He pleaded for some escape, for a second chance to experience life. He exhausted himself with tears. It got to the point where he had to force it out of his mind just to get a hold of his sanity. The boy had to try to do things to distract himself from letting his mind wander. He often went on long walks in a desperate attempt to soak in as much of nature's beauty as he could. He had started playing guitar. It put his mind at ease, sitting and playing out those soft melodies. Music always had that affect on him. It became that music strictly altered his mood. Something about the passion connected with him. I believe it was music that got him through that time. I think it nurtured his ailing soul.

He reached beside his bed and clutched the smooth slender neck of the wooden guitar. Hoisting it up, he laid it across his stomach and began strumming methodically. The past four months had also made him robotic. His eyes had a permanent glaze. In order to overcome those early days of fear and sorrow, he had had to become almost lethargic. He had to learn to accept his fate and take life as long as it was given to him.

The next day would mark his first day of treatment. The week before, he had gone to the doctor and had his blood drawn again. The doctor said it was to do some final tests and decide the best course of action. From there, he would better know how long he had. His mother still considered the treatment a possible cure. He knew it would only be a delayer. He had come to terms with the realization that it was only a matter of time. He wondered if the doctor would have the decency to admit it. Closing his eyes, he hummed softly, strumming his guitar until he drifted off to sleep.

He rose to his feet in the center of a dark hallway. Behind him, he could hear bottles clanking and the thumping of music muffled by the sound of voices and laughter. His hand was wet as he dragged it across the cotton of his sweatshirt. He was somewhere unfamiliar. Staggering, he took a few uneasy steps forward. The hallway seemed

19

to stretch on forever. The walls had no end; they faded into the blackness that collected only feet in front of him. He stopped and turned to face a large wooden door. He assumed the door was wooden, but he could not be certain because the majority of the material was plastered with an oversized poster of Jimi Hendrix. The boy paused to stare at the man with his guitar held comfortably in his hands. Jimi's fingers moved euphorically down the neck of the guitar as he swayed his body and shook his head at the boy. The boy focused his eyes more intently and Jimi played on, the psychedelic notes bending in the air, his head still shaking. A toilet flushed somewhere in the corner of the boy's mind and the acute sound of two girls giggling swirled around his head. He spun around in a circle and caught his hand on the cool doorknob. Jimi stood lifeless in the poster, his eyes transfixed on the neck of his tuneless guitar. The boy twisted the knob and pushed the door open.

There, on a sofa opposite the door, sat the boy's immediate older brother. Two girls sat on either side of him; in front of them stood a glass top coffee table. His brother was slumped over the table, holding a green tube in his nostril. The tube scratched along the glass top as his brother moved it in a wild frenzy, vacuuming fine particles of white powder from the table up into his nostril. He felt the muscles in his body tighten. He could hear the sound of the air slurping its way through the tube. As the last trails of powder were sucked from the tabletop, his brother lifted his head to meet his eyes. The boy could feel the acid gurgling in his stomach. Turning, he ran back down the hallway. He had to find air. A sea of people greeted him at the end of the dark corridor. He pushed his way through as shoulders, hands, and legs rubbed against him. He was lost in a maze of bodies. A girl with thick eye shadow called out his name, but he ignored her and pressed on. The acid in his stomach was trickling up the back of his throat. He spotted a large red door across the room. Slamming through the crowd, he raced toward it and fell bumbling out into the night.

He shot up quickly in his bed and his eyes scanned the room. There was nothing but the red glow of his alarm clock in the darkness. It was only a dream. As real as it may have seemed, it was only a dream. He repeated the words to himself as he laid his head back down against the pillow and tried to swallow the bitter taste of acid that had formed in the back of his mouth.

The next morning he was slow getting out of bed. As he climbed into the shower, he thought about the significance of the day. This was his mother's sliver of hope. After today, she would be looking for signs of improvement. If she did not see them, he thought, she would break. He would have to fake it. He would have to make her believe he was getting better for as long as he could. She was seated stiffly on the sofa when he came down the hallway. Her jacket was on, zipped up tight, and her hands clutched her keys. She rose as he entered the room, and the two walked silently to the car.

They did not speak the entire ride to the office. When they arrived, the nurse escorted them directly back into one of the examination rooms. He winced as he passed the worried faces that dotted the waiting room. He climbed up in the chair and stared blankly at the wall. His mother's eyes were glued to the floor. It was only a few moments that they sat in silence before the doctor came lumbering in. He held his clipboard at his side and looked directly at the boy and then at his mother as he closed the door behind him. His steps slapped loudly against the floor as he moved quickly to the sink, where he washed his hands. The water splashed as the doctor swished it around the basin, rinsing off the suds of soap. Something was wrong. The boy's eyes widened. What had happened to the doctor's solemn tone? Something was not right. The boy could feel his mouth going dry. His palms began to sweat. He could feel the tension rising from his mother as she glared at the doctor. He found himself glaring as well. Something had gone terribly wrong. Sliding on his glasses, the doctor plopped down casually in his chair. Casually. The boy could barely resist the urge to scream. He couldn't take it anymore. Just as he opened his mouth to speak, the doctor stopped him.

"I have been a doctor for 27 years," he began, flipping through the papers on his clipboard, "and I have never seen anything like this."

He lowered the clipboard and pulled off his glasses. The boy rubbed his hands against his pant legs. The doctor rubbed his forehead.

"The leukemia," he started again, this time staring into the boy's eyes. "The leukemia is gone." The boy's throat tightened. "I don't know how, or why, but it's completely gone. I can't even find traces. Maybe the first results were wrong; maybe it's a miracle. I...I don't know. But your leukemia is gone."

Impossible. The boy felt dizzy. The room seemed to be darkening. He blinked, trying to clear his vision. Across the room, his mother erupted in an outburst of tears. She fell from the chair to her knees and cupped her face in her hands.

"Of course, we will have to keep a close eye out to monitor for any signs," the doctor began loudly as if to reprimand the mother for her hasty sense of relief.

The boy had stopped listening. The edges of his vision quivered in a slow, fluid ripple as he sat in silence. How could it be gone? You can't tell someone that they are going to die and then change your mind. How could that be? Life doesn't work that way. People have plans and goals and ambitions. You can't flex their allotted timeline. You can't tamper with their expectations. The boy's thoughts were choppy. How could he live when he had already resolved to die? Did the past four months mean nothing? He could hear his heart beating inside his ears. The low steady rumble of the doctor's voice vibrated somewhere in the back of his mind. He could barely hear the sobbing of his mother's relief. He could hardly feel her arms as she stood and embraced his motionless frame. He could feel only emptiness. It was as if all sensation and passion—all love of art and beauty—had drained from him in that instant. He looked down at his mother's hunched frame wrapped around his shoulders. Enveloped in his emotionless void, he could not feel compassion. He could not sympathize with her pain. He could not cry. He had become robotic so that he could cope with what was happening; he was not sure that he could reverse what he had done. What if it was too late?

He did not notice when the doctor left the room. His mother's sobs had calmed to light whimpers. She must have felt relieved. Parents should not bury their children. He wasn't sure what to feel. It was certainly not that he wanted to die, but could he go on the rest of his life wondering if some day it would come back? What if, when it did, it didn't go away as easily? Would he have the strength to ready himself again? His mother was looking at him now, patting underneath her eyes with a tissue. Her mascara had bled down her cheeks. He turned to her and tried to force a smile, but his lips would not budge.

three

Times had gotten difficult. It is a challenging thing, to grow up and leave your childish ambitions behind. It's a tough transition for anyone, especially at a young age. At one point, the world is your stage and you can become anything you wish to be. The future is an uncertain clay that you mold with your mind and shape with your plans. Anything that you can dream of, you can become. Everything that you fear, you can eliminate. You are invincible. Then, in what seems like a flash, you have boundaries and limitations. Money becomes an issue. Time becomes finite. You have to make decisions that you never planned to make for a future that you never envisioned. Suddenly, people are making demands of you. The future becomes a poised trap ready to spring at any moment, with promise to ruin every single thing that you have built. It becomes a constant hazy inevitable mist that conceals itself while still boldly pronouncing its eventual fruition and adversity. And you are supposed to reconcile this transition. I realize it is not instantaneous. I understand that, technically, this alteration happens over time. However, for some people, the realization hits them in an instant. Some people are ready; some are not. When that realization comes, those people who are not ready sometimes do irrational, impulsive things that they would never do otherwise. It's a much harder awakening for some than it is for others. For the boy's friend Ben, it was particularly difficult.

The phone clanged loudly, stirring the boy from his sleep. 3:34 in the morning—who could be calling? With his eyes closed, he swept his arm across the nightstand in search of the phone. The alarm clock tumbled to the ground as his hand clasped the cordless receiver.

Pressing the answer button, he muttered a sleepy greeting.

"Hey." It was Ben.

"Hang on," the boy answered, lowering the phone and straining to hear. It didn't sound as though the noise had awakened his parents. "What's going on?"

"I think you should come over here. It's—it's real important." His voice was strained and thin.

The boy grumbled an agreement and hung up. Dropping the phone to the floor, he looked at the clock again. It had the makings of a long night.

He was more or less still asleep as he got up and pulled on a sweatshirt and some jeans. He slipped on his shoes and slid silently out the door. He couldn't wake his parents. They wouldn't like him going out at this hour, especially on a school night.

The crisp chill of the night air aided in waking him. He shoved his hands in his sweatshirt pockets and tried to pull the fabric tighter around his frame for warmth. Lifting the handle gently, he opened the car door and climbed into the driver's seat. He winced as he slid the key in and started the engine. The darkened windows of the house remained unlit. He was clear.

Ben lived with his parents roughly ten minutes away. His parents were the type of parents that everyone wished they had. They were genuine, loving people. Every time the boy would come to the house, Ben's mother would greet him with a lengthy, affectionate embrace, followed by a series of motherly ramblings about why hadn't he come to visit sooner and how he'd better be eating enough, to which the boy would shrug and laugh and tell her that, yes, he had been eating enough and, no, he was not staying out of trouble. Ben's father was no different. He was no stranger to long embraces and would tell the boy when he was proud of him and just the same when he was not. They never yelled, except in laughter, and that was only due either to his mother's slight hearing deficiency or to the fact that something hysterical was always happening and they were racing to see whose comment was more clever. Sometimes, they would sit with Ben and the boy until the early hours of morning just talking about the challenges and excitement they faced as kids. The boys would tell them about the things that they had done and seen, without inhibition, and Ben's parents would laugh or offer unobtrusive input on what the boys should do. The boy loved that house. Every time he walked through the door it felt like coming home. Something told him this visit would be quite different.

The tires crunched the gravel into the pavement as the car slowed to a stop outside the townhouse. As the boy turned off the ignition and stepped out of the car, he heard rustling in the bushes beside the concrete steps that led to the front door of the house. Stopping at the curb, he stooped down and whistled lightly through his teeth. The rustling quieted for a moment. Still stooping, he crept a few steps closer to the bushes and whistled again. It was another moment before Mittens came bounding out from the branches. The family cat's four white paws not only signified his name but also made him easily identifiable. The boy scooped the cat up in his arms and rose to his feet. His leg muscles tightened and throbbed as he arched his back, stretching his tired frame. The cat purred softly, acknowledging recognition of the boy. As he scratched gently behind the cat's ears and down its back, the fur felt warm and wet. The dim light beaming from the front porch caught flashes of ruby red thinly painted on the boy's fingers as he lifted them from Mitten's body. Blood.

The cat scurried back into the bushes as the boy dropped it to the ground and sprinted across the sidewalk and up the concrete steps to Ben's front door. His imagination was racing his eyes as he burst through the screen door and scanned the living room. He could hear the sound of running water. The boy dashed down the hallway, his arm still elevated, causing trails of blood to trickle like tears down his hand. He froze in the doorway to the kitchen. Certain images in life are so profound and impacting that, when witnessed, they burn into the memory's permanent eye. These images are carried with the observer for the rest of his life. As the boy stood in the wooden picture frame of the doorway, he saw such an image. Standing, hunched over the kitchen sink, was Ben's broken frame. His eyes were enveloped in tears and his shoulders heaved as he desperately tried to pace his panicked breathing. A damp washcloth was pressed firmly to his bloody wrist. A knife lay across the countertop, its handle covered in red fingerprints and its blade still fresh with thick droplets of rich claret red. In those first moments of uncontaminated terror, it is nearly impos-

25

sible to truly achieve anything. The boy's legs petrified, rooting into the ground like ancient tree trunks. He could not speak. His mouth was void of moisture. His choppy, ragged breaths grated against the lining of his throat like sandpaper. In that immobile helpless instant, the boy thought about all they had been through. The images flashed through his mind like photographs. He remembered the first time they met. It was at a party, and the two boys had bonded instantly. They had spent the better part of that night sitting outside, laughing. He remembered always laughing. He remembered driving and listening to music, inside jokes, skipping classes, and bonfires. The two of them used to do a music routine to Jerry Lee Lewis' "Great Balls of Fire". One of them would make the piano sounds with his mouth while the other would sing the words. They were always entertaining people, not so much for those people's entertainment but more so for their own. When it was just the two of them, they tackled more serious issues. They talked about goals, dreams, and purpose. They used to talk about growing old, marrying sisters, and always being friends. He wondered what could have happened to bring Ben to such a place. It was such a lonely place. He thought about the dark things in life, the difficult things. He thought about the endless search for greater meaning, the seemingly hopeless desire to surpass mediocrity, and the possibility that life was nothing more than precisely what it was—dark and empty. It was these things that they talked about in private. These things were what brought them closer together.

The boy blinked. He didn't remember moving, but he was beside Ben now, pulling the washcloth from his friend's arm and wringing out the blood, which flowed in swirls of water down the drain. The cuts were sloppy but deep. Three clean slits ran diagonally along his arm, all spreading open in unison like mouths each time his heart pumped blood to the severed veins. Like a choir, they opened, and blood spilled out like a chorus, singing of all his sorrow and despair. I wish I could have seen it. There is something sickeningly beautiful about scenes like those. If you have never seen such a thing, then you have no comprehension of what I'm referring to. But if you have witnessed the beautiful face of tragedy, then you know my disappointment upon not being present. The boy pressed the cloth harder against Ben's arm as he lifted it into the air in an attempt to lessen the flow, but he could not stop the bleeding. Ben had stopped crying. His face was turning white. He was losing too much blood. The boy reached for the phone on the wall.

"I have to call an ambulance." The blood on his fingers stuck to the phone as he pulled it from its base.

"No," Ben's voice sounded inhuman, almost robotic. The boy turned to him. "Please."

The phone clicked as it locked back in place against the wall. There had to be another way. Ben grunted through his teeth as the boy gripped the wound tighter. His adrenaline was draining almost as quickly as the blood from Ben's face. The struggle was exhausting them both. How long can you fight something before it destroys you? How long do you hold on when you know you've already lost? The battle no longer becomes about winning. It becomes about salvaging what you can of yourself. It becomes about fighting for a part of yourself, even if you cannot win, because it's something that you cannot afford to lose. The battle becomes the war; and you cannot lose because, if you do, then you've lost something permanent and there is no point in fighting ever again. But if it's going to be your last fight, by God, you better make it glorious. You better fight harder than you ever have in your entire life. It had better consume every morsel of your being for as long as it takes. You better keep swinging till the bitter end. If it's going to take you, let it know you were there. Let it know that you will not be forgotten. Let it know that you were something.

The boy snatched a towel from a nearby drawer. Ben had slumped against the counter, his eyes fluttering. The boy propped the arm up on his shoulder. Gripping the towel at opposite corners, he mustered up his energy and pulled. The fabric popped as its fibers gave way, splitting it in halves. Taking one half and breathing deeply, he methodically wrapped it around the wound. It had to be tight. He could see the bleeding slowing as the fabric bridged the skin on either side. His hands were steady as he looped one end around the other, making a knot. One step at a time. Sometimes you just have to win. Tying it off securely, he slouched back against the wall. He gasped as if taking in air for the first time. Ben was propped against the counter, his head tilted back toward the ceiling. Neither spoke. They stood like that in silence as minutes passed like hours. They didn't need to say a word.

27

They understood one another. They were equals now. They had both stood at the brink of death and been pulled back. They had tiptoed into the void of oblivion and ventured back to the shore. That made you a different type of person, and it gave them a better understanding of one another. It didn't matter why. The question never crossed the boy's mind. It could have been for any number of reasons. People are always so confused as to how anyone could ever come to the place where they are capable of harming themselves. It perplexes me. Have you walked out your back door? Have you turned on the news? Have you not come to the sickening realization that this is a deteriorating existence, worsening with every second? It is a desperate, lonely place to come to, but it is by no means surprising.

Ben dropped his head down wearily, glazed bloodshot eyes gazing at the boy. The color was returning to his face. The bleeding seemed to be under control. He looked exhausted. The boy moved to his side and helped him to his feet. His steps were shaky as they walked down the hallway and out into the living room. If he would not go to the hospital, the boy would have to watch him through the night. He eased him down carefully onto the couch and examined the towel around his arm. Some blood had drained through, but the wound seemed to be sealed. He dropped down into the chair across from Ben and rubbed his eyes with the palms of his hands. His shirt was stained with blood. Ben had closed his eyes.

"It's just so dark," his voice crackled in a hoarse whisper.

"I know," the boy replied. "I know it is."

He watched the slow rise and fall of Ben's stomach as his friend drifted off to sleep. He sat up and watched all night.

For most people, music is a form of entertainment, but for others, it is something much more intimate. For some people, music is the soundtrack to their existence. For some people, music relates on a much more complex level. It is something that those people can find peace in, something that they can turn to when all else fails. For those people, life without music is a much more arduous journey; it is much less colorful. These people find the music that understands

28

them and has the same beliefs, the same memories, and the same hurt that they have. They bond with that music and it becomes almost a part of them, as if it belongs to them. For the boy and his best friend Ben, this certainly became the case. They never spoke about what happened. They only developed a profound, mutual respect and fascination with the brief potency of life.

They never told anyone the story. Ben wore long-sleeve shirts over the bandages until the wounds healed. After that, if anyone noticed the scars and asked any questions, the boy was quick to intervene, and together they would tell an elaborate story involving a very steep hill and a skateboard with a faulty wheel. They would laugh every time they told it, and so would their audience. The part when the wheel popped off, sending Ben soaring through the air headfirst to a clumsy landing, skidding his wrist along the pavement, was always the favorite. By then, people were usually doubled over in gales of laughter. The boys were such entertaining storytellers that no one ever thought to ask why there were no other wounds or how concrete could make such clean razor slashes. No one even considered doubting. Why would they? Instead, they would usually walk away red-faced, wiping tears of laughter; and the boys would stand, plastic smiles painted on, until they were out of view. They became quite good at faking those smiles and those outbursts of laughter.

When they were alone, they spent time theorizing about what things would be like had they not survived, what life would be like without them. They lay on their backs on the floor and listened to music that understood the seemingly meaningless progression of life. If they were saved by coincidence, they thought, then they had no real purpose and were entirely expendable. If they were saved by design, then what was it for? There had to be some magnificent plan that they were a part of. Had it happened yet? Would they know it when it did?

There are two very distinct paths down which this train of logic can take you. The first is the darker, more reasonable of the two. It leads to the conclusion that the world is a fleeting, misguided ball of chaos. Nothing that you build or obtain or experience is worth anything, because at any random frenzied point you could die. The dark things in life engross you. Memories filter to recall only hardships, and your shortcomings haunt you daily. Waking up is often difficult, and food makes you ill. The second is much more optimistic but equally as dangerous. It leads to the notion that each moment is a stolen one and, as such, should be exploited to its maximum. The near-death encounter makes you invincible. Nothing can stop you, because you have already stood once at the threshold of death and walked away unscathed. Each day is another set of opportunities, and you seek to utilize as many as possible before the inevitable end. If you believe that nothing matters and life is short, you become a reckless leech of experience. You set unachievable goals and unrealistic expectations. You crave perfection. Hours spent sleeping are wasted moments of life, and every encounter must be a magnificent one. Because of the nature of each of their experiences, the two boys split in which paths they took. Ben's self-induced introduction caused him to be the pessimist. His fascination was with death and its boundless domain over life. The boy chose the other path. His fascination was with life and its limitless malleability. This made them a balanced pair and became their only contrasting attribute.

Adam Duritz, of Counting Crows, wailed softly on the radio as the two boys lay stretched across the floor. That was how much of their free time was spent. The clock on the VCR blinked a steady "12:34."

"You can't say 'best ever,' " Ben began. "What about the greats, the legends? Without them, music would be nothing."

"Exactly my point." The boy's tone sounded as if they had had this argument before. "I've got tons of respect for the legends, but they are legends not because they stand out but because they did it first. But if we are talking strictly lyrically, no one can compare." Ben paused for a moment.

"That may be true," he admitted, "but there are definitely some close seconds. I'm just saying 'best ever' is dangerous."

"Fair enough," the boy complied.

"I was thinking," Ben started. He was fingering the scars on his arm. "At my funeral, I want you to pick the music—something good like 'Another one bites the dust'."

The boy craned his neck to look Ben in the eye. Ben returned the glare.

"You can't be serious." The boy said, shaking his head slightly.

"Why not?" Ben sounded confused. "I don't want it to be all slow singing and depressing. People should laugh. I don't want them making it something it is not." The boy chuckled. "What? I'm serious. When I die, please don't let them make me a saint. Make them remember who I truly was. And for the love, promise me, you will play the song."

"Alright Ben," the boy began. "I promise, if I'm alive I'll play the stupid song at your funeral. Maybe Grandma and I will even dance." The two boys broke out into laughter.

31

four

There comes a point in almost everyone's life where they feel as though there is no hope. All people get to that point where they long for something so desperately that they will do almost anything to quench that longing, anything to escape it. For Ben, that longing for something more was so great that it nearly caused him to forfeit. Some would call that weak. I say he was stronger than most. I say that the ability to evade most of the vices that people resort to and offer yourself as a sacrifice to appease the merciless clutches of existence is a much bolder resolution. For others, the vices seem more appetizing. As I said before, this was a very difficult time for many people close to the boy.

The car's engine gurgled out a low hum as his brother turned the ignition. He could still taste the yeast in the back of his throat from his last drink. It was a Tuesday night; he didn't anticipate any difficulties getting home. He had survived yet another entertaining late-night party. Even with his windows up, he could still hear the thumping music from inside the house. It was beckoning him to come back in for one more drink, but it was getting late; he needed to get home. Switching on some music of his own, he backed out of the driveway.

Now, I don't know the boy's brother personally, so I have to tell you this story as I have heard it. That's the best I can offer. As his car rounded the corner down the old country road toward home, its tires drifted slightly across the twisted yellow lines. The honk of the oncoming car startled him. He swerved hard back to the right. The tires kicked up gravel off the side of the road as the oncoming car sped past. He veered back to the left, but the tires lost their grip. The back wheels slid out as the car spun around so that it was stopped perpendicular to the road, blocking both lanes. For a moment, he sat, panting. Time slowed as the headlights rose over the hill less than a half-mile down the street. His headlights shone off into the trees along the side of the road. The approaching car wouldn't be able to see him under the darkness of the night. He reached for the shifter. Frantically, he tried to put the car in reverse. The headlights were bearing down on him. The car was coming too fast. Its beams shone brightly in his face as he placed both hands up against the driver's side window and closed his eyes.

You can imagine the impact better than I can. I imagine that the metal twisted and moaned as it wrapped itself into a tangled formation. I imagine that the glass splintered and burst as the pressure climaxed and exploded, pounding through the car windows. The tires sung and echoed like a falsetto tenor vibrating in the vaulted ceilings of an ancient church as his car twirled in sweeping, graceful circles. I imagine that in an abrupt instant all motion came to a halt, the car radio humming static in sharp contrast to the blaring silence that hung thick in the midnight air. I imagine that it remained that way for quite some time. But I cannot say for sure; I have never been in a car accident before.

The ringing of the phone stirred the boy from his thoughts. He leaned the guitar gently against the wall and climbed up from the couch. He had been paralyzed there for the better part of the evening. He pulled the phone from the wall. As he put the receiver to his ear, the chaotic urgency of the situation flooded from the earpiece. Sirens wailed, and frantic voices called out over the chopping of what sounded like an approaching helicopter.

"Hello?" The boy could feel the anticipating shake in his voice.

"Help!" The strangled voice was almost unrecognizable. "You've got to come here! I got into an accident! Get Dad, you've got to come!"

"Where? Where are you?!" His heart was quickening.

"Greenwood. Right in front of the lumberyard. Hurry!"

The boy slapped the phone against the wall and called for his father.

As their car crested the hill, the flashing lights exploded through the windshield. It was a scene of cataclysmic horror. Glass

33

riddled the asphalt. Long thick trails of rubber melded to coarse pavement and led to a faded red pickup truck. Its front end was no longer identifiable. Instead, it was a mangled sculpture of steel. The passenger side of the windshield was shattered, leaving a gaping hole outlined in rigid glass. Blood stained the fragmented shards and restored the dull red color of the contorted hood. The boy felt his muscles tighten. A few paces from the truck, a young man squatted between the tire tracks. His face was planted firmly in his hands and his whole body trembled as two police officers towered over him, pens dancing wildly across miniaturized pads. A third officer stood a few yards away, cross-armed and pensive, as a woman danced in front of him, intensely telling the story of the accident. From the glow in her eyes, the boy could tell she had not been directly affected by the incident. It's a curious thing, the way people are invigorated by tragedy. It's a real mystery. I don't believe it is because people are genuinely concerned for the well-being of one another, because when tragedy is put directly in the face of human beings, they are prone to attempt to ignore and avoid those involved. But within the safe distance of a window-frame view of tragedy, tucked safely in the security of their homes and own comfort, people are thrilled. They love it. That woman was clearly one of those people. Her arms flailed about as she described the details of the impact.

"Like I said, I was washing dishes at the kitchen sink, right over there..." the woman began as the boy opened the car door and stepped out.

The officer pulled his pad and paper out of his pocket. As if she could add anything useful the fifth time she told the story. The boy scanned the scene. Now outside of the car, he was much more a part of the urgent horror.

Rain drummed lightly on the roof of the car like the ominous pounding of an ancient death march. The flashing sirens beamed into his eyes. He squinted and cupped his hands across his brow. The concentration of light burned his vision. Both ways down the road were empty black. The only visible light came from reflections of the spotted houses dancing on the puddles in the pavement. In the distance, he could barely distinguish the silhouette of someone sitting, hunched on the embankment along the side of the road. His father had already started off in that direction, his hands tucked coolly in his pockets, shoulders relaxed in an eerie, overly serene way. Their father had always been that way, naturally passive. He understood that life was inevitably unpredictable and that it had to be taken for what it was. He rarely rushed, counted each thing that happened as an opportunity, and taught his children that they could achieve anything as long as they were willing to work for it. He was almost to the embankment when the boy caught up. The boy's brother hardly stirred as they reached his side. He only looked up at them, and with pockets of tears in his eyes he said, "I think I really hurt her." The boy and his father helped his brother to his feet.

"Let's get you home," their father said. "There is nothing more we can do here now."

The drive home was deafeningly silent. His brother rode in the front seat with his head rolled back and his arm stretched out through the open window. His other hand was pressed gently against his forehead, covering his eyes. The boy rode in the backseat and watched the dispersed droplets of rain collect and make tiny rivers that flowed across the span of his window. Twice his father pulled the car off onto the gravelly shoulder at the request of his brother so he could empty his stomach into the rain-washed grass. The boy had never seen him so shaken. It was a scary thing, to see him so weak. He wondered if that weakness acted as a reminder of the fragility of life. He thought maybe it was a necessary thing—to be brought to such a place of horror and helplessness to be reacquainted with the reality that something far more powerful than us dictates all outcomes. Like the raindrops in the wind, we are forced into formations and clusters that we never intended to be a part of, by a thing infinitely beyond our grasp. Rolling down the window, he reached his hand out and swirled his finger through the gathered droplets.

Once parked in the driveway, their father turned off the car and slumped slightly against the steering wheel. He looked relieved.

"Come on in," he said. "I'm sure your mother is worried."

Sliding the key out of the ignition, he climbed out of the car and into the house. Now alone, the two brothers sat, each wrapped in their own thoughts. The boy felt useful just sitting there with his brother, being there in supportive silence. He could not imagine the tragedy of what he had just gone through but he felt intimacy in those drawn-out moments in the driveway.

"Did you see that truck's windshield?" His brother broke the somber quiet.

He was staring at him through bloodshot eyes in the side view mirror. The boy nodded. The image was burned in his mind, the shards of splintered glass coated in ruby red.

"There was a girl," he started again. "She was in the truck with her boyfriend. I-I guess she wasn't wearing her seatbelt. A helicopter came and took her away."

His words sputtered out like a child trying to explain something he could not comprehend. They sat in silence for a moment before the boy responded.

"I'm sure she will be fine." The words came out before he could stop them.

How could he make such a claim? Maybe she would not be fine. He had no insight into her medical condition. He instantly regretted making such a generic statement. For all he knew, the girl could be dead. He just had to say something comforting, even if there was no way he could prove it. Whether the boy believed it or not, it seemed to somewhat ease his brother's distress. He had closed his red eyes and his breathing had steadied.

As they strolled down the sidewalk, enveloped in the tranquil expectancy of spring, the two boys talked casually. The wind was so gentle on their faces that the trails of winter were not even apparent. The birds were already making their way north, across the sky, and people were migrating outdoors. A woman in shorts and a T-shirt pedaled briskly by on a bicycle. A man nodded a "hello" as he leisurely pushed a stroller past them and down the sidewalk. Outside of the old church across the street, a bake sale was underway. A long white-clothed table stood cluttered with circular plates and square dishes of homemade cookies, brownies, and marshmallow treats. Behind the table stood three older women—no doubt the masterminds behind the merchandise—and a girl about the boys' age. Ben stopped the boy short with his hand.

"Look over there," he said, pointing to the younger girl.

The boy strained his eyes, peering across the street.

"She doesn't look familiar. Should I know her?" the boy asked, turning back to his friend. Ben's eyes were still locked in place.

"No," he said, biting his bottom lip, "but I'd like to." The boy chuckled.

"Well," the boy looked back at the girl, "come on then."

He was halfway across the street before Ben tried to stop him. He had always been the more outgoing of the two. That came from his ideology that every moment should be treated as your last. Ben caught up to him just as he stopped at the table.

"Lemon bars, eh?" the boy asked, motioning to the plate of yellow rectangles on the tabletop.

Her long sun-fire yellow hair bounced gracefully around her shoulders as she turned to him. A smile stretched across her entire face. She had one of those smiles that touched every inch of her countenance, every part except her eyes. Her eyes were filled with brilliant whirlpools of deep sky blue. They looked familiar to him, swirling with that vast sapphire sadness. It reminded him of those rare sunny rains, the radiance still beaming from her hair and smile while it rained in her eyes. Or those last days of August, when the beaming sky is quivering with the looming approach of autumn. I do not believe I can do her justice. She was a gorgeous tragedy.

"Yes," she said, hoisting the plate with pride, "and they are spectacular! I know because I made them." She extended the platter to the boy.

"No thanks," the words stretched out slowly as he eyed her with caution.

There was something oddly familiar. For some reason, he found his thoughts drifting to that day he'd been given back the metallic heart that had symbolized his love, that day in the field when the fingers of his first love had uncurled to reveal that he could not mean to her what she meant to him. He remembered sitting up on that twisted old tree branch and getting lost in the immensity of the boundless field before him. It was a moment he had not thought of in years, but for some reason, standing there, it rushed back to him in an instant. He suddenly became aware of Ben's presence.

"What's your name?" the words sputtered out as the boy re-composed himself.

He rubbed his hand subconsciously over his short hair. The girl snickered.

"No lemon bar, no name." She picked a rectangle up from the pile and broke a piece off between her teeth. "Mmmm," she closed her eyes, "delicious." Grinning, she motioned to the plate with her head. "Eat one first."

"The thing is," the boy chuckled, "I am not really a big fan of lemons. Especially when th-" The girl reached out and pushed the half-eaten lemon bar into his mouth.

"Eat one," she erupted into laughter.

The boy stood, crumbled cookie in his mouth. He grimaced as his jaw worked, chewing through the zesty center. Even if he remotely enjoyed the cookie bar, he could not let his face show it. He swallowed hard and opened his mouth, proving that he had, in fact, eaten the lemon bar.

"Very good," the girl clapped her hands together. "You cannot tell me that was not delicious."

The boy closed his mouth and stood in expectation.

"Chloe," she began again, "my name is Chloe. And yours?" She extended out her hands, her face beaming with victory.

"This is Ben," the boy said, stepping aside and inching Ben forward. The honoree glow drained from her face. The boy wiped his mouth with his hand. "Nice meeting you." And with that, he turned on his heels and walked away.

"Hey!" she called after him, but he was already halfway back across the street.

Chloe quickly became an inseparable part of their group. She, too, knew all the words to every Counting Crows album, and she sat with them as they sang away those early days. They listened to The Cure and The Cranberries and talked about where they had been and what they had seen. Music seemed to have the same effect on her as it did on the boys, so they talked about its seemingly absolute correlation with their lives. She liked to write, just like the boy, so the two of them shared their intimate works. They would write together, taking turns writing lines, playing on each other's emotions and vision. Eventually, like everyone else, she noticed the scars on Ben's arm. The boy had started to tell the story of the skateboard, but he lacked the proper passion. It didn't feel right to keep secrets from someone who had grown so close to them. Ben had kept his eyes on the floor. He was barely through the fabricated story's introduction when the girl cut him off.

"What really happened?" the girl had asked again, rolling up her sleeves to reveal scars of her own, as if the three had needed anything more to bond them.

It turned out that they were much more the same people than they had realized. Chloe had secrets as well, secrets that the three of them discussed in their dark little circles of trust. They only spoke of her secrets in those shaded circles and, since I was never a part of those gatherings, I cannot say what exactly it was that they spoke of. All that I can say is that in those dark circles, something changed among them. Something dynamic happened that altered their way of thinking. They became a sort of support group for one another—a very necessary support group.

The boy sat with a pencil pressed firmly between his fingers and a guitar strewn across his lap. The dim lights barely caught the glistening silver of the gray markings etched along the open notebook that lay across his desk as his pencil scratched its surface. He paused for a moment and reread what he had just written. He tapped the eraser of the pencil against the desk as he muttered the words out loud. Dropping the pencil, he slid his fingers around the neck of the guitar and strummed the soft steel strings. Nodding, he eased the guitar down and snatched up the pencil again. The lead moved quickly as he scribbled notes across the page. This was how most of his songs were written. This song in particular was about passion and how every person must have passion for something—everyone must have that unexplainable gravitation toward something. No matter how mundane that something may seem to others, to that one individual that something is the driving force to everything else. He tapped the pencil against his chin before scribbling out the words, "For me, it's the little things, if I could find out what it is for you...."

A soft knock on the door interrupted his thoughts. His mother's frame shadowed the doorway as she stood, staring at him from across the room. He set down his pencil and turned to her.

"The hospital called today," she began, her voice cool and firm. "The girl from the accident is going to be fine." She paused for a moment, her face softening.

"But," she began again, "she was pregnant."

The boy felt his chest tighten as his eyebrows pressed toward the center of his forehead.

"Was?" he sputtered out. Sometimes he could be such a child.

His mother nodded from the doorway.

"The trauma was just too much. They were afraid this might happen, but they had to focus on saving the mother, because otherwise there was no point. I know it's a terrible thing, but you need to be strong for your brother."

"Where is he?" the boy slid the guitar to the floor and wiped his hands along his jeans.

"He's out," she replied. "I don't think it is something he necessarily wants to talk about. It's just something that happened, and now it's over. It is horrible, but I don't think you need to bring it up. I don't think he wants to talk."

His mother was right. His brother didn't want to talk. No one did. In fact, that conversation was the first and only time anyone in his family ever spoke of the accident. Everyone has a different way of dealing with life. I wonder if the boy remembers that day and those feelings. I wonder how deep down he planted that memory, how often it haunts him. I wonder if he remembers running down the road. The slapping of his shoes against the old pavement must have resonated in the muffled clouds in his ears. I'm sure that his legs tingled as his veins pulsated with pure adrenaline, forcing his muscles to flex and crank.

When he stopped, he was under a large maple tree, panting heavily. He steadied himself against its thick trunk with his hand. The coarse bark felt soothing against his soft skin. How fragile is the innocence of life. He felt kindred to the pain that he knew his brother must have been feeling. Another soldier of youth lost to the recklessness of age. He thought about the significance of the life that had been lost. As if the sanctity of the life was not enough, theoretically, an entire lineage had been destroyed—an entire saga of life, hardship, and love. While the life itself held clear value, perhaps the greater loss was the loss of the experience and impact of that life—experiences and influences that may never occur as a result. Perhaps that life took with it something utterly irreplaceable. That is what people say about many of those close to us now; why not the same for those taken from us? Is ignorance bliss? Because we never saw their value, do we feel no apparent loss of it? Must something be tangible before it can evoke emotional attachment? The weight was heavy on his shoulders as he dropped to the ground under the shading of the tree. That life was lost before it was even given meant that, ultimately, for some people life would be an entirely different experience. How many would be affected will never be known, but one thing was for certain: that loss would change the course of some facets of history. When weighing the significance of an individual, people often evaluate in terms of what that single individual has, or would have, achieved for the betterment of mankind as a whole, and rightfully so, given the selfish inclination of man. As a result, the greatness of an individual is based on his contribution by way of an invention or discovery that aided in the advancement of society. This would lead to the conclusion that the greatest loss suffered by the untimely death of an unborn individual is the possibility of some new antidote or device. I tend to disagree, and so did the boy. When you consider the history of technology, one inventor is typically trailed by a myriad of others, and shortly after one invention is made, several others are developed with similar attributes. This leads me to believe that, essentially, if one person did not exist to develop an idea, someone else would. If Einstein had not developed the theory of relativity, another brilliant mind would have stumbled across the discovery that has become such an intricate part of our society. Perhaps the greatest loss, then, is not found in the deferment of innovation but in something much more subtle. So, as I believe, and the boy discovered underneath that tree, the real victim is Art, as it is the direct result of one's life experiences and encounters. No two people write the same, or paint the same, or create the same, because it is a perfect mixture of life experience, perception, and individual emotion that composes Art. As such, when that life is not birthed into existence, the art that it would originate is lost. Had Shakespeare not lived, whose tragedies and comedies would have softened the hearts of English royalty and narrowed the economic gap? Had Myron or Michelangelo never been born and never smoothed their hands around a ball of clay or a block of marble, then would we have as great an appreciation and as vast a knowledge of the physics and anatomy of the human body? Perhaps we would, but not without the unique creation of some other artistic mind. It was these realizations that fell upon the boy as he drifted off to sleep underneath that maple tree.

His fingers closed stiffly around the slender pen as he lifted it from the floor. He paused as his eyes moved quickly, scanning his new surroundings. He was squatted down on one knee beneath a short round red table. Blue and white lights danced in patterns along the cold concrete floor in rhythmic unison with the pulsating music that cranked overhead. The soft, hypnotic vibrations that palpitated in his chest soothed his initial apprehension. He rose slowly to find that he was not alone. The large warehouse-like room was full of people moving robotically to the enchanting strands of beats and notes that oozed from the pinholes of the speakers which stood in tall slanted stacks like lifelike statues looking down on the crowd. Taking a few tranced steps backward, the boy dropped down onto a plush orange leather bench. Next to him sat a girl with straight jet-black hair and ruby lipstick. Her long dangling earrings swung and cut through the sheen walls of hair as she turned to him. Her thick lips arched into a slight smile as she gazed at him with familiar expectancy, tucking her hair behind her ear. With her other hand, she pressed a long slip of paper against the red table. Furrowing her brow, the girl looked to the ground under the table and back at the boy. Reaching out his arm, he extended the pen. The girl nodded her head, smiling as she took it from his hand, and mouthed the words "Thank you." As she dropped the pen point to the table and swirled it about in fluid loops and motions, the boy felt a slight tingling against his chest.

The methodical pounding of the bass intensified, resonating deeper in his core. The vibrations rattled his ribcage. He turned back to the crowd. Their mechanical synergy was mesmerizing; he could not escape their draw. The concrete was hard beneath his feet as he stood and walked out on the floor and toward the swarm of dancing drones. There was something almost electrifying about the atmosphere in the room. The tingling in his chest grew to a warming sensation. It was something within the tribal vibrations, almost as if something was being awakened. With each step, the stirring in his chest became more apparent. The warm prickling increased to a steady burn that fluctuated with the surges of melody. The music itself had become less relevant, secondary to the swelling presence beneath his chest, almost as if the music had become a byproduct of what was happening inside him. The blue and white lights began swirling faster. He moved closer to the crowd. The stacks of towering speakers seemed to be arching over farther, as if closing in on him. His vision blurred. He thought his chest might explode. Sparks rained down from the speakers overhead as he stepped in among the mob. The sizzling burning in his chest subsided to a low rumble as he scanned the nameless faces in the crowd. The air caught in his throat as his muscles seized tight and his eyes caught sight of her. Her hair swirled a brilliant shifting brown and auburn as she turned her head toward him. Flickering sparks showered down like little stars and dusted the ground between them as her eyes gazed into his. He no longer heard music. They were the most magnificent things he had ever seen—deep warm hazelnut centers outlined with a burst of natural forest green. Like daisies in spring, they bloomed gracefully in the whites of her eyes. Water welled in the corners of his eyes, and his eyelids quivered as a smile stretched across her flawless face. It was impossible. Her nose crinkled slightly, and faint dimples appeared in the lower parts of her cheeks. Her soft, glistening pink lips stretched into the most beautiful smile he had ever seen. It was more than he could bear. He wiped his eyes with the back of his hand in an attempt to hide his tears and returned the smile. He could not peel his gaze away. She was a goddess. He was sure he looked like a fool, standing there, gaping. She chuckled as if she had heard his thought. He chuckled at himself. He chuckled at the world. He chuckled at the fact that anyone could say there was nothing good in the world. He chuckled at the notion that anything could ever be wrong with a smile that bright, eyes that profound, and a girl that perfect. In three bounding steps, they were in each other's arms, both laughing hysterically. It felt so warm and secure and pure in that embrace. The boy would have never been able to let go had he not had as equal a necessity to see her eyes again. The cool clean scent of heaven wafted from her hair as he pulled her in again. It was magical.

They spent hours together just staring, dancing, hugging, and laughing. The boy no longer noticed the robotic drones around them with their rigid movements. Instead, he noticed things about her, like what made her laugh, or the way her eyes flashed when she smiled; her intelligence, or the overwhelming sense of belonging that he found in her presence. He was enthralled with the fluid motions of her arms and hips, enthralled with their inescapable synergy. The music was still a distant humming, but they danced to a music that swelled up from within them, from underneath their chests. For hours, he lingered in her haven of bliss. For hours, he wrapped himself in her passionate attention.

For hours, they danced in their unabashed spotlight of devotion. Suddenly, she stopped. She looked deep into his eyes, as he had discovered only she could, and smiled—this time, a softer, more somber smile. It did not touch her eyes. It did not form her dimples.

"Goodbye," she whispered. "I will see you soon."

He nodded. He knew it was time. Tears collected beneath his eyelids. She kissed him softly on the cheek. He smiled back. He squinted his stinging eyes and tried to burn her image into his mind. There was no need. He would not forget her. He blinked, releasing the tears, and she was gone.

When he awoke, his cheeks were damp and his chest ached. The sun had long since descended the lazy horizon. The crickets and frogs were out in their nocturnal symphony, while the fireflies twinkled in the sky in a rhythmic luminous display. The blades of grass tapping gently against his skin still retained the warmth of the day as a slight breeze stirred them along the ground. Even with the frog's and cricket's song, he could still hear the faint whispering rustle of the foliage audience. He could not escape the unbearable feeling of loss.

"No one is that perfect," he whispered to himself as he rose to his feet.

Breathing deeply, he stretched out his arms and inhaled the crisp night air. As he filled his chest and lungs, his eyes narrowed. He felt a slight rumble inside his ribcage. Exhaling, he placed his hand against his chest. Nothing. He chuckled, shoved his hands in his pockets, and started walking toward home. He wondered if the rumble had been something he created as a result of his dream or if it was mere coincidence. He wondered if, because of the dream, he would start a miserably effortless search for the perfect girl who didn't exist. It's often the things that we ourselves have created that destroy us, the boy realized. He thought about the car accident and how many more there must be like it. He wondered if it was worth the benefit of the convenience of automobiles at the cost of human lives. Shimmying open his window, he climbed through and into his room. We have to live with the consequences of the things we create, the boy thought, however fatal or beautiful they may be. Smiling, he flopped down on his bed and stared up at the ceiling.

The next day was an ominous one in that household. His mother spent the day vacuuming, not out of necessity but as a means to drown out the blaring ring of tragedy. His father spent the day out in the yard, pulling weeds and watering plants. It was not out of the ordinary for him to spend his day that way, but this particular day his hands moved much more slowly, packing the dirt much more gently than usual. The shades were open and the sun was up, but the house was still dark, as if the glass window panes blocked those rays of light from penetrating and illuminating his room. The boy spent his afternoon trying to write a poem, then a song, that could express the rare experience he had had the night before, but his mind was distracted by his brother's accident. He was sure it was on everyone's mind, the way they all avoided one another.

The spicy aroma of cayenne pepper and paprika drifted up the stairwell and into the boy's bedroom. His mother was making chili, his brother's favorite. Earlier that morning, the boy had tried to talk to his brother but his attempt was not welcomingly received, so the boy decided it best to keep his distance. Sweeping his notebook up off his desk, he yanked open one of the drawers and dropped it in. He couldn't concentrate. Most nights his mother would call him and his siblings for dinner, but tonight he thought he might spare her the discomfort of breaking the dreadful silence and considered the clanking of dinner plates a suitable summons. As he descended the stairs, he heard stirring in the other bedrooms down the hall. It seemed they were extending the same courtesy. The boy reached the bottom of the steps and sat down silently in his chair, waiting as the rest of his family filed in behind him.

"It's nothing special," his mother started, setting the large pot down on the table. "I just threw it together with some leftover stuff I found in the refrigerator."

Their silent response proved that they knew it was not true. The boy only stared at her. She looked exhausted. Her eyes were weary from lack of sleep and her shoulders heavy with the burden of her child's pain as she eased down into her chair. The dinner proceeded in silence. No one said a word. The boy kept his eyes fastened to his plate until he had finished every bite. Only then did he scan the table to find that everyone shared the same evasive position. His brother had not touched his food. The boy cleared his throat. No one noticed. His fork clanged loudly against the empty porcelain of his plate as he dropped it and rose to his feet. Walking a few steps around the table, he stopped at his brother's chair. Everyone had lifted their heads to look at him. Bending over, he wrapped his arms around his brother's hunched frame.

"I love you," he muttered, "no matter what. I can't begin to imagine what it's like." He paused for a moment. "But, if there is anything I can do to make this easier, anything, I'll do it. No matter what."

His brother did not respond, but the boy did not need him to. He had done the best he could. Dropping his dishes into the sink, he opened the door and walked outside.

Ben and Chloe were already there by the time he reached the weathered red barn. He could hear them laughing as he trudged down the old paved driveway. Already he could feel a sense of relief from the grave atmosphere of his house. As he slid open the barn door, the warm acceptance of friendship rushed around him. He always felt most at home among his friends. Their laughter quieted as he relayed the news from the hospital. Chloe shook her head in disbelief, her sad eyes squinting with sympathy. Ben stretched out on his back and stared through the holes in the roof in silence. Death was not a thing they feared or were even surprised by. It was something they knew to be natural, something they felt familiar with and accepted. But even for them, the death of innocence was always an extreme tragedy.

"How is your family taking it?" Chloe asked, as the boy sat down beside them. He smirked.

"My mom vacuumed every room, my dad weeded the garden about seven times, and my brother stared at his wall," he explained. Chloe shook her head again.

"That well?" They all three chuckled.

"I don't get it," he continued. "How can you just not talk about something that's screaming so loudly to be said?"

"I guess some people just think it's easier not to," she shrugged. Sometimes she could be surprisingly optimistic.

"They're crazy," the boy said, dropping to his back next to Ben. "Anything good?" he asked, looking up through the holes in the roof.

"Nah," Ben replied, "not really."

Chloe inched closer to the boys and craned her neck to see the blank midnight sky. Had it not been for the gleaming moon floating high overhead, darkness would have filled the night and the barn.

"I think I fell in love last night," the boy said, his eyes still searching. There was a pause.

"With who?" Chloe chuckled.

"This girl," the boy began, "in my dream last night."

He knew it sounded ridiculous, but he didn't know how else to say it. Chloe eased her way down to the barn floor and plucked a daisy that had grown up through the cracks in the old lumber.

"Yeah, that's just the girl of your dreams." Ben said, stretching his legs. "You know how people always say 'the person of their dreams'? That was yours."

"I know what you mean," the boy shook his head, "but this was different, like something I have never felt before. I think she was real. Maybe more real than anything else I have ever experienced."

There was another pause. Ben had turned his head toward his friend. Chloe lay on her back, her eyes transfixed on the daisy's face as she spun its stem between her fingers.

"It's like all this time," the boy tried to explain, "I've been trying to figure out what love really is, and in an instant some random girl in a dream showed me. I've been trying to puzzle out what it feels like and if it still exists, and I think that's where I was wrong. I don't think it's a feeling anymore. I think it's something much deeper, like an inescapable gravity. I think it's something that you get lost in, and once you've found it you can never do without."

The boy laughed at himself and looked at his friends. Ben was squinting with captivated eyes. Chloe had slid the flower in her hair and was propped up on one elbow, facing the boy.

"I know it sounds crazy, but she was the first thing that I thought about when I woke up today, and I think that's what love is. It's like a window, and once you find it and look through it, everything is different, everything is brighter." The boy shrugged. He was not sure it was something he could explain; and even if he could, he was sure it sounded absurd.

"Does this girl have a name?" Chloe asked, dropping back down to the floor. The boy shook his head. "Well, she needs a name," Chloe smiled. "How else will we know when she comes around? What should we call her?"

"How about Sally?" Ben suggested. "It's a common name."

"Sally is good," Chloe nodded. "It's a start. Anything else?" The boy folded his hands behind his head.

"She had brown hair and amazing green eyes, with deep brown pupils." The boy thought for a moment, "And she plays guitar."

"A musician?" Chloe's eyes lit up. "Excellent. Sally." She said it again, nodding with approval.

Just the thought of her possible existence made the boy's heart quicken. He wondered if someone so perfect could live among such a tainted world. He looked up through the hole in the roof. This time, he was not searching for stars; he was staring at the moon—perhaps the same moon that she, too, could see, the same moon that shone down on her angelic face. The boy sighed.

"That settles it," Ben nudged him. "Go find her."

Most of their days were spent out in public. People fascinated them, and they loved to go out and interact with society. It made them feel better to be able to explore, in spite of their secrets, and do small, insignificant things to brighten up daily life. They started volunteering at nursing homes and global aid agencies. At night they would sit in a circle and, with the soft hum of Robert Smith in the background, they would just understand and sustain one another. It was how they would cope—seeking out the good things in life in order to contrast the dark. It was reassuring to know that brighter things did, in fact, exist. However, this sort of social exploration also had an adverse effect on the boy and his friends. To go out meant that they saw the world as it truly was. To brighten the lonely faces of the nursing home halls and troubled faces in soup kitchen lines required that they first look into those faces and discover their hurt. It meant taking on that pain as your own, at least to some degree. Ultimately, it reinforced their understanding of death. Charity was their solace, but at the same time it worsened them to take on the burdens of so many others as their own. They watched people suffer and waste away to nothing. They watched families neglect their own because of age, mistakes, or poverty. They watched people die as they struggled to fight the losing battle of increased quality of life; but at least they were making a difference. They made friends only to lose them. They fed hungry mouths only to watch them starve. While it made them stronger, it also made them darker. It seems it's always just when you are on top that you have to taste the cold realization of the bottom.

B.B. King wept gracefully through the electric strings of his guitar as the boy did his best to bend the notes in unison. He could hear the ancient sorrow of the blues oozing through the speakers. As he slid his hand down the neck of his sunset golden electric guitar, which he fondly called "Julia," he could feel the pain of generations struggling to find their place in a world that despised them. It was seeping through the warm, laminated wood and massaging his fingertips as the strings vibrated softly beneath them. Sometimes he would get lost like that for hours, but today his heart was distracted. It had been five months since the accident, and no one had said a word more about it. Anytime it seemed that, by chance, the conversation would drift in that direction, some member of the family would awkwardly redirect the topic. The boy's concern, however, stemmed from the effect that this sort of evasive behavior seemed to have on his brother. Something had changed in him. He was rarely home anymore, and when he was, he was spending most of his time alone in his room. He was out late with friends whom the boy had never heard of before and could often be found mumbling on the phone at odd hours of the night. Needless to say, the boy had become suspicious. The charade had gone on for too long. It was time that someone said something. The boy propped his guitar against the wall and flipped the power switch on the radio.

As he eased back in his chair, he thought back to when the two of them were younger. Four years his senior, his immediate older brother had a great impact on him growing up. The boy had always admired and sought to try to keep up with him. He remembered sitting up late watching his brother play video games. He rarely got a turn and did his best to stay quiet, but he just loved the sense of security and comfort that he found in spending time with his brother. Even when he was being picked on or ignored, the boy loved every moment. He laughed as he thought back to the pranks and mischief his brother used to talk him into being a part of. Those times gave the boy such a meaningful bond to his brother. It took him years to realize that the bond was not a mutual one, but the boy supposed that was usually the case—younger siblings typically form more of an emotional attachment. For the boy, it became such a powerful connection that he even shared in his brother's pain. He hurt when his brother hurt. He remembered times when his brother was being punished and the boy would attempt to sacrifice himself in his stead, to ease his brother's suffering. Many times he would succeed and take the blame, and while it was a welcome favor, it was never received with much gratitude; but that didn't matter to the boy. It was his brother, his best friend, and as far as he was concerned, that was thanks enough. His brother was in trouble and he needed him, maybe now more than ever. Smiling, the boy stood up and started down the hall toward his brother's room. He stopped a few steps short of the doorway.

"Tonight? You know I'm always in," his brother's voice drifted from the bedroom, "especially if you're scoring."

Scoring? The boy inched closer to the doorway. A triumphant laugh bellowed from the pit of his brother's stomach. It didn't even sound like him.

"Yeah, I think I know where she lives," he started again. "In that neighborhood right across from the high school, right?" He paused. "Yeah, second house on the left? Cool. Got it."

Something didn't seem right. The boy inched closer.

"If not, don't even worry about it. I got us covered. I was talking to my...hang on," the boy could hear his brother walking across the room.

He slid back away from the door just as it swung shut. He moved back to the closed frame and strained to hear but could only make out the low muffled rumble of his brother's voice. Scoring? Covered? Something was not right, and he had to find out what.

Pushing his arm through the sleeve of his hooded sweatshirt, the boy scooped his keys up off his dresser. His brother had left for the party more than an hour ago, and his parents were asleep. It was time to move. He was not sure where exactly he was going, but he had heard his brother say that it was the second house on the left in the neighborhood across from his school. It sounded easy enough. As he started the car and backed out of the driveway, he wondered if he was doing the right thing. Was it wrong of him to listen to his brother's conversation? He hadn't meant to eavesdrop; he just happened to overhear. For some reason, he thought back to the first day that he and his friend traveled across that field. Venturing into the unknown was always a dangerous decision. Had he known the consequence of this decision in particular, I'm not sure that he would have chosen to make it at all. As he drifted to a stop and put the car in park, it was obvious he was in the right place. Cars lined the street in front of the house and packed the driveway tight. Small black lamps bordered a gray sidewalk that led from the driveway to concrete steps where a group of four or five kids his brother's age stood talking in a circle. A girl stood in the middle of the front lawn with a cell phone pressed to her ear. As he opened the car door, he could hear that she was crying.

"It's like he doesn't even care that I'm here," he could hear her sobbing as he walked across the street, toward the house.

She saw him coming and made her way to the other end of the lawn. No one ever wants help when they need it most. The boy pushed his hands in his jacket pockets. He just needed to focus on finding his brother and making sure everything was fine. In and out. The circle of kids quieted as he strolled past them and up the concrete steps. He could feel their eyes on him. He had to act natural; no need to draw more attention than necessary. Twisting the knob, he found the door unlocked and pushed it open. He was greeted with blaring loud music and the overwhelming smell of alcohol. It didn't look good. He was not yet a fan of house parties. The room was crowded with people. Aluminum cans littered the floor. The boy began to inch his way through, scanning the faces for his brother. In and out. He found it impossible to take a step without bumping into someone. Liquid sloshed out of cups and cans and splashed on his jacket, or on the carpet, as he did he best to dodge it. Where did all these people come from?

"Hey, hey!" he felt someone slap his back. "You want a beer, man?" the voice asked.

"No thanks," the boy called over his shoulder and moved quicker through the crowd.

He didn't see his brother anywhere. A girl with a low-cut tank top and a short jean skirt smiled at him. She had thick red lipstick that shimmered with her stretched lips and forest green eye shadow applied generously to her eyelids. She moved her hips and lifted her shoulders as she casually moved closer to him.

"Wanna dance?" she yelled over the music, as she slid her hands down her waist.

"Maybe later," the boy yelled back and pushed farther through the crowd.

He felt someone's foot beneath his as he stepped down.

"Watch it!" a deep voice called.

As the boy turned to apologize, a heavy hand pushed hard against his chest. He stumbled backward. Fortunately, the density of people kept him on his feet. Maybe he shouldn't have come. He felt someone grab his arm and help him catch his balance.

"Careful there, little guy," another deep voice said. "Too much to drink?" A nearby circle of girls giggled.

"None at all, actually," the boy responded, but no one was listening. "Thanks."

He looked back where the push had come from but a new group of people had filled in. What was his brother doing here? He pushed his way deeper in the crowd.

"Hey! Hey you!" someone hit his shoulder. It was a boy about his brother's age with short spiked blonde hair and a beard.

"Look, I'm sorry if I stepped on your foot or spilled your beer," the boy put up his hands, "I'm just trying to find...."

"What? What are you talking about? No, I know you." His speech was slurred, but at least he was friendly. He grabbed the boy's hand and shook it, pulling him in firmly for a hug.

"Yeah," the boy started, the guy did look strangely familiar, probably one of his brother's friends who had been over the house before. "How have you been?"

"Good, man," the slurred words fumbled over one another, "really good. It's so good to see you. What are you up to?" He took a long swig from the bottle in his hand, the whole time keeping his feet firmly planted on the floor as if he might flip backward.

"Not too much," the boy tried to sound interested, "just looking for my brother, actually."

The bottle popped a hollow echo as he pulled it from his lips and dropped his head back to the boy.

"Yeah, he's here. He's here. I think um," he was talking way louder than necessary, "I think," he rubbed his chin, "yeah, he's back in the bedroom there to the right."

"Oh, alright. Well, thanks," the boy said, starting to inch away.

"Yeah man," the kid grabbed the boy's hand again with a damp palm and pulled him in for another hug. "Be careful."

The boy nodded and moved quickly back into the crowd, wiping the liquid on his hand against his shirt. He made his way back across the room and down the hallway to the bedroom door. A large picture of Jimi Hendrix was plastered against the wood. Something seemed oddly familiar. He heard a toilet flush from the door behind him and two girls laughing. Déjà vu? As he twisted the knob and pushed the door open, he remembered. It was happening just the way it had in his dream. His brother sat in the middle of a sofa, opposite the door, with a girl on either side. He was hunched over a coffee table, one hand pressing against his right nostril while the other held a rolled up bill to his left, inhaling white powder from the glass surface. The boy froze. How could he have forgotten that horrifying dream? How was he not more prepared?

Now, I'm not exactly sure what you call this white powder where you come from. I've heard it called many things—ice, snow, blow, angie, blanca, candy, dust, yay, crystal, jelly, lace, lady, number 3, pearl, shake, star, and yes, cocaine. I, personally, have a more clever name for it. Where I come from, we call the sort of substances that distort reality and ease suffering with their instant but fatal relief the "Remedy"; this one in particular is known specifically as "powdered Remedy." For the sake of argument and the love of simplicity, we'll use my terminology. After all, this is my story.

After he had sniffed those last morsels of the powdered Remedy from the table, his brother lifted his head and the two locked eyes. They both were paralyzed with shock. The boy could feel his heart starting to ache. Tears welled up in his eyes. He struggled to restrain them. His brother dropped his head.

"What the hell is going on?" the girl seated on the left said, looking from the boy to his brother. "Hello? Can you shut the door?"

The boy turned and walked back down the hallway.

"Hey! Hello?!" the girl called after him.

"Shut up!" he heard his brother's voice. "Hey! Wait!" but the boy didn't stop.

He walked back out into the sea of people. His breaths were panicked and shallow as he began to shove himself back through the crowd. His legs kept a slow methodical march, as if he himself had no control over their actual movement. His eyes were transfixed on the door, marking his target. A heavy weight shifted the boy off balance as another drunken buffoon stumbled over him. Alcohol permeated from his skin as he caught himself on the boy's shoulders. The boy turned his face away. His head swooned with nausea. Pressing his hands firmly against his assailant's torso, the boy heaved with all that he could muster. The body fell limp onto the ground. He moved closer to the door. His breaths were getting weaker. Hands and shoulders and bodies pressed up against him. Liquid soaked through the stretched fabric of his sweatshirt and tingled against his skin. The girl with the heavy eye shadow caught his eye again and smiled. He looked away. He tried to swallow the ball that had formed in the center of his throat, but it only shortened his already strangled breathing. How had he come to this place? His body temperature started to rise. He felt as though he may faint. Unzipping his jacket, he pressed on farther. The initial shock of what he had just seen was only amplified by the fact that it was not the first time he had seen it. He remembered the dream well: his brother sitting there, those same girls on either side of him, hunched over that table. It was more than he could bear. Flinging open the front door, he spilled out and clasped the banister of the front porch, gulping in the night air. It rose out of him like a volcano spewing gurgling lava from the depth of its cavernous belly, and he bowed over the patio railing and emptied his stomach in the bushes. The circle of people on the sidewalk had made their way inside, and the girl on her cell phone had wandered to some more private destination. He spit the acid that had collected in his mouth into the mulch surrounding the bushes and wiped his lips with his thumb.

Dropping down on the concrete steps, he lowered his head into his hands. His heart was wrenching. You can spend your entire life with someone and still never know the deepest crevices of the capability of their heart. Up the sidewalk, the boy could hear the scuffing of shoes against the hard asphalt. He lifted his head toward the darkness. Out from the shadows, a young man, a few years older than the boy, emerged. His green and white striped polo shirt made him visible as he strolled from the darkness and hung loosely down to a pair of dark blue jeans. The scuffing came from the white soles of his wide gray sneakers, which he barely lifted off the ground in a lazy stroll. He was scrolling through a cell phone with one hand and muttering to himself as he approached the steps. The boy turned his head to look back over the lawn, his eyes still wide with shock. He could still taste the lava in his mouth. He skimmed his hand along the short hairs on his head as the young man dropped down on the steps next to him. He had slipped his cell phone back in his pocket and replaced it with a pack of cigarettes. Flipping open the lid, he slid one out and pressed it between his lips.

"Nice night, huh?" he said, fishing for a lighter in his other pocket. The boy nodded and folded his arms across his knees. "How's the party? You know these clowns in there?" He pulled the cigarette from his mouth and motioned to the door behind them with his thumb. The boy shook his head.

"Not really, I mean, I used to," he managed to croak out through the dry passage of his throat. The young man nodded.

"Isn't that the funny thing about people? Just when you think you know them," he blew a cloud a smoke from his mouth, "they change, or you do, or life just changes you both." The boy turned to him. Who was this kid?

"I'm Jack," pushing the cigarette back in his mouth, he extended his hand to the boy. The boy took it and shook it slowly, nodding his head. "Rough night?"

The boy nodded again. He realized that he must look it; if his silence wasn't enough, he was sure his skin was pale and his eyes felt dry and itchy. Jack chuckled and reached back in his pocket.

"You look like you could use one of these," he said, pulling out the pack of cigarettes.

The boy eyed the box. "Camel Turkish Gold," it read. Jack flipped back the lid again and extended it to the boy. His head was spinning; he could not get the image of his brother lifting the powered Remedy from the glass tabletop out of his mind. He just wanted to erase his memory, just forget what he had seen and destroy his dream. He was angry, and he was not sure why he was angry, or at whom. He was angry at the world altogether for having brought his brother to the place where he would do such a thing, angry that something could have such power and sway as to cause such decisions. He wanted revenge. He wanted some way to get back at the world for what it had done to his brother, to those elderly people in the nursing home, to those poor people in the soup kitchen, to Ben and Chloe, and to him. Pinching his fingers around the slim circle of the cigarette filter, he pulled it from the pack and shoved it between his lips. Jack was smiling. He pulled out his lighter, sparked it with his thumb, and lifted the flame to the end of the Turkish Gold. Maybe the boy and his friends were trying too hard. They could not help everyone. You have to learn to save yourself before you can offer any real assistance to anyone. If you can't help yourself or those close to you, what good can you be to someone hundreds of miles away? The boy was learning that by the second. The tobacco sizzled as he pulled air through the smoldering end. He held the smoke in his mouth for a moment and looked back out over the shadowed blades of grass. As he slowly inhaled, he could feel the singeing tar clawing at his throat. He thought about the white stripes that scarred Ben's and Chloe's arms and the swollen tracks that he knew were forming inside his brother's nostrils. He thought about the baby who had lost its innocent life and about his encounter with leukemia. He drew the smoke deeper into his body. He filled his chest. He thought about his strange connection to a girl that didn't exist, and he exhaled slowly. His stomach tightened as his reflexes tried to force air out in a fury of coughs and hacks, but he restrained. After the smoke had completely cleared his lungs, he allowed himself a few quiet coughs, but he did he best to mask his inexperience. He already felt lightheaded. He slid the cigarette back between his lips and inhaled again, just as deeply. He was making scars of his own.

"Don't worry," Jack chuckled, patting the boy on the back, "you'll get the hang of it, brother." He rose to his feet and flicked his cigarette out into the yard. "Good luck. I'll see you around," he said and he strolled out into the darkness.

The boy sat back with his elbows propped up on the gritty step behind him and inhaled another drag. Titling back his head, he could see the black canvas of sky speckled with a multitude of stars gazing down like eyes intently inspecting his being. He blew smoke across his view to muffle the clarity and made his own clouds, allowing the eyes to see only as deep as the air would allow. He coughed a little, and each drag burned his lungs, but he smoked it down to the filter. Even then, he knew this was an altering moment in his life. In smoking that cigarette, he was doing something he hated because he had seen something he hated in a life that he was trying desperately to love. He had given in for the first time and succumbed to something that had once made him weep to watch. Life simply could not be the same from here. He could almost feel the callous forming on his youthful heart, his once youthful heart. How much would this change him? Did it mean that he had abandoned all values and morality and become a part of the world that evoked such a change? He hoped not. Where was that youthful boy? What had become of his childhood playmate and his locket on a string that he had wrapped delicately in his pocket for a girl he thought he loved? They were gone now. They had left him and become distant, dreamy memories like a foreign fairy tale heard once before. He did not believe he would ever be given a chance to go back.

The door behind him swung open as he flicked the cigarette to the blades of grass, and his brother rushed out onto the porch. The boy kept his eyes on the front yard. He could not turn around and face his brother for fear that he would lose control of his freshly trained emotions.

"Look," his brother's voice was calm, "I'm sorry that you had to see that, but it's not what you think. That stuff—it's not that big of a deal."

The boy nibbled at his bottom lip in an attempt to calm its trembling. It was not the sadness of what he had seen that made his lip quiver. His brother's voice and stuttered explanation showed that he knew the boy was disappointed, and from his tone the boy could tell his disappointment saddened his brother, and that was what broke his heart. He hated to hurt his brother, even with proper reason.

"Plus," he pleaded, "it's not something I do very often. It's nothing to worry about. I only do it every now and then. It's not an everyday thing."

"That's how it always starts," the boy tried to keep his voice calm. "It starts as every now and then and before you know it...." he trailed off.

He wasn't sure if that was true or not but it seemed right. Addictions don't happen overnight. His brother moved closer to the steps.

"You're right, you're right, it's dangerous. I need to cut it out." His voice was insincerely consoling.

"I mean it!" the boy jumped to his feet and spun around to face his brother. "What are you thinking? Don't you know what that stuff does to you?" His grief was melting into anger.

His brother moved closer until he was within inches of the boy.

"Of course I do! That's why I use it!" his whispers were harsh as he leaned to the boy's ear. "Do you have any idea," his voice softened and the boy could hear a slight shake in his throat, "what it's like to wake up every morning knowing that you killed an innocent baby?"

No. The boy blinked slowly. No. He had no idea. He could not begin to imagine. He tried to respond, but the words caught in his throat. No, he could not fathom the horror, the nightmares, the guilt. He could not imagine having to relive that night over and over again. His face softened as he shook his head and stepped back from his brother.

"Look, I know I need to quit," he had steadied his voice. "I just need some time." His brother searched his eyes for compassion, his glare hypnotizing. The boy nodded. "You can't tell anyone. This is my thing. Anyone you tell will only be hurt by it. You've got to promise not to tell anyone."

The boy did not respond; he couldn't. His mouth moved softly but no sound escaped.

"Remember that night at the dinner table?" his brother continued. "You said if there was anything you could do to make this better, you would do it, no matter what. Remember that? Well, this is that thing. Just promise to keep it between you and me for a little while, and then I'll be through with it. You'll see. Just let me deal with this, that's the only thing I need you to do to make this better, alright? It's my battle."

The boy nodded, "It's our battle."

That night the boy went to Chloe's house and sat on her patio, as they often did when her parents had gone to sleep. The boy tried to hide his disheveled hair, his bloodshot eyes, heavy steps, and the lingering taste of vomit in the back of his throat, but as soon as he closed the screened patio door behind him, his friends could instantly tell something was wrong. Ben was the first to ask. The boy remembered his promise and assured them that he was fine. Chloe reinforced Ben's concern by asking if he was sure and telling him that he seemed distant. Again, the boy remembered his promise and told her that he was just tired, that's all. That seemed to pacify their questions, but the boy could still feel their concern.

After a few minutes of silence, Chloe suggested a movie and the three moved in to the living room sofa. It was obvious to the boy that neither of them had let go of the belief that something damaging had happened to him that night; Chloe cuddled up next to him and laid her head positioned peacefully on his chest, while Ben sat at the other end of the couch, transfixed on the television screen, fingering his scars. The boy knew it was not going to be easy, hiding his brother's secret, but he had made a promise and he meant to keep it. He did not know what it was like to feel the things his brother was going through, but the boy would do his best to understand and empathize. He would do his best to take on his brother's pain and help him in whatever way he could. Had the boy known that he would have to keep this promise for two and a half years—two and a half years of watching his brother waste away, of constant worry, late night pickups, and indefinite loans—had he known that this promise meant two and a half years, I don't believe that he would have made it. But he did make it, and back then, his word was his bond and he knew that, and so did his brother—perhaps even more so. It started that night and it became a routine from there; anytime his brother was on his mind and someone would ask what was wrong, he used the same excuse, "Just tired."

five

He adjusted the strap along his back and hoisted the guitar over his head. The spotlight was hot against his face and blurred his vision as he waved again to the crowd of fifty-some that populated the room. Their eyes were on him as he bit his guitar pick between his teeth and strolled across the stage. Months ago, their stares and calls and applause would have made him nervous, but it was something that the boy was getting used to. Dark basements, alcohol-soaked platforms, colored lights, drunken hollering, broken glass, and free rum and cokes had comprised their weekend nights for the past five or six months. It turned out that, apart from being a veteran smoker, Jack was also a decent singer, and he knew a few guys who could make some fairly good noise on various instruments. The boy had run into him at his usual music shop one day, while ogling a custom signature Gibson Les Paul electric guitar, a few weeks after their initial late-night encounter. Jack could see the lust in the boy's eyes and invited him to "come jam" with a few of his friends. The B.B. King riffs and Counting Crows inspired chord progressions seemed to impress Jack's friends. They stopped inviting their old guitarist playmate, and within weeks they were calling themselves a band.

While Jack had the better voice, he wasn't much of a writer, so the boy brought the songs he had written and taught them to the group. It was only about a month before they were playing shows in the dilapidated basements of bars and rundown saloons. They would come out on stage and the boy would play with ease, songs that he had written years before, and Jack would sing the lyrics with passion, as if he himself had written them. Some songs held deeper meaning to the boy and, while he was not nearly as talented as Jack, he would insist on singing them himself. Jack agreed, and while the boy sang he would lower his microphone, squint his eyes, and nod in rhythm as if affirming their decision.

After the show, when desperate girls would flock around him, Jack would put his arm around the boy and say, "This is the guy. He is the band. He writes the music, the lyrics; I just sing them. He's got the artistic mastermind. All I've got is this old mug and a spectacular voice." At this, the girls would giggle and swoon and quite literally throw themselves at the smooth-talking crooner, who received them with open arms. The boy would nod and make his way back to the stage where, he would sit and strum his muted guitar and talk with stragglers about music or artistic inspiration.

The boy was four or five years younger than the rest of the band, so at first he was not old enough for the complementary rum and cokes. This dilemma was quickly resolved when the boy found a fake ID, began sipping down the tall skinny pint glasses through wide plastic straws, and became known on stage as "Matt."

Once backstage, he scooped a bottle of water up from the coffee table and flopped down on the sofa.

Jack burst through the door, rubbing a towel across his face and over his head.

"Good show, brothers," he said, dropping down next to the boy.

The boy nodded, spun off the bottle cap, and threw back a swallow of water.

"Good show," the boy nodded again. "I was thinking, at the end of our encore there, we should break it down one more time before we speed to the outro. It just feels a little awkward only doing a two-measure breakdown." Jack patted his hand against the boy's leg.

"You wrote the song, you clever bastard. Play it however you want." The others chuckled. "Now, you got that tasty green, my brother?"

The boy fished his fingers down into his tight jean pocket. No one ever intends to be the pusher; it's just something that sort of happens. It starts because you know someone who has the best merchandise available. This guy, he likes you because you're appreciative and he sees a bit of himself in your reckless passion for life, so he gives you good deals. Next, you make the dangerous mistake of mentioning it to your friends; then they want to try it. Yeah, of course it's good. It's the best they ever had. So, what starts as your private little gold mine turns into the California Gold Rush and everyone wants a piece; and you, you are their only outlet to the glorious gleaming heap. So, it starts as a favor here, a favor there, for your close friends, and before you know it, you're going out of your way, wasting gas, and risking your neck for a bunch of freeloaders. Then it becomes more frequent, so you up the price, you know, just to pay your expenses, make it worth your while, cover gas. Before you know it, you've got people you don't even know calling your cell phone talking about how they have heard of you. You need the money so you do it. Then they start asking for other Remedies, things you have no experience with, but you do your best to accommodate, because now you've got a reputation to uphold. That's how you become the pusher. The boy tugged the bag from his pocket and threw it on the table.

"Gorgeous," Jack said, snatching it off the wooden top and holding it up to the light. "Piece?"

The bassist slid a piece of blown glass onto the table and Jack pressed the planted Remedy into it with his thumb. As the smoking device made its way around the room and to the boy, he pondered where this newfound hobby had originated.

After the incident with his brother, he stopped volunteering. He suppressed his concern for the well-being of humanity and spent more time in his room, writing. He still spent time with Chloe and Ben, but when he did, he never mentioned his newfound hobbies for fear of their disappointment and disproval. Chloe had an uncle or cousin or someone who got pretty hard into Remedies. It wouldn't do her any good to know that he had started, so he kept it a secret—two separate lives. He had always heard that the sticky green plant stimulated creativity, and people he trusted had told him it was something everyone should try at least once. He had already been smoking cigarettes from time to time and they acted as a doorway into other things. He was more skeptical now. He liked to try things for himself and he didn't like the idea that there were still so many options in life that he had not experienced or understood. So, he tried it and he liked it. He hadn't seen any harm. As chaotic as the world was, one could use some serenity, something to help cope.

He took the device in his hand and put it up to his lips. The thick smoke oozed from the mouthpiece like a clouded waterfall and swirled in whirlpools inside his mouth. It poured down his throat, filling every corner of his lungs. The boy exhaled and added to the foggy haze that was collecting above them. He slouched back on the couch and laid his arm across his forehead. The warming sensation that trickled down his throat and through the center of his chest was a welcomed one. It meant that soon he would feel only numbness. The glass had made its way back around. He took it in his hand and repeated the process. His hands tingled. The walls seemed to quiver. The haze burned his eyes. The device came back around. Three, four, five times. Jack tapped him on the arm and handed him an acoustic guitar. The boy chuckled. This seemed to happen every time. A wide grin spread across Jack's face as he nodded. The boy grasped the neck of the guitar and laid it across his leg.

"Pick?" he held out his hand.

Jack sprung forward from the couch and scanned the coffee table and the floor. The bassist patted his pant legs near the pockets for a few minutes. The drummer illuminated the end of the glass device with the spark of a lighter and stared onward with bloodshot eyes. The boy looked down at his outstretched hand. A pick was pinched casually between his fingertips.

"I got one," he said.

The three spectators celebrated as the boy's fingers moved across the neck of the guitar and he plucked out the soft beginning of Bob Marley's "Redemption Song". His fingertips felt liquefied as he glided them across the metallic strings. Jack set the device down in front of the boy. He stopped playing and picked it up. Spark. Smoke. Cough. He had forgotten where he left off, so he started at the beginning again.

Jack sang the first line. It was the wrong time for the lyrics to start, but the boy improvised and continued playing. The other two swayed in carefree unison. Jack did not stop singing as he placed the glass against the boy's lips and ignited the end. The boy did not stop playing as he inhaled. Spark. Smoke. Spark. The green turned to

black; Jack tapped it against the wooden table and pressed the planted Remedy in again with his thumb. They all sang together as the
boy strummed the melody to "One Love". It was humorous, the boy
thought, to watch the three attempt to relate to a life with which they
had nothing in common. He played a wrong chord. No one noticed.
The cold glass touched his lips again. Spark. Inhale. Smoke. They were
no longer his hands sliding up and down the neck of the guitar or
his fingers dancing perfectly across the vibrating strings. He was now
a spectator, watching an ever-familiar performance from someone he
had once known. He had melted into the fabric of the sofa cushions.

"Don't stop!" the three called out to the stranger once the
song had ended.

"Yeah, don't stop," the boy agreed, and the stranger played
"Don't Push" by Sublime.

The boy loved that song, and he muttered along with the
slurred singing of the others in the room. His chest no longer burned
but by the time the stranger had finished the third song, the boy's arms
were heavy and tired. He guided the guitar to the floor.

"Let's go," the boy suggested, rubbing his itchy eyes.

"You sure?" Jack asked, chuckling to himself. He didn't seem
hesitant but more concerned by the behavior of the others.

"Yeah, come on," he said and he peeled himself from the sofa
cushion.

By day, they were high school students, grocers, retail junkies,
and Target® team members, but by night they were rock stars, burn-
outs, idols, and Remedy-dealing lunatics. Smoke billowed out from
behind them as they pushed open the door and drifted out onto the
dingy dance floor. A few fans were lingering near the edge of the stage
when the boy and his companions strolled over to start collecting their
equipment. Jack greeted the small crowd.

"Hey, thank you guys, thank you all for coming and giving us
some love tonight. We really appreciate it. Unfortunately, we are not
cool enough to have groupies, which means we have a ton of clean-
up that we need to get done, so I apologize but we won't be able to
hang out tonight. Unless," he eyed a couple of the young girls in the
crowd, "anyone really feels like hanging around for a little while until
we get everything packed up." He raised his eyebrows. It just never was

enough.

The boy turned his back to the gathering and pulled his guitar case to the edge of the stage. Flipping up the clasps, the boy pushed it open. Inside was a folder with tattered papers cluttered between its covers. He picked it up and weighed it in his hand. It was his collection of the original copies of all the songs he had written years before, which they now performed. He would never have guessed that this is what would have become of them. He massaged his forehead with his hand. He could feel his heart beating at the top of his neck.

"Excuse me," a voice stammered behind him.

The boy turned to look over his shoulder. A boy, only a couple of years younger than him, stood staring with wide eyes. His fire red hair stood messily on end and clashed with his dark blue eyes and tan freckles.

"My name is Hank," the red-haired boy continued, shoulders hunched high as he awkwardly shuffled closer to the boy.

The throbbing heartbeat had moved from the top of the boy's neck to the center of his skull, muffling his ears. He looked over the kid's head, scanning the room for Jack. He was supposed to get rid of these stragglers. He rubbed his eyes. They wouldn't stop itching. The boy turned back to his guitar case and started wrapping up cables.

"Sorry to interrupt," Hank started again. "I know you are probably really busy. I just wanted to say that I am a huge fan of your music and your lyrics. They're so profound. I just started playing guitar," his voice was dwarfed by the clouded buzzing in the boy's ears.

"Right," the boy muttered over his shoulder, "what'd you say?"

Hank moved closer.

"I said, I just started playing guitar and writing music," his voice was shaky, "and it's just so inspiring to be able to meet someone I admire so much. I'm working on starting up a band just like yours. I come to as many of your shows as my mom will let me, and a few that she won't." The boy dropped a cable in his case and rubbed his head again. What was that noise? "I'm sorry. I guess I just wanted to say that it's a pleasure to meet you and see if you could tell me what it takes to make it as a band?" He tried opening his jaw wide to make his ears pop but his mouth was dry and his tongue felt swollen.

"Huh?" he turned as if just noticing the red-haired boy. "What did you need?"

Hank pushed the toe of his shoe into the carpet and lowered his sad eyes to stare at his hands, which he fumbled in front of him.

"Just some advice, I guess," Hank shrugged his shoulders up higher.

"What? Some advice?" the boy repeated, easing his guitar down into its felt lining. He flipped the latches shut and pulled the case off the stage by the handle.

"Some advice," he said again. Hank was staring with eager eyes. "Let's see. It's all about having fun. Do your best to have a blast before it all goes up in smoke."

With that, the boy snatched up his guitar, pulled his cigarettes out of his pocket, pressed one between his lips, and walked away, searching his clothing for a lighter.

He walked out the back door and to the van parked in the alley. Jack was climbing out of the front seat as the boy slid his guitar case in the back.

"Jack!" he called from the back bumper, "have you got my lighter?" He poked his head around the side of the van.

"There you are," Jack called back, tossing the plastic lighter to the boy.

He caught it and walked toward Jack, who swung his arm around the boy's shoulder and escorted him to the side of the building. Two girls stood, whispering to one another as the boys approached. Their thick lipstick, glistening cheeks, and high heels divulged their unsuccessful attempts at looking older. The boy recognized them from the lingering crowd.

"Ladies," Jack began, "this is my partner." He turned to the boy. "These girls would like to come out with us tonight."

The boy cupped his hand at the end of his cigarette and sparked the lighter.

"It's a pleasure to meet you, ladies," the boy started, puffing out smoke. "I do apologize for my friend, Jack. Most of what he says is bullshit," the girls giggled, "but we'd love to hang out tonight. I've got to warn you, though; I don't know how late I'm gonna last."

"No worries," Jack replied. "We'll call it an early night." They both laughed.

A few blocks away from that dark, dingy basement was a hole-in-the-wall bar (the band's preference), so after they finished loading up the van, they moseyed down the street. The boy slid a barstool out for one of the girls and, with a grinning "Thank you," the two sat and talked. Jack shouldered up to the other girl and struck up a conversation, while the bassist and drummer ordered a few injections of liquid Remedy. The glasses clanked together as they met in the middle of the oblong circle and the six thumped them against the wooden bar top and poured them down their throats. The acidity made the back of his jaw tingle. The girl giggled as she stacked her glass inside of his several seconds later. He looked at her with disappointed eyes and shook his head and she giggled again. She tucked her hair behind her ear and stared intently at the boy while they talked.

"Did you like the show?" he asked her. She nodded.

"You guys were awesome," she clapped her hands together, "marvelous guitar solos!"

The boy paused and peered into the girl's eyes. Their deep brown color looked dull in comparison to the sunburst green he was searching for, but, just to be sure, he proposed the question.

"Do you play?"

She gagged on her orange and red swirled drink as her eyes widened.

"Me?" she coughed out. "No way! I played piano when I was younger but I'm way too tone deaf for anything serious." Just as he thought.

He nodded and smiled politely. There was a tap on his shoulder. Clank. Thump. Swallow.

"So, you think this is what you want to do for a living?" she asked, wiping her mouth with the back of her hand.

The boy chuckled. Practically all of the money they made in a given night was spent hours later at the nearest bar.

"It would be nice," he tried to smooth out the laughter in his lips, "but not everyone thinks my guitar solos are as marvelous as you do, so it's probably unrealistic."

This time she laughed loudly. The glasses lined up in a row in front of them again.

"To the possibility of the unrealistic," she said, and they drank.

67

Clank. Thump. Swallow.

She ran her fingers along her collarbone and twirled them in her hair. The boy eyed her over the rim of the glass as he drained the tingling liquid down his throat.

"Can't you see we're in the middle of a conversation?!" Jack's voice carried over the crowd. "Beat it."

The boy rose instinctively from his barstool. In front of Jack stood a young man with wide shoulders and beady eyes, his head cocked sideways in a threatening glare, which he honed in on Jack.

"Excuse me," the boy muttered to the girl, moving closer as Jack sprung up from his stool.

"I believe I was talking to the girl," the wide shouldered man's voice grew with each word.

The boy could see the shapes of others at the bar rising to their feet in the shadows behind the man. He scanned them each quickly; he was already sizing them up. Jack had a real knack for starting trouble. He heard the stools behind him scoot out. One, then the other; the bassist and the drummer had risen to their feet. The boy could hear anonymous voices in the darkness murmuring the words "roll up." The girl had backed away from Jack. He followed her with his eyes.

"Well, now you're talking to me!" Jack said, pressing his palms against the man's chest and shoving him backward.

The boy rushed forward as the man regained balance and launched a hurling fist toward Jack. The boy caught it in the jaw as he gripped the shirt between the wide shoulders with both hands and tackled the aggressor to the ground. The rushing of footsteps in front of him signaled that the man's companions were coming to his aid, but the boy wasn't worried. This was not their first bar fight. They were not amateurs. The bassist and the drummer leaped over him and met them head on. Jack dropped down next to the boy with fist cocked and delivered a blow square to the man's forehead. The boy wiped the corner of his mouth with his knuckles and jumped to his feet. One man held the bassist with his arms behind his back while another pounded his stomach. The boy drew back his clenched fingers and hammered them against the assailant's kidney. The man arched his back and grunted, twirling toward the boy, who greeted him with a firm blow to the chest. He slumped to the ground. The bassist wriggled free from his oppressor and fired a volley of punches. A strong fist caught the boy in the side of his ribcage, and he spun and extended his arm with force. His knuckles crunched against flesh and muscle. Another man was marching quickly toward Jack and his opponent as they wrestled about on the floor. With two steps, the boy dove and caught the man around his arms and stomach and the two dropped to the floor. He yanked his leg free and crushed it hard against the boy's shoulder. He flinched and pulled himself up to the man's waist. As he lifted his fist to deliver on the man's nose, a strong hand hooked his elbow. Another hand grabbed the back of his shirt and lifted him up. He jerked his arm free and twisted his body to throw a punch, but two more hands gripped him by the shoulders and lifted him to his feet. A firm push sent him stumbling across the room toward the door. Two tall bulky men with matching black shirts were stalking up behind him—security.

"Now!" one of them yelled.

He hadn't heard anything they had said before that, but he assumed they wanted him gone. He staggered out into the street. Seconds later, Jack came toppling out, followed by the bassist and the drummer.

"Not bad, not bad," Jack said, swaggering over to the boy, who was working his jaw painfully.

His cheek was bruised and his hair was a mess, but he still managed a smile. The bassist and the drummer came trotting behind them, as they blundered down the sidewalk, calling insults and threats back to the empty street behind them.

"Wait!" the girl came running from the bar.

When she caught up to them, she winced at the boy's face.

"Are you OK?" she asked. The boy nodded.

"I think so," he replied. She smiled and pulled a pen out of her purse.

"Here," she said, pulling a cocktail napkin out of her pocket and jotting down a number. "Call me sometime. I'd like to see you again."

The boy folded the small square napkin and pushed it into his pocket.

"He will," Jack said, swinging his arm around the boy's neck and continuing down the concrete.

"You took quite a blow for me," Jack laughed as they walked. "I guess I owe you one."

The boy looked over his shoulder. The girl still stood on the sidewalk, biting her lip, watching as they rounded the corner to the alley. The boy pulled the napkin from his pocket.

"You should call her," Jack said, glancing at the number.

"Nah," the boy replied. He unfolded the napkin and pushed it across his mouth, wiping off the blood. Crumbling it up into a ball, he shoved it back in his pocket. "She's not the one."

"You're really something," Jack laughed loudly, "really something. The one," he repeated in disbelief as he popped the handle of the van door and climbed into the driver's seat.

The boy felt his pocket vibrating as he eased down into the passenger seat. His shoulder ached. He pulled his cell phone out of his pocket. It was Ben.

"Hello?" the boy pressed the phone to his ear.

"Hey, how's it going?" His voice sounded eager.

"It's alright." The boy shifted painfully in his chair.

"How was the show? You guys heading home?"

"Yea, it was good. What's going on?"

"Not too much. I met a girl tonight."

"Really? What's her name?"

"Lynn. She's an old friend of Chloe's and we really hit it off." Ben was smiling as he spoke. "There's something about her. I think you will like her a lot."

"Sounds good. I can't wait to meet her."

"Yeah," Ben chuckled, "we'll double date or something. You can bring Sally."

"If only she would stop hiding," the boy sighed and they both laughed, even though it made his shoulder throb.

He clamped his phone shut and slid it back in his pocket. Flipping on the radio, he pushed in his Pearl Jam CD and slouched back in his chair. As he stared silently out the window, he moved his fingers up and down an imaginary guitar neck in unison with the music the rest of the way home.

The single greatest fear among mankind is that of the unknown. To leave the familiarity and security of one environment for the instability and uncertainty of another is a horrifying thing. It is this fear that makes death such a haunting inevitability, because it is the greatest of all unknowns. It was that same uncertainty that made the boy fearful of crossing the field and of following his brother, the same uncertainty that made the farmer apprehensive about completing the barn. Unfortunately, these expeditions into the unknown are necessary quests in order to bring about change. Oftentimes, change requires first new environments and surroundings to evoke new experiences, which, in turn, cause change. These voyages into uncertain territories force people to make new decisions in places they are unfamiliar with. Those decisions, then, forge the future of the individuals who have made them and affect the eventual outcome of essentially everything. This method of determining fate seems somewhat haphazard. As a result, people tend to believe that there must be some ultimate blueprint because, otherwise, there is no order or structure, only the chaotic impulses of a barbaric species. Personally, I do believe in a grand design, namely because I can see traces of it working beneath the fabric of life. I believe it must be there, because something good usually evolves in the end. It must be there because, many times, situations frequently find order when they should not. It must be there because, without some sort of structure, there is no hope.

The boy slouched back in his chair and stretched his legs out under his desk. There was no comfortable position. He bit his pencil between his teeth and massaged his temples. A low hum drifted from the front of the room as the teacher droned on. Every now and then, her spiritless sermon would pause for the clicking of pasty white chalk scratching against the coarse dark expanse of underpaid salaries, undercut renovations, and lowered academic standards. The more diligent students copied her mechanical motions with the chalk frantically on white sheets of paper with black pens. The boy had always done very well in school without the copying or the studying. The things they talked about and tested on made sense to him naturally. Teachers would recite information, the boy would compare it with his experiences and observations, and the filtered material would be ingrained in his mind.

"Did you study last night?" his classmates would ask.

The boy would shake his head. Was there a test?

"Man, you're crazy!" they would say. "I was up all night studying! You're toast!"

Then the tests would circulate, and the boy would scribble down his answers quickly and hand it in while his classmates were still scratching their heads, digging for answers buried shallow in their brains the night before. When the tests were returned days later, they would heave sighs of relief or drop their heads in shame. The boy would fold his test in half and discreetly stuff it into his bag. When they asked how he did, he would shrug and say, "Alright." He had to hide his success because if, by chance, they caught a glimpse of the "A" written proudly across the top of the sheet, they would glare and mutter, "I studied for hours; you didn't even know there was a test."

"Maybe you should stop studying," he would mumble.

At this, they would gawk and gasp and some unsatisfied spectators would call out, "Seriously, how is that possible? How did you do it?" The boy would shrug apologetically, but in his head he would say, "I was studying all of this while you were swinging from playgrounds." He would never voice such a thing out loud of course; it sounded too arrogant, and he had always found arrogance unbecoming.

The blanched white walls echoed the seldom tick of the clock that hung just overhead, amplifying the confinements of the passionless room. To the students, each emphatic jolt of the second hand symbolized their never-ending struggle with the slow movement of time. It bound them to that room, restricted them from adulthood, and prolonged their youthful woes. It must be the opposite for the teacher, the boy thought. More than likely, the ticking seemed much faster to her. It symbolized all the unfinished things in her life or all the things she felt as though she had done wrong. He wondered when that transition came in life, from where he and his fellow impatient classmates were to where their complacent teacher was. Was it a gradual process, or had she woken up one day and realized that time was passing much more quickly than before? Either way, he was quite sure Time would always be his enemy.

"Pssst," the girl next to him called for his attention. "Great show last night."

He smiled and thanked her, rubbing his eyes with his fingers. He barely remembered playing the night before. They were two different worlds, the band and school, and it was always a difficult reconciliation when the two collided, which inevitably they did. As soon as his friends from school heard that he was in a band, his credibility soared. Strangers in the hallways called out his name and slapped his hand in the air or cornered him and talked about which of the band's songs was their favorite and why. He was always polite, but it was awkwardly empowering to be given so much attention.

On nights that the band wasn't performing, the boy would go to his classmates' parties and they would cheer as he strolled in with bottles of liquid Remedy. Sometimes Jack would accompany him, and groups would crowd around and watch in amazement as the two emptied rows of injections down there throats or played guitar and sang out melodies. The young girls would bat their eyelashes at Jack and, with glazed eyes, he would smile back. Something about the contrast between the girls' innocence and the two boys' recklessness made the boy uncomfortable, so, at times, he would advise the girls to go home or distract Jack enough with injections that he would be rendered incapable of causing any harm.

"I really don't get it," Jack said one night as they were leaving one such party. "I know you see the way some of these girls look at you, and they're hot!" The boy chuckled and sighed. "I'm serious! How come you never make a move? I know that you're picky or whatever, but come on!" The boy paused.

"It's not just that," he started. "It's that none of these girls are what I want."

"Because you want some girl that exists in your head," Jack interjected and the boy laughed.

"No, I just don't want to settle. I don't want to do what everyone else does. Think about it: So much of a relationship is convenience. You meet someone who you encounter in daily life and you show interest because you live or work in the same general area. They annoy you less than most other people, so you start dating. Before long, you're calling it love, getting married, and having kids—because

73

it's easy and convenient. But what if you lived in another state or country or even two towns over? It would be someone else, and you'd be calling it love. It just seems too flimsy. I believe there is something better." The boy drifted off. Jack was staring at him intently, slightly nodding his head.

"I get it," he said after a few minutes. "That's pretty profound." He nodded again. "I get it, but I'm not going to stop making moves on local girls." They both laughed.

Once home, the boy flopped down on his bed and pulled his notebook out from underneath his mattress. There was no doubt in his mind that the past few months had been some of his best. He was young; he was invincible; and, as he said, each day was about having as much fun as possible. Some terrible things had happened over the years, but terrible things happened to everyone. Each day was still a magnificent one. When the weather was warm, they would cook out and count stars. When it rained, he would drive with his sunroof open and dance in the streams of mud and water that would trail across the asphalt. When it snowed, they would wander in the woods searching for untouched, virgin snow and race through blanketed fields.

"Each day is a unique opportunity," he would tell his friends. "Some are much more difficult than others, but we've got to exploit them all to the fullest, because, honestly, we don't get that many of them."

This was his mentality for living his life, because it made him most happy. However, there was still an undeniable part of him that ached for something more. He could feel it pushing through in his heart and mind and, thus, in his writing. Something needed to change. Pulling the pen from the metal spiral, he clicked down the ballpoint and scribbled on the page the first words he had ever written about her:

With my friends,
we don't say goodbye.
A casual wave, a smooth high five
let's us know that we're alive
and nothing more is needed.

With my friends,
the party is all ours.
Rolled up plants, beer-stained cards;
we're all sleeping in the yard
and we won't remember a thing.

"What's it worth?" she says.
But she doesn't understand,
when we're all the same and you've got no name,
what good is a friend?
"Not all," is her reply,
but she has been misled.
The lights go down, the music up
and I just bob my head.

With my friends,
We don't need a thing.
My cell phone's on. Give me a ring,
and we'll take care of everything,
except our own demise.
With my friends,
We are always late—
had other plans, another date.
They know we don't perpetrate
and so then nothing more is said.

"Is this it?" she says,
but I just start the car.
She's floating free, but I'm tied down.
I just can't go that far.
"Not true," is her reply.
She thinks I've got a chance.
She can't be right, she can't be wrong,
but I don't need romance.

With my friends,
we just are not close.

75

Each one, we love ourselves the most.
Each of us, another's boast,
but at least we all are clear.

With my friends,
we just do not care
if love is fake, and friendship bare.
As long as there are people there
and the party never ends.

"Wanna go?" she says.
I guess it is that time.
With my friends, it's so hard to tell
which are true friends of mine.
"Not friends" is her reply.
That word just was not clear.
They pull me down, she picks me up
and we are gone from here.

      As I stated earlier, in order to bring about change, one must accept the fact that it requires a transition from the known to the unknown. It is rarely a pleasant conversion and, more often than not, it leaves permanent scars. But the transition is necessary, just as the change itself is necessary. It is usually not expected and typically not in the fashion that you would prefer, but most things aren't.

      The flaps of the cereal box lid popped open as the boy squeezed the cardboard sides and shook the colorful pieces into his bowl. Only on Saturdays did he have enough time in the morning for breakfast. Monday through Friday, he was typically rushing out the door fifteen minutes later than he should, determined to make up the lost time on the road. On Sundays, he would go with his parents to church. They used to all go together as a family, but his siblings had all moved away except his slightly older brother, who had stopped regular church attendance months ago. The boy had done his best to maintain participation. He wasn't sure if church was necessarily vital, but it had helped him cultivate his faith and values, and that was extremely important to him. Without it, he would not have survived those particularly difficult times. It's really quite sad how people tend to forget the necessity of something when they are not witness to the immediate gratification of that necessity. However often he may have forgotten it, his faith was an immense part of his being.

The milk swirled in colors around the rim of the bowl as he poured it over the cereal. Shoveling the spoon into the mound, he hoisted the first dripping bite to his mouth. It crunched between his teeth as he picked up the cardboard box and began scanning the back. It never was anything very interesting, but it usually entertained him for the duration of his meal. He was halfway through the crossword puzzle when his parents marched into the kitchen and stopped at the table. He glanced up at them and blubbered a "Good morning" around a mouthful of sopping cereal. Neither one of them were looking at him.

"We need to talk," his father said, clearing his throat.

That was never a good sign, both of them, double-teaming him, and at breakfast. He immediately felt defensive. What had they found out? Who had they spoken to? He needed to maintain his cool composure.

Keeping his eyes glued to the cereal box, he nodded and managed a meek, "About what?"

They eased down into chairs on either side of him—surrounded. From the corners of his eyes, he could see that they were avoiding his face. His mother looked distraught. Their artificial confidence only added to his anxiety. He stuffed another bite into his mouth.

"You probably are not going to like what we have to tell you," his father started. The boy shifted in his chair. It was worse than he thought. He felt woefully unprepared. "But, we have been thinking about it for some time now, and," he paused. And what? He couldn't stand the suspense. What could be so horrific? He lost composure.

"And what?!" he blurted out.

They kept their calm demeanor.

"We have decided to move."

Cereal splashed onto the table as he dropped the spoon into the bowl. No one seemed to notice.

"We know that you like it here, and you are almost halfway through your junior year, and you have your friends and school," his mother chimed in, "but it's only two hours away and we really feel like it's what's best for the family."

He couldn't form words. For as long as he could remember, he had lived in that house. He had made friends and commitments, and he was doing well with the band. He couldn't just leave those things behind. Two hours away was too far.

"It will be tough to switch schools your senior year, but we found one that we really like," his mom started again.

He couldn't switch schools. This was all happening too fast. His words finally caught up to his thoughts.

"I'm not going anywhere," he said firmly. Not the most brilliant interjection, but at least he was speaking. His mother sat back in her chair.

"Look," his father's voice stiffened, "we are not moving without you, and we are moving." Anger welled up in the boy's eyes. His mother put her hand on his arm.

"I know it is a big thing to ask of you," she said, "and we would never do it if we didn't have to. It would be a better life for all of us there. It has been a long struggle for us to get to this point, and it will be hard for us to say goodbye, but this is our chance, probably our only chance, to get out of debt and have the life we have always wanted. It's the only choice we have. We can't stay here. But if you say no, you're not going, then we will forfeit that chance and figure out a way, if it means that much to you. It will be difficult, but if you say no, we will have to find a way."

Both their eyes were on him now, drilling to his soul. He dropped his head into his hands and stared into the shallow pool of milk that had collected on the kitchen table. He should have just said "No."

six

Naturally, Ben and Chloe were the first to hear the news. The three sprawled out on the pavement, in the middle of the street that crisp autumn night, and they talked about the move. Orange, brown, and red leaves drifted along the coarse, black asphalt while others still clung desperately to thick tree branches, quivering with the anticipation of winter. As if the thick heavy clouds overhead were not enough, the beaming white streetlight several houses down the road scattered its light far enough that it was impossible to detect any stars. The boy could feel the chill of the Earth changing seasons as it seeped through the pavement and clawed at his back.

"You're not actually going to go, are you?" Chloe asked as she folded her arms anxiously across her stomach.

"I don't think I have a choice," the boy said in a vacant voice.

For the first time, he could not express his inward turmoil outwardly to his friends, which made communication extremely difficult.

"It won't matter if you go. Nothing will change. It's only two hours away. We'll still see each other all the time. It just means a longer drive." Ben sounded optimistic.

Chloe announced her disapproval by hugging her arms tighter across her stomach and turning her head away from the boys, but she remained silent.

"I hope you're right," the boy replied, trying to force some emotion into his voice.

He had to avoid seriously considering the possibility of leaving because the consequences were just too great.

"Of course I'm right!" Ben chuckled, "Where else am I going

to find someone as opinionated as you?" The boy managed a smirk, and Ben's laugh trailed off.

"Look," Chloe spoke up, "I know it would be selfish, but I say, just tell them that you aren't going, and make them stay. They will have to, right? Just tell them no."

The boy knew he could never bear the guilt of hindering his parents' aspirations because of his own youthful selfishness. They were right. They had traveled an arduous road to get to where they were in life, and this was their chance. If this was what his family truly wanted, he could not be the one to take it away from them. If this was their dream, right within reach, then they deserved it.

"I'll try," he said, but his voice was riddled with defeat, and they knew it.

They knew he would have to go. So, they sat in silence. The boy wouldn't move away for another five months, but they realized that day that things would never be the same. It was on that day that the three starting say goodbye to one another. They knew it would be a long painful process of letting go, so they began it there, lying on the cold concrete. There they began prepping their hearts to be broken. Typically, there was no shortage of conversation, but that day none of them could formulate the right words, so they quietly mourned.

The boy had his eyes squeezed closed when the first drips of rain freckled his face. He titled his head back and inhaled the wet air. Ben tugged a hood out from under his head and pulled it up over his hair. Chloe craned her neck to search the murky sky for rain clouds. The drips grew larger and more frequent, but the three remained glued to the asphalt altar. Water leaked through the fabric of the boy's shirt, the cool liquid channeling down his chest. The rain fell faster and trickled in streams beneath them to storm drains along the edges of the pavement. The boy pushed air between his lips to blow away the small pool that was collecting in the crevice. His clothes were soaked through. Chloe's chest heaved as she started to giggle. The boy opened one eye and turned to her. She lifted her dripping sleeves to her mouth and exploded into laughter.

"Come on, you lunatics!" she said, climbing to her feet. "It's pouring!"

The boy lifted his head to watch her. She spun around in a

circle, her drenched blonde hair stuck flat against her cheeks.

"I'm pretty sure you're the lunatic!" Ben said as he hoisted himself up from the ground.

This time they all three laughed. Chloe grabbed the boy by the hand and pulled him to his feet.

"Just feel it," she said, stretching out her arms.

They laughed as the droplets crashed in puddles against their upright faces. Something was definitive about that moment. It was as if the rain had come to wash away their youth, as if it symbolized the end—the end of something marvelous. They raced back and forth across the street, splashing water on one another from the puddles that had collected on the pavement. They jumped in the tiny pools and slid along the slick grass with their shoes. Chloe and the boy pretended to dance in the street while Ben laughed hysterically from the curb.

"And I am the rain king!" Ben sang out to them.

"Yeeeeeeeah!" Chloe and the boy sang back, and the three laughed again.

By the time they were finished, their clothes were dripping wet. The fabric stuck heavy to their skin as water cascaded down the fully saturated threads. As they turned to walk back down the street, the way they had come, Chloe moved beside the boy and scooped her hand around his waist. He hooked his arm around her head and hugged it against his chest. Looking down to her face, he noticed two small trails leaking from her sad eyes.

"Are you crying?" he asked. She forced a weak smile and shook her head.

"It's only rain," she said, and the three continued down the stormy road.

Their next few months were cherished ones. They did their best to ignore the solemn unspoken awareness of their impending future and focused on enjoying each day as it came. Ben had started dating that girl he had met, Lynn, which gave them a default topic of conversation. His big brown eyes would light up as he told them about their first, second, and third dates. He would lick his lips nervously and smile whenever the boy or Chloe would mention her name. Every now and then, she would come out with the three of them, but that would completely alter the group's dynamic. Chloe would become less talkative, while the boy would sit and force conversation with the intruder. It had nothing to do with Lynn in particular—she was a very kind, polite young girl; she could have been anyone. Ben was in love, and they couldn't have been happier for him, but they had spent years developing the connection that they had, and their time was dwindling. They tried not to allow distractions that kept them from fully enjoying their last few months. In those awkward moments when the move was clearly on their minds, or when someone would mention upcoming plans outside of their limited scope of time, they would fall silent and stare at the ground until the awkwardness had passed. Sometimes when Chloe would hug him, she would close her eyes and squeeze extra tight, or Ben would linger when shaking his hand and nod with reminiscent eyes. The boy believed that this must be their way of enduring. As if, with each hug and handshake, they were letting another piece of him go; and each time, when they walked away, he felt a little emptier.

Jack took the news much better. Initially, he suggested changing their names, skipping town, and touring the world as traveling musicians, but after the boy explained how that probably wouldn't solve the problem and how he believed traveling musicians died with the Renaissance, Jack became more optimistic.

"It's not a big deal," he said, holding his breath. "We'll still practice once a week, we'll just make it an all day thing; and you'll be able to network there and find new venues and whatnot," he blew a cloud of smoke out above them, "and we'll still play out here. It will work out. Before long, we'll get signed and we can move wherever the hell we want and have someone pay us to make music."

The puff of smoke swirled overhead, mingling with the air above the pickup truck bed, as the two boys lay on their backs against the ridged lining. Jack passed the rolled white paper back to the boy. He pinched it between his fingers and pressed it to his lips. Puff. Inhale.

"Do you think I'm a narcissist?" he asked, pulling the paper from his lips.

"Sorry, brother," Jack said as he turned to him. "I didn't bring my dictionary today."

The boy chuckled. Exhale.

82

"It's basically someone who is in love with themself." He passed the rolled paper back.

"You?" Jack asked, drawing air through the ember. "No, you've got a bigger problem. You're in love with an imaginary girl."

They both laughed. Puff. Inhale.

"I don't actually think I'm in love with myself. I just have always had this notion that I was supposed to be something bigger than most people. I have always believed that I was above mediocrity, and that I was born to achieve something meaningful. That's why this music thing..." the boy paused and passed the shortened paper back, "it's something." Jack nodded.

The boy wasn't sure if his friend understood or not, but at least he acknowledged that he had heard. He opened his mouth for further explanation but was cut short by the loud thump of a large hand grabbing the side of the pickup truck. The boy turned his head with startled eyes while Jack cupped the rolled white paper, hidden in his palm. The hand belonged to the upper half of a rather broad middle-aged man. His plain white T-shirt was the only thing that was easily distinguishable in the thick darkness, but it was clear that he had noticed them.

"What is going on here?" he said in a voice just as much perplexed as it was angry. "What the hell are you doing in the back of my truck?!"

"Wait a second..." the boy said as he and his companion rose casually to their feet. The boy looked thoughtfully at the truck bed beneath him. "This isn't our truck?" he said, turning to Jack, who scrunched his brow and mimicked the boy's confusion.

"No, this isn't your truck!" the man raised his voice. He glanced up and down the side of the truck again, just to be sure. "This is my truck!"

"Oh," the boy scanned the bed again, "...huh," he said nonchalantly.

The man glared in bewilderment as the two boys climbed slowly down the rear of the pickup.

"Oh yeah," the boy said once they were down from the truck, "...not even the right color." Jack muffled a snicker.

"I ought to call the cops on you punks! Get the hell outta

here!" He yelled as they sauntered down the sidewalk.

"Take it easy, man," the boy called back to the man as they walked away.

"That gets funnier every time," Jack laughed and flipped the paper back out between his fingers.

"We can't catch a break," the boy said glancing over his shoulder at the man, who was watching them from the rear of the truck. "Here," he pinched the rolled plant between his forefinger and thumb and squeezed it between his lips. Puff. Puff. Inhale.

"Not a problem," Jack replied. "I spotted another one parked right up here around the corner." Exhale.

"Excellent," the boy smiled as they walked down the street.

The air was arctic and jagged as it whipped mercilessly against the wooden planks that comprised the cabin walls. Each swirling barrage carried with it pounds of snow that heaved in blows against the jostling door. I watched the boy; he did not seem concerned. His eyes were buried in a sea of shuffled papers scratched with scribbled words, as they had been for the past several days. I rose from my post in the corner and threw another block of wood into the fireplace. I had done my best to keep him comfortable and his pencil working but, as usual, my efforts went unnoticed. Someday, he would learn to appreciate all that I have done for him.

In the middle of his pencil's fury, his hand stopped short and his attention drifted to the ceiling. I moved swiftly to his side and caught him by the chin. His eyes were nearly as cold as mine as he met my stare. He didn't use to be able to look me in the eye, but that changed over the past year. I released his face gruffly and nodded to the pages on the desk. His eyes flashed defiance, but just for a moment, then he nodded and pressed his pencil back to the paper. He knew that I was right.

His hand sketched across the pages as I paced behind his wooden chair, checking the words from behind him. His mobile phone danced across the desk as it vibrated against the wooden top. He grabbed the phone up in his hand and lifted it to where he could see. I watched over his shoulder. "Mae," it read boldly across its face. The boy smiled. I slammed my fist down hard against the desktop, but he did not react. I no longer existed to him. I swept my hand across the wood, spewing papers into the air, and walked stiffly to the door. The boy pressed the side of the phone with his thumb, quieting its vibrations, and placed it gently back onto the desk as the pages floated lifelessly to the floor. He leaned back in his chair and folded his hands behind his head. He actually thought he was accomplishing something. What a fool. As I slammed the door shut behind me, he was squatting down, collecting papers from the floor, his face beaming, his fingers working the center of his chest.

Mae was a masterpiece. I have met some fantastic people in my time, but none have compared with the brilliant composition of that girl. She was dignified, intelligent, comical, charming, lighthearted, and beautiful—all the things the boy needed in his life, and he knew it. Even in the midst of his stern determination, she could penetrate the void and ignite flames in that coal black furnace of his heart. No one could deny the intensity of the passion-soaked connection that radiated between them, and anyone who dared try need only look into the deep centers of their eyes and see their kindred minds. In an instant, she could completely alter the boy's state of mind. No one he had ever encountered had as dynamic of an impact on his life. His friends called her his lost cause. He called her his only hope, for he still believed in many of the things he had when he was young, only now they were buried beneath the smoldering rubble of his dreams, destroyed by his reckless decisions. I believe I owe the girl; she is the one who formally introduced me to my dear friend. But, before I get to that, I suppose I must first tell of Mae and the boy's encounter.

He was sixteen at the time, or maybe seventeen (age has little relevance with these sorts of things) for argument's sake, we'll say sixteen and a half. He was sixteen and a half when she fell into his lap. It wasn't one of those expected things or one of those things that you anticipate or even consider; it's just one of those things that happens.

It was still a month and a half before the move, but he could already feel the distance. Chloe had been spending less time with the boys; she had found a new group of friends to split her time between. Ben sought to make the most of their remaining weeks, but he and Lynn were just starting the lengthy, involved process of learning the craft of love, which consumed a considerable amount of time. But the boy would not allow his jealousy to interfere with their happiness. Jack and the band had already accepted the fact that he was leaving and were making plans accordingly.

"You know I consider you my brother," Jack had told him, "and this band is nothing without you, but I was thinking maybe we could get another guy to start practicing with us—just in case, for any show that you might not be able to make."

The boy agreed; the proposition did make sense. He had expected that he would not be able to attend every practice, and he didn't see why they shouldn't be able to play shows just because he couldn't make it. As a result, most of their recent practice sessions had been spent patiently teaching "the new guy" how to fill his spot. Everyone in the boy's life was doing what needed to be done to adapt, except for him. He was living in a world that was learning to live without him.

He dropped down in his computer chair and flipped on the switch. Scratching at the prickle in his chest, he logged on to the Internet. The technology had been around for quite some time, but it had only been a year or two since his family could afford it. As he opened up the "people-finder" page, he wasn't quite sure what he was looking for. He just wanted some way to connect, something to take his mind off the current pressure of life. He certainly wasn't searching but, it's like I said, sometimes you must leave the familiarity and security of one environment to bring about new experiences and, ultimately, a change. All you can hope is that the change is for the best.

He clicked the mouse pointer on the "common interests" box and paused for a moment before typing in the words "Counting Crows." Pages upon pages of made-up, self-inflicted, computerized nametags appeared on the screen, most of which included one or more of the words "cute," "baby," "hott," "angel," "pimp," "seXy," or some altered variation of the word. He chuckled to himself. It is amazing how egotistical people can be when they are hidden from physical contact, behind electronic screens. He shook his head and chuckled again at himself for even trying. He didn't even know what he was doing. His eyes still scanned the first page of the list as he moved the mouse pointer to delete the search results. He stopped short as one of the names on the screen caught his attention. A rose amongst thorns, one name stood out from the rest. Apart from lacking all of the typical keywords, this name was modest and clever. He rubbed his hand across his collarbone and clicked on the name. He blinked as a small square text box appeared in the center of his screen. A thin black cursor flashed in its corner like a beacon in the bleak monotony of existence. His fingers grazed the keyboard as he typed out the word:

Hey.

"Hi. :) do I know you?" she responded.

No, you don't. Sorry. I found your name through this search.

Oh. This isn't one of those advertisements, is it?

Ha. No, not at all. I'm sorry. I was searching for Counting Crows fans and I thought your name was clever, so I figured I would say hi.

Oh, cool. Thanks. Well, hi. How are you? :)

I'm doing alright. A little embarrassed. I've never done anything like this before. Feels kinda stalker-ish.

Ha ha. Well, that's because it is. But that's ok. ;) So you're a crows fan?

I'm sorry?

You're a Counting Crows fan?

Oh, yeah! Sorry, I guess I don't know the lingo. But, yeah, they are my favorite band.

You'll catch on. ;) Mine too. Adam Duritz is pretty much the love of my life.

Ha ha. Well, I'm not going to go that far. But he's definitely a genius.

Fair enough.

So, what's your name?

Mae.

Aren't you going to ask me mine?

Nope. Already know it.

How?

I looked through your profile...had to make sure you weren't "stalker-ish." ;)

   And?

   I'll let you know. :) but so far so good.

   Ha ha. Glad to hear it. But now I feel like I've got to catch up. I didn't know we were screening each other beforehand.

   Ask away!

   Alright, where are you from?

   Texas.

   Never been there. Any fun?

   Not so much. How's Maryland?

   Not much better. How old are you?

   18.

   Cool. Last question, how do you feel about random guys bugging you online?

   Actually, they are pretty cool. ;)

   Incredible! You got all three questions right.

   Sweet! What do I win?

   Um, I'll get back to you on that.

   It better be good.

   Oh, it will be. ;)

   I'm looking forward to it. It's getting late. Shouldn't you be in bed?

   Me? No. I don't do too much sleeping.

   Me neither. No big Saturday plans for tomorrow?

   Actually, I'm going with my parents to look at our new house, and drowsiness may actually help in making me less aware.

   Not a big fan of the new house?

   Not a big fan of the move.

   Sorry. How come?

   Because it means leaving everything behind.

   That's always difficult.

   It's just that I have these friends, and school, and this band, and if I go it means that I let those things go.

   Not necessarily. Tell me more about this band.

   It's me and a couple of guys. We play small shows in the area.

   Awesome. I have a lot of friends in bands. What do you do?

   I play guitar and write the lyrics. And occasionally sing.

Very cool. I was in a band once.
Oh yeah?
Yeah, back in ninth grade. It was me and two other girls. We called ourselves "Sugar Pill."
Sweet name. ;)
Ha. We were terrible.
I'd like to hear some songs. What did you play?
Ha! Not going to happen! Guitar.
Nice. You still play?
Not so much anymore.
That's a shame. You should pick it up again.
Maybe I will. :)

As he was browsing through the numerous B.B. King tracks available online, he noticed one he had never heard before. It was a duet with the king of blues and some guy named John Mayer. The track had a nice sound and this John cat could sing, so the boy searched for more of the new talent's music. One song instantly jumped out at him and he downloaded it to a CD.

That night, as he climbed into bed, his mind felt more at ease. It felt good to escape into the company of a stranger who knew nothing of where he had been or what he had done. She had no expectations or judgment. He could be himself entirely without fear of how she would respond. It was the breath of fresh air he had been looking for.

He slipped his headphones over his ears and clicked the play button on his CD player. Every now and then, he would come across a song that said exactly what he was feeling. He considered it to be a little gift from people far more talented than he. It was as if they said, "Here, I will write for you what you're feeling, because you damn sure can't write it yourself." The track he had downloaded was called "Love song for no one" and it hummed gently in his ears the words he felt but couldn't write.

He closed his eyes and smiled as he started the song again. He had found two things that night that he hadn't been looking for, and yet he still did not realize the magnitude of either. The anxiety in his mind had settled, but his chest was throbbing wildly.

The next night, he left right at the end of band practice; he didn't stay to partake in their usual planted Remedy session. He tossed the baggie to Jack and waved goodbye.

"Where you scooting off to?" Jack asked, "Hot date?" The other three snickered.

"Perhaps," the boy said coolly and walked out the door.

When he got home, he dropped his guitar case on his bed and slumped down in his desk chair. His eyes surveyed the contents of his room. Many people had warned him that he'd better start packing. Scanning the shelves and drawers of books, clothes, and keepsakes, he supposed they were right. He did have plenty of work to do, but he knew he wasn't going to do it. Pulling a cardboard box out from his closet, he plopped it on the floor and glared at its empty walls. Should he choose to fill its hollow body, it would mean that he had given in. It would mean that he was accepting the change; it would mean that he was actually going. He stared at the box a moment longer before shaking his head and kicking it aside.

Now, I cannot say for sure that he was looking for her at that moment when he flipped on his computer. It is a possibility that he was just searching for something to distract himself from even considering the notion of packing. Maybe it was coincidence that he logged on roughly the same time he had the night before and found Mae waiting there, but I don't believe so. That's not how these things work.

Every night, for the next week, they explored one another until the twinkling hours of morning. Hours seemed like minutes, sitting there, getting to know the innermost workings of another human being. That was the beauty of their interaction. Because they were 1,500 miles apart, they developed a surreal connection. Neither one had come from the same places as the other. A few hours a day, they could escape from the anxiety, madness, and monotony of their cryptic pasts and prosaic lives and rest in the arms and mind of someone with whom they could relate. There were no conditions, no obligations or inhibitions. Within a week, the boy had become more authentic with a girl he had met on a computer screen than he believed he had been with anyone, ever. He talked about his past with her—something he had rarely done. He told her about his band and his schooling—worlds that rarely collided. He told her about Ben and Chloe, and his brother—something he never did. She always responded positively, with some encouragement about the boy's reaction to the different situations. She seemed to understand why he had done the things he had and what it had made of him. It made him feel acknowledged and justified.

"I don't think I'll be around tomorrow night...just in case you happened to be online. ;)" he told her at the end of their conversation one night.

How come?

It's my going away party =/

Oh my. Skip it! ;)

Ha. I wish I could. It's supposed to be a surprise.

Ha ha. I guess that didn't work out so well.

Nah. I'm way too suspicious for surprises.

That doesn't surprise me at all. = p

Gee, thanks.

No problem. Well, hopefully it won't be too bad.

I'll let you know.

Alright. Good luck! :)

Thanks. Have a good night.

The lights were off in the building as he parked his car out front. He missed Chloe. He hadn't seen her in weeks. Everyone had their own way of coping; Chloe just had a solitary way. He had expected that, toward the end, she might retreat to the dim recesses of her journal. That was her way—not that he could blame her. He certainly had his own methods of acceptance or denial, but he missed her. The gravel crunched gently beneath his flip-flops as he walked to the front door. Chloe had told him that she couldn't allow people to get close to her, because "closeness equals vulnerability and vulnerability eventually equals heartbreak." He had done his best to convince her that it wasn't the case, and now he was leaving her. She had every right to hide indoors. She was certainly safer there. The metal handle was cool in his hand as he gripped it and tugged the door open.

"Surprise!" they all called, and he did his best to imitate someone not nearly as skeptical as he, someone more easily fooled.

He was greeted with a barrage of hugs, high-fives, and hand-shakes. It was kind of his friends to go through the trouble, but he still did not truly grasp the reality of the situation. He scanned the roomful of people. Chloe was nowhere in sight. Apart from that, the party was all it should have been. They ate, they drank, they laughed. Ben stood up on a chair and tapped his glass.

"Excuse me," he said, "listen up!" The room quieted. "I just wanted to say something really quick. I wrote a speech, but there is no way I'm going to be able to read it. So, here it is."

A few people chuckled as Ben passed a folded piece of paper to the boy.

"You've got no idea what your friendship means to me," Ben started again. "You have never let me down." He paused. "You saved my life," his eyes fluttered.

The boy could see a wall of tears rising from beneath his bottom eyelid. The room was awkwardly silent. The boy could feel the uncomfortable shuffling of feet and the tense glares focused on Ben, who stood silently on his chair podium.

"What about that time I tried to kill you?" the boy called out, smiling to his friend.

The room erupted into laughter, but only part of it was genuine; the rest was simply out of relief. Ben smiled.

"Could you be more specific?" he called back, climbing down from the chair.

The crowd laughed harder, and the two boys embraced.

The rest of the night went smoothly. Eventually, the boy did ask Ben where Chloe was. Ben did his best to fabricate some excuse that was clearly rehearsed and shallow—something to do with plans she simply could not get out of. The boy only nodded. It wouldn't matter soon anyway. It was almost time to say goodbye. The boy glanced at the clock on the wall.

"Is it time?" Ben asked, followed by a deep sigh.

The boy nodded again. The room had already started to empty. Rain crashed down on the rooftop overhead, which only quickened their steps in getting to their vehicles safe and dry. As they filed their way out the door, his friends left him with all of the typical cliché parting words: "Keep in touch," they said, and "Come back soon," "Best of luck" and "I'll come visit"—all the meaningless insincere remarks that people make because they don't know what else to say. It's funny how often people say things they don't really mean, but the boy accepted them all with "I will," "Thank you," or "Please do." Each time that the door opened to let another person out of his life, he could hear the loud splashing of the raindrops against the gravel.

"Do you remember that guitar I bought a year or so ago?" Ben asked once the last person had made their way out and the steel door of his heart had smashed shut.

Ben had gotten the instrument from a private craftsman who was a friend of his father and owed the family a favor. As a result, Ben had gotten a great deal on a beautiful guitar, which he never played. It was one of those things he had always meant to do but never really learned. The boy had tried to convince him to give it a try but, apart from the boy's occasional awestruck fondling of the instrument, it had sat in a dusty case in the corner of Ben's bedroom. The boy nodded; of course, he remembered.

"It's yours," Ben said, signaling to the case propped in the corner. The boy's jawed dropped.

"No way!" he gawked at his friend. "I can't take that! That thing is worth some money. If you aren't going to play it, you can at least sell it."

"This is not a discussion," Ben said, grabbing the case by the handle. "I want you to have it. You know it didn't cost me much, so let's not make it a big deal. I wanted to get you something meaningful, and you've always loved this guitar."

He passed the case to the boy, who fought to keep his lip from quivering. It really was happening. The two boys hugged again.

"Thank you," the boy said.

"Thank you," Ben replied. "I'll miss you." The boy nodded in agreement.

"I'll miss you, too."

The boy pushed the heavy door open and stepped outside. A wide wooden awning stood sturdily above the entrance and shielded him from the rain. Just beyond the reach of the angled structure, a figure shivered in the darkness. The boy moved to the edge of the concrete slab. Chloe stood, drenched to the bone. Her hair plastered heavily to her face, her clothes saturated, shedding water in streams off her limbs and down into the muddy earth. Her shoes squished like juiced lemons as she shifted from one foot to the next. Her eyelashes stuck together in thick black clumps as she stared at him with those gorgeously tragic eyes. She glanced up at the sky before asking.

"Shall we?" she said, extending her palms to him.

He gazed at her for a moment, then leaned his head out from under the awning just enough to see the sky. She stood with arms parallel to the streams that trickled between her feet. Turning his eyes back upon the girl, he smiled as his head began to nod. She smiled back as he clasped her hand and the two ran off, splashing through the puddles as they danced in the rain.

"Promise you won't change," she said.

"I promise."

"Swear we'll always be friends?"

"I swear."

"Forever?"

"...and ever"

"Cross your heart."

The boy made an "x" across his chest with his finger.

seven

Reality struck hard the next morning. His alarm screamed for him at 6:30 a.m., followed by the possibly more piercing call of his mother's voice. In a whirlwind of brown cardboard, clear tape, and black coffee, she and his father had their entire home packaged for relocation. The boy had barely finished his breakfast when they swept him from his chair and into his new life.

The first several weeks were much worse than he anticipated. It was foolish of him at the time to think that if he were to leave, life back home would do anything besides go on functioning just as well without him. He should have seen it coming in the way that all the aspects of his life seemed to be preparing for a life without him. Back then, he still had faith in the dependency of people. He still talked to Ben and Chloe but certainly less frequently, and it was only due to a strenuous effort on his part to keep that communication alive. Not that they could be blamed. They had lives and distractions, whereas he sat in the middle of his ghost white room, inhaling the fumes of new construction and plastering pitiful poetry of things already assumably forgotten on his wall, as a dizzy white fan spun overhead. He would sit and wait and write and coat his white walls in words, just to have something less taunting to look at. He wrote his heart out on those flat panel white brushstrokes in hopes that some day it would be put to use. The band seemed to be the only thing that maintained any consistency, probably only out of necessity. They still practiced when possible and played as many shows as they could. It was an-ever-so gradual process, but eventually, he learned to survive in his new environment. It was brutal and lonely but, even worse, it took some of the warmth out of his eyes and left a callous on his heart.

There is a gravitational pull that some individuals possess that draws similar groups of people toward that individual. For the boy, that gravity was much stronger than it was for most, and it led to his initial demise. The only positive aspect of the move that he could foresee was that it would allow him an opportunity to vanquish certain aspects of his life that he was displeased with—a fresh start, if you will. It would give him the chance to eliminate the need for Remedies, escape his habitual bad company, and quit pushing. But, this was not the case. Unfortunately, his gravitational pull was much stronger than his willpower, and by the time his first day at his new school started, he had already met new replications of his previous contacts. There are a million Jacks in the world. The one that found him first was named Will. A friend of the boy who was from the area had introduced them, and it wasn't a week before the first phone call came.

"Hey—hey, what's up, dude? It's Will."

"Hey, man. Not a lot. What's going on?"

"Not much. I just had a quick question....Do you have access to any greens?"

The boy chuckled. "Greens"—this kid knew the lingo. There is a certain, unspoken code that is used in dealing with these types of things. There are specific "targeted" words that must not be used. "Greens," however, is an ambiguously implicit word and thus safe.

"Um," the boy sighed.

There were some things he just could not escape. He glanced over at his computer, still disassembled in the corner of his room, and scratched his chest. Will interrupted him before he could finish.

"I know it's a weird request. It's just that I'm having a hell of a time finding anything. I would really appreciate it. I wouldn't ask if I wasn't desperate."

The boy made a groaning sound with his throat.

"I'm really trying to get away from all that...nonsense," the boy tried to sound polite.

"That's cool, dude, and I totally respect that. But...I'm *really* desperate and I can't find it anywhere. I would owe you big time." The boy sighed again. "Could you put me in touch with someone who could hook me up, maybe?" That was completely against the rules.

If the boy vouched for the kid, he knew that his source would make the exchange, but it simply was not a polite thing to do. Not to mention that would mean that he, in turn, would be indebted to the supplier, which everyone knows is one thing that you never want to be.

"It doesn't work that way." They boy ran his hand slowly along the top of his head. He really should set that computer up.

"I know; and I'm sorry. It would just be a one-time deal if it was possible." It's never a "one-time deal." "Just this once?"

The boy grimaced. How desperate did he have to be to resort to begging?

"Alright. Just this once." His shoulders dropped; another battle lost. "But, I'm going to charge you what I pay for the stuff."

"Why would you do that?" Will's voice was a blend of shock and gratitude. "I don't mind paying a little extra for your trouble."

"No," the boy said forcefully, "no more profit off that shit. It's too enticing."

"Well, thanks, man! That's really awesome of you."

"But," the boy continued, "you've got to come to get it."

"Not a problem. Not a problem at all. Thanks, dude. Seriously, I owe you one."

"It's not a big deal." The boy flopped down on his bed. "I'll make a call in a bit. Hit me up sometime tomorrow."

"Awesome. Thanks again, dude. It is much appreciated."

"Right on. Take it easy."

He flipped his phone shut and heaved it to the idle pillows at the top of his bed. Rubbing his eyes, he sat up and exhaled. The computer would have to wait until some other time. He pulled his notebook out from its drawer and began constructing another wall ornament.

School was difficult. By senior year, cliques are already formed with the cement binding that allows only the fewest of the favored access. The "jocks," in their ridiculous, stiff, cotton jackets with bold yellow lettering, proclaiming their loyalty to some amateur sport of some trite academy and a meaningless number, sat in the cafeteria and ate their apples and bananas in a dire attempt to appear more athletic than one another. From their nearby table, the "preps" forced the loudest laughter in the room from the pits of their stomachs—a blatant sign of weakness—as they fought to hide their disgust or jealousy of one another's clothing. The "intellects" kept their faces buried in their lunches, lifting their eyes only to discuss homework or look longingly at the more popular groups. Martyrs for their intelligence, they sat, their bulky backpacks filling the empty seats at their table, their silence proving their strength. The tragedy is that any one of them would have traded their superior intellect for just a taste of acceptance. In the secluded corners of the lunchroom, my personal favorite comical group congregated. So consumed with their own injuries, the "Goths" barely noticed the other tables. Victims of privilege, they sat, sulking in their luxurious crannies of despair. Promoters of individuality and critics of organized conformity, they mulled about in their flocks, unified by their hatred of unity. It was difficult to distinguish the few authentically wounded from the imposters, as they all bore the same weighted shoulders. If only they were to look around them and see that their naïve afflictions were minuscule in comparison to the troubles of the rest of the world, they would be a much happier collection of people. It was amusing to see them sitting at the fringing lunch tables in their ancient, black, Germanic tribal garb, their eyes full of disdain for an inevitable world, eating vanilla pudding out of plastic containers with plastic spoons. This was his battleground.

For the first few weeks, he observed, noting their behavior, their weaknesses. If he truly wanted to change his habits, he would have to first find prospects with qualities dissimilar from his previous company; then he would need to identify and use their weaknesses to gain access to their group. It seemed like a logical plan, but the boy neglected to account for this intense gravitational pull. They trickled to him from all regions of the lunchroom and drew him in—Emma and Nate from the "jocks"; Claire, Joe, and Lily from the "preps"; Spencer from the "intellects"; and Jim and Paige from the "Goths." Representatives from each crowd, they gave him access to an immense network of individuals. His plan was foiled, but he could not have imagined that it would have worked. No matter which walk of life or circle they come from, everyone needs a Remedy.

The boy wiggled the cord from the keyboard into the back of his computer tower and placed it gently on his desk. Reading assignments and math problems had consumed most his free time throughout the week; but today was Saturday, which meant that he could start on his ever-growing "to-do list." Every room in the house was completely unpacked and assembled, except for his. Strips of deflated bubble wrap and crinkled tape lay on his floor, strewn between large, brown cardboard boxes packed to various heights with dismantled memories. He scanned the floor around him for the computer power cord. He grunted as his phone vibrated fervently against his leg. He fished it out of his pocket with his fingers and flipped it open to his ear.

"Hello?" he tried not to sound annoyed.

"Hey." It was Will.

"What's going on?" he asked, as he sifted through one of the boxes on the floor in search of the cord.

"Nothing. I'm here."

The boy glanced across the room at the clock on his nightstand. 12:34. He was early.

"Yeah, alright." He snapped the phone shut and dropped it back into his pocket.

Surveying the computer, then the boxes around the room, the boy sighed. Maybe he should just buy a new power cord. He stepped over the clutter and opened his closet door. The small metal heating vent twisted and popped as he yanked it free from the wall and lifted the old shoebox from the dark, cold, flimsy ductwork just below the vent cover. The metal resonated in the hollow canal, vibrating as he pressed the cover back into place. Snatching up the box and his keys from his dresser, he hurried up the stairs and out the door.

Will was leaning against his car, puffing on a cigarette, when the boy rounded the corner.

"Hey," the boy said, and the two slapped hands and got into the car.

Will dug into his pocket and pressed a stack of loose twenty-dollar bills into the boy's palm. There was no longer any real need to be discreet; this was their seventh time meeting under these circumstances. One favor had turned into seven. It's never a "one-time deal." The boy counted the money and paused. He counted it again—three hundred eighty dollars. He thought for a moment; he had only paid three hundred and forty. He tugged two twenties from the stack and tossed them back to his friend.

"Come on, dude," Will started, "everyone else I have ever gotten from makes at least that! I'm going to make twice that just off what I don't use!"

"Nah, man, I told you. Not to you." The boy flipped the shoebox open, grabbed a baggie from inside, and passed it to his friend.

"Thanks, man. What are you up to today?" Will asked, eyeing the planted Remedy with salivating eyes.

"No plans," the boy shrugged, "just getting some unpacking done. Why?"

"Still? You might as well leave it packed up for the next time you move." Will snickered. "I'm going to meet up with some friends." He held up the baggie and winked before stuffing it into his glove compartment. The boy chuckled. "They are actually really cool people and I've been wanting you to meet them. Wanna come?"

The boy hesitated. Staying home meant digging through large boxes of memories he was not sure he was prepared to face, in search of his computer cord. It didn't matter how badly he wanted it set up; he would welcome any distraction.

"I'll cruise," he said, lighting up a cigarette.

"That's my boy," Will laughed, turning up the radio as they backed out of the driveway.

That night, he came home early, but the house was quiet. He slipped down the stairs and into his room. His eyes burned as he flopped down on his bed. It felt like a tomb in there—still and dark, surrounded by walls of clutter, feeling estranged, the stale air of cardboard and plastic tape swirling, stirred only by the steady inhale-exhale of his dying breaths. The methodical click of the clock thumped like the tribal march of a funeral procession, muffled by layers of rock and ancient soil. The dust had nearly settled on his eyes when a light tap echoed on the tomb door.

"Hey, you up?" It was his brother's voice.

The boy lifted his mummified arm to his eyes to shield them as he forced them open.

"What's up?" his voice croaked.

The light was sharp as his brother flipped the switch and stepped into the room.

"Hey," he said, eyeing the floor and stepping carefully over the brown squares, "um, I need to borrow some money."

The boy sat up quickly.

"What?" It had been two months since his brother had asked for money. The boy had taken that as an unspoken sign that his brother was overcoming his addiction. "Why?"

"I'm broke," his brother laughed uncomfortably, "I'm out of gas. I'm trying to go out and I don't get paid till next week."

The boy weighed him for a moment. He hated being so skeptical, but he couldn't take the chance of contributing to that poison. It had nothing to do with the money. Money meant nothing to him. If it was possible for him to survive without it, he would have given every penny away. It makes monsters out of people, he thought.

"You wouldn't lie to me, right?" The boy reached in his back pocket and pulled out the stack of twenties he had gotten from Will.

"Not a chance," his brother said, taking the money from his hand and thumbing through it. "Thanks, man. I'll get you back when I get my check." No he wouldn't.

The boy smiled and nodded. It felt good to pretend like he was making a difference every now and then.

"Also," his brother added, fishing through one of the boxes, "you may want to finish unpacking." He lifted a long slender black plug from the cardboard.

The boy's eyes widened.

"Where did you find that?!" he jumped from the bed and snatched the cord. "Sweet!"

"Like I said," his brother inched towards the door, "unpack."

The boy nodded, but he was already preoccupied with frantically connecting power to his computer.

The power light beamed a solid green as he squatted down into his desk chair. Commotion ignited beneath his ribcage as he logged online and Mae's name appeared on his screen. There was still life left in that tomb after all.

"Hey" he typed as fast as his fingers could skim the keys. It had been months.

"Hey!" she replied, like a fresh breeze through the stale room. His eyes fluttered as the dust swirled free from his lashes and his stiff fingers worked the keys.

And where have you been?

Me?? I've been here. Where have you been?

Ha ha. Trying to relocate my life.

How's that going?

Pretty awful. ;) How have you been?

Good. Busy, but good.

How is the ole' lone star state?

Ha. It is.

For some random reason, I was talking to my uncle the other day about you and he said that he's been to Texas a few times.

Uh oh. ;) What did he think?

Um, he said it wasn't bad. Told me at one point they were driving and a herd of tarantulas were walking across the street.

Ha ha! Really?? A herd?!

Yeah, that's what he said. Do you not see many?

Never.

Never?

Not one. Ever.

Ha ha. He is a little extreme. I guess I should have known better. No one waits for ten minutes while a herd of huge spiders crosses the street.

Ahahaha. Who knows. So, have you gotten settled in?

Just about as much as I can, you know? It's just such a strange, unfamiliar place to me. But I am managing.

That's good. I'm sure it is difficult. Have you gone back to visit at all?

Not really. It's a lot harder than I thought it would be. There is just so little time, and everyone there is preoccupied with their lives, too. Which is no good, because I don't really have anyone to talk to about that stuff.

Well, I'm here. :) And I'll listen whenever.

Thanks. You may not know what you are getting yourself into, but I appreciate it.

It's cool. I'm not worried. :) How's the band?

Not bad. We've still been playing when possible.

You know, I would still love to hear some stuff.

Come to a show some time. ;) I'll give you VIP treatment.

Oh yeah?

Yeah! It will be sweet. Instead of coming in through the nice tidy presentable front entrance with everyone else, you can come through the dirty, dark, hole/backdoor with us. And instead of using the bathroom that they clean, you can use the one backstage that even we are afraid to use.

Excellent! ;)

Oh, and we will even let you help lug all of our equipment to the van!

Sign me up.

Ha ha. But hey, at least the drinks will be free and I will sing you a couple tunes.

Sounds good.

It would be nice to have someone there who appreciates good music and lyrics. You come, and I'll sing every word to you, like no one else is there.

I would like that.

You say that now, but that's because you've never heard me try to hit those high notes. ;)

I'm sure it's angelic. :)

They spent the next three hours talking, exploring the deepest crevices of one another's mind and character. In a sort of unexplainable way, she made him feel at home. In spite of all the madness of the move and his friends and dirty habits, his mind was at ease when they talked. He never lost interest and always felt like himself, maybe for the first time in his life. But it was impossible. It had to be impossible to feel that connected to someone so far away—someone he had never met.

"You know, I was thinking, you aren't happy where you are, and I hate it here; what do you say we just get married and ditch both these towns?" he typed at the end of their conversation. "Go discover someplace new."

Ha ha. I'm in. ;)

Alright, we'll start making plans tomorrow. ;)

Tomorrow?

Yeah, I will talk to you then.

Oh, you will? How can you be so sure?

Because I'm going to sit online and wait, even if it takes all night.

Ha. OK, well, I guess I'd better show up.

Damn straight. ;)

For the next two weeks, she consumed him. He couldn't focus in school. On nights when his friends begged him to come out, he stayed in and studied her heart. He envisioned her eyes through the passion and vigor that exploded from her words, her smile through her graceful wit and uplifting spirit, and her skin through her tranquilizing compassion. She was a being, created in his mind by words strewn across a glowing computer screen, a body, assembled by imagination, into a form of unspeakable beauty but imaginary nonetheless—imaginary and entirely out of reach.

"So, not to freak you out or anything," Mae typed late one night, "but I was at school the other day and this guy was sort of hitting on me, so I told him I had a fiancé in Maryland who wouldn't be too happy."

Ha ha. Did you really?

Yep. So, if a stranger from Texas comes knocking on your door, you will know why.

Tell him he'd better bring some friends and a gun. Everyone's got one of those in Texas, right?

Pretty much. ;)

I didn't know the whole fiancé card was a legit excuse.

It is now ;)

Alright, well I'm going to have to use that one next time. That is, if a girl ever tries to talk to me again. I'll never meet one if I keep hiding inside every night so I can talk to you. ;)

Man, trying to cheat on me already?

Ha ha. Doubtful. ;)

That story doesn't freak you out, does it?

Not at all.

I figured I could tell you. I knew you would think it was funny.

Totally. You can tell me anything.

Ditto. :) You know, I really feel like that is true.

Good, because it is. And me too. :) I was just thinking, you said if a stranger from Texas came to my door, but, even if you came to my door, I wouldn't know it was you.

That's true. Hmmm, this has the makings of a great prank. Ha ha.

Kidding! So what, you want to trade pictures or something?

I guess. It makes sense right?

Sure. Just promise you won't stop talking to me?

Why in the world would I ever do that?

Once you see my picture. It's pretty bad.

You better be kidding. Apart from the fact that I'm sure you are absolutely gorgeous, there is no way I would ever stop talking to you. You're keeping me sane.

Eh. You'll see. You've got to give me some time though, to find a picture that I don't hate as much as the rest. I will e-mail it to you tomorrow.

Alright. I'll do the same. How exciting. ;)

It actually is. : p

I'm glad you think so. I didn't want to seem like a loser.

Ha. Not at all.

Good. By the way, how's the tarantula population been this week?

At an all-time low. ;)

Really? Ha ha. That's a shame.

The boy shifted uncomfortably in his chair. Even through a computer screen, he felt as though she could peer through the very core of his soul. He had told her nearly everything there was to know about his life—everything except the one thing that he was trying to destroy. Every other individual he had every trusted had only been privy to certain aspects of his life. He wanted this to be different. It was time that he threw himself upon the altar of self-consciousness.

"I know I can tell you anything," he typed.

Sure. What's up?

There are a lot of things about my life I'm not proud of.

Like what?

Decisions, friends, habits—things like that.

Everybody has those.

I know. But I feel like mine are worse.

I doubt that. I have made a lot of bad mistakes, but as long as you can realize them and move on, then you are better for them.

Yea, that's what people say. I just feel like I tell you everything and I just wanted you to know that I'm going to fix things.

I'm not worried about that. It doesn't matter what it was. You are a good person, and I'm sure you will do the right thing.

Thank you.

How many times do I have to tell you? Anytime. ;)

Go get some sleep.

OK, be careful. I have a feeling it's going to be a rough night. Come back to me tomorrow night in one piece.

I will. ;)

The boy turned off his computer and pulled out his cell phone. His grip was firm and steady, and he scrolled through his contacts and selected Jack's number. It only rang twice.

"What's up, brother?" Jack's voice was loud over the music that played in the background.

"Hey, Jack. Can we talk?" The boy plugged his ear to better hear the voice on the other end.

"Yeah, sure, hang on." There was a pause, "Hey! Turn that shit down! What's going on, dude?"

"Look, man," the boy paced across his room. "I'm done. I'm done pushing. I'm done with all the favors. I'm just done."

"Whoa, whoa, whoa," Jack's voice straightened, "what are you saying? What's the matter? Are you telling me that's it? You're done?"

"Totally done."

"Are you sure about this, man? You can't just do that." He sounded worried. Jack never sounded worried. "There are going to be some angry, dangerous people. You can't just be done."

"I'm sorry, man. I'm done."

"Don't apologize to me; it's you I'm worried about. I don't think you can just be done."

"Well, I am."

"Alright, if that's what you want," his voice was hesitant.

106

"What do you want me to tell these guys? Because they are going to ask, and if there isn't a good reason, they are going to get upset."

"Tell them..." the boy paused for a moment, "tell them I met a girl and that I don't need that stuff anymore."

"A girl?" Jack mocked.

"Yeah, a girl," the boy said with confidence.

"Alright, dude, I will tell them. I don't think it's going to fly, but I'll do my best. You know I'm behind you no matter what."

"Yeah, I know. Thanks." The boy flipped the phone shut and open again and called Will.

"Hey, Will." He said when the phone stopped ringing. "Hey, why don't you swing by for a minute?"

The boy was waiting in the driveway with the shoe box in his hand when Will pulled up, cigarette dangling from his lip.

"What's this?" Will asked, as the boy handed him the box.

"That's it," the boy replied coolly, "no more favors." Will nodded.

"No more?" he asked, taking the box with both hands, "You sure about this?"

The boy nodded, "That's it."

As he lay in bed that night, he felt cleansed. Things were already looking brighter. He had finally found a reason to make things right. How had he even gotten himself into that situation? He couldn't remember. For the next hour, he laid on his bed in the dark with his phone placed gently on his chest. If there were going to be angry or threatening calls, they would come rather quickly. But the phone did not stir, not once, and he drifted off to sleep wondering if this Texas angel had saved his life.

The next morning, he woke up before his alarm sounded. He felt renewed and refreshed, with a restored fervor for life. It was an easy day at school; the bell seemed to ring much earlier than usual, and before he knew it, he was driving home with the windows down, his hand dancing as it cut through the racing air. Once parked, he hurried inside, dropped his bag down at the door and rushed to his bedroom. He flipped on the computer and sank down into his chair, his legs fidgeting beneath the desk. Logging into his e-mail, he scanned the sender names and clicked on the one from "Mae." She had sent the photo.

107

The e-mail seemed to take much longer than usual to load. It scanned, line by line, as it loaded the picture in fragments. The boy squinted and leaned closer to the screen. He shook the mouse in anxious anticipation. His heart was racing, and he was not sure why. His breaths quickened as his chest tightened. He could see the top of her head. He groaned as sharper pains zigzagged across his ribcage. Eyebrows. His lungs expanded as her eyes were uncovered, then her nose, and mouth. His eyes widened. His chest was murmuring. Yanking his phone from his pocket, he clumsily dialed Ben's number.

"Hey!"

"Ben! I found her!" The boy laughed.

"What? Who? What are you talking about?"

"I found her! I found Sally!"

eight

The boy rubbed his hands against the smooth fabric of his pants and kept both his feet together on the thin carpet that layered the church floor. It was one of those rare Sundays where his brother accompanied him and his parents. He always felt slightly less comfortable those weeks, as if his brother was catching him cheating—as if his presence rendered him transparent and exposed his closeted secrets.

"You have no right to be here," the boy imagined the accusation. "I know what you've done."

"You're no better!" his brain fired back. "You've got the darkest secret of all."

They sat in silence, two impostors in the most revealing place in the world. The boy lowered his eyes to his anchored shoes. Even if his brother made those accusations, the boy could not combat them. Deep down, they were guilty of the same crime, but that didn't matter. God's love was not contingent on their behavior. He knew that no matter what he did or how hard he tried, he could never earn the love of a higher, more righteous being. That was not possible. On his worst day or his best day, no matter how he walked through those double doors, he knew he was always equally unworthy, and thus equally loved.

"I just want to be a better person," he whispered to himself.

That is always much harder than it sounds. He turned to his brother, who scratched the rosy skin underneath his nose and sniffled. It didn't matter how they came through the door. Everyone had the potential to feel loved, and everyone had the ability to change.

He always felt a little more satisfied with life after a good dose of church. It reinforced his fundamental beliefs that he had done his best to preserve over the years. His steps were light and cheerful as he strolled through the sanctuary doors and out into the parking lot. Though it was only early afternoon, the sun felt warm and radiant against his face. It was the one moment of the week where he felt most content with who he was. School was almost over, summer was on its way, and he was loved by a higher power. Smiling, he pulled his silenced cell phone from his pocket and flipped it open—five missed calls. He scrolled through the call log; they were all from Will. Pressing the "call" button, he held the phone to his ear.

"Good Lord!" Will said after a few rings. "I've been calling you all morning!"

"I noticed. Sorry, man. I was in church. What's up?"

"Church?!" Will sounded surprised, "You? In church?"

"Yeah. What's that supposed to mean?"

"Nothing." Will chuckled, "Nothing at all."

"No," he tried to mask his offense, "why is that surprising?"

"No reason. Man. No reason at all."

The boy scanned the parking lot. All the people were making their way to their cars. Mothers and fathers walked proudly with their children, who were clearly anxious to trade in their Sunday slacks and blouses for play clothes but were well-behaved nonetheless. Young couples drifted across the gravel, Bibles in hand, laughing, celibacy pronounced boldly in the air that hung between them. One of the fathers caught the boy's eye and waved. He smiled nervously and waved back.

"Anyway," Will started again, "are you going to Joe's party tonight?"

"Yeah," the boy replied slowly. "I was planning on it."

"Are you picking up booze?"

"Uh, maybe." He kicked some loose rock with his shoe. "I'll let you know."

"Alright."

The boy slipped his hand in his pocket and fumbled his keys between his fingers as he walked to his car. His eyes moved back across the lot. Most of the vehicles had emptied from their spaces. The sun had moved behind a patch of clouds.

"Everyone back inside," he thought. "I need another dose,

please."

Scooping a bottle of water out from the refrigerator, the boy dropped down in his desk chair and switched on the computer screen. He skimmed over the names on his contact list. Mae wasn't there, but Chloe had left him a message. I read it over his shoulder. It said, "I miss your poetry. Send me some new stuff?" The seal crackled on the water bottle as he spun off the lid and threw back a swallow. He hadn't written in months. Snatching up his phone from the desk, he dialed Ben's number, but his friend didn't answer and the punctual ring of the phone resonated against his eardrum. He dropped the phone back onto the desktop and wandered outside.

His parents' new house—he still refused to call it his own—stood wide against the ground. It was the first of the houses in their neighborhood. The other plots of land were occupied by small mounds of copper-colored dirt and little, bright orange flags that flapped loosely around flimsy metal poles. Soon, the men would come with their yellow hats and blueprints and erect a house very similar to his parents'; for now, the mounds and flags and open space facilitated one of his new favorite ways of passing time.

He lifted his club, tee, and a handful of balls from the stash behind the bushes and stepped out onto the lawn. Sinking the tee down into the splintering grass, he balanced a dimpled white ball on its top and looked out over the rows of flagged mounds. The rubber squeaked as he gripped the club with both hands and lined its head up with the ball. The boy had never really played much golf; it was a fairly new interest. Something about that moment of transference, when the force of his arms shifted to the crushing contact of the club that sent the ball soaring, made him feel a sense of release. Each relentlessly smashed ball represented a personal grievance about the current condition of his life. All of the suppressed difficulties that had come with the move were compressed into a small round ball that sailed as high and as far as he could force it. One after another, they glided over the mounds as he hammered the club as hard as his arms could swing. His brother's secret addiction skipped across the dirt and landed in a tuft of stiff grass. The idea of leaving all that he knew and loved behind for something new hooked right and cut around the side of the house. His indescribable feelings for a girl he had never met cleared the farthest mound and bounced once above the piled dirt. By the time he teed the unbearable pain of missing Ben and Chloe, he was panting and his pile of grievance balls was gone. His phone rang against his leg but he ignored it. He didn't even look at it. It didn't matter who it was. Yes, he was coming to the party. No, he didn't know what time. Yes, he was probably getting booze. No, he wasn't taking requests. Throwing the club roughly to the ground, he marched back inside and down into his room, his tomb.

The chair squeaked softly as he dropped down at his desk and ran his hand over his woolly hair. A haircut was just another thing on his list of tasks. Shaking the mouse briskly against its pad, he revived his computer screen. It illuminated a familiar desolate glow. A smile leaped to his face as her message box appeared.

"Hey!" she had typed. "Are you there? I hope you aren't ignoring me."

"Never in a million years," he typed back, rolling the chair closer to the screen.

Thank goodness. I thought maybe you had decided to stop talking to me. ;)

Ha. Good one. Always with the jokes. ;)

Ha ha. How is your day?

Not bad. Yours?

Good. How was church?

It was nice. My brother came.

Oh. So, you felt unworthy and exposed? ;)

Yeah.

Why is that again? I never really understood.

I dunno. It's hard to try to do right sitting next to someone who has seen everything you've done wrong.

You are too hard on yourself.

Maybe so, but I don't think I can help it. Plus, it keeps me motivated to make changes.

Well, don't make too many changes. I kinda like you the way you are. ;)

Kinda? Wow. Thanks a lot.

Ha ha. OK, really. I really like you the way you are.

The boy drummed his fingers against the desktop and smirked. She really was fantastic. She could completely captivate him there, glued by the electricity that transferred from her fingertips on plastic keys to his white-lit computer screen. For two hours he sat, enveloped in that electricity.

"So, why do you think it is that you have never found love?" she asked.

I'm too picky.

How so?

I need someone who is funny, someone I will never get tired of talking to, someone who is smart and loyal and caring, someone who really understands me and values the same things.

That doesn't sound like too much to ask for.

You wouldn't think so.

Not at all.

You know what the most frustrating thing about it is?

What?

I found a girl just like that. But she's 1,500 miles away, in a state I've never even been to.

You think you've got it bad? I've got the biggest crush on a guy I've never met. ;)

I sure hope you're talking about me.

There is no one else.

Honestly Mae, it may sound crazy, but the best moments of my day are spent here, talking to you.

Mine, too.

I go to sleep every night wishing we could have talked longer and wake up every morning anxious to get back in this chair.

Me, too.

And it's not even a very comfortable chair. ;)

Ha ha.

I mean it. It's awful. ;) But you are worth every wincing second. I can't even explain it.

My heart is beating really fast.

I hope that's a good thing.

It is. It is. I just can't believe this is happening. I didn't think it was possible.

I'm sorry. I hope this isn't out of line at all. Please tell me if it is.

No, not at all. It's perfect. Absolutely perfect. I've been thinking it for a long time. I just never thought you felt the same way.

I do. More than I've felt anything in a really long time.

So, what do we do now? Should I pack my bags? ;)

Sure! :)

I wish. Unfortunately, right now, I am getting yelled at to come to the dinner table. I'm sorry. I know it's not the best timing.

Don't be. It's totally cool. I should get going myself. We will have plenty of time to talk.

When?

Tell you what, here's my phone number. Why don't you give me a call whenever you have some time?

Call? Like a phone call? That's a big step.

I think we are ready. ;) Go eat.

Alright. Be safe tonight.

Before switching off the computer screen, the boy looked again at the picture Mae had sent him. Her head was propped casually against a weathered wooden beam. Strands of hair hung, loosely bordering her soft cheeks and distant eyes that stared calmly at the ground. Her lips fought a slight smile that appeared in the very corners of her mouth. Something about the entirety of her expression was transfixing. The boy stared for a moment before printing the picture. He almost didn't notice his phone vibrating in his pocket. His eyes lit up as he fumbled it free from the denim and checked the caller ID. It wasn't her. It was Joe.

"Hey," he flipped the phone open and to his ear.

"What up, man?" Joe sounded excited. The boy could hear AC/DC blaring in the background. He shuddered. "You coming or what?"

"Yeah, I'll be there." He scooped her picture from the printer tray and scanned her face again. "I just need to get dressed first," he said absently.

"Well, hurry up!"

"I'm coming, calm down. Man! You are needy."

"Call it whatever you want. Just get here!" Joe chuckled.

"Alright! Hey, I'm changing the music as soon as I get there."

"What?!" Joe argued, "this is classic!"

The boy snickered as he clamped the phone shut and dropped it back into his pocket. He pulled the top drawer of his desk open and fished through the clutter of pens, paperclips, and guitar picks until his fingers closed around a roll of tape. Pressing the picture of Mae firmly against a blank space of wall above his computer with one hand, the boy tore a piece of tape with the other and flattened it along the trim of the paper. Stepping back, he folded his arms and gave one last thoughtful look before he moved to his closet, shaking his head and laughing at himself.

Mr. Marley sang about the lack of pain in the embrace of music and the boy adjusted the volume on his car radio to his liking. Although he could not fully grasp the intensity of application those words would have to his life, the boy still bobbed his head in agreement and drummed his fingers lightly on the underbelly of the steering wheel. He had real feelings for a girl who had real feelings for him. Nothing could rattle that state of bliss in which he steered the car. Everything was as it should have been. Maybe it wasn't such a bad thing that he had moved. The flashing of his phone on the passenger seat interrupted his thoughts. Spinning the volume knob to the left, he turned down the music and raised the phone into view. It was a number he had never seen, an area code he didn't know. He had deleted certain contacts from his directory after his minor lifestyle adjustment and, as a result, had forced himself into the habit of not answering calls from unknown numbers. His adversaries were crafty ones and had fooled him one time too many by calling from mysterious numbers, looking for "one last favor." His eyes shifted from the flashing screen to the road and back again as he debated in his mind. The number was clearly out of state. Honestly, how much harm or annoyance could anyone cause from another state, even if it was one of the worst of them? Plus, there was the slim chance that it was the voice he was aching with curiosity to hear.

"I hope I don't regret this," he muttered to himself as he opened the phone to his ear.

"Hey," the voice said, followed by a nervous giggle, "it's Mae."

The boy's sigh of relief was quickly strangled by sheer panic. It was really her. There was no longer a shield of glass and wires and text. There was finally a voice to host her enamoring words, a gorgeous voice.

"Hello?" the voice asked.

"Hey!" the boy chuckled. "Wow. I can't believe I'm actually talking to you."

"I know," she giggled again, "me neither. Is it weird?"

"Yeah! I mean – a little. But not in a bad way," he fumbled. "How are you?"

"I'm good." He could tell that she was smiling. "How are you? Are you busy? Can you talk?" She laughed at herself.

"Yeah, I'm fine. I'm just driving to my friend's house. He's having a party tonight. I'm glad you called."

"Me, too," her smile had gotten bigger.

"It's very cool to hear your voice."

"Is it what you expected?"

"Not really," he said slowly. "I expected more of a southern accent. Your voice is much...softer, much more subtle."

"So you aren't disappointed?"

"Not at all," he chuckled, "it's a fantastic voice." They both laughed out loud.

"Thanks. So, what's this party tonight? Any particular reason, or just for fun?"

"It's just for fun. My friend Joe usually has people over on the weekends; nothing too crazy. He's got a nice patio, so we sit out there and drink some beer, play some music."

"Sounds like a good time."

"It is. You want to come?"

"Sure!" she giggled. "I'll be right over."

"If only it was that easy." There was a pause on the other end.

"Yea," Mae sighed. "I'm sure it will be a good time anyway."

"After tonight," the boy replied, "I think I could have a good time doing anything."

"This is pretty incredible," she was smiling again. "I'm glad I called."

"I'm so glad you called. Now I've got your number, you can't

116

hide from me. You're going to get sick of me calling you every day."

"No way!" she started.

"What's up, man?!" Joe's voice interrupted the conversation. "Where you been? What are you doing?"

The boy motioned him away from the car window.

"I'm sorry," Mae sounded flustered, "are you there?"

"Yea, sorry. Joe, I'm on the phone!" he explained. "My friend came up to my window."

"Oh. Did you just get there?"

"A minute ago."

"Sorry! You should go!"

"No, it's fine. What are you doing tonight? I mean, besides coming over here."

"What? Oh! I wish. Um, I'm probably just hanging out at home," she replied.

"That's cool –"

"Heeeeeey, man!" another voice cut in. "What's going on?" The boy pointed harshly to the phone by his ear. "Come on, man!"

"I'm sorry," he apologized again.

"It's OK. They obviously need you," Mae chuckled. "Go."

The boy shook his head and laughed, "Alright. Maybe I can call you later tonight?"

"Sure, if you get time. I don't know how late I'll be up."

"Oh. Well, I'll give it a try. If not, then tomorrow?"

"Sounds good."

The boy slipped his phone into his pants pocket and opened the car door. The summer night air was clean and refreshing as he stepped out. The humidity of the day had faded with the sun in a dusky haze of brilliant orange and red, leaving only faint traces of pollen and greenery that interlaced with the tepid breeze across his face. Pulling a cigarette from his pack, he pinched it between his lips and frisked his pockets for a lighter.

"What's the deal?" he croaked between his teeth. "I can't have a phone conversation without getting mugged?"

His hand slapped loudly against his comrade's as he held the cigarette loosely between his lips.

" 'Bout time. Where you been?" Joe responded as their hands

cupped together. The boy snapped his fingers before dropping his hand to his side (a ritual among him and his friends).

"Here you go, you procrastinating bastard," a voice from behind him said, and a chilled can floated through the air. Spinning around, he caught the can in his fist and called out a "Thanks."

"I'm here now," he said, breaking the seal of the liquid Remedy as he made his way across the lawn, greeting friends with handshakes and hugs.

The narrow trail of grass bordered a sidewalk that ran parallel to the back of a short row of townhouses. Clusters of people dotted the pathway that led to the concrete slab that was Joe's back patio. Tiki torches and lawn chairs were strewn about the cement and the surrounding grassy area. The tobacco singed and popped as he lit the lingering cigarette with the flame of a nearby torch. He realized the obscurity of the phone conversation he had just experienced and was doing his best to hide his obvious excitement. Joe was the first to ask.

"So, who was that on the phone?" he said, squatting down on the patio chair across from the boy.

"Kind of a crazy story," the boy replied.

The cool liquid filled his mouth and bubbled as it drained down his throat.

"Oh, yeah?" Joe pulled out a cigarette of his own.

"Little bit," the boy chuckled.

A small crowd of people had collected on the patio.

"What kind of crazy?" Nate stumbled across the concrete and closer to the boy.

"Uh," the boy smirked, "crazy as in long."

"Did you meet a girl?!" Claire asked from the cluster. The boy chuckled as he poured another swig of liquid down his throat. "You did, didn't you?! Are you serious?" her eyes widened as she stepped closer.

The boy raised his eyebrows as he looked at her over the can.

"Tell me everything!" she squealed, slapping him in the stomach with the back her hand.

His muscles tightened as he suppressed his reflexes and swallowed the mouthful. His eyes scanned the faces of the bystanders; they were a completely captivated audience, just as he knew they would be.

Like Jack, these friends were also quite critical of the fact that the boy did not take advantage of the "available single girls" that he often came across; and like Jack, he had told them that he refused to just settle for someone and that one day he would find the connection he was looking for. So, the simple mention of the possibility of a serious interest in a girl was enough to nearly choke anyone who knew the boy. The group grew larger and they stood, silent except for the occasional flick of a lighter lighting a cigarette or pop of a can opening, as the boy told the story of Mae.

By the time he had finished, he noticed that he had emptied his can and his freshly lit cigarette had burned down into the filter. The audience stood with wide eyes and reflective smiles, watching attentively as he pushed the filter through the opening of the can.

"Yeah, so, that was her," he finished, as he tossed the can into a trash bag and fished another from a blue cooler that sat on the patio. "Like I said, pretty crazy."

"Wow," Joe shook his head, "that is crazy, dude. Are you like, dating this girl?"

The boy shrugged his shoulders and shook his head slightly. "Is that even possible?" Nate asked after a few seconds. "It would be a really tough thing to try to maintain."

"Yeah, it is crazy, but I definitely think it's possible. I think it's amazing. So many people that I know are in these relationships that are just convenient, you know? They work together, or live close by, or know the same people. But this is different. The idea of having feelings for someone who is completely inconvenient is a reassuring thing for me. It really is. Life isn't easy, I know that. I don't think it should be. If everything was already carefully put in place, then we would have no appreciation for anything because we would never have to work for it. It is so refreshing to do something where it's like, everything about the situation indicates that it is probably not the most conducive outcome, but I still have such strong feelings so I'm going to do it."

"Awww," Claire couldn't contain it any longer, "that is so sweet! You should definitely date her!"

The boy chuckled at her excitement and slid his hand nervously into the back pocket of his jeans.

"Long-distance relationships suck, dude," Joe mumbled, rising to his feet. "It's just not worth it." His arms extended slowly into the dark purple air as he stretched what seemed to be every muscle in his body.

"I'm sure that it's tough," the boy started, "but...."

"Unbearably tough," Joe cut in. "You've got to talk on the phone for hours and hours, you're always fighting because you're both frustrated, you can't really check up on her, and there is hardly any physical contact!" By now, most of the small crowd had broken up into side conversations or wandered off in the yard. "Is that what you want? Not me."

The boy poured another mouthful down his throat to quell the dissent climbing up his chest.

"I think that if you believe in something or love something enough, it doesn't matter what it takes to achieve it, as long as you find it in the end," he replied coolly.

"Well," Joe burped, "I hope you're right. But I still don't think it's a good idea."

"We'll see," the boy sighed as a smile caught his eye from across the concrete. "I'll talk to you later. I'm going to go say 'hey' to Lil."

Joe hoisted his bottle up in the air and raised his eyebrows, toasting the boy as he moved across the patio. Within the first few weeks of school, Lily and the boy had become close friends. They had been in the same physics class and, after the second or third week, had completely abandoned the subject in exchange for a solid hour and a half of sidesplitting laughter. No matter what was happening in class that day, the two of them could turn it into their own private comedy show. Time flew by from 12:45 to 2:15, even when they wished it wouldn't, and the two grew closer. By graduation, they were best friends, and when neither of their parents showed up to the ceremony, the two had stretched out on the grass just outside of the building and passed a bottle of champagne back and forth, their regalia hanging loose, symbolizing their carefree youth and unconfined possibilities.

Her brown and blonde-streaked hair fell in light, thin corkscrews down her shoulders and her hazelnut brown eyes caught the boy's as he strolled across the concrete. Her thick red lips flashed a smile. The boy emphasized a wink from tip-toes, over the heads of the cluster that stood between them, and she lifted one eyebrow and pouted her lips.

"Hey there, darlin'!" the boy said, once he had scooped her into his arms.

"Hey!" she said, returning the hug. "What's up?"

"Not a lot," he replied, pulling back. "How did your thing go today?"

Lily was a singer, so there was always some church choir performance or wedding or something that needed her services. Sometimes, when it was just the two of them, the boy would bring out his guitar and play while she sang.

"It was good," she said dismissively.

She was never very interested in talking about her singing. It was one of those things that she did because everyone told her she could, even though she disagreed.

"More importantly," she said, her eyebrows arching, "what is this I hear about a girl? Now, I know you did not meet someone and not tell me."

"Wow, word really does get around quickly here, doesn't it?" the boy laughed.

"Wait! What?" Lily smiled. "So it is true?!"

"Come on, Lil. If I had a girlfriend, you would be the first to know."

"So, what are they talking about?"

"You know that girl Mae that I told you about?"

"Yeah, the one you talk to online, right?

"Right. Well, we were online earlier and we were talking about the possibility of feelings for each other. Then, she called me on the way here."

"That's awesome!" Lily said. "And that totally counts as news that I should have heard first!"

"Sorry!" the boy shrugged his shoulders. "I didn't really have time. It just happened. Then everyone came over and they were asking me questions about it."

"Yeah, yeah," she smirked, "so, how did the conversation go?"

"Really well. It was a little weird, just because I've been talking to her for months but had never heard her voice," he smiled proudly.

"It was really good."

"You are too cute," she giggled. "I've never seen you like this."

"Me, neither," he chuckled.

"So, what happens next?"

"I'm not quite sure. I'm going to call her back tonight or tomorrow."

"Well, call me right after," she smirked again. "Don't make the same mistake twice." The boy nodded his head and rolled his eyes. "I, on the other hand, have some big news that I've been waiting since yesterday to tell you about."

She reached into her back pocket and pulled out a carefully folded envelope and handed it to the boy, who eyed her curiously as he unfolded it and pulled a paper from inside. She bit her bottom lip. Her eyes were glazed with excitement. It was a letter from somewhere in Pennsylvania. He skimmed the first line, "On behalf of the University, I am very pleased to inform you...." his eyes widened.

"I got in!" she interjected. "I'm going to college!" She clapped her hands together and did a little dance with her shoulders.

The boy dropped the paper to his side as his jaw dropped open. Her face was beaming with pride as he wrapped his arms around her and lifted her off the ground.

"That is great, Lil!" he said once her feet were back on the concrete. "Congratulations! Are you excited or what?"

"Thanks!" she wiped her hair from her face. "Yes, very excited. It came yesterday. I have been waiting till I saw you to tell you." She carefully put the paper back into the envelope and folded it again into her back pocket.

"Well, I'm glad you did. Sorry that I'm not as patient with secrets."

"What about you? Have you come to any decisions about school?"

"Nah," the boy dropped down onto a lawn chair, "not yet."

"You do know that it is July, right?" she said, sitting down on the end of the chair.

"Yes," the boy swallowed some more liquid. "I'm looking for a school that has solid liberal arts and English programs and has a good Business program. That way I can double major and do what I love while doing something practical. The problem is, I haven't really found any that I like."

"That's what this college is like," her voice was gaining speed. "You should totally come with me! That would be so awesome!"

"Ha!" he poured another swallow. "Like you said, it's July. I could never get everything together in less than a month. Not to mention that I'm sure the deadline has passed."

"Yeah, but I was thinking about deferring until January anyway. That would give you enough time to apply and whatnot, and then we could both go for winter semester!" her voice grew more definitive with each word. "It's a small, private, liberal arts college, but they have a really good business program, too. You would definitely love it! It's a beautiful campus, and we would have so much fun!"

"Seriously?" the boy sat up and looked into her eyes.

"Definitely!" a broad smile filled her face.

"Alright," he lifted up his can. She raised hers, and the two bumped them together in the air, splashing liquid around the inside of the aluminum. "I will fill out an application tomorrow."

"Sweet!" she threw her arms around his neck and kissed his cheek. "We are going to have the best time ever!"

"Easy there," he chuckled, "don't go celebrating yet. I may not even get accepted."

By the time he had said his goodbyes and gotten into his car, it was probably too late to call Mae back. Although it was an hour earlier where she was, a late mention of song requests had kept him glued to the guitar for longer than he had planned, and he was fairly certain that she had plans rather early the next day. Before he could completely put the idea out of his mind and toss the phone onto the passenger seat, it began vibrating in his hand.

"What's up, brother?" he answered.

"Hey," Jack replied, "what are you doing?"

"I'm headed home. What's going on?"

"I was just listening to our demo, and I just remembered how fantastic it is."

"Yeah," the boy chuckled, "it's not bad."

"Not bad? This thing is brilliant. I was thinking," he sounded excited, "we should start practicing twice a week."

"Twice a week?!" the boy choked. "There is no way. We have a hard enough time with once a week."

"I'm just saying," Jack was trying too hard to sound convincing, "when you are a signed band, you've got to start putting in the extra hours."

"Listen, man, it's just not possible," the boy caught himself. "Wait a second. Did you just say 'signed band'? Are you serious?" The phone was silent.

"Are you serious?! Yes!" the boy shouted. "How?! When?!"

"I got the e-mail today," Jack laughed. "They want us to come in next Monday to play a couple of songs and go over some paperwork or something!"

"I can't believe it," the boy muttered. "I knew if we kept sending it in that eventually they would have to listen to it."

"We did it, brother!" Jack chuckled. "We landed a contract!"

"It really is fantastic," the boy suddenly felt a long overdue boost of confidence about their musical ability. "I mean, we played well on that demo."

"You're damn right we did!" Jack exclaimed. "And it's finally paying off!"

"That is so awesome!" he couldn't believe it. "Did you tell the other guys yet?"

"Nah, had to call you first."

"We should all sit down, before we go in there, and go over some stuff, make sure we are on the same page," the boy was thinking ahead.

"Sounds good," Jack replied. "We could do it Friday night, before the show."

"Oh yeah," he had forgotten about the show. "Good idea!"

"It will be our last show as low-budget, no-name musicians," Jack laughed.

"Then it will be a fabulous show."

"Oh yes, it will be," Jack said. "I've got to go call these knuckleheads and let them know. They need to start practicing, like now."

"Right on. I'll talk to you later, dude."

He hung up the phone and glanced through the steering wheel at the clock on his dash. It was late. He couldn't believe they actually had a chance of getting signed. What a night. Driving home, he had every right to be completely ecstatic. His window was down, his sunroof open. The air that whipped through his car was just cool enough, and the sky was riddled with gleaming pinpoint stars. The moon was just a sliver that hung above him, and his headlights cut through the darkness of a straight, open road, but the boy's eyes kept shifting from the clock to his phone. All he could think of doing was calling Mae to celebrate.

nine

During the last few months of school, while the boy was playing with the band, talking to Mae on his computer, and dealing with
the final phases of acceptance of the move, all of his friends were making college plans; so, after graduation, while his friends were getting
acceptance letters and dorm room furniture, the boy was frantically
trying to make plans for his future. The week after his final exams
he had gotten a job running his uncle's outdoor produce market. It
wasn't much of a job, but his uncle had practically made him partner
the first day, so it was good money. The days were long but peaceful.
The boy would wake up and drive to the market at eight in the morning to help his uncle unload the produce that the man had already
been up for hours collecting. They would lift wooden boxes of corn,
peaches, apples, pears, peppers, and eggplant and carefully arrange
each item into colorful displays atop empty crates and rough planks of
wood. The larger items required both of them. His uncle would stand
in the bed of the large truck and heave watermelons or pumpkins, one
after another, while the boy would stand in the grass and catch them,
then place them in piles on the ground. Once the truck was unloaded,
his uncle would go retrieve more produce from local growers or head
home for a mid-morning nap, while the boy would finish stacking the
smooth apples and peppers in tiered spreads. From ten o'clock till
sundown, he would sit with his thoughts, beneath an old maple tree,
and suck the pure sweet juices from plums, pears, and peaches, stopping only to wait on the occasional customers or replenish the displays.
It reminded him much of his childhood, just sitting there, thinking.
Lately, he had been using that time to try to sort out what he should

do next, since he had graduated. That question had been haunting most of his free thoughts for the better part of the previous month. He had promised himself, and his friends, that he would have figured it out by July. It was this promise that had led to Lily's prodding question about whether or not he had made any decisions about school.

It was the morning after that particular night that the boy woke up half an hour later than usual and had to scramble frantically to ready himself for the day. His shower was cold, his clothes were disheveled, his breakfast was nonexistent, and he had only skimmed five minutes from his half-hour deficit. His head was clouded and his heart was hammering as he jumped into the driver seat and sped from his driveway.

When he pulled up to the market, his uncle was already halfway through unloading the crates. The boy braced himself for the fatherly scolding that he expected his uncle had prepared as he yanked a box of pears from the rear of the truck, but the man said nothing. He only looked at the boy for a lingering moment, a pear between his teeth, and continued his work in silence.

His father's brother was a potter by trade. He had traveled to more than 30 different countries, studying ceramics and cultural art, and was fairly fluent in Japanese and Arabic. He had even built a studio, with a kiln, where he sculpted some of the most masterful dishes the boy had ever seen. Unfortunately, people no longer have much interest in art, and those who do usually can't afford it, so the man had taken up the produce business. Still, he was an artist at heart, and his long, springy, prematurely gray locks of hair that protruded from the top of his head like a bush proved it as he lowered another case to the ground and walked back to the truck.

"Do you ever get the feeling that you should be something more?" his uncle asked. The boy snickered.

"All the time," he answered.

"Hmmm," the man stopped and scratched his chin. "When I was young, about your age, I used to think I could do anything. I used to think that some day I would be someone really famous that had made some huge impact on history, you know? I thought I would make it into history books." The boy nodded. "I was curious if maybe it was a hereditary thing."

"I think so," the boy admitted. "I've always felt like maybe there was some sort of higher calling for me, like I was supposed to do something extraordinary. But I'm also a bit of a realist, so I have resolved to settle for making it into diaries rather than history books."

The boy pulled the last box from the truck and stacked it on the ground. His uncle hadn't moved. He stood, his eyes squinting, his mind obviously working.

"Well," he said abruptly, "I'm off."

Pulling the keys from his pocket, he climbed into the truck and drove off, leaving only a spiral of dust.

The boy took his time with the displays. He carefully placed each fuzzy peach inside the wicker baskets and thought about what his uncle had said. It was clear that the man still held onto at least a piece of his youthful dream. It was a dangerous thing, the boy thought, to hold onto something for so long. He wondered if the man had ever truly had a fulfilled moment in his life. He could certainly sympathize with his uncle, except that the boy had a slight advantage. While they both shared an equally strong love for art, the boy realized that the ancient custom was long since dead, while his uncle still clung to the futile hope of fame.

It was mid-afternoon by the time he had unpacked all the crates and boxes, and the early afternoon rush of stay-at-homes and healthy business types on their lunch breaks had come and gone. Next, the soccer moms would come in their mini-vans like a flock of vultures and pick apart the displays in search of the ripest, most nutritious items for their rising-star athlete kids. The boy didn't have the heart to tell them that soccer would never be taken seriously in the United States. Fortunately, toward the end of the day, he could count on the after-work shoppers to be slightly more forgiving of the fruits and vegetables and take home some of the items that the soccer moms disregarded. Lastly, as the boy was packing up, there were always the workaholic stragglers who would mosey through around sundown and gather up the least desired products of the day to take home with them to their large, empty houses. They may have achieved all the advantages and finer things in life because of their devotion to success, but at Uncle Dave's Awesome Produce, they got the last pick from the scraps of the less fortunate. The irony always made the boy chuckle.

As I said, it was sometime between the stay-at-homes and the soccer moms when the boy slouched down against the tree and opened a crate of corn. He lifted an ear from the box and weighed it in his hand. Before the corn was put out for sale, his uncle required that the boy cut off the husk that collected into a long stem on each ear. The boy did agree that it made the corn look more appetizing. He lifted the knife into the air and flicked the blade across the husk, sending it spinning to the ground. It was an expensive knife, one of those sharp ones, slightly serrated; the kind that can cut through a penny, so chopping corn husks was a fairly effortless task. He tossed the modified ear into an empty crate and grabbed another from the pile. A woman had pulled up in a mini-van and gotten out and was perusing the eggplant. She must have stopped in before picking up the kids. The boy hacked another husk. She was on her cell phone, and the boy had learned that it was best to not even try to help people when they were talking on the phone. He watched her and waited.

"I don't think that should be a problem," she said, halfheartedly squeezing the purple skin of a large eggplant. "I talked to Mae yesterday."

The boy's ears perked up.

"My Mae?" he muttered jokingly to himself. Impossible. There was no way. He chuckled again at himself for even considering the idea.

"Yeah, I'm picking up the kids for her today and she's going to pick them up tomorrow," the woman continued. Different Mae.

"Told you!" the boy thought to himself. "My Mae," he mumbled again and smiled. There was a comforting sense of security in saying it that way. He wondered if there would ever come a day where he would be justified in calling her that. Not that the girl could ever be owned, but that there could be such a strong affiliation, that the use of "my" would instantly identify her. He picked up one of the slashed husks with his left hand and aligned it with the sleek blade of the knife. The boy and his uncle had tried to make a habit of ensuring that the blade was sunk into the dirt or sheathed into a loose husk when it was not in use to prevent accidents and protect the costly knife. With his right arm he pulled back the handle and jabbed forward with enough force to penetrate the stalk.

129

"Excuse me, sir?" a woman's voice called.

He had forgotten about the woman on her cell phone. His eyes lifted from the knife to look at her just as the blade was splintering through the husk. The muscles in his face winced and the palm of his hand tingled. The woman's face melted into panic.

"Call 911!" she shrieked, fumbling for her phone somewhere in the bottom of her purse.

A knot began forming in the boy's throat as he slowly dropped his eyes back to his hands. The angle of the knife had changed at the last second, when he had looked away, causing the thin ridged blade to glide down the front of his thumb, bisecting it into two bloody halves that hung loosely away from the knife. From there, the blade had in fact gone into the husk, but again at an angle, so that the first inch of the tip had pierced through his hand. The stiffness of the sturdy steel had pinned his hand in a C-shaped position. Rotating his palm, he glanced at the shimmering tip of the blade that protruded through the other side. His head rolled with nausea and his stomach convulsed.

"No!" he called to the woman, his throat shaky with fear. "Don't call an ambulance!"

The woman's face was an even blend of horror and confusion, but she stopped clumsily dialing on her phone and lowered it to her side.

"It's fine," the boy lied.

Since the leukemia incident, he had become unnaturally distrusting of hospitals. He turned his back to the woman and wrapped his fingers around the heavy plastic handle of the knife. Steadying his breath, he jerked the knife free. The serrated ridges of the blade hooked inside his hand and pulled with it strands of muscle and tendon that spilled out from the cut like spaghetti. Blood spouted from both sides of his palm, running in thick streams down his arm. The deep slash down his thumb was filled with the rich red fluid that drained down his hand and collected in his palm. He did his best to swallow the acrid acid that was bubbling up his throat. Instinctively, he clenched his left hand into a fist and cringed as his fingertips pressed against the mushy mess of insides that sloshed in his palm. Both of his legs felt as though they may give in as he spun around and moved toward his car, blood drizzling from his clenched fist.

"Y-y-you've got to get to a hospital!" the woman cried out.

The boy moved faster.

"No," he said firmly, "no hospitals! No doctors! I just need to clean it up." He opened the car door with his right hand and climbed behind the wheel.

His grandparents lived less than a mile away but it felt like an eternity, driving with his hand held out the window. Once he finally reached the end of their driveway, he threw the car in park and sprinted to the front porch. His grandmother was sitting in a rocking chair, reading a book, when he came spilling through the door.

"What's happened?!" she said as she jumped to her feet. "Are you hurt?!"

"I had an accident," the boy tried to sound calm as he moved toward the bathroom. "It's nothing."

He knew that the blood that dripped on her hardwood floor would make her believe otherwise.

"You're bleeding!" she exclaimed. "I'm going to call an ambulance!" She shuffled toward the phone on the wall.

"No!" the boy said more harshly than he intended. "Please, no. I don't need an ambulance."

He kicked the bathroom door closed behind him and turned on the faucet in the sink. Aqueous bursts of bloody water poured from his hand and swirled in spirals down the drain. It reminded him of Ben. Nausea bubbled in his stomach and his head swooned. There was so much blood. He hunched himself over the sink and let the cold, soothing water crash against his wounds. He could feel the blood draining from his body. There was a tap at the door.

"Are you OK?" his grandmother asked. "Open up! I have some bandages."

"I'm OK," the boy lied again.

He looked into the mirror above the sink; his face was pale and sick, his vision blurry. He blinked his eyes and shook his head faintly. He looked back down into the sink—still more blood. Dark clouds appeared in the outskirts of his vision and moved across into the center of his eyes. He slumped onto the sink before falling backward against the bathroom door. He heard his grandmother working the handle over his head. His fingers uncurled, releasing the bloody

131

tendons and tissue and sending sharp pains up his arm. He clenched his jaw and winced, and then everything went black.

※

When he regained consciousness, he was in the backseat of his mother's car. His head was pounding, and it was a difficult task for him to sit up. He looked down at his hand. It was wrapped in tight white bandages. His mother looked concerned as she watched him in the rearview mirror.

"How do you feel?" she asked nervously.

"I'm alright," he said without thinking. "Where are we going?"

She didn't respond. The boy scooted painfully to the window as his mother turned the car toward a tall building. The boy read the name in bold letters along the top of the structure and shook his head slowly. She wasn't concerned about his hand; she was concerned about how he was going to react because she was taking him to the hospital.

"The bleeding has stopped for now," she said into the rearview mirror, "but they need to look at it. They need to stitch it up. Please. For me."

He slouched back down into the backseat and stared out the window. It had been two and a half, nearly three, years since the leukemia, but he remembered it well. It scared the boy to think of that lethal power that a doctor had where he could, with all his knowledge and scholastic wisdom, decide for you your fate, with the possibility of being wrong. They had been wrong about him. He would never forget that. He had promised himself on that day that he would do everything that he could to avoid a repeat. It wasn't that he disliked doctors; he was sure they did a lot of good for a lot of people. They were just not for him. The idea that with three words someone could cause him to completely forfeit the hope of a happy, healthy life made him sick. He had made himself a promise, but he would break it for his mother. Cradling his bandaged hand against his chest, he nodded slowly.

"I love you," his mother said softly. "Thank you." She looked back into the rearview mirror but the boy had shut his eyes.

For two hours, the boy and his mother sat in the crowded waiting room. The thin seat cushions did very little to pad the metal poles that ran beneath them. A small TV mounted in the corner displayed fuzzy images of the local news, while rows of people sat in chairs along the wall, pens tapping against clipboards as they struggled to answer the inquisition on the paper beneath the clamp. A stack of magazines with smiling celebrities and gardening tips stood boldly out of place on a coffee table in the middle of the room. The boy read one of the headlines: "Spring styles that will make you look 10 pounds thinner." He chuckled.

"That is just what these people are looking for," he thought to himself. "You may bleed to death, but at least you'll know what clothes you should have worn last season." He looked up at the bold red letters that hung just over the row of chairs—"Emergency Room."

"Good thing there are no real emergencies in here," he thought, glancing around the room. "They'd be in some trouble."

"That's us," his mother tapped his leg.

The boy hadn't even heard them call his name. His knees cracked as he rose to his feet and stretched his muscles. A nurse stood, chomping gum, impatiently holding the door open with one shoe while tapping the other against the hard floor.

"Better not keep her waiting," the boy muttered as he and his mother moved toward the door.

"You know," he continued once they were within earshot of the nurse, "there are a lot of people out here that I think are much worse off than me. I don't mind waiting so that they can be seen." He failed to admit that his patience was due largely to his reluctance in seeing a doctor.

"The doctors will see everyone as quickly as they can, in the order they came in," the nurse said coldly and walked briskly down the hallway.

The boy and his mother followed the woman, who led them to a small examination room, where they waited another twenty minutes.

"Good thing it's only my hand," the boy sighed.

He knew it was fear that was making him sarcastic. It kept his mind off of what was actually happening.

"OK," a short, stocky woman said loudly, as she waddled into the room, wearing the same garb as the nurse who escorted them, "as you can see the doctors are very busy tonight, so I will be seeing you,

OK?" The boy nodded; as if he had a choice. "Let's take a look."

She began unwinding the red-stained bandages from his hand. The thick blood on the last strip stuck to the spaghetti strands that were coiled in his palm and stretched and tugged as the woman pulled the bandaging quickly, to rip it free. The boy's legs kicked and his back arched in pain.

"OK, it's off," she said. "That's quite a cut."

"Thanks," the boy grunted through his teeth. Damn sarcasm.

She doused a gauze with some solution and briskly dabbed the wounds.

"OK," she said again, reaching for a long wooden swab that was essentially a Q-tip® at the end of a wood stick, "this part is going to hurt."

The boy grimaced and squirmed as she used the wooden end of the swab to push the strands of muscle, tissue, and tendon back into the cut in his palm. He balled his right hand up into a fist and bit down hard on his knuckles. By the time she had finished, his left hand was tingling and pulsating with each panicked heartbeat, and the knuckles on his right hand were white and dotted with teeth marks. Next, she smeared a gooey gelatin cream on the cuts before stretching pieces of surgical tape across the wounds.

"OK, that's it," she said proudly. "All we need to do is get a splint on there, and you will be good to go."

His whole arm ached.

"Wait, what do you mean a splint?" the boy blurted out.

"Oh, it's nothing really," she said, lifting up a long, thin piece of metal with a curve on one end. "It's like a cast. It runs along your arm like this and we wrap it with bandaging to keep the hand in place. It's just to make sure the wound doesn't open back up and get infected."

"I can't wear that," the boy argued.

"It will heal much faster if you do," the woman said calmly.

"I can't," the boy said again.

"You really should," she was losing patience, "at least for a little while."

"Alright," he held out his arm, "I will wear it for a few days, but it's got to come off before Friday."

"What's on Friday?" she asked casually, as she wrapped the bandaging in tight circles around his wrist and the splint.

"I'm in this band," he said, "and we have a show on Friday night."

"Hmmm," she sucked her teeth, "do you sing?"

He could tell that her tone had switched back from personal to professional.

"No," he eyed her suspiciously. "I play guitar." She scoffed.

"You left-handed?" she asked. He shook his head.

"Then not on Friday you don't," she continued.

He fell quiet for a moment.

"That's OK, I guess," he said slowly. "I have a fill-in; as long as I can play next Monday."

She shook her head.

"You're not getting it, are you?" she said. She grabbed his arm to steady it. "Wiggle your pinky." He glared at her. "Go on, wiggle it."

The boy concentrated on the smallest finger of his left hand. He focused all his energy on that single muscle. He could feel his tendons burning beneath the cut in his palm.

"Not easy, is it?" she asked. He shook his head hopelessly. "That's because there are severed tendons and muscles. They need to heal; and even when they do, I'm not sure that your pinky or ring finger will ever function properly. I'm sorry, son, but I don't think you will ever be able to play guitar again."

The boy kept his focus on the white wall opposite the examination chair. Never play guitar again? His eyes started to burn, but he fought back the tears. This woman would not see him cry. She didn't deserve to. She didn't know him; she did not know his determination. She was wrong about him, doctors always were. He would show them. He had before. His hand would be fine. They would see.

"You're wrong about me," he croaked out, steadying the quiver in his bottom lip. "I'll play."

"I hope I am," she said carefully, "I really do."

"You are," he climbed down from the chair. "You'll see."

The ride home was quiet; there wasn't much to say. He sat in the passenger seat and stared at his bandaged hand while his mother drove. He would not let himself be discouraged. It was like he had

135

said to Joe—if you believed in something enough, you could never stop fighting for it. He spun the knob on the radio and scanned through the stations. He stopped at the abrasive electric guitar of Third Eye Blind and rested his head against the headrest. He moved the paralyzed hand up and down an imaginary guitar neck in unison with Mr. Cadogan. He would play again.

Ben was the first person the boy called once he was alone in his room. His friend had been there the first time the doctors had given him bad news, so it was only natural to call him first. Ben listened attentively while the boy told the story of his day.

"They are wrong," Ben said once the boy had finished, "and you will show them that. I know that better than anyone. They don't know how much guitar means to you. You won't be done that easy. Did you tell them that you beat leukemia? Do they know that? They seriously think that a couple loose tendons are going to stop you?"

The boy laughed at his friend's vigor. He knew there was a reason he called Ben first.

"Thanks, man," the boy was starting to feel better. "Even if it takes time, I will play again. I'm just worried about this weekend."

"What about this weekend?" Ben scoffed. "Let the kid fill in for you. So what?"

"Yeah, but what about Monday? That's when we are supposed to go meet the producers."

"Monday is a week from now," Ben said reassuringly. "That is plenty of time for you to heal up and play."

"Hopefully," the boy sighed, "but I've got to call the guys either way and let them know what happened. I've got to let them know I can't play on Friday, at least."

"So, tell them that," Ben agreed. "Tell them you can't play on Friday but you are good to play on Monday."

"Alright," the boy said, checking the clock. "I've got to go call them. Plus, I want to call Mae before it gets too late."

"How are things going with all that? You haven't talked about it much."

"With Mae?" the boy responded. "Really good. How are things with Lynn?"

"Good," his friend was smiling. "We, uh, we are really happy."

"Cool, man, I'm glad to hear it."

"You know, Chloe has been looking for you."

"Yeah, I know," the boy admitted. "I'm trying to find time to call her back. It's just so busy with work and the band and everything. Tell her that I'm sorry and that I'll call her soon, OK? Maybe the three of us can get lunch next week?"

"Sure," Ben sounded doubtful. "We will figure something out."

The boy hung up the phone and flopped down on his bed. Holding his hand up over his head, he tried moving his pinky again. It was as if there was something blocking communication with the finger. In his mind, he knew how to move it, what it would take, but no matter how hard he focused, the finger wouldn't budge. He tried again; this time he started with his thumb. The swollen appendage pivoted at the first knuckle but the slice and tape across the second prohibited any bending. His pointer finger moved rather easily. The middle finger was slightly more difficult but would bend at both joints. He took a deep breath and concentrated on his ring finger. He flexed and twisted every muscle and tendon, but the finger did not move. He dropped his arm to his side and exhaled. He could feel the warm, wet blood leaking from the cut. It would take a few days. He picked up the phone and dialed Jack.

"So, uh, is that it?" Jack asked once the boy had finished explaining his inability to play on Friday. "Are you done, or something?"

"Done? What? No!" the boy was confused. "How could I be done?"

"Oh, uh," Jack laughed, "I don't know." He was obviously Remedied.

"No, man," the boy said, somewhat annoyed, "I'm going to play on Monday."

"Cool," Jack chuckled again. "We'll see." We'll see? The boy ignored the ambiguous comment.

"Later," he said, flipping the phone shut.

The phone call to Mae always proved to be the most soothing. He told her the story of the accident and she listened closely, interjecting with gasps of concern and moans of sympathy. He did his best to spare her the graphic details. Apart from not wanting to upset her stomach, he certainly didn't want her to worry.

"I'm worried about you," she admitted after the story.

The boy laughed at himself.

"Why?" he coaxed. "I'm fine. I'm pretty sure it just needs to heal up. You know me, and you know how important music is to me. I will play again."

"I know," she said, "but I still need to make sure you are alright."

"I am." There was a slight squealing noise in the background. "What's that noise?" he asked her.

"That's William," she giggled, "my guinea pig. I told you about him."

"Yeah," he remembered, "but you never said he squealed!"

She laughed loudly.

"He does that whenever he gets excited," she chuckled self-consciously.

"That's cool," the boy said. "I do the same thing."

"Oh yeah?" she laughed. "When you get excited?"

"Yep," he nodded his head as if she could see him.

"I'd like to see that," she was smiling.

"You will someday," he said jokingly. She laughed again. "Look at us," he continued, "look at how well we are doing. We are talking on the phone like pros."

"That's true," she agreed. "I knew we'd get the hang of it."

He could hear her wince through her teeth.

"What's wrong?!" he asked quickly, jerking up from his bed.

"Nothing," she grimaced. "My chest has been hurting a little today."

"Hurting, like how?" he fumbled over his words.

"It felt like maybe heartburn earlier," she explained, "because it was just a burning in my chest, you know? But then the past few minutes it has gotten worse, like a churning feeling."

"That's weird," the boy said slowly. "Are you alright?"

"Yeah, I'm fine. It's getting better."

"Good. Maybe I make you sick?" he teased.

"No way," she said quickly. "Maybe a little nervous, but not sick."

"Mine was actually hurting a little earlier, too," he said thoughtfully. "Wait, nervous? Why would you be nervous?"

"I don't know. It's just crazy to talk to you, to hear your voice." Each word was filled with such passion.

"I know. I know," the excitement was more than he could stand; it came out in burst of laughter. "You don't even understand. I, literally, do not feel happy or satisfied with my day until I talk to you. I have all these daily problems, you know, like everybody else, and sometimes my friends can be disappointing, but at the end of the day, when I get to talk to you, all of that melts away and I am right where I need to be."

There was a pause on the phone. He flexed his stomach and chest muscles as a sharp jolt shot across his chest. It was as if mentioning his previous pain reawakened it beneath his ribcage. He hunched his shoulders and took deep, steady breaths. It was roaring inside of him, flames lapping against the inside of his chest cavity. His vocal cords were vibrating inside his throat. He was ready to scream.

"I love you," she said softly.

His vocal cords closed, and the air rushing up from his lungs caught in the middle of his throat.

"I mean, like, as the sort of person that you are," she continued quickly. "I really enjoy talking to you and feeling like we are spending time together. You make me laugh and I have such a good time every time we talk. There is a difference between loving and being in love, you know?" she fumbled. "I love a certain group of people who are close to me and who I have a special connection to, and you are one of those people. You have been for awhile now."

He shook his head slowly. What an idiot. How could he have let that moment pass him by? He certainly couldn't explain to her that air had caught in his throat, that he had choked.

"Pick it up where you dropped it," he thought to himself.

"Yeah," he agreed, "I love you, too." He knew he meant it more than it sounded. He felt like he had to redeem himself. "And I don't say that often," he continued. "Not even to my friends. I love them, but the connection that I feel for you is something very different." He noticed that the seething in his chest had settled to a gentle purr.

"I'm glad to hear that," she was smiling again.

"Are you?" he said excitedly.

"Uh huh," still smiling.

Seeing as how it was their last summer of high school, the boy and his friends were sure to exploit it to the fullest. Once Mae finally decided that she should, in fact, go to bed, the boy slipped on his shoes and jacket and drove to Claire's house. Cars were parked zigzagged across the front lawn of the house when the boy pulled up. As he climbed out of the car, he tugged his jacket tighter around his body. The air was as crisp as the previous night but was not nearly as warm, which was why the party had been moved from Joe's house to his much more wealthy girlfriend's mansion. The boy did not know what Claire's parents did for a living, but whatever it was made a lot of money and kept them away from the house most of the time. He shoved his hands in his jeans pockets and marched up the long driveway.

"Bet it's warmer in Texas," he muttered, smiling to himself.

Joe answered the door after just a few knocks.

"Heeey, man!" Joe slurred. "I didn't think you were coming!"

In order to avoid the interruptions of calls while he was talking to Mae, the boy had told his friends that he didn't think he was going to make it.

"What happened to your hand?!" Joe shouted. So, the boy told the story of his accident a final time as he and his friend smoked a cigarette on Claire's front porch.

"Insane!" Joe blurted at the end of the story. "Does it feel any better now?"

The boy shook his head.

"Still can't move them," he responded, holding up the makeshift cast.

Claire pouted out her bottom lip and wrapped the boy in a sympathizing hug.

"What ever happened with that girl last night?" Claire asked. "Did you call her back?"

The boy laughed nervously.

"Actually..." he started, "is Lily here?"

"Yeah," Joe said loudly. "She's inside on the phone with her jackass boyfriend. Want me to get her? Actually, here she comes."

All eyes were on Lily as she opened the front door and stepped into the cold air. Her eyes were red and she sniffled as she stepped down onto the porch. The boy could instantly tell she was upset.

"What's going on?" she asked the crowd of eyes. "Hey!" she spotted the boy, "I didn't know you were here already. How is your hand?"

"Yeah, it's alright" the boy said gingerly. He pulled her in for a hug and whispered in her ear, "Do you want to talk?"

She held him for a moment and regained composure.

"Are you kidding?" she whispered back. "You just got here. They will never let me take you away."

"Later then?" he asked as she pulled away from him. She wiped her eyes and nodded. "So, I've got to tell this story, and I wanted to make sure you were here to hear it." He said loud enough for everyone to hear. "It was too late to call her last night, so I called her tonight."

"What's her name again?" Claire tried to whisper.

"Mae," Lily responded before the boy could.

"Yeah, so I called Mae tonight," he began again, "and we talked for a little while and it was good. Then, I told her that I really feel comfortable with her and that I feel connected and close to her and that the best part of my day is spent talking to her."

"Hey!" Joe yelled. "Come on, man! What about me!"

"Shut up!" Claire yelled back.

"You know I have a good time with you, too, Joey boy," the boy laughed. His drunken friend raised his can to the boy and winked. "So, then she pauses for a minute, and my chest starts hurting. I guess because I was nervous or whatever, but it was hurting really bad. Then, all of a sudden, out of nowhere," he held up his arms, "she says that she loves me."

In simultaneous unison the girls cried out "awww" while the guys called out an assortment of "ahhh" and other barbaric heckling.

"So, wait!" Lily jumped in. "What happened? What did you say?"

"Well," the boy smiled bashfully, his ears burning red, "at first, I didn't say anything."

"You didn't say anything?!" Claire exclaimed. "What?!"

The boy held up his hands and chuckled nervously.

"Hold on," he tried to calm the two girls. "I choked. My chest was killing me and air caught in my throat."

"You choked?" Lily's jaw dropped. "Like gagged choked? Seriously?"

The boy rubbed the top of his head and squinted one eye.

"That's bad, isn't it?" he asked quietly.

"Yes!!" Claire blurted out. "Pretty bad!"

"I tried to!" he pleaded. "I couldn't! I was too nervous or excited or whatever! Hopefully, I didn't botch it."

"I'm sure it's fine," Lily assured him. "How was the rest of the conversation?"

"Really good!" he trailed off. "It's always really good."

His eyes scanned the faces of the crowd as they made their final comments and muttered their reactions to one another. There was no question that the boy cared for his friends. As his eyes moved from one to the next, he thought back to the good times and emotionally attaching experiences he'd had with each of them. He remembered the time when he and Joe got kicked out of three different stores for reenacting *Braveheart*, shirtless and decorated in war paint. One night, after an exhausting day of finals, the two had driven four hours to the beach and watched the sun come up over water, just to find some serenity. Or how, the next day, Joe had fallen asleep on his desk midway through his history final. He would never forget that time at school when he was having a bad day and Lily hijacked the announcement microphone and sang "You Are My Sunshine" to him over the intercom of fifth period. She had done a week of detention for that stunt. They had certainly had some bonding, memorable moments together and yet, still, the boy could not obtain the depth of affinity with them that he had found in Mae. Even as he stood there, talking with them, a large part of him wished that he was spending that time with her. True, he had never seen her face to face or shared the same cool breeze or been to any of the same places or even seen the way her body moved as she walked; but he had studied her heart, mind, and soul, and found something inside of those three things that he could not be without. He drove home that night, resolved.

For the next two nights, he didn't go out. Instead, he lay down on the floor inside his closet, so his parents wouldn't wake up, and talked to Mae.

"Can you hear me better now?" she had asked, after the boy complained about the poor reception of her cell phone.

"Yes, that's much better," he tried to keep his voice down. "What did you do?"

"I'm standing on my desk," she laughed, "and I'm not moving an inch!"

So, while he curled up on the small carpeted square that was his closet, amid his shoes and old school books, Mae stood, balancing on top of a wooden desk, eye-level with the light on her ceiling, and the two talked for hours, never once bemoaning their necessary poses. When the batteries on their phones would surrender to the hours, they would rush to the nearest outlet and attach themselves to it until they were replenished.

"I need to get a second battery," she would yawn, "so that I always have one charged."

Every night they would sit and drain each other of information, the other soaking up every drop, until they were satisfied that they knew all there was to know about how the other felt on every subject they could think of. But they were never satisfied; they always wanted to know more.

"Do you see many mullets in Texas?" the boy asked.

"Mullets? Like the hair style?" she laughed. "Um, I'm not sure. I haven't really noticed. Not any more than I think you'd see anywhere else."

"Haven't noticed?" he teased. "You've got to keep a better eye out for those things."

There was never a dull or quiet moment, because they connected in a way that most people only dream of.

"My parents were asking who I have been talking to," she had said.

"What did you say?"

"I told them the truth," she said boldly.

"And?" he replied.

"They trust me."

It was understood that Thursday night was "guys' night out,"

143

so when Joe called him Thursday afternoon to ask if bowling was an acceptable selection for that week's festivities, the boy had no choice but to commit. He had every intention of spending time with his friends at the bowling alley that night, but as soon as they got there, the boy spotted a glorious mullet hanging from beneath a cowboy hat and absolutely had to call Mae, which resulted in his spending the first hour pacing the men's room floor, laughing with her on his cell phone. Will had come in twice, and Joe once, to tell him when they were starting new games without him and to pester him about being on the phone, but they didn't even faze him. His legs never once tired of treading that sticky linoleum floor. That disinfectant smell of the bleached porcelain that filled the room did not rattle his stomach. He was exactly where he wanted to be, because he was as close to her as he could have been. When he finally hung up the phone and joined his friends, who were already in the middle of their fourth game, he wore a smile that their envious taunting could not touch.

On the drive home, he rode in the passenger seat of Joe's truck. The windows were down and the wind was whipping briskly across his face. The truck engine roared against the asphalt to the background of Incubus that blared from the speakers. The boy fished into his left pocket with his right hand and pulled a cigarette from the pack.

"So, what's the deal, man?" Joe asked, turning down the volume.

The boy cupped his bandaged hand around the end of the white stick and sparked his lighter. "What do you mean?"

"With this girl, I mean, I guess you really like her right?" his friend kept looking from the road to the boy.

"Yeah," the boy said, blowing out smoke, "I really do."

"How come?" Joe asked. "I mean, she's like a million miles away, but you don't talk to other girls, or even look at them anymore; and you seem OK with that. But you don't see her either, so it's like, why?"

"She's worth it," the boy thought for a moment. "It's like, you've dated a lot of pretty girls, right?" Joe laughed and nodded his head proudly. "But you dated them because they were pretty, right?" He nodded again. "But then, you got to know them and you found out that they were mean, or snobby, or just didn't match your personality,

144

you know?" The smile drained from Joe's face as he nodded a third time. "This happened the other way around. I met a girl who had all of the qualities I love, you know, smart, funny, laid back but still fun loving, caring; and I got to know her—well. Then, to be honest, man, I was already hooked. Then I saw her picture, and it was just a bonus that she was absolutely gorgeous. This girl is everything, man, everything I need."

Joe didn't respond. His face was introspective as he pulled a menthol cigarette from his pack and lit it. He took two deliberate drags and looked at the boy with a furrowed brow.

"So, what next?" he was asking himself as much as he was the boy.

The boy took a long drag off his cigarette and stared out the window. That was the inescapable question. Next what? The streetlights and traffic signals zoomed by in streaks of white, green, and yellow against the pinkish, light-polluted sky; there was so much light for a sleeping city.

"I don't know," he finally replied, and Joe nodded knowingly.

The boy's cell phone vibrated and he opened it to find a text message from Chloe. "Sorry about your hand," it read. "Good luck tomorrow. Let me know if you are going to play." It was Thursday; the show was tomorrow, and Chloe had remembered. He needed to call her, but it felt too late. He wouldn't play the next day, but if he meant to play on Monday, it was time to get his fingers working; but first, he needed rest.

He awoke the next afternoon apprehensive. It was time for him to defy medicine a second time. For the previous three days, he had tried to be as careful as possible with his wounded hand, to accelerate the healing process. Today was the fourth day, and it was time to try. He untucked the bandaging and began cautiously unwrapping his wrist. The tightness of the bandage had made his skin wrinkled and pale. The stagnant air of his bedroom felt like a cool breeze against his suffocated skin as the metal splint fell to the floor with the uncoiled bandaging. As he examined the wounds, he recalled the horror of the accident. Surgical tape ran in thin strands around his thumb, so that it was almost entirely covered in blood-spotted white strips. The hole in his hand was covered by folded gauze squares, held in

145

place by crisscrossed pieces of the same thin tape. Hoisting his guitar with his right hand, he awkwardly shifted it across his legs until it was somewhat comfortable. Lowering the neck down gently, he eased it into his cupped left hand and took a deep breath. It felt good to hold the guitar. He reached up slowly with his right hand and pulled the pick free from the strings with a pop that made them vibrate, echoing inside the guitar's hollow body. He steadied them with his palm before strumming the pick softly down the strings. It was still in tune from the previous week. Next, he turned his eyes to his left hand that held the neck of the guitar. His fingers were paralyzed and crowded together. He took another deep breath and concentrated. His pointer finger was slow as he hooked it around to the front of the guitar and pushed it down into position on the string. He sighed. His middle finger was weak and shaky as he pressed it down on the next string. He smiled and nodded as he strummed the chord. Wincing, he readjusted the guitar in his hand and focused his muscles on positioning his ring finger. The tendons in his wrist bulged beneath his skin as he flexed his arm to move the damaged muscle. The finger did not respond. Wiping his brow with his other hand, he tried again; still no response. It was as if something was blocking the signal inside his palm. Attempting the same routine with his pinky yielded the same result, and he lowered the guitar to the floor hopelessly.

That afternoon, he did go to lunch with Ben and Chloe, and the three sat and reminisced about the past. They never once talked about the band or the effect of his injury; the boy assumed they could read the consequence in his heavy shoulders. Instead, they talked about Ben and Lynn, Chloe and her writing, and Mae. The boy talked incessantly about her, and, despite his obvious discouragement about the band, they could hear the enthusiasm in his voice. For hours, they sat and talked as if they had never been apart. They told the boy stories about things that had happened or changed since he had left and he told them about his new friends and experiences. It was good for the boy to feel some sort of inclusion in the life that he had left behind, but he could not help but feel a slight sense of resentment that they still owned the world that they had once shared with him.

On the ride home, the cigarettes were more satisfying than usual. The fiery smoke that singed the hairs in his throat seemed to acquit him of his memory. Once inside, he barricaded himself in his room and plastered written emotion on his walls. Scribbled words on torn white paper and strips of clear tape fumbled in his damaged hands as he struggled to empty his mind onto the walls of his tomb. Once he was satisfied, he slipped on his jacket and drove to watch his band play.

He was late getting there, and Jack and the others were already on stage. His friend looked so proud, standing up there, singing songs that the boy had written. The boy flipped up the hood to his jacket, positioned himself against a wall at the back of the bar, and surveyed the room. It was a good turnout; roughly sixty people crowded the open floor in front of the boy, each one seeming at least fairly interested in the clowns on stage. The energy level was high, and Jack could sense it. He dipped the microphone as he sang and played air guitar with the music. It was a fantastic show after all.

"Something to drink?" the bartender asked, leaning toward the boy.

"Rum and coke," the boy nodded and reached for the fake ID in his pocket, but the woman was already across the bar, scooping ice into a glass.

Typically, he found that whether or not they checked his ID depended on his level of confidence. If he reached for it before they asked, they would usually dismissively wave it away with their hand; or if he ordered a complex drink confidently, they would never even ask. It was all in his composure. He nodded a "Thank you" and picked the glass up off the bar, pouring some of the liquid down his throat. A finger tapped softly on the boy's shoulder and he turned to see a thin, red-haired, freckle-faced boy standing meekly behind him. The boy vaguely recognized him from other shows and nodded politely.

"I knew that was you. Why aren't you playing?" the voice asked.

The boy pulled up his jacket sleeve, revealing the splint.

"Whoa! Are you OK?" Hank exclaimed.

The boy nodded and smiled.

"Hopefully," he called over his shoulder.

The band was playing one of his favorite songs, and they were almost to his big solo.

147

"You don't remember me, do you?" the voice called from be-hind.

The fill-in played the solo well, missing only one of the ending notes.

"I would have played it better," the boy thought.

"You can't play at all" his brain retorted. The boy turned again, scanning the spiky red hair and blue eyes. They must have met before, but the boy could not recall. He searched his memory for a name; nothing surfaced, but he nodded his head anyway.

"It's Hank," the freckled boy said nervously. "I come to all your shows. We met once. I was starting up a band and wanted some advice."

"Oh yeah," the boy lied. "How is that going?"

Hank smiled at the recognition; the boy had fooled him.

"Slow," Hank said. "You know, not all of us have natural tal-ent."

The boy laughed awkwardly. Natural talent? He certainly would not call it that. Sloppy outward splattering of inner turmoil—that was a more accurate name for it.

"Have they been on long?" the boy motioned to the stage.

It was best to change the subject when people started calling him talented. Hank turned as if just noticing the people on stage.

"Uh," he thought for a moment, "this is the fifth song."

"What'd we open with?" the boy chuckled.

" 'From What I Remember,' " Hank quoted the song title care-fully, enunciating each word to prove he was familiar with the band's catalogue.

The boy nodded. It was a song he had written about the band's regular use of Remedies.

"W-which is a great song," Hank stammered on, "like, one of my favorites. Is it true you wrote that on a napkin at a bar?"

"Yeah," the boy laughed, "I did." He set his glass back down on the bar and lit up a cigarette.

"Thank you," Jack panted into the microphone at the finish of the song. "It's awesome that everybody came out tonight. This is a big night for us." He held up his arms to include the other members on stage. "We actually have a meeting with some producers on Monday." What was he doing? "...hopefully we can get a contract signed and a record underway...."

The crowd cheered loudly. Hank slapped a "congratulations" on the boy's back. Jack took a bow, followed by the bassist, drummer, and fill-in, all in unison.

"Thank you," Jack continued. "So, we're, uh, working on some new songs." They were? "...making some changes...." Changes? "...and we're really excited!" He looked back to the three band members behind him and laughed. "We're going to take a break for a bit, take some shots, and we'll be back in a little while." Jack finished, and the four walked backstage.

Twirling the half-smoked cigarette down into the ashtray, the boy moved quickly to the door at the right of the stage.

"What the hell is going on?!" he said, barging into the small room where the four sat, huddled around a coffee table.

Jack was already thumbing some planted Remedy into a glass bowl.

"Hey, brother!" he said. "You made it! Grab a seat, join the circle!"

"Jack!" the boy said more harshly. "What the hell is going on?!"

"What's it look like?" he said absently. "Trying to get ready for the second set."

The other three kept their eyes glued to the table; no one would look at him.

"Jack, we need to talk. Now." The boy stood stiffly while Jack rose to his feet and followed him out the back door of the bar.

"What was that up there?" the boy asked once they were out in the alley. "It's supposed to be you and me, Jack. What are you doing?"

"Whatever I can!" Jack fired back. "I'm trying to take this band somewhere. You...you're just too damn far away, man! How are we ever supposed to...."

"Don't start that shit!" the boy interjected. "We talked about this a long time ago!"

"How are we ever supposed to get anywhere if we aren't making progress?" Jack said loudly. "I'm just trying to build from what we started!"

"Is this a joke?" the boy scoffed. "You're up there talking about new songs, Jack! New song?!"

"We are working on new songs," Jack's fished a cigarette out of his pocket.

"Who is?!" the boy choked.

"Me," Jack said, sparking the lighter, "and the new guy. He's not bad."

"Are you kidding me?!" the boy gawked. "Are you kidding me?! The new guy?! The fill-in is writing songs? The fill-in?!"

"We need to be consistent. You aren't here." Jack said. "And when were you going to tell me?"

"Tell you what?" the boy was in shock.

"About your hand!" Jack motioned to the cast. "About how you'll never play again!"

The boy should have known Jack would hear it from somewhere. Everyone's business was everyone's business.

"I'll play again," the boy muttered.

"I'm sure you will," Jack said calmly, "but right now, we've got to do what's best for the band. We can't pass up the opportunity on Monday. We voted on it and everyone in there agrees. The kid has got to play, so he's got to replace you."

"That's my music," the boy's voice was shaky; "those are my lyrics."

"I know. I'm sorry." Jack said tonelessly, "They will be waiting for you when you get better."

The boy shook his head slowly. He couldn't believe what he was hearing.

"I hate to do this," Jack said, blowing smoke from the corner of his mouth, "You're like a brother to me," he stretched out his hand, "I hope this doesn't change things between us."

The boy laughed and shook his head in disbelief.

"After everything we've done," he chuckled again and half-heartedly swatted at the notion of a handshake as he walked away, down the alley.

"It doesn't have to be this way," Jack called to him from beneath the floodlight attached to the brick outside the bar.

"Yes it does," the boy replied.

He wasn't sure if Jack heard him or not. He was already almost to the end of the alley and enveloped in the shadows.

ten

The springs in the mattress made the cardboard box bounce slightly as the boy dropped it onto the bed. Because of his lack of desire to settle into his parents' new house, most of his belongings were still transitory, which made it fairly easy to relocate. It required only that he sort through and decide which boxes came with him and which were packed into his parents' garage. He found himself wanting to leave most of them behind.

The room was small and simple—four white walls, one wooden door, one curtainless window, and a fluorescent light in drop ceiling. A metal clothing rack that swiveled on four wheels shared the wall opposite the door with the window and compensated for the lack of a closet. The bed was small, but took up the entire side wall, except for the small area where the clothing rack fit at the foot of the bed. The head of the mattress squeezed tightly between the wall and a dark, wooden dresser that shouldered up to the door frame. Opposite the bed was a small bookcase, and the only open area in the room. It wasn't much, but it was his. He surveyed the room again and smiled proudly; this was college.

The acceptance letter had come months beforehand, but he had still been unsure about the decision. He didn't know much about the school, had never visited, and was discouraged by the perpetual warnings he had been given that unless he wanted to become a teacher, an English major was pointless. Lily had broken up with her "jackass boyfriend" and had, coincidentally, started dating the boy's brother. The two got along well, and it seemed as though they had helped absolve one another of their pasts. His brother had been completely "clean" for the past four months and Lily had stopped crying on the phone about a boyfriend who mistreated her. The two of them had teamed up in coaxing the boy to accept the school's offer; Lily wanted his companionship, his brother wanted someone to baby sit his new girlfriend. Neither was a viable reason, but, in the end, the boy could not think of a better response to the never-ending question of "what next?" Not to mention that with the loss of the band, a large number of his friends going away to college, his hatred of his new house, and the fact that no matter where he went Mae was a telephone line away, he had little reason to stay where he was.

"Where do you want this?" his father asked, holding up the boy's guitar case as he walked into the room.

His parents had been generous enough to transport him to the school and help him unpack. Freshmen weren't supposed to have cars on the small college campus, so he had left his parked at home and had let his parents drive. After the first semester, he meant to finagle a way to have a car there anyway.

"Just throw it in the corner there," he said, mindlessly opening and closing his left fist.

The wounds had healed, and so had the muscles and the tendons, leaving only white slashes of scars across his thumb and palm. He had regained most of the use of all his fingers and had started playing guitar again, but it was not as satisfying as it once was. Learning to play again meant practically starting from scratch. He had to start from the beginning, this time with the limited mobility of his fingers. It had been a frustrating, lengthy process, and even after he had completed it he was still not to the level of skill that he had once achieved. However, without regular performances with the band, there was little reason to strive for such a goal. He had considered calling Jack once he was comfortable playing again, but the band seemed to be functioning fine without him. He had heard through mutual friends that they had gotten their record contract and put out an album, but he had yet to find a copy. There was no reason to; he knew he would not be mentioned and he couldn't bring himself to listen to them play without him. He had also heard that, while their music was doing well, the individuals were not. A contract meant more money, and for the band more money meant more expensive and thus more dangerous Remedies, which was not what the boy needed. Instead, he filled his free time, and the vacant holes inside himself, with Mae. The two had decided to make their relationship an exclusive one and began calling themselves a couple. They had taken that first, awkward "I love you" and incorporated it, more gracefully, into the quiet whispers of their conversations. When he did pick up his guitar to play, the boy restrained his fingers from dancing out the melodies to songs he had written for the band and wrote new love ballads about Mae instead. The only recognition he needed was in her smile.

All of the dorms were full by the time the boy had completed his registration, so the college had offered him a bedroom in a house, on campus, with three other freshmen. It seemed to be the optimal situation; he would have his own space and privacy and yet still be directly on the college grounds. In coming to the school, the boy was hoping to continue to improve his lifestyle by letting go of a few more of the vices that bound him. He had already given up the planted Remedy and been forced to forfeit the late-night mischief with the band. The boy believed that a strict, private college with stringent policies against smoking, drinking, and nearly all nocturnal activity would aid him in surrendering the final few. The privacy and freedom that came with the house would only mean that his goal would require more self-control and discipline than he had foreseen, but he had hope for real change. The other three tenants had hopes for change as well. They, too, saw the school as an opportunity to progress and strengthen their personal faith. Unfortunately for the lot of them, they were randomly selected to be placed in their own house, together. It had all the makings of a fun-filled disaster.

"Ryan," the first of the roommates introduced himself.

He was an obvious "intellect". A head shorter than the boy, he stood, a handful of computer wiring coiled in his grip, as he watched the boy shift boxes around his crowded room. Ryan had come to the college to jump on the hot ticket that was computer science. Online business was booming and the Microsoft® giants of the industry were gobbling up college grads faster than they could be bred. However, Ryan was different than most of the other computer intellects the boy had met. While he did somewhat enjoy the technology, Ryan had gotten into computers solely for the money, and he had no problem admitting that.

"It makes monetary sense," he would say. "I will be making a minimum of eighty thousand as soon as I graduate. Easily."

The boy raised his eyebrows as he began loading the drawers of his dresser. It did make sense.

"How's it going, guys? I'm Seth," the bulky brown-haired roommate came sliding excitedly into the room, tossing a football in the air with one hand.

The boy looked up from his drawer of clothes and introduced himself as Seth flopped down on the boy's bed. His diamond stud earring and savage gum chomping labeled him a "jock," but there was something less typical about him. He was much more kind-hearted and innocent than the boy would have expected. He had come to the college to experience "life away from home" and to escape some harmless, small-town mischief that he had gotten into in high school. Apart from that, he had gone to college because everyone told him he should; he had no major, no clue as to what he wanted to study or what he was good at, and no urgency about answering any of those questions. The boy found himself drawn to Seth's simple enjoyment of life.

Luke moseyed down the hallway and leaned in through the doorway, his eyes scanning the layout of the room. The boy examined him carefully. His hands were wedged into the pockets of his tight rusted jeans and he wore a generic football jersey that covered his square frame. His face was pensive and confident as he looked over the heads of the room's occupants and studied the walls and furniture closely.

"These rooms really are small, aren't they?" he smiled.

The boy's eyes traveled once around the four walls before he chuckled and rose to his feet to introduce himself.

"I'm Rob," Luke said, shaking the boy's hand.

"Ridiculously small," the boy said, motioning his head toward the room behind him.

Luke laughed and nodded. Ryan and Seth moved to the doorway and introduced themselves as well, while the boy squatted back down to the task of filling his drawers.

"You said your name is Rob?" the boy asked, his eyes on the clothes he was squeezing into his new dresser.

"Yeah," Luke replied.

"It doesn't suit you," the boy lifted his eyes to his new roommate. "You look more like a...Luke, to me."

Ryan smiled and nodded in agreement. Luke looked from one to the other and shrugged his shoulders.

"Then call me Luke," he exhaled after a few moments.

"Luke," the boy said again, smiling and folding a sweatshirt into his drawer.

The brutal snowstorm that waged war against the small wooden cabin for the better part of the previously ten days had finally come to an end. The snow had settled in a thick mound around the exterior walls, and the sun could be seen again through the windows. It was still months before the season would end, but we had survived some of the heaviest snowfall that we had seen yet. The boy seemed relieved; I didn't have the heart to tell him that the worst blizzard was yet to come.

I was out surveying the aftermath of the storm when he awoke, but I could tell when I returned that he had not had his morning coffee. The mug still sat, overturned on the countertop, and he sat in his chair, his pencil working. No coffee meant that he was not relying on substances, which meant that he was feeling optimistic. My steps were slow and quiet as I crept up behind his desk chair. His eyes were reminiscent and his lips formed into a light smile as his hand traced the same letters over and over. I held my breath as I craned my neck to peer over his shoulder at the words his lead was tracing. "Pelican ?" it read. The question mark was surrounded by a thick, dark circle. I could hear him muttering to himself; he was trying to think of a word he had forgotten. I drew in a slow, contemplative breath and he spun at the sound. His eyes met mine, and I cowered at their vigor. He watched me calmly as I glided cautiously away from the chair. Days when he was optimistic were simply days I could not be around. Snatching up my cigarettes from the counter, I walked briskly to the door. Just before I slammed it shut behind me, I glanced back at the boy. His eyes were still on me. He winked and I shook my head in disgust, trudging out into the fresh-fallen snow.

———∞∞∞———

"When will I ever get to see you?" Mae whined softly into the phone.

The boy took a deep breath and sighed. It was a conversation they had often, where they expressed their bittersweet frustration of not being able to see one another.

"I don't know," he moaned back, "hopefully soon, or I'm going to explode!" He was thumbing through the computer printout pictures he had of her.

He smiled at the picture of the two of them together; she had taken pictures of him that he had sent her and pasted them with pictures of herself.

"You're going to explode?!" she giggled at his dramatic response. "Then I will have no reason to live!"

The boy chuckled at her adorableness.

"The trouble is, we are broke college students!" the boy laughed, "but we've got love and that's all that matters!"

Mae laughed loudly at his exaggerated enthusiasm, but money and college were the issues. They had looked at flights to visit one another but could not afford the cost or the time off from school.

"I am so in love with you," she said, "like so in love with you. And all I want to do is get my arms around you, but I can't." Her voice trailed off.

"I will figure something out," he sighed. "I will find the money somehow. I love you."

"I love you," she replied, but William was squealing in the background.

Within the first month of moving in, the school informed the boys that it intended to demolish their house after that semester. This not only made them leery about their living situation for the following year, but it instantly destroyed any respect that they may have had for the school-owned property. Paintball shootouts, baseball pitches, bicycle races, touchdown passes, and golf balls had riddled the walls with cracks, holes, and, at times, chasms. The boys thought they were doing the college a favor by clearing out some of the drywall. Unfortunately, the college didn't see it that way, so the boys did their best to hide their destruction with posters and tapestry.

The afternoon following that conversation with Mae, the boy lay on his back on the floor of what they had come to call the "studying room"; his feet crossed and propped up on the only windowsill in the room, his hands folded on his chest. The name was entirely inappropriate as virtually no studying was ever actually achieved in the room. Instead, they used the room to sit and talk or watch the occasional movie on Ryan's computer. Luke rocked slowly in a squeaky, swivel chair, flipping halfheartedly through a clothing magazine, while Seth sat opposite him, shooting holes in the fibrous tiles of the drop ceiling with his paintball gun and chuckling to himself. Ryan assumed his usual position at his desk, fingers moving swiftly across his keyboard, typing in a language the other three did not understand.

"We need money," the boy said.

It was a school policy that first-semester students were not allowed to have jobs. Not to mention that Luke was the only one of the bunch who had been able to sneak his car on campus, which made job transportation nearly impossible.

"Maybe we should sell drugs," Luke said absently as he turned another page of his magazine.

Seth laughed at the idea. The boy thought for a moment but ignored the suggestion. If he could find a way make some money, he would be able to see Mae, but he wouldn't be any good to her in jail. Plus, he had promised himself that he was through with dishing out paid favors.

"I copied that CD that you wanted," Ryan called to the boy, lifting a silver disc from his computer's CD tray and placing it on the desk.

The boy eyed the disc.

"I have an idea..." he said slyly, and swung his legs down from the wooden sill.

Seth lowered the paintball gun and watched the boy as he sat up quickly.

"What if," the boy started slowly, "we started selling copied CDs to people? Like, with tracks that weren't produced or hard-to-find versions of songs."

Luke lowered his magazine and lifted his eyes to the boy.

"How?" he asked.

"Easy. We already download music. All we have to do is find an open online market where consumers are selling to other consumers and we're good. We can download anything people want," the boy explained. "Ryan, help me out."

Ryan had spun around in his chair and was nodding attentively.

"Yeah, it's doable," Ryan agreed, "very doable. That's not a bad idea at all!"

"Isn't that illegal?" Seth said slowly.

"It's becoming illegal," the boy corrected. "There are no laws about it yet. There will be soon, but not yet. I mean, it's frowned upon, but it's better than selling drugs." He knew he had only made the comparison for his own conscience.

The boys spent the next two hours working out the logistics of the plan. They found an online consumer-to-consumer marketplace that they liked, decided on a few trial CDs, and discussed possible loopholes to avoid any legal confrontation. The more they talked, the more they realized the delicate intricacy of their operation; it took careful scheming and planning. There were copyright laws, customer satisfaction concerns, quality and shipment issues, and questionable availabilities that they had to address. It was not going to be an easy task, but once they felt comfortable with their overall plan, they decided to test it out. They selected a list of fifteen trial CDs and Ryan posted them online.

"Alright," he said once he had finished. "Now, all we have to do is wait."

The four boys smiled as they looked contently at each other.

"Well," the boy glanced at the clock on the wall. "Let's eat."

They walked to the cafeteria feeling optimistic. They made jokes, laughed, and soaked in the last dwindling rays of sunlight as they strolled down the smooth sidewalk. They had only lived together for two months at that point, but the four had grown immeasurably close. Had you asked the boy then, he would have said they were his brothers.

"Hi, Ryan!" a plump girl with braces and glasses said as she walked by.

"Hi," Ryan mumbled politely, awkwardly lowering his head and quickening his pace.

"Hey, Ry," the boy teased, "I think she likes you."

Seth laughed loudly.

"Shut up. I hate you," Ryan muttered, smiling and shoving his hands in his pocket.

"She seems like a nice girl," Luke goaded, and the boy chuckled.

"Yea," the boy agreed, "Ryan, maybe we should invite her to dinner."

"I'm going to kill you," Ryan smirked, and they all four laughed.

Every college has a meal plan, but most are not as expensive as the one at the college that the boys attended. With no jobs and no parental assistance, they simply could not afford it. In order to remedy this predicament, they all shared one meal plan. Ryan had convinced his semi-wealthy parents that he needed an unlimited meal card, with as many cafeteria visits as he wanted, and they had agreed to pay for it. So, Ryan would go into the entrance of the dining hall, where they would swipe his card, while the other three boys would stand at a locked door around the corner. Once inside, Ryan would nonchalantly flick his card hard against the ground so it would slide under the door, and the boys would repeat the process until they were all in. To limit this blatantly fraudulent act to once a day, one of the boys would carry a backpack with empty cereal boxes and milk jugs, which he would fill up as he made his way through the lines. The other three would gather enough food for themselves and the fourth onto their trays, and they would move to a table and eat.

"Where's Lily?" Ryan asked, biting into a steaming slice of pepperoni.

Naturally, the boy's high school friend had become a part of the group. She had spent most of the first two weeks of school over at their house and had grown close with the other three boys. But recently, she had been going home more frequently to see the boy's brother.

"She's with my brother," the boy replied, popping a grape into his mouth.

"I can't get over that," Luke shook his head. "Doesn't that drive you nuts that your best friend from high school is dating your brother?"

The boy shrugged his shoulders. It bothered him when he allowed it to.

"Sometimes; I mean, it is weird. But they are two of my best friends, and they seem happy." He shrugged again.

Luke shook his head sympathetically.

When they finished eating, they put their trays and dishes on the mysterious conveyer belt that took them somewhere to be cleaned and walked home. The boy had nearly forgotten about the CD selling experiment by the time he strolled into the house and into his room. He was staring intently at a picture of Mae that he had taped above his bed when Ryan called.

"H-hey! Um, you guys gotta come in here!" he cried from the "studying room."

It took a moment for the boy to snap out of the enraptured state that her eyes had captured him in. By the time he scrambled into the room, Ryan was awkwardly pacing along the carpet while Luke and Seth stood, jaws dropped, laughing and pushing one another in the illuminating glow of Ryan's computer screen.

"Look at this!" Luke said, motioning the boy to the computer.

The boy moved to the screen. Ryan paced up behind him and used the mouse to point out the visuals.

"Look," Ryan said nervously, "all of the CDs sold!" He moved the mouse down the columns of listings. Each one was green. "But look at how much they sold for. Look at how much they owe us!"

The boy's eyes followed the mouse as Ryan moved it to the "Total" box at the bottom corner of the screen. He read it out loud: "$679.43." His eyes moved to the clock. It had been two hours.

"In two hours?" he chuckled. "We made six hundred seventy-nine dollars and forty three cents in two hours?! We're in business, boys!"

The three boys cheered and hugged excitedly.

"It's too much," Ryan stammered, "It happened too fast!"

"It's perfect," the boy said calmly. "Don't worry, man. It's perfect."

Ryan nodded, and the two hugged in celebration.

"Now, tomorrow," the boy said to the other three, "we figure out how to pull it off."

That night the boy was especially ecstatic to talk to Mae.

"Hey, cue-pie," she answered.

"Hey, gorgeous!" he said. "I've got to ask you something!"

"What is it, baby?"

"When is your spring break?!" he asked excitedly.

"Um," she sounded suspicious, "the second week of March, I think."

He flipped through some papers on his bed, "Excellent! Mine, too!"

"OK," she said slowly. "What are you getting at?"

"I think I found a way that we can see each other," he held his breath, waiting for a reaction.

"What?!" she giggled. "How? That's amazing! But how?!"

He breathed a sigh of relief.

"We found a way to make some money. It's not exactly the most honest way," he explained.

"Are you putting yourself in any danger?" she asked. "Could it hurt you?"

"No," he replied. "I don't think so."

"Alright then," she said. "I trust you. Do what you think is right. Just get to me, or get me to you."

He breathed another sigh of relief. That was one of the reasons he loved her. He knew she trusted him completely. She had never once doubted his love or questioned his intentions; she had no reason to. Every ounce of his energy was entirely devoted to her, and she knew that. He would have done anything in the world for her. They never fought, never lied, never neglected one another, because they loved each other truly and wanted nothing more than to make the other happy. It was true love to the fullest.

"I can't believe I'm actually going to see you," he exhaled as the weight lifted from his chest.

"I love you," she gasped, "and I always will."

eleven

Business was booming. The morning after their first night of sales, Ryan had copied the CDs, the boy had added a few personal touches to make them more authentic, and the four had walked down to the school post office. To deter any suspicion, the boy had told the nice old woman behind the counter that the four of them were in a band and that they sold their CDs online. He was very polite and told her that, hopefully, they would be in at least once a week making shipments. She seemed interested in their story and was even kind enough to give them a discount on each CD they shipped. Their system was flawless. Ryan would set up the listings, copy the discs, and take payment; Luke would create the CD labels and organize the discs with the mailing addresses; Seth would take them to the post office to be shipped; and the boy would decide on which discs to sell, download the music, and resolve any customer complaints. Sales had been so successful in the online marketplace that Ryan had designed a website on the school server so that students could make purchases as well. Between the website and the open marketplace, they had saved roughly nine thousand dollars in the first two and a half weeks. Life was good for the boy. He was making money, he was always among friends, and he was in love—true, undeniable love.

"Looks like CD sales are treating you fellas well," Lily said as she eyed a few minor additions to their living room after a party one night.

The boy smiled and tipped a bottle of liquid Remedy to his lips. From the beginning, the boys had agreed to keep their operation a secret to avoid any competition or attention from the college, but they could trust Lily, the boy had assured them of that.

"It's pretty crazy," the boy agreed, dropping down on the sofa next to Luke. "It's gone much better than we expected."

"You guys better be careful," she laughed as she sat next to the boy. "You could probably get into some serious trouble."

"Nah," Ryan disputed from a nearby chair. "The laws aren't concrete enough yet. We'll be fine."

"So, what are you going to do with the money?" she asked all three of them now. "Just split it up?"

Ryan sat back in his chair as if just considering the question for the first time. Luke tossed a handful of corn chips into his mouth and observed the boy.

"I was thinking..." the boy said casually, "maybe we could use some of it to plan something crazy for spring break. Maybe something like the beach?"

He watched as his friends' eyes lit up and they agreed with a barrage of "yeah"s and "great idea."

"I'll go start looking for places to rent right now!" Ryan hopped to his feet.

They had made plenty of money. Their plan had worked. It was time for the boy to reveal his true intentions.

"I was also thinking," he stopped his friend, "I'm going to use part of my portion to buy a plane ticket for Mae to come here, so she can drive down with us."

The room fell silent. Ryan froze and his mouth fell open, but Lily was the first to speak.

"You're going to fly her up?!!" she squealed. "You're actually going to meet her?!!"

The boy smiled proudly and nodded as Lily threw her arms around him.

"Your portion?" Ryan scoffed. "No way, man! We'll include her ticket in the cost. You want her to be there, she's in. We'll split it up with the rest of the costs. Then we'll divide up whatever is left."

"Yeah!" Luke agreed before the boy could object. "At this point, I'd say we are about as eager to meet her as you are!"

"I doubt that, but thank you. You really don't have to do that. I was planning on paying for it."

He really wasn't all that surprised; they had all been like family to him. He would have done the same for any of them.

"It's already done," Ryan said flatly. "Just find a plane ticket, tell me how much it is, and I'll add it into the cost."

The boy sank back into the couch and smiled. He loved Mae; he loved his friends; he loved life.

Lily had class early the next morning, so, with a yawn and a hug, she scurried out the door and back to her dorm. Ryan sat, tapping the keys furiously as he searched his computer screen; Seth was fast asleep in his bed; and Luke and the boy sat in the white frame of a wide screen-less window, smoking cigarettes. It hadn't taken long for their common habits to emerge. They had all come to the school with the same goal—to eliminate certain substances. In all fairness, they had been able to refrain from most of their past experimentation, but the smaller, seemingly less harmful habits had slipped through and been deemed acceptable. Ryan still drank liquid Remedy, Seth still picked petty fistfights, and Luke and the boy still smoked cigarettes.

"You've got to explain something to me," Luke said after a drag, lingering puffs of smoke billowing from his mouth as it opened and closed. "Every time I talk to you, I can tell that you're in love. Anyone can. All they have to do is look at you. Seriously, you love that girl more than I think I have ever seen anyone love anything." The boy grinned as he watched a crumbly trail of ash float down from the window and land softly in the grass. "But you have never even seen her. How can you be so in love and so sure about a girl you've never met?"

Luke didn't understand, but no one seemed to; the boy did not expect them to. It wasn't a decision or even a feeling. It wasn't even something that the boy fully understood, certainly not at the time. It was like a part of his body, some vital organ that he could not live without. It didn't matter what her face looked like when she laughed, or how her body moved when she walked, or the flavor of her skin; all that mattered was that she never leave him, because her existence brought breath to his lungs.

"If she has the perfect skin tone, or beautiful hair, or her lips fit exactly across mine, that's just a bonus," the boy tried to explain. "I'm so wrapped up in her—just her—everything about her, that it doesn't even matter at all." His hands danced in front of him as he

165

spoke, "I'm so sick of love being this thing that people need to feel, or see, or touch, and as soon as they don't see it or feel it anymore, they just throw it aside and hunt for someone new. That's not how it's supposed to work. That's not love. Love is this thing that finds you and literally embeds itself into the very core of your being and becomes a part of you. Then, everything you do, you do with that love in mind, whether you want to or not, because it is as much a piece of you as your arm or your mind or your soul. That's how it is for me, so it leaves nothing to be desired. I want to see her, more than anything, but what drives me the most to make it happen is that she wants to see me, because I would do anything within my power to give her everything that she wants. That's love, for me. That's how it feels, and that's why it's so easy."

Luke's eyes were narrow as they inspected the boy; he pouted out his bottom lip as his head moved slowly up and down. The boy scanned the grass below, shifting nervously as he inhaled another drag.

"You're crazy," Luke smiled.

"I know," the boy agreed, and the two chuckled.

"I want to talk to you guys about something serious," Ryan recited a familiar speech as he rounded the corner and saw the two. "I love you guys, and I want you to be healthy. Don't you know those things kill you?" he teased.

"Shut up," Luke laughed. "What do you want?"

"I think I found a place for spring break," he clapped his hands together. "Come check it out."

The place was perfect—four bedrooms, two bathrooms, a full deck, a nice living room and kitchen, and mostly importantly, it was on the beach. The three boys scrolled through the pictures and were quickly convinced. They had found the house; now it was just a matter of filling it. Mae was ecstatic to hear the news. Of course, at first, she tried to object to them spending so much money for her attendance, but the boy quickly explained that it had been his plan since the beginning, and she accepted. Lily had declined the invitation because she couldn't bear the thought of a week away from the boy's brother and Seth had already made plans with his girlfriend from back home, so Ryan, Luke, and the boy picked a handful of friends from the school and planned the trip. In addition to the house rental and Mae's plane ticket, the boys also agreed to use their profits toward any recreational Remedies they wanted.

"We should do it up right, go all out," Ryan said during one planning session, "a last hurrah!"

The boy raised an eyebrow.

"What do you mean?" Luke asked.

"I know we are all clean and whatnot, but it's spring break. What if we went a little crazy and made a few bad decisions—just for old time's sake? One last go around. A sort of sending off of the things we leave behind." Ryan's speech was poetic and heartfelt, but it still made the boy's stomach churn.

"A last hurrah," Luke smiled slowly. "What'd you have in mind?"

"Nothing too risky," Ryan coaxed, carefully eyeing the boy, "some green maybe?"

The boy's throat clenched. It had been a long time since he had thought about planted Remedy. He had entirely given it up. He had no need for it anymore; Mae had expunged any reason he'd ever had for Remedies.

"Sounds good to me, but I don't know where to score any anymore," Luke said.

The boy was speechless as he helplessly watched the conversation progress. He had promised himself that he was finished with that stuff. What would Mae think? Would it upset her? Everything he did, he did with love in mind.

"I don't either. I usually just smoked other people's," Ryan admitted.

The boy winced. People like that were the worst; he called them "scavengers" and they were his least favorite kind of smokers. They never bought because they never wanted to hold for one of three reasons: either they didn't have the money, had criminal records, or were too judgmental or self-righteous, only wanting to dip into the squalor of the Remedied when they found it most convenient or available. It was the third of these that upset the boy the most—thinking they could step down amid the filth and decay, that they judged and ignored, whenever they wanted, for a taste of something to ease the pain of their plastic, cookie-cut, pious, bloodthirsty existences. Not only do they allow someone else to carry the weight and risk of their Remedy until they are ready to use it, but they have the audacity to cast judgment on that same someone. The boy shuddered. He realized that both of their eyes were on him, clearly waiting for a response. Mae would understand; he knew that.

"Yeah, fine. I'll get it." He was such a sucker.

His two roommates slapped his hand and patted his back in victorious celebration. The boy pulled his vibrating cell phone out of his pocket. It was Mae; perfect timing.

"Just the girl I'm lookin' for," he opened the phone.

"Hey," she sniffled. Her voice was hoarse and weak.

"What's wrong?" the hairs rose on the back of his neck, and his chest welled up with anger. He wasn't even sure why.

"It's nothing really," she sounded elusive; "I'm just having a hard time."

The boy plugged his finger in his ear and walked back to his bedroom.

"With what? What's going on?" he asked

"I really don't want to upset you. I just wanted to hear your voice," she sighed.

"Mae, you've got to tell me what's going on. I'm freaking out."

"Alright, but I'm embarrassed, and please don't let it upset you," her voice was slow and hesitant. "I was telling my parents about spring break the other day, and they flipped out and tried to tell me I couldn't come."

"Why not?" the boy already knew the answer to the question before he even asked it.

"They said because they don't know you or where you come from. They said I can't come." She sounded nervous. "What are we going to do? My mom is worried. I told her to just trust my judgment. My dad, he's angry. He doesn't like the whole idea at all."

The boy couldn't blame them; he'd be the same way with his daughter some day.

"Is there anything we could do to convince them?" the boy squatted down on his bed, biting his nail, his foot tapping rapidly against the thin carpet.

"My dad probably won't budge, but if I could just convince

my mom.... She just needs some reassurance. She just wants to feel comfortable."

"Alright," the boy bit his thumb. He knew who to call for comfort and reassurance. "I'll work it out. I love you. I will call you back later."

"OK. Love you."

He flipped the phone shut, then open, and dialed home. His mother answered promptly after two rings and he began to explain his predicament. She listened quietly as he paced the floor of his bedroom, then the hallway, telling the story of the past few years. As absurd as it felt to tell his own mother about his life, it seemed necessary to tell it from beginning to end, explaining the feelings and actions that had led him to that very point. He spared no detail and used the most potent of words when describing his love for the girl. His chest burned as he tried to translate the depth of his emotions into language. By the end of the story, he was panting and disheveled, standing in the middle of his hallway. His mother was silent for a moment, as she digested all the information her son had spewed.

"Alright," she cleared her throat, "tell me what you need me to do."

His shoulders felt slightly more at ease.

"Call her mom," he said. "I need you to convince her that you're my mom, that I'm harmless, and that this trip is OK."

"OK," she sounded confident. "What's the number?"

Even after he had hung up the phone, he couldn't stop pacing. What if it didn't work? He had to think of another plan. He tried to sit down and work on midterms and papers that were due before the break, but he was too consumed by his anxiety. He called Ben to try to distract himself, and the two talked about what they had missed in one another's lives. The boy told him about the trip and Mae, and Ben assured him that it would work out. Things seemed to be going well with Lynn, Ben's girlfriend, and his friend explained that he was actually headed to pick her up. The boy apologized and hung up the phone. Before he could return it to his pocket, the screen illuminated with a call from Mae. Her timing truly was impeccable.

"It worked!" she giggled into the phone. "I don't know what you said to your mom, or what she said to mine, but it worked! She said I could go!"

The boy inhaled a deep lungful of relief. Once again, their story had saved them.

"It's a good thing," his voice was shaking with relief and excitement, "because I didn't know what else I was going to try."

"It was perfect. You—you are perfect," she said, "and now, everything is perfect." A smile stretched across his entire face.

"I love you," he chuckled.

"I love you! And...!" her voice gained speed, "I can't believe I'm going to see you in two weeks!" Two weeks.

Since he was very young, he had always dreamed of finding an impossibly perfect kind of love; now he had found it. He had been waiting for nearly ten years; he could wait another two weeks. Hanging up the phone, he flopped down on his bed more content with life than he had ever been. He laughed; it was only going to get better. His brother was clean; Ben was well and had found a girl; the boy had survived leukemia, been in a successful band, pushed his luck with Remedies and come out relatively unscathed, and fallen completely in love. He chuckled at the ironic progression of his life, his surreal life. His stereo speakers hummed David Gray's "This Year's Love" softly, as the boy drummed his fingers lightly on his chest. Reaching up the wall beside his bed, he tugged at the printout of Mae until the tape peeled from the plaster. Lowering it to his face, he kissed it once and searched deep into her eyes.

"Hey, man," Ryan called from the doorway where he and Luke stood. The boy lifted his head to see. "How much do you think we will need for green?" Ryan continued. The boy dropped his head back to the mattress. "We were thinking like 150. Is that enough?"

"Should be," the boy nodded.

Closing his eyes, he tried to return to his blissful state of mind, but the song was over and his thoughts were on the Remedies.

"Might as well get it over with," he muttered to himself.

"Well I'll be damned," a voice answered after a considerable number of rings. "I thought you didn't love me anymore."

"Hey, how's the garden look?" the boy had no interest in small talk.

"It's coming along," the voice snickered. "Spring blossoms just came in. What's it matter, though? I heard you found a girl, made you quit."

"I did...and I have. They any good?" the boy looked nervously around his room. He just wanted the conversation to be over, but he couldn't show it.

"Daylilies; you do remember daylilies, right?" the voice teased.

The boy thought for a moment, "I remember. I'm looking at a 50 split."

"Aw, shit!" the voice exclaimed. "Does this mean you're back?!"

"No," the boy said quickly, "I'm not back. It's a one-time thing, for a friend."

"Ha ha, that's how it starts man," the voice laughed. "We both know that."

"I'm not back," the boy said calmly. "Is it doable or what?"

"Alright, alright, a 50 split? That's it?" the boy could hear air sucking between teeth. "That's not even really worth my while...but you were my boy, and I can't blame you for bein' in love."

"Thanks," the boy said, slightly relieved.

"I do also have a few experimenters that you might like. Some, uh, white tul-."

"No thanks," the boy interrupted.

"Alright then," the voice chuckled, "I'll get that to you. Take care of yourself."

"You, too," he said. "Thanks again. I'll see you around."

"Eh, man," the voice called before the boy could hang up. "Welcome back."

"I'm not back," the boy said strongly.

He could hear the voice chuckling as he hung up the phone.

twelve

Two years of never meeting and eight months of learning love had taken them far beyond the need for human contact. Never even grazing her lips, for eight months the boy probed her mind and dissected every cranny of her being. He inspected her character inside and out and found it unblemished. She came to him more pure and justified than anything ever had.

Love is funny, how it finds you and completely envelopes you. The boy could remember a day when he tried to give his heart to a girl in the form of a naïve silver trinket, and she had rejected it. He prayed that this time would be different; he knew it would. Mae was more than he could ever have considered, or anticipated, or even dreamed. If he should be so fortunate as to have her explode into his life, perhaps Fate was directing the two of them toward a love-infested future. Perhaps Fate was the one who would have them collide. He was a freshman away at college just truly scratching the surface of the craft, the art, of love and sensibility; and she was an innocent angel from Texas with so much love, just looking for something meaningful—something magical—to sweep her from the confines of her small town.

"Tomorrow! I'm going to see you tomorrow, like actually see you! Not cling to some wrinkled picture in the middle of the night, in my bed, with dried lipstick marks all over your glossy face, but actually see you, actually trace my finger along that jaw line that I have studied a thousand times." Her voice always made the boy tremor but, mixed with the anticipation, he could barely breathe.

"I know," the words must have formulated themselves, because he had no speech, "after all this time of loving an imaginary portrayal of pictures, I don't know if I'll be able to handle it. It might be too much. For so long I have dreamed of this day, I cannot believe it's actually happening!" He spoke to the picture on his wall; the phone just happened to be listening.

I'm somewhat leery of describing the sensations that the boy felt, because I don't believe that most people have ever experienced them. They were beyond surreal, beyond explanation. But they are part of the story, so I must attempt to embody them. I heard the boy awkwardly attempt to describe it once. He said it was like when he was younger and would have nightmares, horrifying nightmares that the world was ending or that his parents were actually aliens. He said it felt like that moment when you first wake up from one of those nightmares and realize that it was only a dream. It was like that security that everything is going to be alright, that everything is as it should be, that despite the lingering horror of what you left behind, it was worth experiencing to get to that relieving, belonging, sense of happiness. That's the best way I can think of to describe it; I did not know the boy at the time, and I've never felt anything of that sort.

"So you've got all my flight information and everything right? I can't believe this is actually happening!" Her words flowed through the receiver.

A week beforehand, the boy had given her his credit card number and told her to buy whichever flight she found that was the most convenient for her. The plan was that she would fly either to BWI in Baltimore or HIA in Pennsylvania where the boy would pick her up, bring her back to his house, and they all would start the drive down to the beach early the next morning. She had found a number of flights—some that flew into BWI, some into HIA—and she had discussed them with the boy. Once she had made her decision on which worked best with her schedule, she had called him and given him the airline and flight number, which he'd scribbled down on a piece of scrap paper. Opening his top dresser drawer, he pulled out the small slip of paper.

"Yes I do, and neither can I." It was like a dream. "And I cannot wait to tackle you when you get off that plane." He felt like he was meeting his best friend for the first time.

"Me neither. Alright, I am going to go pretend like I can actually get some sleep tonight, just to make tomorrow come faster." They

173

were like children on Christmas Eve. "I love you and I WILL see you tomorrow."

"I love you so much. Goodnight."

Hanging up the phone seemed like it should have been easier than usual, but it was just as difficult as ever. He could have talked to her all the way, until he had her securely in his arms. Love is funny like that; you never get enough.

Living with three other guys can make a house rather difficult to keep clean. Luke stayed up with the boy most of the night helping tidy up and listening politely as the boy talked for hours about how devoted his heart had become to some flimsy pictures, a telephone number, and some text on a screen.

"So, tomorrow, what if there is no physical attraction? Did you ever consider the possibility that when you two actually meet face-to-face there won't be anything there?" Luke had asked the boy.

"Never," he replied.

She knew him better than anyone ever had; and her ideas, her charm, and her mind were the things that stole his heart. Any physical attractions were simply additional benefits. She was already perfect to him.

The next morning the boy woke up earlier than usual and beaming. Flipping open his phone, he found a message from Mae and smiled. 'I'm on my way to you!!' it read. His shower was refreshing and quick and he nearly jumped into the clothes he had spent half an hour picking out the night before. Luke had been kind enough to offer to drive the boy to meet his destiny and came bumbling out of his room sometime mid-afternoon.

"I knew you'd be awake. You should have woken me up," he rubbed his eyes and muttered to the boy who was nervously rearranging the clutter that crowded his room.

"It's fine," the boy said, stepping back to scrutinize his new arrangement. "We've got a little time."

"Alright," Luke yawned, "let me get dressed."

Once Luke had grabbed the nearest pair of jeans, a T-shirt, and some flip-flops, he trudged out to the car with the boy fidgeting and following quickly behind.

"Do you mind if we make a stop?" the boy asked, once his

seatbelt was eagerly fastened.

"Sure thing," Luke popped the car into reverse. "Where to?"

"A grocery store or something," the boy grinned. "I need to get flowers."

Luke shook his head and laughed, "You're ridiculous, man."

The car lurched forward as Luke sleepily slid his foot off the clutch and onto the gas pedal, but the boy didn't notice. He was busy drumming his hands rapidly against his knees. Luke eyed him cautiously and flipped on the radio. "The Middle" by Jimmy Eat World played through the speakers.

"Great song!" the boy exclaimed, rolling the window down and letting the sunshine in. Luke smirked and opened the sunroof, just to humor him.

He was just finishing singing along with every word when Luke shifted the car in park outside of the supermarket.

"Be right back!" the boy said, hopping out of the car and strolling into the store.

Fresh bouquets and baskets of flowers greeted him just inside the door. Brilliant shades of orange, red, and yellow shone from crisp green stems bundled in strategic clusters. The soft, natural smell of greenery wafted from the assemblage as he drifted closer. Sliding one of the bouquets from the bunch, he twirled it in front of his face.

"You need help with something, dear?" a shaky voice asked from behind him.

He turned to find an elderly woman with a blue apron, hunched over a small countertop, working a strip of ribbon with a pair of scissors.

"Uh, I'm headed to the airport to pick up my girlfriend," it felt good to call her that, "just getting her some flowers." He held up the bouquet and smiled.

"Oh, those will never do!" she eyed him over the rim of her narrow glasses and set down the scissors. "Come over here."

The boy chuckled and dropped the flowers back down into the display.

"You're going to pick up your lady," she explained as she shook a fresh sheet of tissue paper out on the counter, "you need flowers that show your excitement—not just for today but for the rest of your lives together!"

The boy watched closely as she carefully stacked bright orange, yellow, and blue flowers onto the paper.

"This one," she held up a red rose whose pedals were still wrapped tightly into a bud, "this one is for what is yet to come."

She winked and placed the flower into the bunch. With a sprig of baby's breath, the bouquet was complete, and she rolled it up into the paper. She stared at it proudly before handing it over to the boy.

"She'll love it," the woman said with a smile.

"I know she will," the boy smiled back. "Thank you."

He was still grinning and admiring the flowers when he sauntered back out to the car. Luke rolled his eyes and shook his head as he watched the boy climb back into the passenger seat.

The parking lot was fairly empty; it was a much smaller airport than any he had ever seen. Luke found a nearby parking spot and the two moved quickly into the entrance. The boy was hardly through the door when his eyes started their frantic search. His heart felt like it may explode from his chest. He moved quickly up and down the promenade, glancing at the escalators and stairs, looking for a flight monitor. Nothing.

"Calm down, man. You OK?" Luke chuckled, "Are you even going to recognize her?"

He didn't even really hear the question. His palms were glistening and his breaths were short. The airport was empty. She had said she would call when she landed but he could not calm his apprehension.

"Sit down," Luke flopped down on a row of blue cushioned chairs that lined the perimeter of the room. "Wait for her call."

The boy awkwardly sat in the chair next to him. How could an airport be so empty? His head swiveled back and forth as he searched up and down the terminal, but there was no one there. As if just remembering his phone, he fumbled it free from his pocket and checked the screen—no missed calls, no messages. He kept it out in his hand and his eyes darted from its screen to the terminal and back again. His leg would not stop bouncing against the floor. He could find no comfort in the cushioned chair; he could not stop his muscles from shifting. A sharp pain shot across his chest. Luke said something, but the boy didn't notice. He checked the time; he watched the minutes turn over to the precise time her plane had been scheduled to arrive. He scanned the terminal again. Nothing.

"Sometimes planes are late," Luke said reassuringly. He could see the worry on his roommate's face.

The boy did not respond. Why were there no people? Where was everyone?

It seems unfortunate that certain aspects of this story must be told from hearsay, but, at times, it is the best I have to offer. I must reiterate that I did not know the boy at the time and did not know of Mae, but in order to tell this tale coherently, I must rely on how I heard the boy tell Mae's side of the story to a friend years later.

"I love you and I WILL see you tomorrow!" Mae said.

Her heart was fluttering inside her chest as she spoke softly into the phone from beneath her covers. When she was not standing on her desk to talk to the boy, she could often find herself lying in bed, curled up against the bordering wall. She attributed this position to the belief that as she listened to his voice through the receiver, her body naturally inched its way in the direction of the phone in an attempt to get closer to him. She would not stop until she was pressed against the white plaster.

"I'm curled up to the wall again," she giggled.

"That is the most adorable thing ever, by the way," the boy chuckled, "and I can't wait to replace that wall."

She smiled and nestled closer to the blockade.

"Tomorrow!" she said again. "Are you nervous?"

"A little, but more excited than anything," the boy admitted.

"What if I am not what you expect?" she tried to hide her apprehension.

"That's impossible," he said calmly. "All I expect is you."

She knew that the boy loved her, but she could not escape the feeling that maybe, someday, something would change his mind.

"OK," she tried to swallow her uncertainty, "I love you. I will call you when I land!"

"I love you so much. Goodnight."

Her mother was anchored in the frame of her doorway when she hung up the phone. One hand up on her hip, she stood, her gentle face contorted with worry as she studied the suitcase at the foot of the bed. Mae tucked her cell phone under her pillow and sat up expectantly.

"You are really going, aren't you?"

Mae nodded sympathetically; she knew that there was more to her mother's question than was apparent.

She was an only child and, as such, had greater value to her parents. With multiple children, a mother can spread her love evenly across them, but when there is only one, all the natural love and worry that a mother possesses is channeled to that single offspring. In many cases, this overindulgence can cause a certain level of self-absorption and pretentiousness, but it had the opposite affect on Mae. That exemplary love had made her extraordinarily grateful and had taught her how to pass that care on to others. As a result, her and her mother had become uncommonly close, which made the notion of her leaving especially difficult. She understood her mother's concern. Her only daughter was going to meet a stranger, whom she claimed to love, from another state. If the fact that her daughter was in love wasn't terrifying enough, it was to an unknown boy who would assumably be the cause of her eventual departure from home.

"You can't stay there. I don't know what I would do without you. You know you have to come back, right?" Her mother tucked her hair behind her ear.

"I'm coming back," Mae chuckled. "I'll be home in ten days."

It wasn't until after she said it that she weighed its sincerity. Maybe she wouldn't come back; people had done crazier things for much less than true love. She smiled at the thought, and her mom smiled back.

Falling asleep wasn't easy, but she considered it to be one final obstacle before they could be together. If she could just pass the night, she would be nearly in his arms by morning. She could feel the excitement tingling underneath her skin. All this time of talking, connecting, learning, laughing, missing, and loving—and now, she was finally going to see him. The anticipation was almost unbearable. She closed her eyes and imagined herself there with him. Past the waiting, past the speculation, past the anxiety of their initial contact, she imagined herself in his grasp and she drifted peacefully off to sleep.

Rather than selecting the flight that was most convenient to her schedule, Mae had picked the round-trip tickets with the earliest arrival and latest departure so that she could spend as much time as possible with the boy. Her alarm had tolled early, but her excitement had kept that from mattering. She took her time showering and getting dressed; she wanted to soak in every morsel of enjoyment from that day, and her smile proved it. Her mother did her best to ignore it as they loaded her suitcase into their minivan and drove to the airport. Mae sat in the passenger seat, a blue gift bag of presents for the boy in her lap, and thought of the endless possibilities of the day. It could be anything from instant love to hopeless tragedy. He could sweep her off her feet at first sight, or they could do the awkward dance of flirtation. They could embrace and kiss in a movie scene twirl, or miss recognition and nervously try to compensate with a clumsy handshake or hug. There was even a possibility he would not find her attractive. Obviously, she had sent him the more flattering pictures she could find of herself, some of which were taken a year or so earlier. Flipping down the mirror, she looked at her reflection. What if she looked different now? She could feel her mother watching her out of the corner of her eye as she examined herself in the glass.

"I promise that I will be careful," Mae said, shutting the mirror.

Her mother nodded and eased the van slowly onto the airport exit ramp. Mae could feel her muscles tightening; it was really happening. Soon she would be in the air, then in his arms. She gripped the seat cushion beneath her and bit at her bottom lip. Her mother pulled the van up to the airline entrance, the two said as lengthy a goodbye as the traffic would allow, and Mae grabbed her luggage and was on her way.

To ensure enough time for check-in and security lines, she had given herself an extra hour, which had translated into 45 minutes of sitting at the gate, waiting to board. She tried occupying herself to help the time pass, but her anticipation made her scrutinize every passing minute. She had brought a book, but she could not read it because she could not concentrate on the ink on the pages. She had considered wandering the terminal to look for an early lunch, but that would have required that she haul her bags around with her and the thought of food made her stomach turn; so instead, she sat, watched, and waited. The overall hustle of the airport only intensified her anxiety. A woman moved quickly past her chair, chasing after one child while holding another on her hip. Two tall men in business suits walked the concourse, carrying briefcases and talking urgently to one another. Mae watched as a pack of stewardesses rolled suitcases smoothly along the carpet, muttering and giggling to each other.

"We are looking at about a fifteen-minute delay," the woman at the gate entrance announced over the speaker, and Mae drummed her fingers against the arm of her chair.

Apart from the apprehension about meeting the boy she loved, there was also a certain level of nervousness about doing something that everyone disapproved of that she had to reconcile. The girl had never been one for rash or spontaneous exploits; in fact, most of her decisions were made through clear, responsible reasoning. It was not that she was overly analytical or particular, only that she was a clearheaded, grounded girl who was typically not overly emotional. Her friends and family knew this about her, which is why they disapproved. Not that she blamed them; it was an unusual thing that she was doing, but she was doing it for good reason, and some day they would understand that. Love often requires unusual actions.

She nearly sprung to her feet when the woman announced that they were ready to board the aircraft. Gathering up her things, she moved through the line, down the walkway, and onto the plane. Her seat was a window seat, as requested, next to an older dark-skinned woman who smiled as Mae loaded her suitcase into the compartment overhead and squeezed down the row of chairs. Pulling her cell phone from her pocket, she sat down in her seat and checked the time—twenty minutes behind schedule. The dark-skinned woman watched as Mae typed the words "I'm on my way to you" and sent them to the boy. Turning off her phone, she slid it back into her pocket and sighed deeply.

"How are you?" the dark-skinned woman said in a thick African accent.

Mae wiped her hands against her jeans and smiled.

"I'm fine," Mae replied, her voice fluttering with excitement. "How are you?"

The woman smiled and nodded lazily.

"Is this your first time flying?" she asked sympathetically.

"No," Mae smiled politely and steadied her breathing. The woman must have thought that her nervousness was a result of the flying. "I am meeting someone for the first time today, someone pretty important."

"Who?" The woman had a certain maternal care that flowed through her voice.

"My boyfriend," Mae laughed shyly. "It's kind of a long story." She tucked her hair behind her ear.

"Well, luckily, we have some time," the woman smiled wide, the white of her teeth distinctly contrasting the black of her skin.

So, as the plane cruised 36,000 feet over the tiny tracks of civilization, Mae began to tell the woman the story of the boy and their love. At first, her voice was calm and casual, as if talking to a stranger about the weather, but as the story progressed and more emotions became involved, her voice grew more passionate and descriptive. Passengers in nearby seats began to lean closer and listen in as she described the events leading up to that day. The audience of strangers grew exponentially with the passion in her voice as the story went on. Every so often, a voice would interrupt to ask for more details about something she had mentioned or to repeat an earlier portion of the story they had missed. It is amazing how much people thrive for romance. Complete strangers will congregate together and stretch and climb and beg just to taste a piece of true, unabashed, enchanting romance. They were mystified zombies, men and women alike, eyes glazed with fascinated fixation.

"So," Mae said, as she finished the story, "he is picking me up from the airport today!"

With dreamy sighs and misty eyes, the spectators smiled and purred, some touching her arm and smirking enviously as they shifted back into their seats. Mae wore a beaming smile of her own moments later when the pilot announced that the plane was on time

181

and that they were beginning their descent. The dark-skinned woman next to her grabbed her hand, squeezed, and winked as the aircraft began lowering in circles to the ground. Mae smiled back and looked out the window. Her breathing was long but shaky as she watched the buildings and cars below increase in size in the window picture frame. A soft humming rose up through the floor of the plane and up her back where it resonated in her chest. She squeezed the woman's hand tighter and pressed her other hand against her ribcage as the plane sank lower. She was only moments away now. Her muscles were tingling. The woman in the seat in front of her turned around and smiled. She could feel slight tremors dancing through her body as she attempted to smile back. The woman rubbed her thumb gently across the girl's knuckles. Something rattled inside her chest. Pressing her fingers against her ribs, between her quickening heartbeats, she could feel something whipping against the walls of her torso. Closing her eyes, she held her breath as the wheels of the plane made contact with the asphalt runway and the wings slowed themselves through the manipulation of air.

"Come on, girl!" the dark-skinned woman said as soon as the plane had come to a stop and the seatbelt lights were off.

All of the eyes of her earlier audience were on her as she unfastened the buckle. They remained in their seats as she stood up and moved down the row. A muscular man in a tight T-shirt had stood and pulled her luggage down from the overhead compartment. Other than that, no one else moved from their seats.

"Here you go," the man said, once she had made it to the aisle. "Go get him."

Taking the handle of her suitcase, she hurried down the rows of chairs. Applause and calls followed her as the crowd behind her cheered and shouted for the other passengers to clear the pathway. Laughing hysterically, she made her way up the open aisle to the front of the plane and up the walkway. As she spilled out of the gate entrance and into the terminal, she paused to catch her breath. The concourse was swarming with people. It was mid-afternoon and the day before spring break. Business suits and briefcases intermingled with bathing suits and boogie boards as flocks of people moved among the gates. The sweet scent of sticky buns blended with the hasty smell of fast food and filled her nostrils as she moved quickly toward the exit. She could still feel the deep pulsations in her chest as she raced past security and out into the main terminal. Her head spun in quick motions as she scanned the entrances in search of the face she had memorized from pictures. While the concourse was filled with traffic, the terminal itself was fairly empty; she felt confident that she would recognize him. Moving closer to the glass exit doors, she dropped her suitcase and searched again. Her body teetered as she hoisted herself up on her tip-toes and scoured the faces of the increasing number of people filing into the corridor. Her heart was racing; she could feel it thumping inside her head. Her mouth was dry and her chest was expanding with electrifying pressure. She paced back and forth in front of her suitcase, her anxiety growing with each passing second. Frantically digging down into her pocket, she pulled her phone free—no missed calls, no messages. She had said she would call. Flipping it open, she dialed the boy's number, tried to steady her breath, and put the phone to her ear.

No sooner had Luke mentioned the possibility of the plane arriving late than a small crowd of people came pouring over the top of the stairs and down into the corridor. The boy jumped to his feet and centered himself near the bottom of the steps, skimming the faces of each person as they moved past him and out through the glass doors. A girl with dark hair and a suitcase mounted the top of the steps. Her face was uncertain as he followed her down the stairs with his eyes. His heart quickened its pace. He craned his neck for a better view. About halfway down the steps, she looked up and he caught her eyes; it wasn't her. Shaking his head, he moved back to search the thinning crowd. Luke had risen to his feet behind the boy and stood with his hands in his pockets, his face doubtful. The boy's shoulders slumped and he heaved a sigh. Had his phone not been out, still clenched in his fist, he probably would not have heard it ring over the noise of the dispersing crowd. His heart leaped as he read her name across the screen and opened the phone to his ear.

"Hey!" he said, his chest vibrating with excitement.

"Hey!" she echoed the excitement. "I'm here!"

She had returned to her tip-toes and was sidestepping back and forth among the crowd.

"Where?" He spun in a circle scanning the room.

"I just landed," she laughed nervously. "Where are you?"

"I'm at the airport," he smiled. "Right by the main entrance."

"Main entrance...." she was glancing at the labels on the sign overhead. "I'm not sure where that is...."

"Where are you?" the boy was pacing up and down the corridor again, hopping to look up or down the flights of stairs.

"I'm not sure," her voice shook with anticipation. They both laughed. "I'm, um, I think I'm by the main entrance."

The boy ran back to where he'd first come in.

"I'm by the main entrance!" he teased. Luke was chuckling and shaking his head in disbelief. "What do you see? Tell me what you see."

The boy tapped his hand against his chest to keep from jumping up and down.

"Um," Mae giggled, "I'm near some sliding glass doors...." The boy looked at the row of sliding doors behind him. "...there are some big red pillars...."

He spun in another circle. He didn't see any pillars.

"Big red pillars...?" he muttered.

They sounded familiar. He knew he had seen them somewhere but he could not recall. He checked the immediate area again. He had seen them somewhere at the airport before.

"There are yellow and blue signs...." she continued.

The dark-skinned woman who had sat next to her on the plane was walking out from the gates and into the main terminal. Seeing Mae, she gave a concerned look from across the corridor.

He looked at the signs above him—they were all green.

"Yellow and blue signs??" he asked slowly.

"Yea..." her throat tightened, "yellow and green signs that say 'BWI.'"

A wave of nausea crashed over the boy. His head swooned, his mouth dried out, his jaw dropped open, his chest clenched up, and his hands tingled.

"BWI...? In Baltimore...?" he repeated hesitantly.

"Yeah!" her voice reflected obvious concern, "BWI. In Baltimore. What's wrong?!!"

The boy was speechless. He remembered where he had seen the big red pillars before—at the airport at home, not at the one at school. For hours every day of the previous two weeks, they had talked and planned and longed for the coming of that day, but not once had they talked about which airport she would be flying into. He had given her his credit card and told her the two most convenient airports, she had bought the ticket and given him her flight number, but he hadn't even thought to ask which of the two airports she had chosen. He was in Harrisburg, Pennsylvania; she was in Baltimore, Maryland—two hours apart.

"You're in Baltimore...? I...I'm at the Harrisburg airport."

He braced himself. The air caught in Mae's throat and the color flushed from her face. She could not believe what she was hearing. The dark-skinned woman's smile faded when she saw Mae's eyes and she rushed to her side.

"Don't worry!" the boy fumbled. "I'm sorry! I can fix this. It would take me two hours to get there, but I know people who are closer. I will find someone to get you. Don't worry!" He was talking to the both of them. "Are you OK? I don't want you to be alone, but I gotta make some calls to find you a ride."

"Yeah," her throat released the air. "It's fine - I'm fine. I met this woman on the plane. She is really sweet. She is with me now." Mae smiled at the woman who stood next to her.

"Alright baby, let me make a call. I'm sorry. I love you. I will call you back right after." He forced his voice to be calm and comforting.

"OK," she did the same, "I love you."

"Hey," he said just before she hung up. "Welcome to Baltimore."

"Thanks," she laughed.

Once he had hung up the phone, he became slightly more frantic. He just wanted to make sure she was safe. Luke could see the worry in his eyes and moved quickly to his side.

"Is there any way we can take your car to Baltimore?" the boy

185

asked reluctantly.

Luke checked his watch and contorted his lips.

"Not right now," his roommate replied, "I've got class in an hour. We could go after?" He offered.

The boy shook his head. He couldn't make her wait that long. He scrolled through the names in his phone.

"I'm going to call my mom," the boy said quickly. She had heard the story; she would understand.

"I need a favor," he said as soon as his mother had answered the phone. "It's kind of a big one."

"What is it?" she asked, and he explained the details of his predicament.

"OK. She is there now?" she said once he had finished.

"Yeah, she is with some lady she met on the plane."

"Alright," his mother said decisively. "Dad and I will go get her. Then what? Do you want us to bring her to your house—to you?"

"Yeah, if you can." It was a hefty request, but his mother knew the story of their love and she respected his determination; she agreed, and her voice sounded almost eager to be a part of their saga.

As soon as Luke and the boy were back in the car, they each lit up a cigarette and headed home. The boy tossed the bouquet of flowers he had bought onto the backseat and rolled down the window. He chuckled as he tuned the radio to "Rain King" by Counting Crows. He turned up the volume, took a deep drag of his smoking stick, and the two drove home in silent reverence.

When they pulled into the driveway, Ryan and Seth were standing on the front lawn, throwing a Frisbee. As Luke put the car in park and the two climbed out, Seth flicked the flying disc to his roommate, but Ryan had his hands up in a shrug as he looked at the boy, and the disc floated to the ground.

"What happened?" Ryan asked. "Where is she?"

The boy snatched the flowers up off the backseat and closed the car door. Awkwardly ignoring the question, Luke pushed his keys into his pocket and walked slowly up the driveway.

"I'm an idiot," the boy answered as he walked toward the house.

"No you aren't," Luke chuckled. He turned to Ryan, still in his confused stance. "We went to the wrong airport. She's in Baltimore."

"What?!" Seth exclaimed.

"What are we going to do?" Ryan asked.

"My parents are bringing her here," the boy shrugged.

"Look at it this way," Luke said as the four walked into the house, "at least it will make a good story some day."

Once in his room, the boy flopped down on his bed and waited. The bundle of flowers dripped droplets of filmy water on the comforter next to him as he folded his hands behind his head and stared at the ceiling. It was only half an hour or so before his mother called the first time.

"We got her!" she said.

"Thank God!" the boy shot up in his bed. "Is she OK?! Is everything alright?!"

"She's fine," his mother laughed. "Nervous, but fine. The woman from the plane waited until we got here. We're going to stop to get her some food because she hasn't eaten all day, and then we will be there."

"Alright, just hurry!" He dropped his head back to his pillow and massaged his forehead.

His chest felt constricted. How could he have made such a foolish mistake? He wanted everything about that day to be perfect. All he would have had to do was ask which airport. Had he only been more thorough, she would have been with him at that very moment. He picked up the flowers from the bed and smelled them before laying them across his burning chest.

It was nearly dark by the time his mother called him the second time.

"Where are you??" he sprang up from the mattress and raced to the window.

The clenching pain in his chest had intensified to a roaring furnace. Flames lapped wildly against the back of his ribcage.

"We are getting close," his mother replied, "just a few more minutes."

Staggering, he caught himself on the windowsill and steadied his breathing. It wasn't that it was painful—it was far beyond that—it was like a part of him was coming alive for the first time. It wasn't painful at all; it was invigorating. He moved quickly to his mirror and checked his appearance; it was presentable. Grabbing up the flowers from his bed, he paced his bedroom floor, his eyes transfixed on the window, his mind anxiously racing, and his hand petting the center of his chest. He could not have known it then, but that furnace inside his chest—that pulsating tremor beneath his ribcage—that was that cracked half of orb where it all started. That was half of the illuminated ball of energy where it all began. It was coming to life, igniting inside of him.

"It won't be much longer," the boy's mother smiled from the passenger seat.

Mae could not steady the quiver in her bottom lip as she sat quietly in the backseat. The boy's parents were extremely nice and had done an exceptional job of making her feel comfortable and welcome, but she could not quiet the significance of the occasion. It came through in the quiver of her lip, the tremble of her voice, the dampness of her palms, and the fire in her chest. Out the window, she saw the sign marking the entrance to the boy's college and his mother turned again and smiled from the front seat.

"Oh my gosh...oh my gosh...oh my gosh...." Mae could not silence her nervous muttering.

She was only a few miles away now. The constriction in her chest made her breathing short and panicked.

"Oh my gosh...oh my gosh...oh my gosh...." she gasped as they rounded the corner just before his house. "I don't think I can get out of the car!"

"You'll be fine," the boy's mother said soothingly.

Mae nodded politely and tried to maintain her composure, but that second half of orb was raging inside of her. It bellowed with blazes equal its counterpart and caused the same forge of intensity beneath her chest. By the time the car pulled into the driveway, both halves were aglow in full burning brilliance. The boy saw the headlights from his room and raced down the hallway. Mae could not stop giggling as she pushed open the back door of the car and lowered one foot to the ground. As he flung open the front door and she stepped out of the car, I swear the two halves of orbs could be heard humming and crackling in the silence of the night. Mae froze at the sight of him; the boy's legs were anchored to the front porch. She couldn't believe she had actually found her way to him. He couldn't believe she actually existed. It was the girl from his dream; there was no way to deny it. It was Sally. Her black hair was up in little butterfly clips as she stood paralyzed in his driveway. He was under the spotlight of his front porch, flowers dangling in one arm, glued to the concrete.

"She's absolutely perfect," the boy whispered to himself.

"I can't believe I'm here," Mae whispered to the night.

In seven euphoric, ecstatic leaps from either side, they were in each other's arms, twirling in the natural magic of the clear night air. The two halves of orb erupted with sparks that rained down among them like the stars overhead. The boy instantly thought of the dream; Mae instantly felt at home.

"I have missed you for SO long!" the boy laughed.

"Tell me about it!" Mae laughed back.

He could not figure how to allow his hand to release hers as he introduced her to his roommates and gave her a quick tour of the house. It seemed that every room or object he showed her added new meaning to the conversations they had had on the phone over the previous three months. He showed her his room last.

"This is where I lie in bed and talk to you, where I fall asleep and dream of you, and where I wake up and think of you," he told her. She wrapped her arms around him and squeezed as tight as she could.

"Open your present!" she lifted up the blue gift bag.

On top of the tissue paper that protruded from the bag was a small black card. She had made it herself. On the front was one of the more successful superimposed pictures of the two of them. She had printed it from her computer and burned the edges for artistic flare. The boy opened the card. Taped to the inside was a small rectangular card with a note below it that read, "I've been saving this for you since the Renaissance festival in October! =) Don't worry, it's only one."

Peeling the small rectangle free from the tape, he read it, "This card entitles the bearer to one free kiss from any willing man, woman, or beast."

"The best part about that card," she explained, "is that they told me that if the recipient of that card gives it back to the person who gave it to them, they get free kisses whenever they want."

He smiled and raised his eyebrows. Turning his eyes back to

the black card, he read the inner flap to himself: "Hopefully after this week we'll have some real pictures together! =) I can't believe I'm going to see you today (it's 3:37 am). I've been missing you for so long. I love you so much! So I know this card and the little gift are a little cheesy. I was going to do more but I sorta ran out of time and I've had some of this stuff for months. So anyway, I just wanted to tell you that you mean more to me than anything. You mean the world to me. I need you so bad, I love you so much, and I can't wait to see you today! P.S. Be careful when you open the bag. I brought some friends from Texas with me.... Love you, Mae." Pulling the tissue paper free revealed two large plastic tarantulas.

"I told you to be careful!" she said as they both laughed.

Reaching farther into the bag, the boy lifted a book from inside.

"This is incredible," he said as he examined it.

It, too, was homemade. The beige covers were constructed of a hard material that she had wrapped in paper. A row of small holes lined one end of the covers, which she had laced through with black twine to bind the book. Midway down the inside of each cover, a string ran across the backing of the book and was knotted on the exterior of either side so that the book could be tied shut. The front was scourged, again with artistic flair, revealing a misshapen square of black paper on which she had written a collection of Counting Crows lyrics: "There's things I remember and things I forget. I miss you...I guess that I should. 3,500 miles away, but what would you change if you could? I need a phone call...," "I'm in the mood for you...for running away," and "I don't know if I'm wide awake or dreaming, but all I ever need is...everything." The inside cover read, "I love you...I need you...I want you... the most." He had found his heaven.

That night, they lay in his bed together. She smiled at her picture on the wall above the mattress while he traced her face with his finger.

"I love you," he said, "more than I ever thought I could love anything. Probably more than I should."

She leaned closer to him.

"I love you," she smiled, "certainly more than I should."

They closed their eyes and their lips met. It was love to the fullest. Nothing could have been better as they lay in bed together that night. Everything was aligned and in order as it should have been. Sometimes Fate does get it right. They were in love; they were together. The two halves of the orb were connected and whole again.

thirteen

The impartial blaze of the glowing morning sun scattered through the prismatic glass pane of the boy's window and danced against their yawning cheeks as they lay in bed. The house was quiet except for their giggles, chuckles, and whispered "Good morning"s. They savored the first half hour of that day—laying and talking, expressing their feelings of excitement while the rest of the world slept. They did not need the socialization or gratifications of civilization; they found complete satisfaction in one another's company.

"Promise that you will never stop loving me," the boy said.

He was studying the metal tin that sat on his floor. The planted Remedy that it contained had been delivered to him sometime earlier that week. He had told her that they would be bringing it along and she knew what that meant for him, but he had not fully accepted the idea of backsliding. Mae lifted her head from his chest and turned to face him.

"I've done a lot of stupid things," he went on, "and I am probably going to do some more, but I will always be honest, and my heart will always be yours. I just need to know that it's the same for you. I need you to love me no matter how dumb I may be at times."

Her brow furrowed, "I will always love you. There is no doubt of that in my mind, no matter what you do. I will never let you go, no matter how far you run. You don't understand; I would die without you."

She lowered her head back to his rising chest and he stroked her hair with his fingers, his eyes still on the tin. Everything he had worked for and everything he had survived had brought him to that moment.

A light knock on the door broadcasted the awaking of his roommates and the start of their day. Once they were out of bed and dressed, Luke, Ryan, Mae, the boy, and their five other friends that they had invited loaded up the three cars that the trip required. It was the first time that the boy had the opportunity to watch her interact with others. He watched the way her figure moved as she helped carry supplies from the house to the car. He chuckled at how her nose crinkled when she smiled or laughed. When she saw him observing her, she would wink or stick out her tongue or stop to kiss him.

"Good work, man," Luke said when he noticed the enthrallment in the boy's eyes.

"Yeah," the boy nodded, "so long as I don't screw it up." He was mindlessly stroking the scars on his hand.

It was a seven-hour drive from the college to the beach. Luke drove his car and had offered Mae and the boy to ride with him. For the first two hours, they rode together in the backseat, leaving the passenger chair empty. They simply could not find a reason good enough to justify spending one precious moment apart. Luke didn't seem to mind; he talked on his cell phone and tuned his radio while the two lovers held hands and conversed behind him. Sometime in the third hour Mae had fallen asleep, so, at the next stop for gas, the boy moved to the front seat to keep his friend company.

"It's going to be a fun trip!" the boy said once his seatbelt was buckled.

"Yeah, man," Luke responded excitedly, "I'm really looking forward to it!"

Drawing a cigarette from his pack, the boy lit and cracked his window. He turned around in his seat to ensure that the wind did not disturb her; she was dozing peacefully.

"She looks like an angel when she sleeps," the boy remarked, exhaling smoke from his lungs.

"You think she looks like an angel all the time!" Luke teased.

"I know," the boy turned back around, "I can't help it."

By the time she awoke, they were nearly to their destination and the two boys were buried deep in a philosophical conversation.

"I'm not saying that it doesn't make me angry," the boy was

preaching, "I'm just saying that people are a product of their environment. The reason that you are where you are right this moment is because of your surroundings and experiences—bottom line."

She smirked; it was his passion that she loved. He was passionate about his morals and they were almost identical to hers, which was important. She did her best to remain undiscovered so as not to disturb their conversation, but the boy had developed an uncontrollable routine of checking on her and after a few moments noticed her rousing.

"Hey," he said sweetly, "how was your nap?"

"Good," she smiled, stretching her limbs. "How long did I sleep?"

"A few hours; we're almost there."

"I'm sorry," she yawned, "I shouldn't have been wasting our time together with sleep! Who needs sleep?"

He winked and she smiled.

The house looked exactly as they had seen in the pictures—a stilted, single-level with blue siding; a flight of weather-worn wooden stairs that led to a large, equally worn deck; and an unusual number of windows and sliding glass doors. As soon as they opened the car doors they could smell the familiar salty air of the beach. The boy's flip-flops crunched against the sandy driveway as he hoisted open the trunk and carried his bag and Mae's suitcase up the stairs. The words "Pelican Watch" were written in big white letters across the front of the house. The boy studied them as he walked inside; he wanted to remember everything about that week. The sliding front door opened up to a spacious living room decorated with two plush couches, a wooden coffee table, and a meager television. Connected to the living room, and sharing the same four walls, was a slightly smaller kitchen. Vinyl cabinets lined the right wall and overhung a laminate countertop that ran the length of the wall and extended out in an L-shape, dividing the living room and kitchen and serving as an eating area with four bar stools that sat on the living room side. A glossy, wooden dining room table occupied most of the left side of the kitchen and sat in front of the door to the back deck. In either wall, midway between the kitchen and living room, were doorframes that led immediately to three dark, lightweight doors. The doors directly ahead opened to a small bathroom with laminate flooring. The doors to the left and right led to bedrooms. The boy took the doorframe to the right of the kitchen and pushed through the bedroom door on the right. It opened to a cozy room with a king-sized bed and sliding glass doors that allowed access to the front deck. Mae's eyes were exploring as she came trotting in behind him.

"Good?" he asked, assessing the room.

She nodded, and he dropped their luggage down onto the bed. Once the others had agreed on sleeping arrangements, they all congregated back in the living room.

"Well, here we are. We made it!" Luke said.

"Let's celebrate," the boy agreed. "Drinks?"

"Yeah!" one of the girls they had invited exclaimed. "Make me something tasty!"

Mae nodded her head emphatically, and the boy mixed up a couple of frozen chocolate drinks. The girls toasted and began sucking down their liquid Remedies while the boy poured a few rum and cokes for himself and his comrades, who drank them down nearly as quickly.

"Let's play a game!" someone suggested, so they spent the next few hours of the evening sitting at the kitchen table, drinking and playing games.

The more they drank, the more the boy noticed Mae watching him with eager eyes and a devious smile. He shared her same sentiment; they had been longing to get to one another for so long. It was only natural that they should want to spend time together apart from the crowd, but they behaved themselves and remained social, only occasionally reaching under the table to squeeze a knee or rub a calf with a foot.

"Show us that fire trick you used to do," Luke said to the boy once they had lost interest in the game.

Jumping up from the table, Luke rushed into the bathroom and found a bottle of rubbing alcohol. Carrying it back out into the living room, he began searching for the next required item. The boy rose to his feet.

"This will work," the boy motioned to the polyester sleeve of the jacket he was wearing.

It was a trick he had learned in high school. Back then, they had used tennis balls, but he figured any similar material would work. Unscrewing the lid, the boy doused his sleeve with the alcohol.

"What are you doing?!" Mae laughed as she moved from the kitchen to the living room.

The boy winked at her with assurance. The others crowded closer around as the boy pulled a lighter from his pocket, sparked the flame, and touched it to his outstretched arm. The fire spread quickly across the area where he had poured the alcohol and danced in bright blues and greens. What he had learned in high school was that the fire never actually became hot; it only burned the alcohol out of the material. At the time, he and his high school friends had soaked tennis balls in the liquid, set them on fire, and tossed them around, never once burning their hands. After a few rum and cokes, he had applied the same principle to his jacket sleeve, and his friends cheered and laughed as he moved his flaming arm in circular motions through the air. Mae's wide eyes were equally full of excitement and concern as she watched. One of the basic stipulations of the stunt that the boy had forgotten was that the performer had to be mindful of how long he allowed the fire to burn. Eventually, all the alcohol would evaporate into the flame, and the tennis balls would start to singe unless more liquid was applied. This fact had completely escaped the boy's mind and, after a full minute of entertaining the crowd, he started to feel a slight tingling along his forearm. Within a few seconds, the tingling became a searing sensation and the boy shook his arm wildly until the flames were out.

"Whoa, dude!" Ryan said, observing the jacket sleeve.

The polyester had melted into a narrow black-trimmed hole that stretched a quarter the length of the sleeve. The skin beneath was red, and the hairs on his arm were burned off.

"I burned myself," the boy chuckled, holding his arm up to Mae.

"Oh my goodness!" she exclaimed, checking the wound. "Are you OK?!"

"I'm like steel baby!" he wrapped his arms around her and lifted her off the ground. "Nothing can stop me!"

Rolling her eyes, she threw her arms around his neck and kissed him. The jagged edges of the hole in his sleeve scratched against the tender skin of his burn as he held her up in the air, but he ignored it. Any amount of pain was worth feeling her lips against his. He dropped her back down to the ground and she staggered backward, giggling and wiping the corner of her mouth.

"I need a cigarette after that fiasco," Luke said to the boy. "Wanna come?"

The boy nodded.

"I wanna come!" Mae said, tracing the boy's hand with her fingers.

"Well, come on then," he kissed her on the forehead and the three walked outside.

The soothing night air was warm and carried a light oceanic breeze as Luke and the boy walked down the wooden steps and placed cigarettes between their lips.

"That stunt did not go as planned," he said, flicking his lighter.

"I still thought it was cool," Luke replied, puffing smoking from the white stick.

Mae leaned against the railing of the staircase, about halfway down, and watched the boys. Her smooth black hair was messily collected in a clip at the back of her head, and she wore her black, oval, plastic glasses. Most of the time she did without the glasses; the boy did not understand why. Either way, she was a walking dream.

"Can I have one?" she asked from the steps. The boy's eyes widened. "My mom smokes," she excused, "and sometimes I like to have one when I drink."

Pinching one out his pack, he handed it to her. He certainly was not going to be a hypocrite. He held a lighter to the end, and she puffed the stick smoothly. There was something extra attractive about adding a cigarette to her ensemble. She held it coolly, her other arm wrapped across her stomach, and took casual magnetic drags. Shaking his head, he scolded himself. He would not condemn her smoking, but he certainly could not encourage it.

"But," he thought to himself, "having one 'sometimes when she drinks' was just fine."

Because of the long drive and early start, they all agreed to an early night. Mae and the boy went back into their bedroom and closed the door. She went into the bathroom to wash off her make-up and change into a T-shirt and a pair of shorts while the boy slid off his jeans and climbed under the covers. Once she had finished getting ready for bed, she came back into the bedroom and closed the door behind her.

"Why do you even trouble yourself with makeup?" the boy asked, seeing her for the first time without it. "You are naturally gorgeous."

"Yeah, right," she said with doubtful eyes.

Flipping off the light switch, she climbed under the covers and hugged up against him. The sweet smell of her perfume drifted from her hair as he traced his fingers along her feathery skin. He pressed his lips against her cheek as she nestled her face to his. Prior to their meeting, the two had agreed that there were certain boundaries that their morals would not allow them to cross. Up to that point, they had both stayed pure and true to their beliefs, and they intended to remain that way for one another until they both decided that it was time. They had realized the desire that their love would evoke long before they had met and had resolved to draw the line and test their self-control. I will respect the details of where that line was drawn and what precisely took place behind that closed door, but I will tell you that it was the most beautifully innocent exploration of intimacy that I have ever heard of. I will tell you that they tasted the long anticipated, savory flavor of one another's skin and that he worshipped the graceful movements of her delicate silhouette that appeared in the light that shone underneath the door. They whispered to one another and frolicked between the sheets until the slim traces of sunlight could be seen cutting over the horizon and through the curtain of their glass door. Only then did they surrender to the necessity of sleep and collapse in each other's arms.

The boy was the last to awake the next morning. Mae was in the kitchen sipping coffee and talking to his friends when he came staggering out of the bedroom. Her eyes lit up the moment she saw him, and he could tell she was restraining herself from rushing to him.

"Good morning," she said, flashing an allusive smile.

"Hey," he yawned, moving into the kitchen, "Sorry. I didn't realize everyone was up." He kissed her softly on her lips. "What's the plan for today?"

He picked up an apple from the bowl of fruit on the counter, another business expense. They had given a grocery list and a few hundred dollars to one of the girls who would be accompanying them and she had purchased the week's groceries the day before they had left.

"It's pretty cloudy out," Ryan complained, "no sense in trying to go to the beach today. Plus the water is like ice. I checked it this morning."

"So, you want to just hang out here?" the boy asked, polishing the red fruit against his shirt.

"We might as well," Luke said, flopping down on the couch.

"Maybe we should go out tonight," the boy crunched into the apple, "drive around and see if there's anything going on."

"That sounds good," Ryan said, and everyone else agreed. "But in the meantime...." He picked up his guitar and motioned the boy to do the same.

Taking another bite from his apple, the boy scooped up his guitar and sat down on the couch. The two had decided to bring their instruments for such an occasion.

"I've never heard him play," he heard Mae say to one of the other girls.

Since the accident, he had stopped playing as frequently. It was frustrating to attempt to do something that he used to do so well. Ryan had never been in a band but had played a fair amount by himself and enjoyed it. Sometimes at school he would suggest that the two of them play together, but the boy would usually decline. He preferred playing alone in his room. The only reason he accepted at the beach was for Mae. She sat down on the sofa next to him and watched as the two boys tuned their guitars.

"What do you want to play?" Ryan asked, mindlessly strumming a chord. The boy shrugged.

"Any requests?" Ryan asked the room.

That was always the worst idea. The requests came raining down from every corner of the room and the two wound up playing for an hour.

"Let me hear you play," the boy said to Mae, once they had finally called an end to the crowd's demands.

"No," Mae objected, "I'm really terrible."

199

The boy picked up the two guitars and moved into the kitchen.

"I doubt that," the boy said when they were alone. "Show me what you got."

Sighing, Mae took Ryan's guitar in her lap and positioned her hands carefully. Nervously plucking the strings with her fingers, she played out the melody to "Blackbird" by The Beatles flawlessly.

"That's fantastic!" the boy exclaimed. She really was good. "You've got to teach that to me!"

He picked up his guitar and watched as she chuckled and played the melody again. Mimicking her fingers, he played the first few notes of the song. She smiled.

"Then you go...," she said as she played the next cluster of notes.

He clumsily tried to imitate. Someone snapped a picture from across the room.

"No, like this...," she played it again, and he mirrored the notes. "There you go!"

The last sequence of notes was the hardest. She plucked them three or four times before he caught on. He watched as she played it once more from the beginning, then the two of them played it together.

"Good job!" she congratulated him. "It took me two weeks with my teacher to learn that song and you got it in five minutes!"

"I had a better teacher," he said and kissed her lips.

They spent the rest of the afternoon laughing and playing cards with the group. After dinner, they all went to their rooms and got dressed for the night out. One of their friends was convinced that they would find a nightclub of some sort and insisted that they dress accordingly; so, they all reemerged into the living room in the classiest clothes they had packed, snapping pictures. Naturally, Mae looked like a goddess. She wore a sleeveless red top that tied behind her neck, smooth black pants, and black dress shoes. Her makeup was perfect and her scarce jewelry accented her beauty. The boy could not keep from staring as they loaded into the car. Two of their friends had decided to skip the excursion, making it possible for everyone to fit into two cars. Luke drove his car with Ryan in the passenger seat and Mae and the boy in the back. They led the way while their three friends followed in the car behind them. They turned down the coastal highway, but the road was dark and all the businesses looked closed. Mae and the boy huddled together in the backseat and looked at the stars through the sunroof. Luke pulled in and out of shopping centers and drove up and down side streets while Mae and the boy kissed and swayed to either side with the sharp turns of the car. Ryan and Luke argued in the front seat about which way to go, but the music was loud enough in the back that they were not disturbed. Luke smoked frustrated cigarettes, but the air from his window swirled around the backseat in romantic gusts.

"Did you just say 'birt-day?'" the boy teased Mae.

"Yeah!" she said. "My cousin's birt-day!"

"As in 'birthday'?" he emphasized the correct pronunciation, and she giggled.

"I'll admit, your way is much cuter," he said, and the two laughed.

"Any ideas?" Luke turned the music down and asked the two. They had been driving in circles for almost an hour.

"I say we call it quits. There's nothing going on. Let's head back," the boy suggested.

Ryan agreed and they drove back to the house.

"That was a lovely backseat date," the boy said, opening the car door for Mae.

She still looked gorgeous. The frustrations of the evening had ruined the night for their friends, who had all gone to bed disgruntled. Still wrapped up in the enchantment of their evening, Mae and the boy decided on a walk along the beach. They slipped off their socks and shoes and let their feet press against the cool wet sand. The air was calm and clean as the two strolled along the shore, their hands interlocked. The moon mirrored itself against the docile sea as it lured foamy splashes of water that filtered down into the sand alongside their path.

"Do you really believe in something lasting forever?" she asked as they walked.

The boy watched a wave glide up the beach and stop just short of their feet, leaving only a faint outline of its existence in the sand.

"I have to," he replied. "If I don't have you forever, I don't know what I'll do. Nothing will ever matter at all after what I've had with you."

"Don't worry," she squeezed his hand. "You have me forever. No matter what happens, I will always love you."

The two walked on in silent appreciation of the beauty of the night. The soft hiss of the churning of the sea sang in their ears from one side as the tall blades of grass that scaled the hills bordering the sand swayed together in tapping applause from the other. Occasionally a small sea crab would scurry across their path, appearing almost translucent in the moonlight.

"Look!" Mae said, pointing back.

Their footprints were embedded in paths of wet sand that blended into one single trail behind them. There was just enough light from the dimly lit sky to trace the trail back into the darkness. Taking her camera from her pocket, Mae squatted and took a picture.

"Now there is proof that we were here together," she said, rising to her feet. "One trail." She smiled into his eyes and kissed him gently.

Back in their bedroom at the house, the two repeated the activities of the previous night, only this time she did not leave the room to change and he studied the softness of her curves in the overhead light.

The boy was the last one awake for the second time in a row, but Mae still indented the mattress beside him. Her eyelids fluttered as she watched him stir. He could hear the muffled clanging of pans and strumming of guitars through the bedroom door.

"Good morning, beautiful," he said, stroking her cheek with his knuckles.

She smiled and kissed his fingers.

"What can we do today?" she asked.

The boy turned his head to look through the glass of the door in their room; the sun was shining a blinding white.

"It looks nice out," he turned back to her, "let's go back to the beach."

She agreed and the two got dressed and ventured out into the living room. Ryan was sitting on the sofa, softly strumming his guitar, his eyes mesmerized by the television. Luke lay on the floor, lids half open, hands folded behind his head. The other five assumed similar positions in front of the small screen.

"Anyone interested in checking out the beach today?" the boy asked the apathetic group.

"Uh," Ryan shook his head, "it's too cold today, man."

The others agreed with their silence, so Mae and the boy walked to the beach alone. The air carried a slight chill, but it was counterbalanced by the radiance of the sun. Mae stood in front of the ocean and shielded her eyes as the boy snapped a photograph. They walked again down the sandy shore and found a pile of large black bundles. The boy was unsure as to what the bundles contained, but they looked harmless, so the two climbed on top of them and sat to watch the ocean. They talked and laughed for hours, taking pictures of one another and drinking in the beauty of their love among the beauty of nature.

By the time they had walked back to the house, the sun was setting in the western sky. The air had gotten cooler and the waves less intense.

"You see that way over there?" the boy pointed in the direction of the sun. "That's where you live—just over there; and all I'm trying to do is keep you over here."

She took his hand as they walked and laid her head against his shoulder.

Their housemates greeted them at the door with freshly made cocktails, and with a "clank" and a "thud" Mae and the boy joined in on the debacle in progress. Music played loudly through the stereo and the blender roared as they toasted to being young. Mae finished her first drink quickly and the boy grinned as she popped open a can; she was the best of both worlds. He stirred himself another cocktail and Luke aligned a row of small glasses on the kitchen table. He filled each to the brim with liquid Remedy and passed them around the room.

"To spring break!!" Luke hollered, and all the glasses clanked before the tepid liquid was poured down their throats.

The boys laughed as the girls scrunched up their faces and stuck out their tongues in disgust. Luke lined three more glasses up on the table and filled them to the top. Mae winked at the boy as she moved back toward the couch and he raised his eyebrows in return.

"Hey! Hey!" Luke called. "Here we go!" He handed a glass to the boy and one to Ryan. "This one is to roommates!"

"To roommates!!!" Ryan and the boy cheered. Clank. Thump. Swallow.

"Seriously," Ryan put his hands on their shoulders, "you guys are the best. I'm serious. I wouldn't want to live with anyone else. I love you guys."

"You too, man," the boy agreed. "Another! It's getting too emotional over here!"

So, Luke staggered the glasses again and sloshed them to the brim. Clank. Thump. Swallow.

The frosty liquid drained from the can down the boy's throat as he tilted his head back. Most of the large bottle of liquid Remedy had been divvied into the smaller glasses and thrown down into their stomachs. Someone had suggested a card game, so they sat down at the table and shifted the cards around. Stacks of empty cans crowded the wooden spaces between their slouched frames. Lowering the aluminum, the boy looked at Mae in the seat next to him. She was squinting through her glasses' frames at the cards in her hand and wearing a crooked smile.

"I've got to run to the store," Luke said, sliding his chair back quickly. "I need some smokes. Anyone else?"

The boy watched as his friend rose shakily to his feet.

"You are not driving anywhere," one of the girls said. She picked up her keys from the coffee table. "I will take you."

Luke agreed; the girl hardly had anything to drink. Looping her arm into his, she helped him out to the car.

The rest of the group moved to the living room sofas, and Ryan produced a small glass pipe from his suitcase.

"Shall we?" he asked, flashing it to the boy.

He had done a good job the first few days of avoiding contact with the Remedy, but he had agreed to find it, and they had brought it for a reason. Mae was in the midst of conversation with another girl when the boy went to retrieve the metal tin from his bag. Squatting down on the couch next to Ryan, the boy opened the lid and they inhaled the soothing aroma. Ryan passed the smooth pipe and the boy thumbed the planted Remedy into its chamber. His hands froze as Mae turned from her conversation, but she only smiled and shook her head. Sighing relief, he finishing packing the greenery into the glass and was fingering for the lighter in his pocket when Luke came blundering through the front door.

"Hey, hey!" he laughed loudly. "The girl just crashed her car!"

"What?!" the boy lowered the pipe to the table and his eyes shot to the open door behind Luke. "Where is she?? Is she alright?!"

"Yeah, yeah," Luke calmed the crowd, "it's fine. She just bumped into some post. There is a little dent in the bumper, but she's fine."

The girl stepped through the door as Luke was finishing the explanation.

"Hey guys," she chuckled. "I hit one of those stupid wooden posts with my car."

"You did?!" Luke exclaimed before anyone else had a chance to react. "Who was with you?!"

"Uh...," the girl looked confused, "you were."

"Oh yeah!" Luke said as if just remembering. "Holy shit! I was just in an accident!"

The entire room erupted into laughter.

"Why don't you come over here and have a seat, get in on this," Ryan called to Luke, patting the cushion beside him.

His mildly disoriented roommate staggered across the room and flopped down on the couch as the boy took a deep breath and lifted his lighter to the pipe. Spark. Smoke. Inhale. It had been more months than he could remember. The billowing smoke was soothingly scorching as it oozed into his mouth and down his throat. Air came launching up from his stomach, but the boy restrained the cough. As he passed the smoking pipe to Ryan, he noticed Mae sitting down on the cushion next to him. She eyed the device as it moved from the boy's hand to Ryan's then gave a questioning eyebrow to the boy. The shock nearly made him choke. He emptied his lungs and swallowed before responding.

"Yeah, of course!" he took the pipe back from Ryan after he was finished. "Are you sure?"

"Just one," Mae smiled, taking the smooth glass into her hand.

The boy smirked and sparked the lighter to the chamber. Spark. Smoke. Cough. Mae's eyes turned a hazed red as she slumped down into the sofa and dropped her head onto his shoulder.

"You OK?" he asked her.

She giggled and nodded, her eyes closed. The glass continued its linear circulation without her as she rested on his shoulder. Spark. Smoke. Spark. The boy could feel his tingling head swooning. It had been so long. Spark. Cough. Smoke. Little circles of blur swirled in the exterior of his vision. Spark. Spark. Spark. He could feel the dizziness of his head gurgling in the vacancy of his stomach. Inhale. Cough. Inhale. It was too much. Staggering through the kitchen, the boy spilled through the back door and emptied his stomach over the railing. Coughing and hacking, he gulped in mouthfuls of the clear night air. It improved his stomach's condition but did very little to repair his state of mind; his head would not stop rolling. He stumbled back into the house and down the hallway to the bathroom. It was a difficult task for him to maintain his balance against the sink while brushing his teeth, but he managed to achieve it and found his way back to the couch where Mae now was laying. Luke had retired to his bedroom, and the boy could hear the wrenching of Ryan's stomach in the other bathroom. As he kneeled down in front of the sofa, he brushed the loose hairs from Mae's face and kissed her cheek. Even with his lips pressed against her face, he could not hear her breathing. He pressed his hand against the side of her chest and waited. He could not feel the compression of her lungs.

"Baby! Mae!" he whispered harshly. "Mae!" Her head bobbed slightly, and a grunt came from her throat. "Breathe! You're not breathing!"

She drew in one, long, ragged breath and exhaled slowly. The boy's shoulders dropped and he slumped against the cushion, watching as she inhaled a second, shorter breath. Her breathing became more labored and less frequent the longer he observed, until he was convinced again that she was not breathing at all.

"Baby! You've got to breathe!" he rubbed his hand along her shoulder.

She inhaled another deep breath.

"I'm breathing...," she mumbled, but he believed she had

stopped again.

"Please, babe. I'm getting worried! You're not breathing. Take some deep breaths," he shifted nervously in front of her.

Her lips vibrated together as she blew exasperated air lightly between them and giggled. The boy chuckled with relief. Picking her up beneath her arms, he steadied her against his body and carried her back into the bedroom. He pulled off her shoes and socks and positioned her as comfortably as possible underneath the covers before collapsing on the pillow next to her. Forcing himself out of the bed, he changed into a pair of sweatpants he had found in his luggage and fell back onto the mattress. Within minutes, he was asleep.

The boy awoke sometime in the middle of the night to the light shake of Mae's gentle hands on his shoulder. Her hair swung in her silhouette as she straddled the boy's waist, on her knees.

"Baby...breathe...," she said faintly as she shook him. "Breathe...."

After a few seconds, his eyes adjusted better to the light and he noticed that her eyelids were closed.

"I'm breathing, darling," he chuckled, rubbing her arm with his hand.

"OK...," she sighed and flopped over, off his lap, and back onto her pillow.

No one was very early or chipper in emerging from their beds the next afternoon. The sky was overcast, and the wind was more violent than it had been. The boy could hear it lashing against the house as he lay under the covers of their bed, Mae bundled up next to him, whispering about their future. They spent most of the day that way, locked up inside their room exploring one another and talking. Once, the boy had unlocked the door and tip-toed out into the kitchen for a glass of water for Mae, and the house had been dark and quiet. Two of the girls were standing out on the deck in sweatshirts, looking out over the beach, but the boy moved quickly and returned to their room before they could notice him through the glass doors.

"You made it!" Mae said once he had closed and locked the bedroom door.

"Yeah," he smiled, "it was a close call." Handing her the glass of water, he dropped down on the mattress next to her.

"I don't want you to go back," he said. There were only a few days of their vacation left. "This has been the most amazing week of my life. We got off to a rough start there at the beginning with the flight mix-up and all that, but even that turned out well." They both laughed. "It just doesn't make sense for me to lose you. I don't know if I'm ever going to be happy until I see you again."

"I don't want to go!" Mae set her glass down onto the coffee table and moved closer to the boy. "I would give up everything just to stay here with you. In fact, I plan on it. I plan on giving up everything I have in Texas to come be with you. I would do it right this second if I could, but I can't. My mom needs me right now, and I need to finish college—at least this semester; but don't let that worry you. You come visit me, I'll be back down to visit you, and we will do that until I can buy a one-way ticket to you."

The boy smiled as she kissed him firmly on the lips. She was right; they could make this work. They spent the rest of that late afternoon making sparks beneath the sheets.

It was 8 o'clock at night by the time everyone had come out of their rooms, Mae and the boy being the last of them. Murmured "hello"s and moans about the previous night filled the air and affirmed that they had not yet fully recovered as they drifted from their bedrooms and to the kitchen table. Luke made a plateful of pancakes from the surplus of breakfast food, which no one was ever up early enough to consume, and the group of mumbling zombies devoured them in minutes. They all did their best to remain social, and they achieved it for the first few hours, but by midnight the television was dancing a dismal light across their captivated faces. Mae signaled to the boy and he scooped up his cup of ice water and took her hand.

"You guys are nuts!" Ryan called as they dashed back toward the bedroom.

Mae giggled and the boy bit his bottom lip and winked at his roommate, who only shook his head and smiled.

Behind the locked door, they slipped back into their pajamas and between the sheets. Skin flashed on skin, hands made frictional heat, and the two halves of orbs rumbled in the satisfaction of being unified. Her hair fanned like a halo around her head as she lay on her back and fluttered her eyelids. The boy took a mouthful of ice and water from his glass and hovered above her, his muscles twisting and flexing in the faint glow from underneath the door. Swallowing the water, he trapped a single ice cube against the roof of his mouth with his tongue and lowered his lips to her neck. She shivered at the touch of the chill that the ice brought to his mouth, and the boy smiled slyly. Reaching into the glass that sat on the floor next to the bed, he gathered three more cubes from the water.

"It sounds like they are still up," Mae said as she readjusted her head on his chest. "Will it be awkward if we go out there?"

"Probably," the boy lay on his back, stretching the entire length of his body.

"But I want some water...," she said thoughtfully. "I have an idea!"

She jumped up from the bed and tossed her pajamas back to the boy, who watched in bewilderment.

"If we can't avoid it," she said, putting on his sweatpants, "we might as well make a joke out of it."

She pulled his T-shirt over her head and laughed. The legs of the sweatpants ran loosely down her legs and collected in excess bunches at her ankles. The T-shirt was baggy on her shoulders and hung well past her waist. Shaking his head, the boy laughed and held up the pajamas she had thrown at him; they would never fit him. Giggling, she nodded her head assuredly and coaxed him from the bed.

Her pants were thread-popping tight and stopped midway down his shins, and her thin-strap pajama top left his stomach revealed as they strolled out through the living room and into the kitchen. Chuckling at themselves, they grabbed two glasses from the cabinet and filled them with water. Most of their housemates were still awake, but none of them turned their eyes from the light of the television to notice the clothing switch. Shrugging, Mae and the boy walked back toward the bedroom. Their joke had gone to waste.

"Goodnight," the boy said as they walked behind the couches.

"Night," Ryan muttered, turning to see them. "Nuts." He shook his head and went back to the TV.

Earlier in the week, a few of their companions had driven past a state park where they had seen sand dunes and had convinced the others that it would be a fun place to spend their last day. The air was still cool and windy, so they put on light jackets and sweaters and drove to the park. The dunes were enormous and rolled across the horizon as far as they could see. Sand kicked up into their flip-flops and caught in the cuffs of their jeans as they raced up and down the heaping mounds. They watched a hang-glider soar from one of the steeper dunes and took turns rolling down the sand banks. The boy took Mae by the hand and they dashed through the range. They all played "king of the mountain" and laughed loudly at one another's attempt to scale the crumbling slopes. By the time the sun set over the sierra, their muscles were sore and they were out of breath.

Most of their things had been packed up the night before, so the next morning when they woke up, it was merely a matter of transporting everything to the car. All of the others were quick in loading up their belongings and vacating the house, but Mae and the boy took their time. They spent a few extra minutes in their room, her hand around his waist and his around her shoulder, saying goodbye to their time there. For everyone else, it was a fun but rather uneventful trip—the weather was unfavorable, they spent very little time at the beach, and most of their activities were identical to the things they did at home; but for Mae and the boy, the trip was monumental. It was where they had first spent time together, first explored one another, and first felt what it was like to function as a couple. For them, the trip represented the beginning of something great, and they treated it as such. Standing in the quiet emptiness of the house, they sucked in the last remaining moments of their first encounters with love.

Tossing their luggage into Luke's trunk, the boy climbed into the front seat and they started the trip back. Much like the drive there, Mae slept in the backseat while Luke and the boy talked up front. Because she had bought a plane ticket that flew into Baltimore, Mae's flight home would be leaving out of the same airport, so Luke drove the two to the boy's parents' house. Her flight was not until the next morning, so she spent the night there and the two stayed awake as late as they could, discussing the difficulty in saying goodbye.

"I don't know how I'm going to make it," she kept her eyes on the carpet of his bedroom floor.

"I know," he rubbed his hand across his hair. "Me neither; but don't worry, I will be down to visit you as soon as I can. I promise. We just have to get through this semester."

"Do you love me?" she lifted her eyes to his. "Is this really going to work? It's already so hard."

"I love you more than anything," he took her hand in his. "Of course it's going to work. A man can't live without his heart."

The next morning, they shared the backseat of his parents' car as they drove to the airport. His father pulled the car into the lane for departures and stopped outside of Mae's airline entrance. The two climbed out and he lifted her suitcase from the trunk and set it on the curb. Her eyes were watery as he wrapped his arms around her and held her firmly against his heart. He had not cried in nearly two years—not since he had heard the news that he would be moving. It did not surprise him that he was not crying now; he had come to accept the fact that it was something that he could no longer do.

"It won't be too long. I promise," he said, rubbing her back softly while he held her in his grasp.

"It's already too long," she sniffled. Her arms were locked around his stomach. "I feel like my heart is being ripped from my chest."

Her half of the orb moaned and ached.

"I'm sorry," he pressed his lips against her cheek, "I miss you already. I can't stand the thought of being away from you for too long. I will be there soon."

Releasing their arms, they shared one final, lengthy kiss, and she picked up her suitcase and walked away sniffling and wiping her eyes. He stood on the edge of the curb and watched her until she faded into the motion of the crowd.

The tinted window of the car door blocked the sun from penetrating the backseat as he pulled it shut behind him. He kept his attention on the passing of the vehicles as his father turned on the car's blinker and merged back into the flow of traffic. He could feel a faint murmur inside his chest as he buckled his seatbelt and took slow, meticulous breaths. He knew he would be fine as long as he kept his mind occupied.

"So, how was your time together?" his mother asked from the passenger chair.

The boy slumped down in his seat. He could feel a burning

sensation building in the corner of his eyes.

"Good," he tried to make his voice sound apathetic to avoid any further questions.

His mother could sense his apathy and said nothing more. A smile stretched across his face as the burning intensified, and he felt the stinging tingle of his tear ducts expanding. Taking a deep breath, he turned his face upward and toward the tinted window as the liquid began trickling softly down his cheeks. He could not keep from chuckling. It was not that he was no longer able to cry; he just had not felt strongly enough about anything in a very long time.

fourteen

When you fall in love, it is like nothing else you have or ever will experience. It is as if a new person within you has been born. You no longer have the ability to simply acknowledge the essential parts of yourself. When you are born, you are born with all of the natural components of a being—personality, emotions, and perception. Over time, those natural components blend with your personal experiences and construct your basic beliefs, preferences, and knowledge. But when you fall in love, a new aspect of your creation is introduced, an aspect that had gone previous undetected, and it skews your understanding of existence. Every decision and emotion is now made and perceived through the window of that aspect. No longer do you do things out of selfish preferences or personality, but you do them out of the knowledge that love is guiding you—a love that you have come to depend on for guidance; and when that love is taken away, even if only for a short while, you can no longer function as the human being that you have become. It is a terrifying and dangerous condition to linger in, but until that love returns from its slumbering hiatus, you are never truly whole again.

The boy drummed his fingers on the desktop and tried again to retain the information his eyes were scanning on the textbook page, but his mind was on Mae. It had been ten days since she had boarded the plane and been shipped away from him—ten days. Reaching underneath his bed, he pulled out the square metal tin and set it on the desk. Lifting the lid revealed the hard homemade journal she had made for him and a bag of the planted Remedy left over from their trip. He opened the journal and scribbled the words to one of his favorite In-

cubus songs: "You have only been gone ten days, but already I'm wasting away." As he closed the book and returned it to the tin, his eyes
caught sight of the sealed bag and he shuddered. The mere existence
of the substance was a reminder that he had fallen short of his goal.
He needed to rid himself of it. He had tried pawning the remnants off
on Ryan or Luke, and when both had declined, he had stowed it away
and hidden it under his bed. He had considered destroying it, but he
thought that to be a wasteful display of a lack of willpower; if he was
so tormented by it that he needed to eliminate it, he may as well have
smoked it because either way he was defeated. Holding it up to the
light, he surveyed the contents. It was high-quality merchandise, the
kind that his associates from home would have salivated over. Taking
a deep, resolute breath, he dropped the bag on his desk and pulled his
phone from his pocket. He certainly knew how to dispose of Remedies
without feeling that they had gone to waste. Personally, I think he
should have just flushed the shit.

"Hey, how's it going?" he said once the phone was answered.
"Listen, I know you smoke. I've got some stuff I'm trying to get rid of.
You interested?"

"Hmmm...," the voice responded. The boy had met the kid in
one of his classes, and it hadn't taken long for their common interests
to emerge. "I'm actually good for right now, but I know a few guys that
were looking."

The boy scratched his cheek. It was always risky dealing with
people you didn't know.

"I mean, they are totally legit," the kid continued. "I've known
them for a long time and I'm sure they would be interested."

It was risky, but the boy was desperate.

"Alright," he said, "tell them to come by."

He felt instant relief as he hung up the phone. Pitching the
bag into his guitar case, he clamped it shut and slid the metal tin back
underneath his bed.

While his college was not far from home, the boy still rarely
had the opportunity to see his family. He had no car to drive to visit,
and they were preoccupied with the busyness of their own lives. He
only saw his brother on the occasional appearances when picking up
or dropping off of Lily, so he was excited when his brother called and

invited the boy and his roommates to accompany Lily and him on a weekend trip. He had found a cabin in the nearby mountains and was planning on taking Lily on a romantic excursion.

"We are going up Thursday to Sunday," his brother had said. "You guys should drive up on Saturday and stay the night."

Whether or not his brother was only being courteous was irrelevant. The boy asked his roommates, and Ryan and Luke seemed excited. Seth opted to stay behind due to "too much schoolwork." They were discussing the details of the trip when a knock resonated on the front door. Swinging it open revealed two strangers on the front porch. One wore tight black jeans, a gray zip-up, and a green shirt with a cartoon rainbow across the chest. The other wore equally as tight khakis with a white belt, a blue shirt that read "ban hate," and a tailored black jacket.

"What's up, guys?" the boy asked, looking them over.

"We, uh, heard that there might be someone here who can help us out in acquiring some stuff," the stranger in the blue shirt said, wiping strands of long blond hair across his forehead.

The boy nodded and opened the door for them to come in; he had almost forgotten. They followed him into his room where he flipped open the guitar case, pulled out the bag, and handed it to them. He was finally rid of it. The two tight-shirted boys held the bag up in front of their faces and their eyes sparkled as they examined the greenery inside. The one in the green shirt pressed his hand forcefully down into his tight jean pocket and pulled out some cash, which he handed to the boy.

"Now, don't come back looking for more. It' a one-time deal," the boy said firmly as he tossed the money into his desk drawer. "Anybody asks where you got it, just say somewhere off campus."

The strangers nodded gratefully and hurried out the door. The boy kicked his guitar case shut and flopped down on his bed. How often we become the things we hate.

It was his first trip out to the cabin. The wooden logs were better sealed and much less tarnished then; they had not seen the more tragic winters yet. Back then, the steps were still solid and functional, and the boy and his roommates climbed them and walked through the front door. The layout inside was similar: a cozy sitting area with a small desk beneath a window and a fireplace against the wall. A hallway led to the bathroom, kitchen, and bedroom. It was not much, but it was a relaxing atmosphere. The boy felt at ease as he sat down in the desk chair; it was so quiet and serene. His mind was clear, and he thought only of Mae. Ryan and Luke went back outside with Lily and the boy's brother to start a fire while the boy remained glued to the chair. It was a sense of peace that he had never felt before. It was genuine happiness. He was in college, had his friends, and had no concerns or worries. He was responsible and had solid plans for the future; his brother was finally happy; and, most importantly, he was in love.

By the time he had removed himself from the desk and wandered outside, the others had an impressive fire burning. Ryan strummed his guitar while Luke, Lily, and his brother sat around the flames, drinking cans of liquid Remedy and talking. The boy joined the circle and popped open a can of his own. Bits of spark and ash crackled in small ascending trails from the fire and faded into the chilled darkness of the night as they sat and talked. The boy watched his brother from across the flames; he had not seen him that happy in a long time. His face was plastered with a smile and he threw back his head and laughed, hooking his arm around Lily's shoulder. Lily noticed the boy's eyes on the two of them and gave an apologetic smile. Hoisting his can into the air, the boy nodded and smiled reassuringly at his friend. Luke slapped the boy's back and the two laughed as they talked about their trip to the beach. Ryan strummed his guitar loudly, and they all sang along. They told stories about their childhoods and mimicked the trends of their youth. They talked and laughed and sang until the red blaze of the fire had subsided to a coal black hiss. Ryan had finally stopped playing guitar when his cell phone began ringing in his pocket and he stood up to answer it.

"It's Seth," he said as he opened the phone and strayed away from the circle.

"This was fun. I'm glad we did this," Lily said once Ryan had vanished into the darkness.

"Yeah," the boy agreed, "it was a good time."

He poured the last drops of liquid into his mouth.

"I'm pretty beat," the boy's brother yawned. "You guys ready for bed?"

Luke nodded quickly, "We've got to head back early tomorrow."

With stretches and sighs, they rose to their feet and began walking toward the cabin.

"We've got a problem," Ryan emerged from the shadows behind them.

"What's going on?" the boy turned to meet him.

"That was Seth," Ryan's voice was shaking. "Campus security raided our house today, tore everything apart."

"What?!" Luke said.

Lily covered her mouth with her hand. The boy scrolled through the possibilities in his mind. There were pictures of them drinking and smoking, probably some bottles of liquid Remedy, cigarettes, documents and CDs that implicated their "illegal" business, multiple acts of vandalism done to the property, and probably video recordings of them doing most of those acts—but no planted Remedies; he had gotten rid of those.

"What did they come for? What did they take?" the boy asked quickly.

"I'm not sure," Ryan said carefully. "They knew we were gone. Seth said they asked him why he didn't go out of town with us."

"Those bastards were waiting for us to leave," the boy muttered.

"They took a lot of stuff, trashed the whole place," Ryan continued.

"They can't prove anything!" Luke argued.

"Did they find the video?" the boy asked.

Ryan nodded slowly. Seth's mom had allowed her son to borrow her video camera for a school project. Seth never completed the project, got a zero, and the boys decided to film themselves doing ridiculous activities around the house instead—activities that typically resulted in intentional damage to the building.

"They had real cops with them and they kicked in the door. It's pretty serious," Ryan shook his head.

"Real cops?!" Luke exclaimed.

The boy rubbed his eyes with his hand. They didn't call the county cops for some pictures and booze. What were they looking for?

There was no sense in driving back to the college that night. The campus security guards had taken what they wanted and told Seth that the boys would be hearing from the college in a few days. They would deal with the rest in the morning.

It wasn't easy falling asleep. The boy sat in the desk chair and stared up at the ceiling. It had only been hours earlier that he had sat in that same chair and expressed his gratefulness for the fortune of his life. Now, there was a possibility that things were not as bright as they seemed. As he sat there, he thought about how quickly life can shift from something beautiful to something dreadful. In one pivotal moment, everything can fall out from underneath you. That night, in that cabin, he feared that such a moment had come. If you asked him now, I believe he would say that is where the first threads of his life began to unravel, where it first began to falter. I believe that is why he brought me to the same cabin years later, to pick up where he dropped off.

The house was destroyed. The front door could not close completely due to the broken doorframe where some swollen-headed brute had planted his shoe. Posters, pictures, and tapestries were ripped down from the walls and torn or clearly stepped on. Ceiling tiles lay in crumbled pieces on the floor, exposing cobwebs and cheap light fixtures overhead. The boys scanned the damage in awe as they moved quickly into the "studying room." The ceiling tiles that Seth had shot the paintball gun through were missing, but Ryan's computer was unharmed and the CDs were untouched. Next, they checked their bedrooms; the boy stopped in his doorway. All the drawers to his dresser were pulled out and overturned on his bedroom floor, his guitar was tossed in the corner, and his case was open. He checked the wall; Mae's picture still hung safely over his mattress. He pulled the metal tin out from under his bed and checked the journal and the other pictures he had of her. Everything was there. He met Ryan and Luke back out in the hallway, their eyes full of dismay.

"We'll clean up later," the boy tried to sound consoling. "For now, let's just go eat."

Lunch was quiet. None of them felt strong enough to force

conversation, so they each sat and pondered their own thoughts. They knew their potential consequences. For the first time, they did not fill their empty boxes, cartons, and backpacks with the cafeteria food. Instead, they walked back to the house with leery paranoia. As soon as they had returned to the shelter of their home, the boy called Mae and told her the story while they cleaned up the devastation that the intruders had left behind. She expressed her support for the boy and it eased his worry.

"What are they going to do?" she asked.

"I don't know," the boy replied, "They are going to get back to us. I'm sure we will have a hearing of some sort."

"Well, just be strong," she said. "Don't let them corner you. I love you no matter what happens. Just remember that when they are talking to you. They may judge you, but my love is unconditional."

It took a week for the letters to arrive. By then, the boys had become much more relaxed about the situation and had come up with a plan of action. They had just finished dinner and had decided to check their campus mailboxes for any CD orders or checks they may have received. Ryan was the first to open his box and jerk the long slender envelope from inside. His shoulders sank as he tore open the seal and scanned the letter. He held it up so that the others could see. Snatching it from his hand, the boy glared at the college logo stamped boldly on the top of the page and skimmed the letter, "We are writing to inform you that you are hereby subject to a hearing held Tuesday... violations of college policies...disregarding/defacing college property... possession of prohibited paraphernalia...." Turning the key to his mailbox, he flung it open and pulled out the same threatening envelope. He turned to find Seth and Luke reading identical letters. The hearing was on Tuesday; it was Monday night.

They were especially sentimental that evening; they sat in the living room and discussed their fondness for the time they had spent together. They reminisced about the amusing stories that had happened in the house and laughed at their adventures. It was their way of saying goodbye. Even if they were able to dodge any real consequences, there was less than a month left of school, which meant that their time together was coming to an end.

"Do you really think they will kick us out with so little time left in the year?" Seth asked.

The college meant the most to Seth. Since high school, it had been his dream to attend the university, and he had been fairly clear about the fact that he enjoyed it far more than he had imagined.

"Who knows?" Ryan said, scratching his head.

Ryan was smart; if need be, he could easily find another college that wanted him.

"Are you all planning on coming back next semester? I mean, if we can...," Seth shifted nervously on the sofa.

Ryan nodded; Luke looked to the boy.

"I'd like to," he said affirmatively, but Luke did not respond.

"Can we agree," the boy continued, "that no matter what happens, we had a great time? They can't break us if we stick together. You guys are like brothers to me."

"It's been awesome," Ryan agreed, and the four brothers slapped hands and hugged one another.

The next evening, they walked to their doom, their heads held high and their unity undeniable. They were four branches bound together as they flung open the door of the academic building and strolled down the long white hallway. A tall, balding man with glasses greeted them outside of a heavy wooden door, introducing himself as the "student life office director."

"We are going to take you right in this room here," the director said. "If you just give me one moment, I will check to make sure we are ready for you."

The boy watched as the man swung open the door and walked inside. A long bench-like table curved around on one end of the room. Behind it sat an assortment of eight or nine people, each with papers in front of them. A television and VCR sat in the corner beside the table. Facing the bench of judges and jurors was a single chair scooted up to a small square table. A single chair? A lump formed in the boy's throat. Why hadn't he thought of that possibility?

"Alright," the boy began as soon as the door had closed. "They are taking us in one at a time...."

"What!?" Seth jumped.

"Are you serious?" Ryan trailed.

"There is only one chair in there," he knew he didn't have

much time, "we've got to stick to our story. Don't let them corner you, and don't tell them anything they don't already know!"

The door handle clicked, and the boys fell back into a line.

"OK...," the bald man said, "which one of you is Seth?"

Seth's face was red as he raised his hand and followed the man into the room.

"I'm worried about him," Luke said once they were alone again. "What if they crack him?"

"On what?" Ryan asked. "There is nothing to know."

"He'll be fine," the boy said calmly.

Five minutes passed, then ten, then fifteen before Seth came glistening and panting from the room. A campus security guard escorted him down the hallway quickly past the others, but Seth caught the boy's eye, smirked, and winked. The boy nodded proudly as the bald man came out and called Ryan's name. Luke and the boy leaned against the wall and waited. The boy tried to decipher the meaning of Seth's gesture. His face was difficult to read. He did not seem pleased or acquitted; his smile was fake and his eyes looked worried, not relieved, but his action indicated that he had been successful. Perhaps he was still nervous of the outcome.

Another ten minutes passed before Ryan was escorted from the room. His head hung down and he stared at the carpet as the security guard stalked on his heels. He glanced up at the boy as he strolled by and shook his head lightly. The boy's eyes narrowed and he gave a questioning look, but his roommate had already passed. Luke was called in next, and the boy was left alone in the hallway. He thought about what Mae had said to him. She loved him no matter what happened. There was nothing they could do to him that would compromise her feelings for him. It was such a reassuring realization.

Ten more minutes passed and Luke came swaggering out of the room, his hands in his pockets. The boy straightened himself up off the wall.

"I'll see you in a few minutes," Luke said as he walked past the boy.

There was something strange about his tone. Shaking his head, the boy followed the director into the room.

"Good evening," a voice boomed from the front of the room

as the boy lowered himself into the short, stiff chair.

"Good evening," he folded his hands on the table in front of him and forced his shoulders to relax.

Roughly fifteen feet from where he sat, nine strangers lounged on cushioned chairs and stared down at him from behind a curved laminated oak bench. A security officer stood to the right of the bench, next to the television. Another was positioned just on the edge of the boy's peripheral, his thumbs looped firmly into his belt. The booming voice came from a blonde-haired woman who sat in the center of the semi-circle and eyed him as she spoke.

"I assume you are aware as to why we are all here this evening," she said plainly.

The boy did not respond.

"Well," the woman cleared her throat, "we are going to show you some things and ask you a few questions."

One of the security officers marched over to the boy's table and dropped a stack of pictures down in front of him. The boy was familiar with their tactics; they were trying to intimidate him into giving them information, but what were they after? Steadying his nerves, the boy picked up the pictures and thumbed through them.

"Let's go through them together," the woman said. The boy held up the first picture. It was of him and Luke smoking a cigarette. "I am sure you are aware of our strict anti-smoking policy...," the woman threatened.

The boy scanned the picture. There was nothing to indicate that the picture was taken at the college.

"I am," the boy began, "and this picture was not taken on college grounds. It was taken when we were away on a weekend trip."

The other eight officials' pencils moved wildly across their notepads as he spoke.

"The next picture, please," the woman called out.

The boy flipped to the next picture and held it up. It was of a tower of empty liquid Remedy cans; they had built it as a trophy one night.

"Are you aware that this college also has strict anti-alcohol policies?"

"Yes," the boy responded, "but, again, this picture was taken off campus and..." he scanned the picture again. No one was in the picture; it was just a picture of empty cans. "None of us were present for it."

She rubbed her forehead with her hand and shifted the papers in front of her.

"Actually," the boy flipped through the rest of the pictures, "none of these were taken on campus."

"None of them?" the woman asked doubtfully.

The boy shook his head. She motioned to the security officer, who slid a piece of drop ceiling onto the table. The boy picked it up and examined it. Six green holes perforated the crumbly fiber of the panel—holes that Seth had shot with his paintball gun. Had they found the paintball guns? The boy did not know.

"Can you explain that to us?" the woman asked; her voice was frustrated.

"No," the boy shook his head. He tried to keep his answer short. He did not want to overwork the eight stenographers.

"Well, it looks like some sort of bullet holes," the woman coaxed.

They had not found the guns. The boy picked up the panel and scoured it again. Shrugging, he set it back on the table.

"I don't know much about guns," the boy shook his head.

"Are there presently any guns of any sort or weapons in your house?"

The boy faked a look of concern. He was sure Seth had taken his paintball rifles home by now.

"I don't believe so," the boy said coolly.

The officer dropped two packs of cigarettes—one was the boy's, one was Luke's—onto the table and set a bottle of liquid Remedy down next to them.

"How can you explain these?"

They were doing all the things he had expected, and he was following the plan carefully.

"As far as I understand," the boy said, "smoking is prohibited on campus, but I have never heard anything about storing cigarettes on campus. Are we not allowed to hold them here and drive off campus to smoke?" He was trying to keep his voice submissive.

223

The woman talked quietly with her associates.

"How do you explain the bottle?" she asked after a moment.

The boy picked up the bottle in his hand.

"This...?" he asked. "...this is not ours."

"Not yours?" the woman raised an eyebrow.

"No," the boy went on. It actually was the truth. His brother had bought the bottle and left it for them at their house. Technically, it was his. "It's my brother's. He came to visit and left it here. He bought it; he is twenty-two."

"Unfortunately," she was regaining confidence, "that is irrelevant. Not only is it against the rules for student to have alcohol in their rooms, but it is against the law when those students are not of age!"

The boy shook his head. So, at the most, they were looking at alcohol citations. Not bad.

"Not to mention," the woman went on, "that there is still the matter of the damages to school property. Play the tape."

The security officer pressed a button on the VCR and the video screen blipped on. The boy sat in silence as the panel of officials stared at him while he watched the video of him and his roommates playing football in the hallways, slamming into walls, driving golf balls, and busting holes into the drywall. The boy did his best not to snicker at the awkward hilarity of the situation. When the video was over, the woman folded her hands in front of her mouth and awaited his response.

"Let me start by saying that I am sorry," the boy began. "Those were clearly irresponsible things to do, and I know the rest of the guys are sorry that we did them as well. I apologize to the college as well as you personally. That being said, in our defense, since the day we moved in, we were told that the house was going to be demolished after this semester and that the university would be more lenient than in most cases. Obviously, we took that more literally than we should have." The woman nodded. "But, in all fairness, if you go look at the house now, there is much more damage from when they" he pointed to the campus security officer, "came storming through than anything we have ever done."

The security guard's keys jingled as he shifted awkwardly and glared at the boy. The woman weighed him with her eyes for a moment.

"That may be true...," she seemed conflicted, "but the issue here is the damaging of things that you do not own, which is against university policy. So, we are looking at underage possession of alcohol on campus and destruction of school property." She shuffled the papers in front of her. "Let me ask you one last question..." she leaned forward in her chair and stared at him over the rim of her glasses, "...who is selling illegal substances out of your house? Which of your roommates?"

"What??" the boy's breath caught in his throat and his heart sank.

"We have reason to believe that someone in your house is selling illegal drugs. Do you know who it is?"

The boy's eyes narrowed. That was what they were looking for; that was all they wanted. They had gone through all this trouble to try to nail him for a one-time sale. He should not have sold to those strangers; he knew better. It must have been them; they were the only ones.

"If you can tell us which of your roommates it is, we will drop all of these other charges and everyone else can have a clear record. You seem like an intelligent young man. I'm sure you will make the right decision."

They must have said the same thing to his roommates, but none of them had given him up. That was what each of them were indicating as they passed him in the hallway. He rubbed his hand over his hair. They had each been given the opportunity to clear their own charges if they had only said his name, but none of them had.

"Please! Which one of your roommates is dealing illegal...?"

"No one," the boy cut in defensively. "No one is dealing!"

She sighed, "Then we have no choice but to recommend that the college take full punitive action, resulting most likely in the expulsion of all contributing members."

The boy could hear the anvil pounding in his chest. The possibility of expulsion? He could not allow that to happen. There was no sense in allowing everyone to suffer for his short-sightedness; but what could he do? Was he willing to risk the possibility of jail to keep his friends from getting expelled? He thought about Mae and the advice that she had given him. He thought about his love for her and how it caused him to no longer do things out of selfish preferences or his own emotions but out of the knowledge that his love was guiding him. No matter what they did to him, she would love him till the end.

"No one is dealing," he said again more calmly, "but I can tell you about the illegal substances," his eyes dropped to the table in front of him, "as long you promise me that anyone who is not involved will have all of these charges dropped. I'd like your personal word."

"You have my word," she leaned hard against the bench, as if she was trying to close the distance between the two of them.

"It was mine," he said confidently. "I sold it, but I'm not a dealer." She pulled her glasses off her face and with squinted eyes she watched the boy tell his story. "I'll be honest; I used to use the stuff a couple years ago...."

She listened closely as he told the saga of Mae and how he had given up Remedies and about their love. He told the woman about their spring break plans to finally meet one another and how, at the time, he thought it would be a good idea to bring the planted Remedy along for one last encounter. He told her about how it had made him fear for Mae's life because of her difficulty breathing—or his imagining of her difficulty breathing; he wasn't sure. He talked about how it made him sick, about how there was some left over that he couldn't stand to hold on to, and how he had just been desperate to be rid of it. He told her that he had come to the school with the intention of cleaning his life up for Mae and that he would do it one way or another. Then, he prepared himself for the consequences.

The woman's eyes had been on him throughout the entire story, and now that it was finished, she inhaled a deep lungful of air and sighed. Her demeanor seemed much less threatening and her eyes almost carried a sense of fondness.

"That was a very noble and brave thing you did, young man," she said, placing her glasses on the bench in front of her, "admitting blame to spare your friends. I understand your plight as well; it is painfully obvious that you are in love, which can often make people do foolish things. But I respect that, so I am willing to compromise. I will not expel you; and I will leave any legal action out of the question. Un-

226

fortunately, nobility and love do not negate wrongdoing, and I am in a position where I have to take action against that wrongdoing. So, I will allow you to finish these last few weeks of school here at the university; but I advise you, young man, to look for a new school over the summer, because you will not be able to return to this college next fall. If I find out that you are attempting to register for classes next year, you will not find my temper nearly as accommodating."

The boy nodded slowly. Rising to his feet, he turned and walked out of the room. He may not have been allowed to return to the college the following year, but he still felt victorious; he would be able to finish the semester and transfer to a new university. The alternative would have been much worse—he and his roommates would have been expelled, none of them would have even finished the semester, and he was not sure how many other schools would accept students with that background. Once again, for the third time, the story of Mae and the boy's love had saved him from disaster.

Luke, Ryan, and Seth were pacing outside of the building when the boy burst through the metal doors. His face was ambiguous as he stepped out onto the sidewalk among them. They crowded in around him, wringing their hands, their eyes full of questions. He scanned their eager faces; not one of them had given him up. He had never been more proud of his friends.

"We're good!" he laughed. "All charges dropped!"

"All charges dropped?!" Ryan repeated.

The boy nodded, "Completely clear!"

"Yes!" Seth wrapped his arms around the boy and lifted him off the ground.

Ryan and Luke slapped hands and patted each other on the back.

"Woooooo!!!" Seth cheered. "They couldn't take us! We're not going anywhere!!"

They laughed and hollered as they ran back home. Ryan did a cartwheel in their backyard and Seth hugged the cold brick of the house. Luke and the boy trailed behind, chuckling at the jubilance of their roommates.

"So...," Luke said, "you've got to tell me, dude, are you coming back next semester? Because, if not, then I'm not going to either."

The boy chuckled and shoved his hands down into his pockets.

"No, man, I'm not," the boy croaked quietly into the night air. Luke shook his head slowly.

"Then I'm going to miss you," his voice was shaky as he hooked his arm around the boy's shoulder.

He could feel that tingling sensation returning to the corners of his eyes.

"I feel like a cigarette," he chuckled, regaining composure. "How about a drive?"

Wiping his eyes, Luke chuckled and rattled the keys free from his pocket.

"Sounds excellent," he said.

fifteen

The rest of the semester went smoothly. The fervid surveillance of the college forced the boys to keep their mischief to a minimum, and they survived the last month and a half of school. They had taken their finals, packed up their things, and said their goodbyes to the college and to one another. They had made promises to visit each other, but they all secretly knew in the backs of their minds that this would be their last encounter. Ryan and Seth would return the following semester as roommates, but Luke would transfer to his second-choice university. As for the boy, his possibilities were endless. He had moved back home to his parents' house and his uncle had offered him his job back at the produce market. Before he could accept, the boy had to address a more pressing and essential issue.

It had been two months since he had seen her and his heart was aching. As soon as she told him when her semester would be over, he purchased his plane ticket to Texas and they anxiously counted down the days until his arrival. While it was equally as exciting as the first, it was much more strenuous for the boy to prepare for their second meeting. Their first encounter had occurred in a place that neither of them were familiar with. The second would take place in her hometown, amid her family and friends. Every day when they talked, she would reveal new plans for the two of them to spend time with a relative or friend and, while the boy was eager to be exposed to these areas of her life, he was also mildly intimidated.

"I'm nervous about meeting her dad," he told Ben a few days before the trip.

"Don't be. You will be fine," his friend crunched into a handful of chips.

"I don't know," the boy said. "He has made it pretty clear that he is not very fond of me."

Mae's father seemed like a friendly man; he was just protective of his daughter. On numerous occasions, he had expressed to Mae his leeriness of the boy. He knew nothing about the boy, was skeptical of where he had come from, and disapproved of the overall relationship. Mae had assured the boy not to worry and that her father would come around, but it had done little to ease the boy's apprehension in meeting the man. Her parents' approval was important to him, and all he could hope to do was convince them of his worth.

"How could he not be fond of you?" Ben's voice was skeptical. "You are practically the nicest guy I know! I'm sure he will like you once he meets you."

"That's a little overboard, but thanks."

"No problem."

"So, when are we hanging out?" the boy changed the subject.

"Uh, soon," Ben sounded evasive. "I will make it up there in the next couple of weeks."

For the boy, the most disheartening aspect of moving from his hometown had been the response of his childhood friends. It had been almost a year since he and his family had packed up their lives and relocated, and only twice had his friends come to see him. He had seen them many more times than that, but only because he had been willing to make the trip back home. He understood why it happened that way. They were busy with their lives and not as in need of him as he was of them. He knew that it only took a few weeks after his move for them to fill the hole that it had created. Unfortunately, he had not had the luxury of distractions and was thus more deeply impacted with the feeling of loss. Much of that grief had subsided as he found new friends and became involved with Mae, but there was still a small part of him that yearned for the companionship of his youth.

It was an easy trip from Baltimore to Texas. Mae was waiting for him in the airport terminal, her face beaming as he raced through the gate. Throwing his arms around her, he closed her in his grasp and the two kissed with long-awaited passion. Her eyes were glazed with glee and a wide smile stretched the skin of his face as they laughed with excitement. Completely enveloped in their oblivious bubble of blissfulness, they walked down the corridor with interlocked fingers and through the crowd of swarming people.

"So this is it?" the boy whistled, admiring her minivan.

"Yes," Mae chuckled, "this is it; but don't go knocking, this thing has been good to me." She slid into the driver seat and started the van.

"I didn't say a word," the boy smirked as he climbed into the passenger seat and the van went gliding out of the airport parking garage and down the street.

"We have to pick up my cousin from school. Is that OK?"

In addition to being especially close with her parents, Mae was also exceptionally close with her extended family. As a part-time job, she would pick her cousin up from school certain days of the week and baby-sit until his parents got home from work. She had told the boy numerous stories about their after-school homework sessions, board games, and cherished talks. He was only ten years old, but Mae considered her cousin to be a good friend and a valued confidant.

"Of course! I will finally get to meet the guy who has been hogging up all your time!"

Mae giggled as the boy lounged back in his chair and cracked his knuckles. The sun was up and the windows were down, allowing the thick humid air to swirl in rejuvenating gusts through the cabin of the van. Mae wore her glasses and sat with perfect posture, her chair scooted to the dash, her hands carefully gripped around the steering wheel as they talked and laughed. It is nostalgic for me to picture them that way; they were so young and in love and nothing else mattered because they did not allow it to. The visits back and forth were fairy-tale romantic and infinitely treasured. They had no concerns for money or reasons for conflict because they loved one another with all that they had.

"My friend had a vivid dream one time," Mae said as they drove across a long bridge, "of me driving my van over the side of this bridge."

"Uh, do me a favor," the boy replied, "...avoid this bridge."

She smiled and rubbed her hand over the top of his as the van rumbled on.

231

Her cousin's school was not far, and before long, he was climbing into the backseat of her minivan and sliding the door closed.

"Hey!" the boy introduced himself.

"Hi...," the blonde-haired cousin replied.

The boy chuckled; he would find a way to win her family over.

"He is just being shy," Mae laughed. "You alright?" she asked her cousin. The young boy nodded. "You want to go see grandma?"

He nodded again and she eased her flip-flop from the brake pedal.

Mae's grandmother was one of the sweetest people the boy had ever met. She lived alone in a small blue house off of one of the nearby side streets and greeted them at the door with glasses of freshly brewed iced tea.

"It is a pleasure to finally meet you!" the woman said to the boy after she had released Mae from an affectionate embrace.

The boy's cheeks were flush as she slid her arms around him and gave a friendly hug. It was not something that he was accustomed to, but there was a comforting security in it that made his shoulders ease.

"We aren't interrupting, are we?" Mae began, "I just wanted you to be able to meet...."

"Nonsense!" her grandmother interjected. "You know you are welcome any time. I was just doing some gardening out back." She turned her attention to the young, blonde-haired boy, "You know, our tomatoes are getting pretty big. I'm going to need you to come over soon and help me pick them. Would you like to see?"

The young boy gulped the last mouthful of iced tea from his glass and nodded enthusiastically. With raised eyebrows, her grandmother turned to Mae and the boy and adjusted her wide-framed glasses.

"I would love to see your tomatoes," the boy smiled and set his glass of tea down on the kitchen table.

Mae looped her arm around his waist, and the two followed her delighted cousin and grandmother out the back door of the house.

The garden was more like a vegetable field. Tall stalks and vines lined most of her backyard and were adorned with vibrant tomatoes, squashes, and cucumbers. The rows were plowed with obvious care and the rich, dark soil indicated devoted toiling. Mae's cousin raced to one of the tomato plants and dropped to his knees in front of it while his grandmother pointed out some of the larger vegetables. Mae carefully stepped through the rows of produce, admiring some of the newer blossoms that she had not seen. The boy stood, his eyes wide with awe; she had grown vegetables that far exceeded the quality of those that he and his uncle had sold at their market.

"Mae tells me you know a thing or two about vegetables yourself," she said, dusting the soil from her hands.

"Nothing like this," the boy replied. "I would only embarrass myself. These are incredible!".

"Thank you, but it's just a hobby," she dismissed, "something for the grandkids to enjoy."

She motioned to the blonde-haired boy behind them. He was on his knees, packing soil gently around the base of a tomato vine. His school clothes were already covered in dirt.

"Let's go back in," she moved toward the door. "He will sit out here for hours."

Back inside, the three sat down in the woman's living room and talked. She asked the boy questions about his life and she and Mae laughed as they told him stories about theirs. It truly was an enjoyable time for the boy, and he was sorry to see it come to an end.

"We'd better get going," Mae chuckled when her cousin came wandering in through the back door, his knees stained with mud. "I've got to feed the monster and get him back before his parents get home."

"Alright," her grandmother rose to her feet and gave them all hugs goodbye. "It was so nice to meet you," she said to the boy.

"Nice to meet you as well," the boy smiled warmly. "I really enjoyed it. Good luck with your garden!"

The woman stood on her front porch and waved as they climbed into the car and drove away.

"She is such a nice woman!" the boy said, buckling his seatbelt.

"Yea," Mae smiled, "she really is, and she definitely liked you! You both are two of the most important people in my life, so it was really important to me that you met."

She leaned over and kissed the boy quickly. Her cousin twisted

233

his face in disgust.

"Sorry!" she laughed. "Is that gross?" Her cousin nodded his head, and she laughed again. "I'll make it up to you. We'll get some pizza."

She parked the van outside of the small pizza shop, and her cousin leaped from the backseat and raced inside.

"He loves this place," she said, taking the boy's hand and sneaking in a kiss.

Her cousin was tapping his hands on the counter and staring at the pizza when Mae and the boy walked in. They ordered enough for the three of them, and the boy reached for his wallet.

"No," Mae grabbed his arm. "Let me pay. You paid to get here to me."

The boy sighed and pushed his wallet back into his pocket.

Conversation was slightly more successful over lunch. The boy was able to coax the young boy into telling him about school and the latest fads in youthful trends. The more that the boy asked, the more responsive her cousin became.

"So, does Mae bring a lot of guys around to hang out with you?" the boy teased.

"No. Just you." the young boy responded, before sinking his teeth into a thin slice of pepperoni.

Mae smiled proudly and winked.

After they finished their meal, Mae gave her cousin a handful of change from her purse and he scampered off to the arcade games that clustered the corner of the shop.

"Ha!" the boy scoffed, "I knew it! You paid him to say I was the only guy you've been bringing around!"

She giggled and squeezed his hand beneath the table.

By the time they finished with lunch and drove back to her cousin's house, it was almost time for his parents to come home. Mae reached up to the visor and pressed a white button that opened the garage door. The boy watched as Mae backed the minivan into the garage and pressed the button again, closing the door. She must have been extremely close with her family; none of his aunts or uncles would have ever given him their garage door opener.

"Come on! Hurry!" her cousin jumped from the backseat and

ran to the house.

"What's going on?" Mae asked, turning off the car and opening her door.

"I wanna show him my room!" he called back to them.

"Sweet!" the boy said to Mae, who only smiled.

Grandma seemed to like him, and he had won the approval of her cousin; he wasn't off to a bad start. He climbed from the car and walked into the house. The door from the garage led to an impressive kitchen with marble countertops. The sun shone through two large windows that lined the left wall and reflected off a stainless steel refrigerator just inside the door. A breakfast bar jutted out just beside the windows and was the only barrier between the kitchen and a large living room. Two cozy brown couches sat with their backs to the kitchen and faced a big screen television.

"It's this way!" the young boy exclaimed, somersaulting over the rear of the sofa and landing safely on its cushions.

The boy followed down a hallway to the right of the living room and stopped outside of one of the rooms on the left.

"This is it!" her cousin said as Mae walked up beside the boy.

"Very cool!" the boy exclaimed, examining the room.

Mae watched as her cousin showed the boy the posters on his wall and his toy collection. They were just about to play a board game when his mother came home.

"We'll play next time," the boy said.

"Alright," the young boy agreed, tossing the game back onto his shelf.

Mae's aunt was also very polite. The boy introduced himself, and they talked for a few minutes before Mae apologized and said that they would have to be leaving.

"He really likes you," Mae said once they were back in the van. "I've never seen him warm up that quickly to a stranger. Then again, I do talk to him about you a lot. Yes, I talk to a ten-year-old about our relationship." She laughed.

"Well then, I'm really glad that he likes me," the boy chuckled; now, if he could only get her parents to do the same.

Her house was similar to her aunt's. Nestled in the remote shade of framing trees, it faced an old country road. A short driveway

235

was paved along the right of the front lawn and stopped at a large white garage door. Another button above her head opened the door, and Mae pulled the van inside. The boy shifted anxiously in his chair; it was the moment he had feared.

The wooden door that connected the garage to the house opened to a comfortable kitchen with granite countertops that lined the walls to the left and covered a small island in the center of the room. No walls outlined the right side of the kitchen; instead, it expanded into a spacious living room with plush gray sofas. Opposite the door to the garage was a hallway that presumably was the way to the bedrooms. At the end of the left kitchen wall was a narrow entrance to a compact dining room.

A short woman stepped through the passageway. Streaks of gleaming sporadic gray shimmered in her otherwise brown hair and added discernment to the skepticism in her eyes. Her mouth was a twisted blend of scrutiny and concern as she surveyed the boy.

"This is my mom," Mae said, but the woman needed no introduction.

Her features were slightly more mature and defined, but there was no denying that she was her daughter's mother.

"It's very nice to meet you," the boy said, extending his hand to the woman.

She took it slowly and cocked her head to the side.

"I have heard a lot about you...," she said.

The boy cringed; there were only a handful of acceptable responses to that statement, and they were all scripted clichés, which he despised. He searched his wit for a better reply but nothing came to mind. He considered reciting one of the painfully typical responses like, "Hopefully good things," "Don't believe a word of it," or "Uh oh," but she continued before he had the chance.

"It's nice to finally meet the boy that Mae stays up all night talking to." A cautious smile lightly caught the woman's lips.

Mae giggled, and the boy returned the smile.

The far right wall of the living room was comprised of tall square windows that exposed a backyard with a concrete patio and a rectangular pool; the boy remembered the pool from a story Mae had told about a clumsy raccoon that had gotten too close to its slippery rim. At the end of the wall was a glass door that swung open as Mae's father came quickly through it. His broad shoulders and ruddy skin proved that he was a hard-working man, something that the boy respected greatly. His long hair and thick beard were almost entirely white, not because of age but the kind of white that comes from years of difficult labor. The boy took the man's calloused hand in his and shook it.

"It is a pleasure to meet you," the boy said as the man probed him with his eyes. "This is a very nice house that you have." He pushed his hands into his jeans pockets and scanned the ceiling.

"Thank you," the man's voice was gruff. "What do you think of Texas so far?"

The boy had only heard stories, mostly from Mae, about the "Texas pride" that most residents of the state possessed. It was something that he had not fully understood; he was proud to live in Baltimore, but Mae had explained that Texans exhibited a much more intense level of satisfaction. She and her mother were both watching quietly as the boy responded.

"I really like it," the boy smiled. "It's nice to have some warm weather."

"Well, welcome," a skeptical smile stretched below the man's mustache as he nodded to the boy and walked into the kitchen.

Mae motioned for the boy to follow and led him down the hallway that cut between the kitchen and living room. The first door on the left was the bathroom; straight across from that was her parents' bedroom. The second door opened to her bedroom. It was exactly as she had described it: Two large windows looked out over the front lawn, her square desk sat against one wall and her bed against another, and it was full of creative decorations that she had made.

"This is where you can sleep," she said, flipping on the light switch to the last bedroom on the right.

It was the smallest of the bedrooms with a modest bed, a plaid blanket, and a stuffed toy clown positioned in front of the pillows. The boy looped his arm around Mae's waist and kissed her on the forehead as she flicked off the light switch, her eyes on the carpet.

That night, they ate an early dinner with her parents in the compact dining room. In most cases, the boy was fairly talkative, but that night, he found it difficult to formulate conversation. He had never been in a situation where he cared so much what strangers thought of him, and it made him extremely nervous. Mae's parents were cordial and they asked him questions about his life, but he had trouble responding. He knew that neither of them were thrilled that he was dating their daughter. That fact would usually not have affected him, but he loved Mae more than anything and wanted to be a part of her family, so it caused him to struggle. By the end of the meal, he was sure that they were hardly convinced of his value or devotion to their daughter. He offered to clear the table and do the dishes and when her mother declined, he and Mae slipped back into her bedroom.

"Do you want to go somewhere?" Mae kissed him once the door was closed behind them.

The boy slid his hands around her back.

"It's up to you, darlin," he kissed her soft cheek. "As long as I am with you, I'm happy."

She smiled up at him.

"I missed you so much," she squeezed him tighter; "I need you so badly," she traced her fingers along his shoulder blades.

"I need you, too," he kissed the top of her head. "What can we do?"

She leaned back away from him and chewed her bottom lip.

"Are we ready?" she smirked. "Should we...go somewhere?" she whispered, her eyes watched the closed door behind them.

A lump formed in the boy's throat. He loved her with every morsel of his soul—there was no question of that—but he was nervous. It is a scary thing to decide to give everything you are to another person. There are certain ramifications that often come as a result. Making that decision sometimes has the power to destroy relationships, to destroy love. It is frightfully dangerous how decisions made out of love have the ability to both create and destroy the animation of that love. Something that is so powerful that it has the potential to destroy love is something to be revered; the boy realized that as he stood in her bedroom.

"I love you," he said, "and I am ready to show you that in every way possible."

She kissed him sweetly on his lips.

"I know that I am going to marry you some day," her voice was resolute. "There is no question of that in my mind. I love you so much and I don't want to spend a minute without you. I want to be as close with you as possible. You already have every bit of my heart; I want to give you everything else."

"You are the only one for me and the only one that there will ever be," the boy winked. "Let's go for a drive."

The van cut cleanly through the thick night air, the humidity hanging like the heavy sheets of darkness that flowed in the window frames around them. Cool gusts of air spun against their skin as they weaved down the backcountry roads. They laughed as they looked from the open road to one another with hungry, eager eyes. Out there, there were no streetlights or traffic signals, only the steady glow of the van's headlights and the furnace of passion that welled up inside of them. Every few minutes, Mae would comment about a side street they would pass, explaining why it was not a good choice, and the boy would smile with anticipation. Neither of them were in a hurry; it was a beautiful night and they were just two kids in love, trying to prove it. They left the radio off and listened to the silent sanctity of the purity of love that pulsated between them. The boy no longer felt uneasy; he was absolutely certain that he would never want to share something so intimate with anyone other than Mae. It didn't matter what ramifications their decision may have. They were in love, and nothing could stop them as long as they stood together.

"This one is perfect," Mae smiled as she twisted the steering wheel to the left.

The boy read the name of the side street as they turned down it: "Self Rd." He chuckled to himself and rubbed his hand along her leg. She interlocked her fingers with his and bit her smiling bottom lip as she pulled the van to a stop in a patch of gravel along the side of the road.

Fuzzy clumps of fur from the floor of the van rubbed against the boy's palm as he climbed inside and pulled the back door shut behind them. He could feel the fervent throb of the half of orb beneath his chest as it sparked and churned. Outside the hidden van, the trees swayed with limber grace, their branches surrendering to the will of the wind. The stiff blades of grass extended into the delicacy of the smooth

239

velvet of the night and bobbed with the lapping of the breeze. The two halves of orb circled around one another. A gust of wind whipped against the front of the van and glided smoothly up the windshield and over the ridges along the top of the vehicle. The jagged side of both halves of the orb, where they had been split, aligned perfectly with one another and moved together. Outside, the wind increased and the leaves on the trees rustled with applause as they heaved and dropped against each other. The two halves moved closer, the electricity of their energy jumping in sparks from one side to the other. Gusts of wind rushed gently against the side of the van, and the darkness echoed with its cry. The boy could feel the vibrations in his chest. Sloppy red and blue flames burst from the center of the orb and singed against their skin as the two halves came together in an explosion of electricity. Air escaped their lungs, and the flashes of light blurred their vision. The boy scooped his hands behind her head and pressed his lips firmly against hers; his breaths were short and his skin was glistening.

That particular night, I was making preparations for my first encounter with the boy. At this point, it is still not imperative that you know the details of my person or the nature of my doings, but I will tell you that I was on an oil freighter somewhere halfway between Perth, Australia, and Cape Town, South Africa. I only know this information because it was there that the ship was docked for the duration of that night and the next morning, and I happened to overhear the captain call the mapping coordinates "-40.0446, 84.37." I was then able to esti-mate our location from one of the maps onboard. Otherwise, I would not have been privy to that information. It does not bother me; I have no real concern for things of that nature. I mention it now only be-cause it is something that I just recalled and I vowed to tell the story as best as my memory would allow. Why I was on an oil freighter in the Indian Ocean is a more difficult question to answer. Let me just say that I was on holiday and leave it at that; the story of my trip to Cape Town and my interest in oil is another tale for a later time. As for now, we must remain focused on the story at hand.

While I was floating in the vast darkness of the desolate sea, the warm Texas sun was just stirring them from their night's slumber. The boy awoke to the light tapping of Mae's tiptoes against the floor as she crept into the guest bedroom and slid underneath the covers.

"My mom just left for work," she said, snuggling up beside him.

He looped his arm around her and held her against his chest.

"Are you glad you came?" she asked. "Are you having a good time?"

The boy stretched his legs out under the sheets.

"Uh," he chuckled, "last night was probably the best night of my life!"

"Good. Mine, too." She giggled.

"Are you sure?" he tucked her hair behind her ear. "You aren't sorry?"

"No!" she laughed. "Of course not; not at all!"

They spent that afternoon indoors. Leaving only once to rent movies from the nearby store, they spent the rest of the time in pajamas, absorbing one another. They talked, they laughed, they held one another and watched the videos. Mae taught the boy how to play a game with a wooden board and glass stones called "Mancala," and they listened to music. Even from 1,500 miles apart, they were closest friends; and when they were together, that fact was apparent.

That night, one of Mae's cousins came to the house and the three went into the city. Her cousin drove her car while Mae rode in the passenger seat and the boy sat in the back. From the questions and conversation that she initiated with the boy, it was obvious that Mae had talked to her cousin about him. The three discussed music, and the girls told stories about their childhood. Incubus began playing on the radio and Mae turned up the volume.

"I love the lyrics to this song," her cousin said, and Mae nodded in agreement.

"You are so lucky," the girl tried to lower her voice. "You found someone who writes poems and songs about you." She motioned to the boy in the back seat. "I wish I could find someone like that."

Mae smiled politely and winked at the boy in the side view mirror. Rolling his eyes, the boy winked back.

They passed the next few hours lost on the city streets. With no real destination and little knowledge of the town, the three tore blindly through blocks and alleys, wrapped in the lighthearted invincibility of being young. They drifted past the sky-scraping monuments to prosperity and searched the pavement for signs of life; they looked up to the stars and talked about what they wanted to be in the future. It did not matter that they never actually made it anywhere that night. More than likely, the trip would have been less enjoyable had they actually reached a destination.

The lengthy drive through the city did nothing to discourage Mae and the boy from taking her van out once they were back at her house. The weather was perfect and they sang along to Counting Crows as they drove through the nearby neighborhoods. It was a miracle that a love for the same band had triggered their love for one another, and they loved the band all the more for it. They talked about their favorite albums, songs, and lyrics, until Mae pulled the van to a stop in a vacant parking lot.

It was the tap of the metal flashlight against the glass window that disturbed them. The police officer's eyes were on the pavement beside the van as he waved the beam from his lamp around the window.

"We're all adults, so I'm not gonna ask any questions. But y'all can't be here," he told them and, with blushing apologies, the two drove away laughing until they couldn't breathe.

The vibrations of the boy's phone in his pocket caught his attention, and he was still chuckling when he answered it.

"Hey! Well aren't you having a good time..." it was Joe's voice. "What are you up to?"

"Not too much," he winked at Mae, who was still giggling to herself in the driver's chair. "I'm in Texas."

"Oh, yeah, that's right! I forgot about that! How is it? How's that girl?"

"Good. She's great," the boy replied, his eyes still watching Mae.

"Cool. Well listen, I was thinking we should throw a little summertime barbecue Friday night. Are you going to be around?"

"Yea," the boy shifted in his chair, "I'll be home by Friday."

The smile dissolved from Mae's lips and her cheeks lost their glow. Most of the time, they would get so engrossed in their time together that they would forget its eventual end until it would drop dead in front of them. Neither one of them liked talking about it; it never did any good. No matter how much they loved, needed, and missed one another, they could not escape the undeniable truth that they would have to say goodbye. Nothing could make that any easier.

"So does that sound good or what?" Joe sounded confused.

"What? Y-yeah," the boy stammered, "that sounds good. I'll talk to you later."

Sliding the phone shut, he wedged it back into his pocket. "Raining in Baltimore" by The Counting Crows hummed on the radio.

"As soon as I finish school...," she trailed off.

There was no sense in talking about it; that only made it more difficult.

"...I know...," the boy mumbled.

Mae cleared her throat and tapped her fingers against the steering wheel.

"I'll tell you one thing...," he continued. "You should have seen your face when that cop knocked on the window!"

They both burst into laughter.

She was sleeping sweetly on his chest when we awoke the next morning. He kissed her lightly on the cheek; she must have slipped in once her mother had left for work. A smile drifted across her face at the touch of his lips to her skin, and her eyes fluttered open.

"Good morning, gorgeous," he smiled.

"Good morning," she stretched. "I was having a fantastic dream."

"Oh yeah? What was it?" he asked.

"It was the future...," she yawned, "we were married...lived in a nice house...couple of dogs."

"Is that so?" he smirked as she nodded. "Any kids?"

"Yeah," she giggled, "I think there were a few running around."

"Uh oh...," he opened his eyes wide.

"You love kids!" she patted her hand against his chest.

"In your dream!" he teased.

Mae rolled her eyes. His oldest brother and his sister each had two children, and it was blatantly obvious to anyone who knew him that he loved them dearly and anticipated his own.

"But still," he continued, "the thought of kids is scary. It's getting bad out there," he motioned to the world. "It's got to be hard enough just to teach them the right things, not to mention making enough money to raise them."

Her eyes were solemn as she turned to him. "We'll teach them; they will be surrounded by love. And don't worry about money; you'll make plenty some day playing music or something."

"Not with this hand," he held up his scarred palm.

Mae cupped her hands beneath his and silently traced the white slashes with her thumbs.

"That hurt you really bad, didn't it?" she asked, and when he didn't answer, she pressed her lips gently against the old wounds. "You see these?" she turned her palms to show the backs of her hands; the boy scanned her skin.

"No," he shook his head after a moment.

"Look," she moved her hands closer and rubbed her fingers across them, highlighting certain areas of skin on either hand. "When I was little, I was boiling water on the stove, so I had the burner up pretty high. I left the water on too long and when I went to pull it off the stove it slipped and spilled all over my hands and feet."

The boy strained his eyes and traced a gentle finger along her hand. He could barely distinguish the faint white dashes that sprinkled her skin.

"I can hardly even see it," he assured her.

Your scars are always much more visible to you than they are to others.

Mae had made plans for her and the boy to meet some of her friends out for dinner later that evening, so they took their time with the rest of the afternoon. They drove to a local coffee shop and sat outside at black cast-iron chairs and round tables with green umbrellas and sipped their iced coffees in the beaming sun. After they had finished, they went to a music supply store and the boy helped Mae pick out a new tuner for her guitar. By then, it was time to return to her house to get dressed for the evening.

Mae emerged from her room looking casually elegant, while the boy negotiated his layered tees and faded jeans. Digging down into his bag, he snatched out a bottle of cologne and applied some to his ensemble. He typically did not wear the stuff, but he had gotten it as a gift and figured there was no better time to try it out. With a quick goodbye to her parents, they ventured back out to the van in the garage.

"You smell really good," Mae said once the doors were closed. She sniffed again and leaned closer to him. "Like really good!"

"Well," the boy raised an eyebrow, "I'll have to start wearing this stuff more often."

The restaurant was back in the city, so it took some time for them to get there. Every other street seemed to be named after a president as they drove down the strip. Mae giggled as the boy sought to recall what years each of the random men were in office. Somewhere between Jefferson and Polk, Mae shifted the van into park and the two strolled in to an upscale Mexican restaurant.

The place was certainly authentic: Mexican flowers grew from terra cotta pots that sat on Talavera tiles along the floor; an outdoor garden in the center of the restaurant hosted more native plant life and housed a number of colorful parrots that flapped overhead. Mae's friends were seated at a long rectangular table in one of the more secluded corners. They greeted Mae with hugs and the boy with friendly handshakes as they introduced themselves one at a time. He did his best to remember as many as possible, but by the time they had all sat back down at the table he had forgotten nearly all of their names. Most of them knew him from pictures or stories that Mae had told and they asked curious questions about his interests and his experiences with the girl. They seemed genuinely interested in his responses, and the boy concluded that he was quite fond of her friends—some of whom had invited Mae and him back to their house. So, after they finished the meal and said goodbye to the others, Mae and the boy followed a few of her friends back to the outskirts of the city. The sun had settled below the horizon and the farther they drove from the city, the deeper the darkness became until it was just the headlights from the two vehicles cutting into the night.

"Did you have fun?" she asked as the van jostled down a gravel road.

"Yeah," he replied, "I did. They are really nice people."

"Is it OK that we are going over here? Would you rather do something else?"

"This is fine," he smiled. "They seem like a lot of fun."

Mae pressed her foot on the brake and slowed the van, drifting back from the car in front of them.

"What's wrong?" the boy asked.

The road was dark and empty behind them. Mae did not respond as she pulled the van to the shoulder of the road and unbuckled her seatbelt. Lifting the armrest on her chair she climbed over to the boy and passionately kissed his lips. His eyelids floated shut as she repeated it twice more before hoisting herself back to her chair and buckling her seatbelt back across her chest.

"Is everything OK...?" the boy's voice was dazed.

"Yea," she laughed, "I just really wanted to kiss you."

"That's good," he chuckled, wiping the corner of his mouth.

"By the way," she giggled, "that cologne still smells unbelievably good. I like it a lot."

"Whoa," he teased, "I'm going to need to get another bottle!"

The air was heated and thick as they sat on the back patio of her friend's house and talked. Gleaming stars cut through the canvas of night and shone like bits of particles exploded from the radiant moon. One of her friends pulled a cigarette from a pack and offered one to the boy. He accepted gratefully, and the two puffed swirls of smoke out into the picturesque evening. A loud thrashing in the row of bushes that lined her house interrupted their conversation.

"What was that?!" Mae asked, gripping the armrests of her chair with both hands.

The boy lowered his cigarette and tilted his head to listen closer. It was more like a rustling the second time. The girl who lived in the house turned in her chair to check the bushes behind her.

"What in the world is that?" Mae chuckled.

Smiling, the boy shrugged his shoulders and inhaled another drag from his cigarette.

"Hey!" the girl called to the bushes. "Get out here!"

A small white dog leaped from inside the shrubbery and trotted over to the table where they sat.

"This is my dog," the girl rolled her eyes, "and he's a little crazy."

"Aw! Come here!" Mae patted her hands against her legs and

the dog raced to her side.

She loved dogs; she had two of her own and the boy often teased her about having to share her love with two canines. In actuality, he enjoyed dogs as well and had always wanted one, but his overly cleanly mother would have never allowed it. Mae had assured him that some day they would share custody of hers. After a few minutes of enthusiastic petting, the dog rushed away back into the darkness.

"Man!" the boy laughed when the thrashing started in the bushes, this time more fervently. "He is going nuts in there!"

Mae and her friends laughed loudly.

"What is he doing?!" one of her friends asked.

"Who knows," the owner replied, "digging or something."

They all laughed again. For the rest of the night, any time that they would start a conversation, the excavating dog would interfere with his bush rattling and send them all into a commotion of laughter.

Mae and the boy were still wiping their eyes and chuckling as they walked to the driveway to head home.

"That was a lot of fun," he said once they were in the car.

"Yeah it was," Mae agreed, fastening her seatbelt. "Was it an OK thing to do? You aren't sorry that we came here, are you?"

"Not at all!" the boy replied.

"Well, I just didn't know if you would rather have done something else for your last night."

It was obvious by her face that the words pierced her just as deeply as they did the boy. Their visits could never be long enough. The boy turned his face to the darkness outside his window; Mae kept her eyes firmly on the asphalt that glimmered in the headlights in front of them. In less than 24 hours, they would be apart again, and neither of them knew for how long. It was like being born and murdered each time they saw one another and then days later were ripped apart. It was a frustrating and yet necessary part of their lives, romantic and yet tragic. The boy slid his fingers over Mae's thigh and into her hand that sat in her lap. She clenched her knuckles tightly around his.

"I'm going to miss you...," he said.

"I'm going to miss you so much," she replied.

"I love you...," he declared.

"I love you more than anything," she sniffled.

"...and I will see you again soon."

He kissed her fingers. The tears trickling down her cheeks would not allow her to reply.

sixteen

The car rumbled against the radiating asphalt beneath him as the boy shifted it forcefully and pressed against the gas pedal. It was always more difficult to function in his daily life after he had seen Mae; it was like transitioning from summer to winter, heaven to hell. He had only been back for two days, and the taste of her sweetness that lingered on his lips served as a reminder of how recently they had been together. Fishing his phone from his pocket, the boy checked his rearview mirror. Ben's tan minivan flashed underneath one of the passing streetlights. The boy had asked his friend to accompany him to Joe's party and, surprisingly, Ben had accepted and was following closely behind. Sliding open his phone, the boy sent a message to Mae: "I need to see you again soon." It was only moments before she replied, "Ditto."

Joe's party was typical—smoking crowds congregated on the front lawn, cars were strewn about the driveway and sidewalk, and the scent of liquid Remedy permeated the air. Opening the car door, the boy grimaced at the sound of Metallica booming from inside. With an apologetic frown to Ben, the boy led the way up to the house. Some of his friends had not seen him since he had left for school, so they were overly enthusiastic when he came through the front door. They slapped his hand, patted his back, and hoisted him into the air as they greeted him. The boy introduced Ben, and they exchanged cordial handshakes.

"My brothaaaaa!" Joe rounded the corner. "What is up, dude?!"

"Hey, man!" the boy replied. "How you been?"

"Not too bad!" Joe hooked his arm around the boy's shoulder. "How was your trip?"

"Awesome, it was really awesome," the boy motioned to his friend. "This is my buddy, Ben."

"Ben?" Joe repeated. "How you doin man...Joe."

"Nice to meet you," Ben shook the slightly taller boy's hand.

"So, how do you know this troublemaker...?" Joe waved his thumb at the boy.

"That guy?" Ben chuckled. "He's been getting me into trouble since middle school."

The boy shrugged his shoulders and moved toward the living room.

"Aw, look out! He's back!" a hand slapped against his arm.

It was Shawn, a high school classmate of the boy. He was tall and bulky with long spiked blonde hair and thick fingers that nearly enveloped the boy's as the two shook hands. Beside him stood a short dark-skinned kid with brown eyes, jet black hair, and a muscular frame. His name was James, and the boy was not very fond of him. He was crafty and could usually be found escorting his larger, less intelligent friend around. His mouthy arrogance had gotten Shawn into more fights than anyone could count, and after they were over and the opponent was writhing on the floor beneath Shawn's fists, James would reappear to spew a mouthful of victorious insults. He had become known as the "phantom fighter."

"What's up, James?" the boy nodded, and James nodded back.

He thought it made him looker tougher if he didn't speak, especially with Metallica wailing in the background.

"So, what have you been up to?" Shawn asked.

"Right now...," the boy craned his neck to peer into the living room, "I'm trying to kill this music."

Shawn laughed, and James blew air through his nostrils.

"I think it's in there. We're gonna go grab a few beers." Shawn said.

"Alright," the boy moved to the living room, "I'll see you around."

The speakers must have been turned to their maximum potential when the boy approached the stereo. A piercing popping sound blended with the abrasive electrifying clatter of guitar as he spun the volume knob and switched the disc. Jack Johnson's choppy acoustic strums jumped from the CD player, and the boy smiled with satisfaction. Bobbing his head, he walked into the kitchen and tugged open the refrigerator. As he lifted a cold bottle of liquid Remedy from the shelf and twisted off its lid, he heard someone say his name. Closing the refrigerator door revealed Lily standing a few feet away.

"Hey!" she said, reaching for a hug.

The boy poured a swallow of liquid down his throat before returning the embrace. He had tried to maintain his friendship with Lily, but there were too many complications that came along with her dating his brother. The general logistics of the situation had changed her. Because his brother was older, Lily had been forced to act older herself. As a result, she treated the boy much differently than she had when the two were just good friends. It was an unfortunate thing, but it was undeniable nonetheless. The boy had just accepted the fact and let her go. Other than their occasional encounters at parties or family events, the two hardly spoke.

"How have you been?!" she asked. Something was different about her.

"Really good," the boy smiled. "Things are going really well. I just got back from Texas."

"That's good. Do you know what's going on with your brother?" she changed the subject quickly, "I haven't talked to him since Wednesday and I'm supposed to come to that thing on Sunday...you'll be there, right?" She had changed something, but he couldn't put his finger on it.

The boy swallowed another mouthful. "...what thing?"

"The family thing," she explained, "all your family is supposed to be getting together Sunday afternoon."

He shrugged; he hadn't heard a word about it.

"Your mom called me about it...she is the sweetest lady. Anyway, I can't figure out what is up with your brother. We were out on Friday night...," she rambled on.

The boy scanned the clusters of people collected in the kitchen and the adjacent family room, looking for Ben. These were his friends. His first home—the place of his childhood—had become a distant memory, along with most of the people in it. Chloe and Ben were the only two that he had maintained steady contact with. He spotted his friend laughing in the corner with Joe and Nate. It was strange to see them interact; it is always a little odd to watch two different worlds of friends collide. Ben had been with the boy through some of his most contemplative years, both of them searching for something fundamental in life. Joe and Nate had spent the previous two years trekking alongside him through his happier, more careless times. Neither was completely privy to the existence of each other's era and, as they stood side by side, an ominous chill crept up the boy's spine. It was the first time Ben had ever met any of his friends. He had known these people for two years and it was the first time his best friend from his childhood had ever met them. His eyes narrowed as he poured another mouthful and watched the three thoughtfully.

"So, I was like stumbling down the sidewalk by myself trying to find a cab home because he would not stop talking to these girls...," Lily continued her story. Her hair was shorter. That was it. She had cut her hair. It must have made her feel older. "He was just being such a jackass...." His brother had become her "jackass boyfriend"; and she had become just another one of his brother's girlfriends. Oh the cyclic nature of life!

After he had finally convinced his brother's girlfriend that her boyfriend had not said a word to him about her in the previous two weeks, he excused himself and made his way toward the family room.

"Cigarette?" Joe asked as the boy approached.

He nodded with wide eyes and the two ventured out on the back deck and smoked. When they came back inside, Ben was leaning against the wall in the family room with his arms folded, and his eyes were on James, who sat on the sofa in front of him.

"Lighten up!" James snickered. "I didn't mean anything by it. Learn to take a joke, man!"

Shawn's large frame occupied the seat next to James and he chuckled at the comment. The rest of the chairs in the room were filled with eager spectators.

"It's fine. I get it. I can take a joke," Ben replied. His face was turning red.

"Alright," James muttered, "'cause for a second there I thought you were going to cry!" He slapped his leg as he and the rest of the room laughed.

"Hey!" the boy walked quickly across the carpet, his bottled clenched in his fist. "What the hell is so funny?"

James sat back in his chair and rolled his eyes.

"Did I miss something funny?" the boy turned to Ben, who shook his head and looked at him with injured eyes.

"We were just messing around!" James blurted. "I can't help it if he can't take a joke!"

"Do you know him?!" the boy exclaimed. James did not reply. "I didn't think so. So don't 'joke' with him!"

"Sorry!" James put both hands up in defense. "I didn't realize your friend was so sensitive!"

The boy took two steps toward the sofa; Joe was at his side by now. Ben scoffed and stormed from the room. James grinned, but Shawn did not move. The boy stopped himself.

"You know, you're a real jackass," he said, calmly pointing a finger at James. "I'm out of here."

With that, he turned on his heels, slammed his bottle down on the coffee table, and followed Ben out the front door.

His friend was already across the front lawn and almost to his car when the boy stepped out onto the grass.

"Hey, man!" the boy called. "Hang on! Wait!" Ben quickened his steps.

"Ben! Hang on a second!" the boy raced to catch up to him.

Ben's shoulders dropped and he sighed as the boy came up beside him.

"Hey...," the boy huffed, "look, I'm sorry. That guy is an idiot. He says stuff just to get under people's skin. He is not even really one of our friends –"

"It wouldn't surprise me if he was!" Ben retorted. "You obviously don't have a very strict screening process!" He motioned to the house behind him with his hand.

"Look, I'm sorry about James...," the boy said slowly.

"I don't even care about that guy!" Ben's voice was frustrated. "It's you that I can't believe!"

"Wait. What? Me?" the boy choked.

"Yeah, man!" Ben threw up his hands. "I mean, look at you. Look at the people you are hanging out with!"

"Hold on, James is not someone I hang out with," the boy explained, "and I told you I was sorry for –"

"Not just James! What about everyone else?!" Ben cut in. "Those are the people you want to be associated with?! What about the drinking?!" The boy pulled a cigarette from his pocket. "And I can't believe you are smoking regularly!"

"Is this for real?" the boy chuckled. "Are you being serious?"

"Yes!" Ben exclaimed. "I didn't expect you to have changed so much!"

"What?!" the boy choked. "Well, I didn't expect you to bail on me! You don't like the people I hang out with? You don't like my lifestyle? Where the hell have you been?!"

"Not out making bad decisions!" Ben's face was red. "I've been where I should be – taking care of the people we used to care about!"

"Oh I see…," the boy nodded, "I'm the bad guy. You think I wanted to move? Do you think I wanted to leave you all behind?"

"No…," Ben stared into his friend's eyes, "but I think you left us much farther behind than you had to."

A sting pierced in the boy's chest and burned his eyes.

"I was alone. I was so alone when I moved here," his voice was shaky, "and these people were the only ones who cared, and I will love them forever for it. I don't care what they do; I'm not going to judge them. They were here when you were too busy to be here for me."

"You're destructive…," Ben popped the door handle to his minivan, "you always have been," he climbed into the van, "and you always will be…I'm just glad you found some people who are equally as destructive."

Closing the car door and turning the key, Ben shifted the car in reverse and backed down the driveway, leaving the boy standing silently on the front lawn.

He could hear the crunching of Joe's shoes in the grass as his friend walked up behind him. The boy did not turn around; he kept his face toward the way Ben's van had disappeared and took a long drag from his cigarette.

"You OK?" Joe asked once he was beside him. He nodded his head.

"Your friend alright?" Joe handed him a fresh bottle of liquid Remedy and twisted the lid off one of his own.

"Yeah," the boy's voice croaked.

"What did he say?" Joe peered in the direction the boy was looking.

"The truth...," he replied, and Joe nodded.

"What do you want to do about James?" Joe tipped the bottle to his lips.

"Nothing," the boy shook his head, "it's not worth it."

"You're probably right," Joe agreed. "Cheers."

Their two bottles clanged together, and they poured the liquid down their throats.

"It's good to have you back home," Joe said.

"It's good to have a home," the boy replied, pulling his ringing cell phone from his pocket.

"Hello?" he answered with anticipation.

"Hey!" Mae responded, and the boy melted in her voice, "I've got to tell you what my mom just told me!"

"What is it?!" the boy paced across the lawn.

It didn't matter what sort of mood he was in, she could flip it to pure bliss in a heartbeat.

"Apparently, my dad had a couple of his buddies over last night, and I guess they were asking about you coming to visit," Mae went on, "and he told them, 'I don't like everything about the guy, but it looks like he's going to be my son-in-law, so I've got to learn to.'"

"Well...that's a good start, I guess," the boy chuckled.

"That's a big step!" Mae laughed. "Also! Wait! Sorry! How are you? What are you up to?"

"I'm perfect now that I know your dad is not going to shoot me," he teased. "I'm over at my friend's place. How are you?"

"I'm good!" she giggled. "Sorry. I didn't mean to interrupt. Go back to your friends."

"No way," he said. "I've been dying to hear your voice all day. What were you going to say?"

"Yeah, right," she smiled. "I was going to say that I've already

255

started looking for flights up there in the next three weeks. I'm going to try to come before my classes start; but that means I will only be able to come up for a couple days."

"Fantastic!" the orb leapt inside his chest. "I think that is a fantastic idea! I'll take whatever time I can get!"

"Alright," she laughed. "Get back to your friends. I'll talk to you later."

When he hung up the phone, he did not go back inside the house. He set the bottle down on the front porch, hopped in his car to drive home, and called Chloe along the way.

"Hello...?" she had obviously been asleep.

"Were you sleeping?" the boy grimaced. "Sorry to wake you up."

"It's cool," Chloe yawned. "What's up?"

"I just wanted to say hey," the boy admitted, "and I want to apologize for not calling more often. I know that I've been a bad friend and I just want you to know that I'm sorry and I will try to do better...."

"Whoa, whoa," Chloe blinked, "dude, you are an excellent friend to me—one of the best. I know you are busy; so am I! You don't ever have to worry about that. I wouldn't mind an extra call here or there but you do what you can. I know that. But you are certainly not a bad friend."

"Thank you," the boy smiled, "I needed that."

"No problem. How are you?" she stretched. "Are you writing?"

"A little," the boy shrugged. "I'm sorry. Go back to sleep."

"Are you sure?" her voice was accommodating. "We can talk."

"I'm good," he sighed. "Thank you."

There was a bar not far from the cabin, and on days that I was persistent I could convince him to leave the confines of the wooden walls and empty a few glasses at the scoundrel's altar. We would sit among strangers and friends, and he would pour out the ailments of our existence through casual conversation.

"The weather should be breaking soon," they would say. "Soon the sun will be out to unthaw the summer blooms."

"I haven't seen summer in years," he would swallow into his glass, "or the sun, for that matter."

Then they would ask, "Where you from, son?"

To which he would reply, "Somewhere that is literally enveloped in ice."

The music blended with the clanking of miniaturized glasses and the slurping of straws and provided the perfect euphony to our allusive conversations. I would sit as near to him as his anger would allow and we would talk about the things he could remember. Sometimes, we would share a drink or a familiar song, and our friends would laugh at the mimicked despair that would bellow from our inflated chests. I would slap his back with the palm of my hand and he would laugh at the stinging sensation and add another glass to the tipping stack. A recognizable face would mix liquids that we would pass around the room to people that I knew well, and we'd cheers and toast with fondness and sympathy until our veins were pumping water. If, by chance, a band would assemble in the shaded corner of the bar, he'd watch them with awe while I'd drum on his skull and make him drink twice as much. Either way, I would make sure that he had forgotten his grievances as well as my persistence before we would stumble arm-in-arm back to our coffins in the cabin to be revived. This particular night, there was a thick layer of snow that neither of us had foreseen blanketing the slopes to the cabin, and we howled with laughter as we trudged over the treacherous hills and through the front door. Before he collapsed with exhaustion on the floor by the fireplace, he fell down in the desk chair and scribbled the words,

"One day fades into another
and the seasons change again.
Your name pops up in my head
and I blink you away -
I blink it all away.

It always snows around here
but we all just want some rain,
or would rather be dead;
dead to the cold,

dead to such cold things.

We are all surrounded
- enveloped in ice -
blindly searching for
someone more frozen than us;
someone less thawed,

searching for some means
(means of escape)
from these hollowed bodies
to a place less empty
to fill ourselves.

But we never find any life
- never any love -
except the one toward ourselves,
that's the only one you love,
only one that loves you.
To you it's just a game,
to me it's all the same,
and in the end,
we'll both be dead.
Dead is forever.

     It had been two and a half weeks since he had boarded the plane, hiding his tear tracks behind a pair of large sunglasses, and left Mae sniffling in the airport terminal. In another two weeks she would come sailing from the sky down into his city. She had called and given him the flight information and he had asked questions and meticulously copied every detail to avoid a repeat of her previous visit. He was doing his best to simply pass the time until he could look into her eyes again. He had started working again at his uncle's produce market and was nervously searching for a school to attend in the fall.

     "What's the matter with you?" his mother asked when he

came trudging into the kitchen one morning before work.

"Nothing," he grunted.

He had been up late the night before sifting through the frustration of college applications and had awoken with the worry still heavy on his shoulders.

"It's obviously not 'nothing,' " his mother said, ringing out a rag into the bucket she was using to wash the floor.

"It's just these college applications," the boy sighed, flopping down into a kitchen chair. "They are driving me crazy!"

His mother looked up at him.

"Life is nothing but difficult tasks and decisions," she said. "Some are more difficult for certain people. You will figure it out. Look at you and Mae. I think it is such a big accomplishment that you have already decided who you want to spend the rest of your life with. That is one thing you never have to worry about again, and that's a huge thing! Rely on that. Find comfort in the fact that you have one major decision in your life figured out, and build from there."

The boy could not help but smile.

"You do want to marry the girl, right?" she asked. The boy could not restrain from laughing as he nodded. "Well, alright. Get out there and tackle the rest!"

His spirits were high as he drove to work. His mother was right: If he could hold on to Mae, he could accomplish whatever else life could bring. He was quick in setting up that morning, and he talked with his uncle about his trip to Texas. The man listened with patience and laughed at the boy's excitement as he spoke with unadulterated passion about the girl he loved. As if the excessive talk of the girl drew her to him, his phone began to ring.

"And there she is," the boy smiled at his uncle.

"Alright," his uncle waved, "I've got to get on the road."

The boy waved back before slipping the phone to his ear.

"Hey gorgeous," he answered.

"....Hey," Mae replied, her voice was tired and weak. "How are you?"

"I'm good. Are you feeling any better today?" he asked as he stood under the old maple tree. She had been sick for the better part of the previous two weeks.

"Yes. I think so," she said quietly.

He scooped an apple up from a crate and sunk his teeth into its juicy center.

"That's good, baby," he crunched. "What do you think it was? Like, the flu or something?"

"No...," the words were slow, "I-I'm sorry...I just didn't want you to worry. It's taken care of now. I'm better."

"Worry about what?" he lowered the apple to his side. "What is taken care of? What are you talking about?"

"I....," she released a heavy sigh, "...I...thought that I was pregnant."

The apple bounced gently against a thick gnarled root that grew up beneath his shoe and collected dirt as it rolled away from him. He turned his stinging eyes up to the branches that waved overheard, allowing only glimpses of sunlight to penetrate their canopy.

"For how long?" the boy managed a whisper.

"...Ten days," she replied.

"Why didn't you tell me?" he sighed. "I would have never let you go through that alone."

"I know," she said. "I just didn't want you to worry. You have so many other things to deal with. You are stressed about school and busy with work. I just didn't want to worry you."

"Nothing is more important than you," his voice faltered. "So...what happened? You just...aren't anymore?"

"It's possible that I never was.... But I know I'm not anymore." She kept her voice level.

The boy bit the quiver in his bottom lip.

"Are you OK?" he asked. "Should I come there?"

"No. Don't worry. I'm fine," she replied. "I will be there in two weeks."

A station wagon pulled onto the gravel lot and left a swirling trail of dust that the boy traced with his blurry eyes.

"Are you sure?" his voice was full of intensity. "I can be there tomorrow."

A woman with blonde hair and sunglasses climbed from the front seat of the station wagon and walked toward the counter. Halfway there, she turned back to her car and picked her purse up from the passenger seat.

"I'm positive. Don't worry. It's OK. We don't even need to talk about it. It's over. I just wanted you to know why I was sick," she made her voice sound so casual.

The boy turned his back to the woman as she approached the counter for the second time.

"OK...I love you," he said, clenching the grief with his teeth. "I'm really sorry, but I have to go. I've got a customer."

"I love you, too," a bit of sadness slipped through. "I understand. I will talk to you later."

Wiping the corners of his eyes and taking a deep breath, the boy turned nonchalantly and greeted the woman with a smile.

"How are the apples today?" she smiled back.

"Delicious," the boy coughed.

He kept his eyes on the soil as he placed the woman's apples into a brown paper bag and counted out her change. He managed a fabricated smile and "Thank you" as she walked to her car and drove away. Once the trail of white dust had dissipated into the air and the woman's car had disappeared from the lot, the boy sank down with his back against the trunk of the tree and buried his face into his hands. He could not bear the thought of Mae having to go through that worry alone and, for some reason, he could not stop thinking about his brother's accident—and the baby that had been lost.

seventeen

One of the interesting things about Baltimore is that it is extremely close to the capital of the United States, Washington, D.C. It is something that the people who are not from Baltimore do not realize and that those who are take for granted. Most times, the local residents went often enough in grade school that they give little thought to its beautiful museums and eloquent monuments. Some of the older citizens remember the city from a time when picket lines and rallies still made impacts on the dominating mind of supremacy and regular visits were worthwhile. This is what caused the boy's parents to insist on taking Mae on her first excursion through the capital.

They stopped their car outside of the airport terminal, and the boy sprung from the backseat and rushed inside. Mae was standing at the baggage claim when the boy came leaping down the escalator and wrapped her inside his arms. He could feel her muscles relax against his chest and could hear her sniffling as they held one another and shared their simultaneous feelings of loss and relief. Neither spoke for those few minutes that they remained engrossed in each other's grasp, and when Mae finally pulled back she was wiping her eyes.

"Hi," she giggled at herself and pushed her lips securely against his.

"Hi," he replied and smiled knowingly into her face.

Taking her hand in his, he lifted her suitcase as it passed on the conveyer belt, and the two walked back out to the car.

Washington, D.C., was just as the boy had remembered. They strolled along the brick walkways and his parents snapped pictures of them outside of the aged government facilities. They visited the monuments fashioned to the likenesses of great individuals and read plaques to heroes lost in war. They walked along the large squares where countless historical events had occurred and through the prestigious gardens where they would duck behind the shrubbery to share a kiss. Mae seemed to enjoy herself and was grateful to the boy's parents for suggesting the trip. By the time they arrived back in Baltimore, the sun was long below the horizon and Mae had fallen asleep on the sweet comfort of the boy's shoulder in the backseat.

The boy had only been able to convince his uncle to allow him to take off for two of the three days that Mae was in town; so, the next morning, the two woke up together and got ready for work. They laughed as they splashed water from the sink on one another while they brushed their teeth. They chuckled together while they ate bowls of cereal at the kitchen table. She rode in the passenger seat of his car with the sunroof open, and Counting Crows blared through the speakers, as they danced and sang along on the way to work. Every now and then, the boy would turn down the volume to point out a building or a road that he had told her stories about, and she would listen intently then laugh hysterically when he would turn the music back up and resume his singing.

"You sound just like him!" she commented on his imitation of Adam—the band's lead singer—and the boy shook his head and laughed.

The car rolled to a stop in the dusty parking lot and Mae and the boy climbed out into the warm summer air. His uncle was squatting down along the wooden planks, putting the finishing touches on a squash display, when they walked over to the tree.

"Wow!" he rose to his feet, his smile beaming. "You must be Mae! It is so delightful to meet you!" He shook her hand and turned to the boy, "I didn't believe she could possibly be as beautiful as you described, but I was wrong."

Mae's cheeks flushed a subtle pink as she smiled politely at the man.

"I've heard a lot about you as well," she said to the boy's uncle, who turned to the boy and embraced him in a comical façade of gratefulness.

"She's just being nice! She's just being nice!" the boy teased, trying to escape the energetic grasp of his uncle's arms.

"It really is a great pleasure," his uncle laughed, turning back to Mae. "I have heard a lot about how you two met and the things that have happened thus far, and it truly is an amazing story."

The boy looped his arm around Mae's neck and pulled her close to his chest; she was his entire world.

"I'm not kidding," his uncle continued, "you two have an incredible story...one that you can tell your children, your grandchildren, their children, and their children. I mean, you have the ultimate proof of how love knows no limit or distance or difficulty," his voice was quickened with excitement. "You have the perfect example of how two people just need one another. I can feel it emanating from the two of you. You are two halves that are only whole when you are together. I can totally sense a strange feeling of pure, necessary love between you two!"

Mae's grin was wide as she looked up at the boy. He nodded and kissed her forehead.

"I'm pretty sure we have realized the same thing," the boy smiled as she squeezed tightly around his chest.

Mae sat in a camping chair beneath the maple tree while the boy tidied up the displays and waited on the first few customers. He picked up a pear from one of the layouts and polished it against his shirt before handing it to her. She sank her teeth through the crunchy skin and laughed as the juice drizzled down her chin. The boy chuckled with satisfaction as she sighed with pleasure and took another bite. It was not an egotistical satisfaction; he had not grown the fruit, he had no right to take credit for its sweetness. It was a generous satisfaction in the ability to see her smile. It was the fact that what made him happiest was to see her enjoying life.

When the mid-morning rush came, Mae helped by bagging up orders and weighing produce while the boy assisted customers in picking out ripe watermelons or cantaloupes and pricing them.

"We make a great team!" the boy said once the last customer had left. He hooked his arms around Mae's waist and hoisted her into the air. "We should open up our own market!"

Her eyes mirrored devotion as he pressed his lips against hers. As he lowered her to the ground, he noticed a perfectly ripened white nectarine at the top of one of the brimming baskets. Those were his favorite.

"You've got to try this!" he snatched the nectarine up from the display and carefully handed it to her.

"OK!" she giggled and took the piece of fruit in her hand.

The boy watched as she lifted it to her mouth and took a bite into its soft center.

"Mmmmmm!" she hummed. "That is delicious!"

The boy clapped his hands together and nodded his head.

"Those are my favorite!" he laughed.

"I can see why!" she replied between bites.

Picking up a peach from a crate, the boy dusted it against his jeans and pulled out his bottled water. Pouring the water over the peach, he rubbed it gently in his hand until the fuzzy layer was gone from its skin. The midday shoppers were arriving as he handed Mae the cleaned fruit.

"Try this next," he smiled, and she looked at him with wide eyes and half of a nectarine between her teeth.

"You are trying to make me fat!" Mae teased.

"Its fruit – all natural!" the boy winked.

"Hey, I never said I wasn't going to let you try!" she laughed.

It didn't matter even if she weighed 300 pounds, the boy thought, he would not love her a fraction less.

The boy was even quicker and more polite with the customers than usual. Just the fact that Mae existed is what got him through most days of work; but to have her there—in the same state, the same town, underneath the same tree—kept the smile from ever leaving his face. The midday crowd was short; he was so anxious to get back to her that he dashed through the orders and was back at her side in no time. She was just finishing the last tender bites of the succulent peach and smiled with satisfaction as he sat down beside her. All of the charming things in life were only amplified by the profound affection that they had for one another. Fruit tasted sweeter, the air was more refreshing, and the days were much more gratifying when they were in one another's company. Those were the only moments of their lives when everything seemed to make perfect sense.

The boy's uncle was back in time to assist him with the after-work shoppers and the workaholic stragglers. Once the last patrons had made their way to their vehicles and the sun was splintering over the horizon, Mae, the boy, and his uncle packed up the unsold merchandise and headed home. The summer night air was dry and refreshing as they drove.

"I don't mind that job at all with you there!" the boy chuckled once they were inside the house.

"I wish I could work there every day with you," Mae threw her arms around his neck and kissed him with passion.

"Would you like to go somewhere, darling?" the boy raised an eyebrow.

Mae bit her bottom lip and nodded earnestly.

"Alright," he went on, "let me get changed and we'll go."

Just down the street from the boy's parents' house was a small public park. It was dark when he pulled the car into the entrance and flipped off the headlights. Whenever he was with her, she brought him back to who he truly was. Nestled there in the darkness, seen only by the stars that peered overhead, they navigated one another and delved into the deepest slots of intimacy. A pillar of light flashed across the back window of the boy's car. Once again, neither of them had seen the figure coming until it was upon them. Springing upright in his seat, the boy rolled down his window and squinted his eyes.

"How are you this evening?" the police officer said, flashing his light from the boy to Mae. "I'm a respectful man so I will give you a moment to regain your composure."

The boy glared at the officer's avoiding eyes.

"Alright," he began again after a moment, "it's pretty obvious what is going on, but the park is closed. It closes at dusk; so, you are trespassing. Like I said, I'm pretty sure I understand the situation but I need to take your name, address, and social security number just in case anything is found damaged in the park."

The boy looked at Mae and shook his head apologetically. It was shortsighted of him to let this happen again. He dug his wallet out of his back pocket and pulled out his driver's license.

"OK, so...first and last name?" the officer turned to the boy who had his license extended through the window. "That works just as well I suppose," he said, taking the small plastic card from the boy's hand.

The boy recited his social security number and the officer copied it down along with the information on his license.

"Alright," he said once he had finished, "I'll be getting in touch with you if they report any damages. You all have a nice evening."

With a tip of his blue hat, he spun around and marched back to his cruiser, which had only then become visible in the thick darkness of the boy's rearview mirror.

"We just have all the luck, don't we?" the boy said soothingly.

Mae forced a vulnerable smile and the boy turned the car back toward home.

The next day, the boy's mother dominated the house with the roaring of the vacuum, so the two, once again, began their search for privacy—this time in the innocence of daylight. Up the street from his parents' house was a local grade school. It was a Saturday, which made its parking lot the perfect location for solitude. The boy turned the car down the long, windy entrance to the school and stopped on the far side of the empty parking lot. They rolled down the windows and let the carefree summer air drift across their faces. Placing her hands gently on his thigh, Mae kissed the boy like she never intended to stop. The boy opened the sunroof and they soaked in the purity of the sun. Two hours passed while the lovers sat in their private abode. It was not the most comfortable residency and it lacked the simple needs of survival, but I believe they could have lasted forever in that compact.

"Hello?" the boy's scooped his vibrating phone up from the dashboard.

"Hey, man! So, what's the deal?" Joe snickered into the phone. "Are we going to meet this girl or what?!"

The boy had been somewhat reluctant to introduce some of his friends to Mae, and they knew it. Apart from the fact that Mae's time was a cherished rarity, it was also something that he was not sure he wanted to expose to his friends. It had nothing to do with Mae; the boy was more than confident that she could handle their whimsical personalities with lighthearted patience. His concern was more with his friends' inability to maintain the level of respect that he believed his love was worthy of.

"Uh...," the boy looked at Mae, who wore an understanding smile. "Yeah, man. What is going on? What are you up to right now? Are you at your place?"

"Yeah," the boy could hear voices in the background. "I'm over here with Nate, Emma, and Claire. You want to come by?"

The boy checked the clock; Mae's flight home wasn't until that evening.

"Alright," he tried to hide the reluctance in his voice. "We'll be there in a few minutes."

"Is that OK if we stop by my friend's house?" he asked once the phone was back on the dash.

"Sure!" Mae was always so laid back. "I'd like to meet these friends of yours anyway." She cocked an eyebrow at him and giggled.

Joe was outside on his front porch smoking, and he threw his hands up in the air when he saw the car round the bend. The boy could tell by the sloppy smile that spanned the distance between his ears that his friend was Remedied.

"They are a little bit nuts," the boy laughed, "but they are a lot of fun."

"It's cool," Mae smiled, "I've got lots of friends like that."

"Heeeeey, dude!" Joe hollered as he slapped the boy's hand and pulled him in for a hug.

"Hey, man. This...is Mae," the boy replied as she climbed out of the car.

"How you doin! I'm Joe!" he wrapped his arms around her. "You are all this guy talks about! It's great to finally put a face to the name!"

"You, too! I may have heard a story or two about you as well," Mae said, politely returning the hug.

"Eh," the boy teased, "I don't talk about these clowns!"

"Whatever," Joe slapped the boy's chest with the back of his hand. "You know you love me. You talk about us all the time."

The boy shrugged his shoulders and took Mae's hand. Before they could move inside the house, Nate, Emma, and Claire came out the front door.

"What's going on, buddy?" Nate smacked the boy's hand. "How you feeling?"

"Good," the boy replied. "This is Mae."

"It's a pleasure," Nate nodded. "Would you like a beer?"

"Nah, we're cool," the boy declined. "How are you ladies?" He greeted Emma and Claire with hugs.

"So, how long are you in town for?" Joe asked Mae.

"I am actually leaving tonight," she replied, her eyes sad as she looked to the boy.

"Yeah, we can't really stick around," the boy explained. "We just wanted to stop by."

"Oh. Well, alright, dude," Joe chuckled. "Thanks for coming around. I will talk to you later."

While Mae shook hands with the others and exchanged cordial salutations, Joe pulled the boy close to him.

"I never thought I'd see the day...," he whispered to the boy. "Good work, man!" He motioned to Mae.

The boy smirked and nodded in agreement.

"She really is the world to me," he said as she turned from his friends and walked to his side.

It was such a relieving sense of security to know that she was coming with him. The rest of her time may have been spent with people he did not know in a town he had only visited, but at that moment, right then, she was going with him. He wanted to linger in that truth forever.

"Hey, man!" Joe called as they walked to the car. "What are you doing tomorrow?"

The boy shrugged; there was no tomorrow. There was only then and there, him and her, love and forever.

"I don't want to do this anymore," the boy said once they were back in the car.

Mae spun her head quickly toward him.

"What are you talking about?!" she blurted out. "Don't want to do what?"

"This back and forth," he explained.

"Oh," Mae sighed. "You scared me. Me neither."

"I'm just so tired of saying goodbye to you; it makes no sense. We are in love. We want to be together for the rest of our lives. Why should we ever be apart?"

269

"We shouldn't," Mae shook her head. "You're right; and it's my fault. I'm just afraid of leaving my mom behind, but I have to. I can't keep doing this back and forth either. I need to be with you every day. When I get back, I'm going to start looking for schools up here to transfer to."

"I don't want to ask you to do that...," he began.

"I want to. I need to," she giggled. "I've been thinking about the same thing anyway." She looped her arm around his bicep, "It kills me every time I have to say goodbye to you. I want to come up here and never go back."

The boy kissed her hand while he drove.

"You know that I would die if you were to ever leave me, right?" she said, rubbing his arm softly with her fingers.

"You don't have to worry about that," he chuckled, "I would have no reason to live without you."

As he drove down the street toward his house, the boy noticed an elderly man shuffling slowly along the sidewalk. An outdated jacket covered his hunched shoulders and an old brown bucket hat shielded his eyes from the sun. The lackadaisical way in which his legs moved inside the elastic denim of his jeans was proof that the man had no real destination, but it was the man's face that caught the boy's attention. It was full of hopeless defeat as the boy coasted past. Perhaps the man had recently lost his wife; perhaps the two had once strolled that same sidewalk together. He wondered how long the man would last, how long a heart can pump once it has been broken. He had known of many couples who were married for long periods of time and then passed away within just a few months of one another. It was as if once their spouse was gone, the other simply had no reason to go on and died quietly of a broken heart. When love is true, it becomes as necessary for life as oxygen or a beating heart.

Back at the house, the two sat on the loveseat and savored their last bit of time together. The air was still and quiet as they held one another and tried to begin the agonizing process of ripping the converged halves of the orb apart. Each time they were together, the halves had become more deeply sealed to each other, making it more difficult and painful each time they had to separate them. For the boy, it felt as though his heart was being torn from his ribcage. It may as well have been; his heart was hers and she took it with her wherever she went. With each union and separation of the orb, the two halves became more reliant on and devoted to one another. Mae was not far from the truth when she said that she would die if the boy were to leave her. After a certain level of exposure, it becomes impossible for one half of the orb to live without the other.

eighteen

The squeaking of his shoes echoed in the vaulted ceilings of the crowded mall, but the boy did not mind the attention that it drew. He welcomed the common glances of strangers as he strolled along the gallery. He was proud of the decision he had made and had no objection to admitting it. He wanted everyone to know; he would have stopped each individual shopper to tell them the news if he could have. They bustled around him, bouncing from store to store, while his shoes stamped the straight path ahead of him, hands tucked casually in his jeans pockets. His eyes were two pools of determination, and he kept them locked in the direction he was going. The occasional oblivious customer or wandering toddler would stray across his path, but the boy would dodge them quickly, chuckling to himself; he could not be stopped.

Mae had only been gone a little more than a week, but the boy could feel the emptiness in his chest. He had already planned out his next visit and was eager to prepare the necessary steps before he could depart.

The commotion of the crowd died off in abrupt silence as he walked in through the storefront. Two sales clerks sprang toward him with hungry eyes; it was obvious why he was there. The boy sidestepped them politely and requested the owner—the man had been a friend of his parents' and the boy had promised to come see him on such a day. The polite, balding owner rushed to the boy from the back of the store, his smile beaming, his hand outstretched.

"Nice to see you, young man, nice to see you," he shook the boy's hand. "Is today the day?"

"It is," the boy nodded with pride, and the owner clapped his hands.

The two of them spent the next hour and a half sorting through merchandise. The boy sat at the counter while the man brought out cases and cloths and placed them in front of him. He ignored the vibrations of his cell phone as the man told him about the items and the value of each one. The boy listened carefully and told the man what he liked and did not like about each. Other than the boy, the store was empty, so sometimes the idle clerks would mosey past and give their opinions or pitch rehearsed selling points.

"I really like this one," the boy examined it closer. "I think this is it."

He knew that it would be impossible to pick a ring that mirrored the beauty of their love, but it was as close as he could hope for.

"So, this is the one?" the owner took it from the boy's fingers and held it beneath his lamp. "It is beautiful. She is a lucky girl. You want to go ahead with this one?" The boy nodded. "Alright, I'll get that cleaned up and the setting tightened for you. It will only take a few weeks. Congratulations, young man!"

"Thank you," the boy laughed.

The man picked the ring up with a piece of cloth and walked to the front counter. The boy's heart was leaping inside his chest as he followed behind.

"Now, I am going to give you a discount because I know your parents from long ago, and you kept your word in coming back to see me," the man said as he punched numbers into a calculator, "So...all that is due today...is the deposit."

He spun the calculator around so the boy could read the amount. Reaching into his pocket, the boy tugged the carefully folded bills out and placed them on the counter. Most of it had come from the money he was storing for a new guitar; the rest would have to come from savings and his pay from the upcoming weeks.

"The rest will be due when you come to pick it up," the man said as he counted the bills. Tearing a receipt from the register, he handed it to the boy with a smile.

"Alright," the boy chuckled, "thank you very much for everything!" He turned and began walking out of the store.

"When did you need it by?" the man called from counter. "When are you going to propose?"

A glowing smile spread across the boy's face, "Hopefully, in two months! I've got to get her here first!"

His cell phone was vibrating violently against his leg when he made his way back into the noisy gallery. Whistling to himself, he spun the phone out of his pocket and answered it.

"Hello?" his voice was light and jovial.

"Hey," Chloe's voice was not. "Have you not heard?"

The boy froze inside the swarming crowd of people.

"What? Heard what?!" the boy choked.

"Ben...he took a bunch of sleeping pills last night," Chloe sniffled. "He is fine, but he has been in the hospital since early this morning."

"What?!" the boy gasped. "What hospital?! I'm on my way!"

"We can't go see him," she sighed. "They aren't allowing visitors."

"What happened? How is he?" the boy wasn't sure he was making sense.

"They ran tests all morning," Chloe understood. "They said he is going to be fine. He is getting released tonight."

"Why didn't anyone tell me...?" his voice was weak.

"...I guess everyone knows you guys aren't exactly on the best terms," she said carefully.

The boy exhaled, shook his head, and dropped his hands.

"Look," she went on, "we are all going go get dinner with him tomorrow night. I think you should be there."

"...I will be," he said.

He stumbled out of the mall with worry on one shoulder and guilt on the other. His throat rumbled apologies as he bumped into hasty customers and did his best not to trample the young. His friend had done so well for so long; where had this come from? Why had the boy been so callous toward Ben's feelings? Why had he gotten so defensive? He should have never said the things he did; he didn't mean them. He had just bought a ring to make Mae his wife. He could not care for his friend; how could he care for a wife? The sea of people seemed to be tossing him mercilessly among them, heaving him in helpless swells and dashing him against their shopping bags and cell phone conversations. Staggering, he swam through the edges of the mob and spilled out into the sunlight. Catching himself on his knees, he swooned as he did his best to fill his nostrils with the tantalizing air.

The boy did join his friends for dinner the following evening. He got to the restaurant early and waited outside for Ben. Lynn was with him when he pulled up, but he saw the boy waiting on the wooden bench outside and sent her into the restaurant ahead of him. A light rain was misting from the overcast sky as Ben sat down next to the boy.

"Hey," the boy said.

"Hey," Ben replied, "...you know I didn't mean it."

"I know," the boy looked out over the dreary gray parking lot. "How are you feeling?"

"Good, believe it or not," Ben chuckled. "It really helped me realize how important it all is, you know? Lynn and I have never been closer. It's funny; I've got to screw it up before I can realize how good it is."

"Look, I'm sorry about the things I said to you," the boy's voice shook, "I'm sorry I wasn't there for you. If this had anything to do with –"

"Nah," Ben waved him off. "It was just something that sort of happened. I knew it wouldn't work; I didn't really mean it."

The boy quietly nodded his head as the rain collected in his hair.

"I'm sorry, too," Ben continued. "I did not mean the things I said, either. I was just irritated about what that kid was saying to me."

"Yeah, sorry about him," the boy shook his head. "He is just a hateful person. But I just want to make sure that we are OK."

"Of course we are," Ben hooked his arm around the boy's shoulders. "We can't stay mad at each other for too long."

Chloe rounded the corner and a subtle smile flashed across her face as she saw the two boys rising to their feet.

"Hi," she hurried over to them and wrapped her arms around them both.

"Hey," Ben laughed. "How are you doing, darling?"

Chloe buried her face into his shoulder and did not respond.

"We need you," she said after a moment. "I know it's dark... but we need you."

Ben's face flushed a light pink, and the boy shifted his eyes to the little pools of rain that collected on the sidewalk.

Reunited, the three walked into the restaurant and took their places at the table. Unfortunately, they were not able to sit next to one another, but they laughed across the table throughout the entire meal. Ben talked about his future college plans; Chloe talked about her photography and her writing; and the boy talked about Mae. He did not mention the ring because he was not prepared for the uproar that it would have caused at the table. Certain members that were present at that time would have had the news out much quicker than he intended, leaving him no opportunity to tell it himself. He would wait until it was entirely paid for to start the wildfire gossip. Instead, he told them about the trips back and forth from Texas and the difficulty in saying goodbye. They laughed at stories from their youth and sighed with reminiscent fondness at things they had once done. For that two-hour span at the dinner table, they were best friends again. They forgot the distance and lifestyles that had changed them and they went back to the fundamental roots that they had intertwined. By the time the meal was over, they had laughed so much they ached. The boy wrapped his arms around Chloe and said a long goodnight. He extended his hand to Ben but his friend swatted it away and hugged him with his thick arms. They said their goodbyes and tossed around a number of dates when they could get together again, and then they walked their separate ways back to their automobiles.

When the boy arrived home, his brother was sitting in the living room talking on his phone and watching television. With a wave hello, the boy went down into his bedroom and flopped onto his bed. Lifting a stack of pictures from inside his nightstand, he flipped through them and thought about his life. Most of them were of Mae—pictures from spring break, his trip to Texas, and Washington D.C. He smiled at the photo of her standing in front of the ocean and the one of their footprints blended together in the sand. He laughed at a picture of the two of them playing guitar together. They had accumulated so many of surreal memories in a fairly short period of time. The boy wondered if things would be different when she moved to Baltimore.

He knew that not much would change; he believed that they would still be just as much in love—if not more—and that they would continue to have a selfless, peaceful relationship, but he could not help but wonder how she would react to the daily aspects of his life. His best friend was suicidal, his brother was recovering from a Remedy addiction, and his family was not always supportive. His life was nearly the opposite of what he had seen of hers. She was used to a stable, intimate family. Her friends seemed to be fairly level-headed and moderate. How would she react to his chaotic life? What if it scared her away? How could expect her to move to Baltimore and simply take on his turmoil? Where would they live? It did not matter; the boy shook his head. They were in love, and love conquered all.

He called her that night and he lay in the quiet of his bedroom closet while they talked. He had no doubt that he was doing the right thing; they had spent so many nights trying to figure out a way that they could be together, and now they would finally be able to. He would make one final trip to see her, she would move to Baltimore, and then he would give her the ring. She had found a handful of schools that she liked and had begun the process of applying. Everything was in irrepressible motion.

On his second trip to Texas, they did not stay in her hometown. Mae wanted the boy to see her favorite city in her home state, so they drove to Austin. Her cousin and his wife lived there, so they had a convenient place to stay. The city was just as beautiful as she had described. Smooth hills flowed down into the rhythmical side streets of the uptown borough. The frictionless melodies of deprived musicians could be heard flowing from nearly every bar, restaurant, or café that they passed. The slightly more deprived did not require the luxury of four walls and a stage but rendered their neglected tunes from the blacktop. He could see why Mae loved it so much.

She and the boy had little time to even drop their bags inside the door before their generous hosts swept them out into the city streets to enjoy an outdoor dining concert experience. It was a Mexican restaurant, as most in the area were, and the entire front lawn of the establishment was covered in people. The four spread out a blanket in a clearing along the outskirts of the crowd while a woman in eccentric clothing named Toni Price danced on stage, singing the forgotten bluesy style of Janis Joplin. Mae and the boy shared a bowl of nachos and swayed in the evening sun to the harmonious vibrations of the woman's vocal cords. When the sun set behind the city hills, the two huddled together beneath the dancing stars and drifted into the enchantment of the night. It reminded the boy of his dream from years before—her swirling brown hair, the flickering sparks of stars in the sky, her warm chestnut eyes with bursts of forest green, the crinkle of her nose, and the cool clean scent of heaven. They may have been amid a crowd of fellow spectators, but they only saw each other.

Their hearts were still drumming with the hypnotic rhythm of the asphalt when they sank down onto the pullout bed of her cousin's family room. The soft rattle of the snare drum resonated in the air between them. The heat from the blacktop radiated from their skin as they glided around the fluid sheets. Tangy pulsations leaped from the hollow bodies of wooden guitars and stretched in the distance that separated the two halves of orb. Their hips shook in abrupt unison with the tempo of the city. Their fingers moved up and down the fretboard of the thumping bass as it walked its wild scale. The trumpets wailed and the cymbals crashed with resounding passion as the two halves met. Raspy vocals crunched in among the melody and led the horn section in a frenzy of honks and shouts. The dizzying dance of the keyboards rotated their rumba and sent the flutes twirling in a whirlwind of sound. The saxophone blew its final note and, just as quickly as they had come, they vanished back below the asphalt, leaving only the echo of the cymbal to applaud their heaving shoulders.

The next morning, they abandoned the tangling cling of the bedspread and explored the city. The boy drove Mae's minivan while she guided him through the poetic side streets. She led him to a breakfast bar where they ate egg burritos with peppers and onions and talked about how much they had missed one another. Next, she directed him to a nearby sculpture garden, where the two held hands and wandered through the skillfully crafted carvings, taking pictures of their favorites. The garden was empty and they took their time treading its flowery path. Sculptures of angels, humans, and saints stood on small stands like altars and lined the walkway. One, of two lovers in an embrace, caught the boy's eye and he snapped a quick photograph. When they had seen all of the carvings, the two walked back to the van and drove to the artistic district, to the streets where the music was born. The smell of fresh paint and the agile sound of intertwining harmonies filled the air as they parked the vehicle and spanned the sidewalks. Clothing shops, coffee houses, record stores, restaurants, and various music venues occupied almost every storefront on each street they turned down. They wandered into one of the record stores and the boy's eyes widened with wonder. It was nearly five times the size of the shop he frequented in Baltimore. Just inside the door, to the right, was the checkout counter that faced an extensive selection of rock, pop, and country albums. To the left was a wooden archway that led to an equally impressive collection of hip-hop, jazz, blues, and industrial music. Directly across from the entrance was a wide staircase that led up to the punk, reggae, comedy, and cultural sections. Mae and the boy moved up and down the aisles, snatching out albums that they loved and ensuring that the other had heard them. In the rare cases that one of them had not heard a record that the other loved, there would be a 30-second eager rant about why the album was a necessity. Most of the time when one of them would pick up a case, the other would explode with excitement about it before they had the chance to say a word. It was amazing how they could tell the stories of their lives and the beliefs of their hearts through the lyrics and melodies of estranged musicians.

"This album...," the boy held up Third Eye Blind's self-titled debut, "got me through the first half of freshman year of high school."

"1997...?" Mae thought, "I'd have to go with...." She moved back two aisles and held up *Whatever and Amen* by Ben Folds Five.

"Not a bad choice at all," the boy nodded, "'97 was a good year..." he pulled out *Galore* by The Cure and turned it toward her, "this got me through the second half of it."

"I never really got into them," Mae cocked her head and took the album in her hand.

"What?" his jaw dropped.

"I know you really like them," she said as she examined the case.

279

"They are in my top five...," he burst into another 30-second rant.

By the end, she was giggling and adding the disc to the growing collection of those she would purchase. Neither of them even bothered to mention Counting Crows; it was common knowledge between them that the band's entire catalog was the musical paragon. Instead, they took their artistic connection to a deeper level through other musicians. Never once did either of them mention an artist that the other disliked, and each of them walked out of the store with bagfuls of the other's recommendations.

"I really want you to hear this band," Mae said once they were back in the van, "then I want to show you something." She turned the key in the ignition and slid a disc into the CD player.

Funky bass lines melded with jazzy guitar riffs, a swing-like horn section, and rock-influenced drum loops and exploded in Southwestern groove from the speakers. The boy bobbed his head in unison with the music and snapped his fingers.

"I dig these guys," he said.

"Yeah, I figured you would," she smiled. "They're a local band. I really like them."

"Sweet," the boy nodded. "What are they called?"

"Soular Slide," she said as she drove the cruising van uptown.

"Hmmm," the boy tapped his fingers on her dashboard. "Can you make me a copy?"

"You can have this one," her eyes were on the clock as she turned into a small parking lot. "I've got it on my computer."

She pressed the eject button and the disc came spinning out. Pinching it between her fingers, she handed it to the boy. He stretched his fingers around its edge and rotated it toward his face—it was the same brand of blank CDs that he and his college roommates had used in making the money to afford Mae's first visit to meet him. He thought back to that first encounter, of going to the wrong airport, of Mae racing off the plane to find him not there, of his parents driving her to his house for their first meeting, of their first night together, and their trip to the beach. Along the top of the CD she had written "Soular Slide" in graceful letters; he even loved her handwriting.

"What?" she laughed at his dreamy smile.

"Nothing," he chuckled. "I was just thinking about you."

Her nose crinkled as she smiled and leaned across her chair to kiss his mouth.

"Where are we?" he asked, looking around the parking lot.

"I told you I wanted to show you something," she smiled. Her eyes shifted again to the clock, "Come on. It's almost time."

She yanked the keys from the ignition and hopped from the van. The boy pushed the passenger door open and climbed out of his chair. Mae took him by the hand, and led him up the sidewalk toward a long bridge that stretched over a drowsy river. The sun was nearing the western horizon and Mae glanced at it with shielded eyes. The air was flowing and fresh as the boy filled his lungs and soaked in the beauty of their surroundings. A row of people were gathered on one side of the bridge as they walked out onto its sidewalk and stopped. It was an even better view from there; towering buildings climbed on either side of the river, but from the bridge the sun could be seen as a glowing red and yellow, lingering above the distant hills, and the river could be traced cutting naturally through the quieting city. A soft dusky breeze drifted gently over the bridge and carried the fragrance of summer. Mae took his hand and looked out over the water.

"What are all these people doing here?" the boy asked.

"Every night, just before the sun goes down...," Mae turned and looked at the descending ball; its tip had almost submerged into the horizon, "a colony of bats comes out from underneath this bridge."

"A colony of bats?" the boy craned his neck in an attempt to see the underbelly of the bridge. "Like a 'flock' of bats?"

"Yeah," Mae smiled, checking the sun again. "Like a flock of 1.5 million bats."

The boy's jaw dropped. An explosion of flapping brown wings erupted from beneath the bridge and dispersed out over the water. Mae laughed as the boy gaped at the sea of flying creatures. Their wings beating against the twilight air sounded like the propeller blades of a helicopter as they streamed from under the bridge and out into the world. The sun created a marvelous backdrop as it set in the west, shooting strands of purple, red, and orange across the eastern sky where the animals swirled out in gusts of natural grace. It was one of the most breathtaking occurrences that the boy had ever witnessed.

Mae clenched her hand around the boy's dangling fingers and rested her head against his shoulder. The flood of liberated creatures fanned out into the evening for nearly an hour. Mae and the boy stood arm in arm until they could no longer distinguish the brown wings against the black of the darkened sky.

"I love you so much," he said as he took her hand, and they began the walk back to her van.

"I love you, too," she kissed his cheek.

"I can't be without you anymore," he said.

"I know," she sighed. "Me neither."

"So, let's do it," he turned her to face him. "Let's be together."

Her eyes widened and a smile crept along her lips, "What do you mean?"

"Every moment that I am with you, I am happy. We never fight; we always have a good time. We love the same things, want the same things. We have identical beliefs and values and desires for the future. You are the only thing that matters to me. When I am with you, you consume me; when I'm away from you, I'm only trying to find a way to get back to you. I cannot imagine being with anyone else. I could not imagine someone more compatible. I know that there will never be another girl for me—ever. There couldn't be; not after what I have had with you. It makes no sense that we shouldn't be spending every moment together. Come to Baltimore. Marry Me. Let's never be apart."

"OK," her smile burst into a laugh and she wrapped her arms around his neck. "Alright. Let's do it."

They drove back to her cousin's house with the windows down and their hearts in the sky. Every few moments they would glance at one another and laugh. They could not have been more in love, and they were finally going to prove it to the world. They would be the ultimate representation of what true love really was—selfless, devoted, all-encompassing love.

The boy's fingers plucked softly against the steel strings of her cousin's banjo, while Mae sat on the bed and listened. The boy had never played the instrument before, but it was similar enough to guitar that he could manage. Mae's face was tinted with peaceful bliss as she watched his fingers climb up and down the cool fretboard. The thought of eternity with one another did not rattle either of them; instead, it did just the opposite. It gave them a distinguishable sense of serenity to know that they would be one another's constant for the rest of their lives. No matter how difficult things got, they would always have each other. It was an empowering sense of invincibility.

That night, as the boy lay on his back in bed, he ran his fingers lightly through Mae's hair. Her head was resting gently on his chest, and it rose and fell with the inflation of his lungs. He smiled at the progress of his life. Had he not been alone those early years of his life, he would have never believed, and thus never have waited, for the beautiful things that he had found in Mae. Had he not had leukemia, he would not have become so close with Ben and Chloe and would not have developed such a musical dependence. It was that musical dependence and his love for Counting Crows that had brought him to Mae. Had he not cut his hand, he may not have gone to college; he may have pursued his career in music. Had he not moved and gone away to school, he may not have been isolated enough to dedicate the time and involvement in growing to love the intricacy of Mae. He began to see the sophisticated web that had brought him to the place—to that very moment—and it made him chuckle. Each moment had happened to bring about one result.

"We were meant to be together," he whispered, kissing the top of Mae's head.

"Mmmhmm," she moaned sleepily and buried herself deeper into his chest.

nineteen

I do believe that I did mention earlier that there are points in each person's life where they feel as if there is no hope left. It is not something that anyone desires or anticipates but, much like anything else in life, it is inevitable. It is a chain reaction. Just as the discovery of hope can sweep like disease through crowds, or religions, or nations, so can the woeful acknowledgment of despair spread through the life-lines of a society. It is a dark, agonizing process as it bleeds from one individual to another, and in the end only the strong survive. Luckily for the boy, I was there to pick up the pieces.

From the moment he had arrived back in Baltimore, the ring had never left his mind. It was all he wanted; it consumed him. He had told her of his intentions and she shared his excitement. In less than two months, she would be descending into his city and he would slide the smooth circle of promise onto her finger. The ring was picked out and he almost had enough money to complete the purchase. He had spent the last few weeks of summer and the first two months of school working as many hours as possible to pay for the ring. He had decided to take classes at the local community college to conserve the funds that he did have. He could worry about transferring to another school once she had her ring. Just another three weeks of work and he would have enough. Three weeks after that, she would arrive. The anticipation was almost more than he could stand; it reminded him of the weeks before their first meeting.

The boy lay on his back on his bedroom floor and listened to the new Counting Crows CD, *Hard Candy*. The CD had come out roughly three months beforehand but it had not left the boy's stereo since that day. He had woken up the morning of its release, gotten dressed, driven to the store and purchased it, and I don't believe he had listened to anything other than those 14 tracks since. It was a fairly optimistic album—something uncommon of the band—and it applied to where the boy was in his life. Ben and Chloe had called him the day of its release, and the three had talked for hours about their love for it and their indecisiveness in picking a favorite song or lyric. Ben had explained that while he adored the new album, his heart was still true to their first, *August and Everything After*. Chloe fell in love with the slower, more morose tracks from the new CD like "Goodnight L.A.," "Black and Blue," and "Holiday in Spain." The boy loved it all. He stretched out, rubbing his knuckles against the carpet, and soaked it in. He mouthed the words, "She is standing by the water as her smile begins to curl. In this or any other summer, she is something all together different - never just an ordinary girl," while Adam crooned them through the humming of his speakers.

"Is this their new CD?" his brother asked from the doorway. The boy turned his head so that he could see him and nodded. "Any good?"

The boy never could tell whether or not his brother was a fan of the band. At times, he seemed to enjoy their music and occasionally the boy could hear one of their songs drifting from his brother's room, but other times he mocked the boy for his devotion.

"It's unbelievable," he admitted, and his brother smiled.

"I will have to check it out," he replied.

"There is a pretty dynamic change from their earlier stuff," the boy propped himself up on his elbows, "and I'm sure people will be critical of that, but I dig it. I understand that good musicians reflect their lifestyles and outlooks on life in their music."

"Cool," his brother stretched his back. "Listen, do you think I could borrow like twenty bucks?"

"Sure," the boy picked up his wallet from the nightstand. There was no cash; he had gone to the bank the day before and deposited every bill he had into his account for Mae's ring.

"Actually," the boy grimaced, "I'm all out of cash."

"What about a bank card?" his brother asked timidly, "I'm just out of gas and I'm supposed to take Lily to the mall tomorrow."

"Alright," his phone rang on the floor next to him as the boy slid his bank card from the leather wallet.

It was Mae.

"Hey, cutie pie," he answered the phone. "How are you?"

"Hey!" she sighed. "Much better now."

"How was your day?" he asked as he handed the card to his brother.

"Can I borrow this?" his brother whispered, holding up the boy's gray hooded sweatshirt.

The boy nodded.

"It was OK," Mae said. "How was yours? How was class? How did your test go?"

His brother tapped his arm and mouthed the words "pin number."

"Class was alright," the boy scribbled the four digits down on a piece of paper and waved goodbye to his brother. "I think I did pretty well on the test. It was easier than I thought it would be."

"Of course it was!" Mae laughed. "I'm sure you got an 'A' and I know you didn't study!" He had told her about his pattern with test taking.

"Don't you start giving me grief about it, too!" the boy chuckled. "I can't help it!"

"I know," Mae giggled. "Hopefully the kids inherit your brain."

"Oh, please," the boy coughed, "I'm hoping they get everything from you."

The boy's phone beeped that its battery was low. Hopping up from the carpet, he plugged it into the wall and lay in the corner on the floor, talking to Mae until they both fell asleep.

The next morning, the boy awoke to the smell of bacon. Some Saturdays when his father was feeling overly generous, the man would wake up early and prepare an extravagant breakfast spread for the family. That way, they would all see each other at least once before they went their separate ways. It was always a nice way to start off the day. Climbing from his bed, the boy took a quick shower and got dressed. He walked down the hall to wake up his brother, but his room was empty; he must have beaten him to the breakfast table. He whistled as he scaled the steps in leaping bounds.

"Good morning!" his father said, sliding another pancake from the skillet to a serving plate on the kitchen table.

"Good morning," his mother echoed, shoveling a forkful of eggs into her mouth.

"Morning," the boy smiled at the spread, "this looks delicious."

"Tell that to your brother," his father pulled out a chair and sat down at the table.

"I tried," the boy scooped up a piece of toast from the plate and bit into the flaky crust. "He's not in his room. I thought he was up here."

"No," his mother raised her eyebrows, "he didn't come home last night."

"What?" the boy poured himself a glass of orange juice. "He didn't?"

"Nope," his father shook the pepper shaker over his eggs, "and I told him I was going to make breakfast this morning."

"Sorry," the boy swallowed a mouthful of the juice, "he said something about going to the mall today."

His cell phone rang in his pocket. It was far too early for calls.

"It's not your fault," his father said. "That just means more for us."

The boy checked his phone; it was Lily.

"Excuse me," the boy pushed back his chair and stood up.

"...or not," his father said as the boy walked down the hallway and into the spare bedroom.

"What? Did he lose the pin number already?" the boy answered the phone.

"Hello?" Lily sounded puzzled. "What? Pin number?"

"Yeah," the boy chuckled, "my brother. Are you guys not at the mall yet?"

"The mall?" Lily said. "I don't know what you are talking about."

"Wait. You aren't with my brother?" the boy could feel the boiling acid creeping up his chest.

"No!" Lily exclaimed. "That's why I'm calling...he is really worrying me. He hasn't been himself. He is ignoring my calls and sneaking around. I don't know what to do! Do you have any idea what's going on?"

The boy could feel his head swooning. How could he be so stupid? The acid from his stomach was gnawing at the tissue in his throat. He held his hand to his forehead; it was glistening and hot. A tingling that started in the bottom of his feet crawled quickly up his legs, through his chest, and to the top of his head. His arms were numb, and his palms shimmered with sweat.

"You know, don't you?! What is it?" Lily's throat rattled with accusation.

"I-I've got to go," the boy moved quickly back down the stairs to his bedroom.

"Wait! What?!" Lily choked. "What is going on?!"

The boy snatched his keys from his dresser and slipped on a pair of flip-flops.

"Listen, I'm sorry. I can't talk about it right this second," he took deep breaths and stood still in the center of his bedroom, "I will call you later."

"Alright," he heard her say as he clamped the phone shut and dropped it into his pocket. Flipping off his light switch, he sprinted up the stairs and to the door.

"Where are you going?" his mother asked.

"You aren't going to eat?" his father chimed simultaneously.

"No, I can't," the boy flung open the door, "I've got to run out. I'll be back. Save me some."

He slammed the door and darted to his car. Throwing it in reverse, he sped backward out of the driveway and barreled down the street. His mind was racing as he impatiently drummed his fingers on the steering wheel. It wasn't far. His stomach churned and he unbuckled his seatbelt. In a few quick turns he was pulling into the parking lot. He popped the car into park, jumped from the driver's seat, and jogged to the front door. An old woman was coming out as he approached the entrance. He forced a polite smile and held the door open, doing his best to hide his angst. Once she had cleared the doorway, he walked briskly inside and up to the front counter. Ripping a small rectangular sheet from the stack he scribbled down a series of numbers and handed them to the smiling woman behind the counter.

"Can you check the balance on that account...please?" the boy said, pointing at the piece of paper.

"No problem," the woman smiled. "Just one moment...."

The boy scratched below his bottom lip and tapped his finger against the counter. He tried to prepare himself. The tightness in his chest and gurgling of his stomach told him that it would not be good. How much would be missing? Enough that he would be angry? Enough that he would demand it back? Enough that he would have to postpone buying Mae's ring? How much it was would tell how badly off his brother was. If only the teller knew the weight of her words. Her brow scrunched as she scanned the computer screen. The boy leaned farther across the counter and she straightened her face. She opened her mouth to speak; the hairs rose on the boy's arms.

"There actually...is a negative balance on this account," she held the small rectangular paper with one hand and worked her pen across it with the other.

The boy could feel his chest tightening. She spun the paper and slid it across the counter so that he could see. "-$12.34." His vision blurred as he glared at the number. Not only was his bank account beyond empty, but that also meant he could not purchase the ring and that his brother was in a lot of trouble. His knees quivered, and he sagged against the countertop. His muscles tightened as the gargling in his stomach heaved.

"That means...," the teller went on, "that there was a purchase made with your bank card, but then there was an ATM withdraw before the purchase was processed, leaving the account as negative. There will be a thirty dollar overdrawn fee for every day that it remains nega...."

He could feel that his face was pale as he looked at the woman with perplexity. His brother had emptied his account. He could not marry the girl he loved—at least not yet. Snatching the paper up from the counter, he staggered backward. The woman watched him cautiously as he regained his balance and moved quickly out the front door. Catching himself on a large brick pillar outside of the bank, he hunched over a patch of bushes and emptied his stomach into the mulch.

"Ew!" a woman's voice exclaimed. "Are you OK?!"

The boy waved her away with his hand. Her face was contorted with disgust as he straightened his back and wiped his mouth with the back of his hand. Another woman with sunglasses and a stroller was frozen in the parking lot, staring at him with twisted lips. They watched him with fearfully captivated eyes as they would a hideous creature. Dropping his eyes to the asphalt, he tugged his keys from his pocket and stumbled to his car. They were still staring as he started the ignition and drove from the parking lot. There was no sense in going out to look for his brother; he was sure that he would not find him. Instead, he drove back home, went down into his room, and called Ben.

"Hey, man!" his friend answered.

"Hey...," the boy replied.

"What's up? How was Texas?" his voice was optimistic.

"It was a great time," the boy could feel his eyes stinging.

"That's awesome," Ben smiled. "How is Sally?" His friend still called her by the name they had given her on the floor of the barn years before.

"She's perfect, absolutely perfect," the boy choked, "but I screwed it up."

"What?!" Ben said. "What do you mean?"

"I was going to propose to her in a couple weeks," his voice shook, "I had the ring picked out and everything, but I...can't afford it." Even in his anger, he could not allow himself to defame his brother.

"Oh. Wow! Really? Congratulations," Ben fumbled. "Why can't you just get a cheaper ring?"

"I can't afford any ring," the boy scoffed. "My account is empty."

"Man, that's terrible. How did that happen? I'm sorry...," his voice dropped, "so, I guess you've got to wait till you save up some money. That is not necessarily a bad thing anyway. I mean, are you sure you are ready to get married? That's a big deal. Maybe this is a sign that you should hold off."

"She's coming up here in a month and a half...and my life is in shambles!" the boy blurted out. "I can't hold off! What am I going to do?!"

"Take it easy," Ben said soothingly. "There is plenty of time. Just relax. It shouldn't be this stressful; just slow it down, man. You are getting ahead of yourself. I know that you love this girl, but you are stressing yourself out way too much right now."

"Maybe you're right...," the boy noticed his gray sweatshirt thrown across his bed. His brother had been home and had returned the jacket.

"Of course I'm right!" Ben chuckled. "I mean, I was so stressed with life that I was about ready to give up; but all it took was for Lynn to show me how much she cared. Now we are better than ever. Trust me. Just slow it down. Enjoy it."

"Alright...," the boy snatched up his jacket from the mattress, "I gotta go."

"Alright man, keep your head up," Ben sighed, "I'll talk to you later."

The fabric stretched as the boy pushed his arm through the sleeve and pulled the hood on. Snapping the phone shut, he slipped it into his jacket pocket. Something plastic crinkled underneath the weight of his phone. Pushing his hand farther into the pocket, he pressed his fingers into a soft pouch wrapped in the crinkling plastic. With squinted eyes, he tugged the pouch free from his pocket. His throat constricted and his hands tingled as he scanned the baggie of powdered Remedy. It had been years since he had stumbled in and found his brother inhaling the substance. The boy had promised then that he would keep his discovery a secret as long as his brother would quit. As he stood there holding the baggie up in the light, he realized where his money had gone. He realized that his brother had not changed. It had not done any good to hide his brother's addiction. He thought that if he just supported him and allowed him to give it up on his own, it would disappear. He did not want to cause his brother that embarrassment and cause his family that pain. Instead, almost four years later, they were fighting the same battle. He wondered how long his brother had been fighting alone. Stuffing the bag back into his jacket pocket, he wiped his leaking eyes and walked slowly back up the stairs.

He was waiting on the front porch when his brother's car

pulled up. His eyes were glazed and transfixed on the clouded setting sun as he sat, wrapped in his sweatshirt, on the concrete steps. The weather was still warm but the hint of green that accented the blue sky and the ominous squalls of wind that blew across his face warned of the approaching storm. His brother was spinning his keys around his finger and humming a tune as he walked down the sidewalk toward the house. He froze at the sight of the boy.

"I went to the bank today...," the boy said, his eyes still on the darkening clouds.

"...yeah?" his brother shifted nervously. "What happened?"

"They told me that my account balance is negative," the boy clenched the small rectangular sheet of paper in his fist. "How could you do that?"

"Look, I'm going to pay you back," his brother said, "I told you I needed to borrow some money."

"Some money?" the boy chuckled. "You took all the money."

His voice was calm and his eyes never left the clouds.

"I had a lot of stuff I had to pay for!" his brother struggled to explain, "I was behind on some bills. I owed people money...."

The boy tossed the baggie of powered Remedy to his brother and, for the first time, he looked into his eyes. His bottom lip quivered as he waited for a response.

"...shit," his brother fondled the bag in his fingers, "It isn't what it looks like."

"You know, I actually believed you the first time you told me that," the boy's voice shook. "I was such an idiot! Nothing has changed."

"That's not true," his brother argued. "I was clean for a long time. This...this is just like a one-time deal. Don't even worry about it."

"Don't worry about it?!" the boy choked. "How can I not worry about it? I've got to tell someone. We can't go through this again."

"We?! We?!" his brother laughed and held up the bag. "This doesn't have a thing to do with you! This is my issue! I'll pay you back your money. We will settle that up. It's just going to take a few months. But don't you worry about my issue. You aren't going to tell anyone."

"Yes I am," the boy's eyes were back on the clouds.

"Oh you are?!!" his brother stepped closer. "No you aren't; and you want to know why? Because I'm not going to rehab over some stupid little baggie, and you don't want to break mom's heart! I can't believe you are actually going to judge me."

"I'm not judging you...," the boy's voice was calm.

"How are you going to justify lying about it all these years?" his brother stuffed the baggie into his jeans pocket.

"It was a mistake.... I was trying to do what was best..." he could feel the saline stinging his eyes.

"Just give me a little time," his brother sighed, "it's not that big of a deal. I just got a little bit because I've been having some trouble lately. Don't tell them," he motioned to the house, "They will only judge me; you know that. They aren't going to help. They don't care! You know how they are. They didn't even come to your graduation. I don't need their help. I just need to make the decision for myself. They aren't going to understand. Just like they wouldn't understand if I told them the real reason you transferred home from college."

The boy squinted his scorching eyes and lowered his head. He had decided not to tell his family about the trouble he had gotten into while he was away at college. He told them that the university was not what he was looking for and that he had decided to look for another school. In actuality, he had been politely expelled for the possession of illegal substances. How could he not extend the same mercy to his brother?

"So, we will both keep our secrets and we won't destroy the family," his brother was beside him now.

The boy remained quiet.

"I'm sorry about the money," he continued, "I really did need it; and I will pay you back over the next few months."

The boy nodded and rubbed his eyes.

"Thanks, little brother," his brother patted his back as he walked up the stairs. "Oh, hey! Lily is on her way over...try to be nice to her, alright?"

The front door opened and closed, swallowing his brother before the boy had a chance to respond.

Back down underground, inside his tomb, the boy lay on his bedroom floor for the remainder of the day and contemplated Mae. In just a few weeks, she would be there amid the crisis of his life and he would have no ring to give her. It wasn't supposed to work that way. Ever since he was very young he had developed an understanding of what love was meant to be, and it did not involve all the added trag‑edy. It would be unfair of him to ask her to come and live among the mess his decisions had created. His head pounded with stress. Ben was right; they just needed to slow down and relax. If he truly loved Mae, then he would make his world right before he would ask her to be a part of it. He thought about the pregnancy scare and the responsibil‑ity of marriage. He thought about the meager salary he was making at work and buying a house. He thought about trying to go to school and support a wife. He thought about how his bank account was empty and how his brother needed him. He thought about the selfishness of asking the girl he loved to leave everything behind for the squalor of his life, then he called her.

"Hey, baby!" she answered the phone.

"...hey," he sighed, "I need to talk to you."

"OK," she said. "What's up?"

"I-I love you...," he began, "I just have had a lot going on right now...and I've been thinking that m-maybe we should slow things down. I just don't want to rush into something that I don't think we can handle. I mean, we are a million miles apart with our separate lives and issues...and you are going to leave all that behind to come here, but I don't know that here is alright right now...." He didn't even sound like himself.

"What are you saying?" her voice was bewildered. "Are we breaking up...?"

"No – Not at all!" he stammered. "Well...I don't know what we're doing. I'm not sure what it means. I just think we are doing all this rushing and there is no reason to. W-we should be enjoying every step of this."

"Is there something you are not enjoying?" she was begging to understand, but the boy had boarded his secrets inside.

"No, there isn't. I just want to step back for a minute. I want to make everything stop. It's all just happening too fast and I don't know that I can take it. I just need everything to back up and let me breathe."

He never distinguished between when he was talking about his life and when he was talking about their love.

"OK..." she forced steady breaths between the searing of the orb in her chest. "If that is what you want...then I will obviously give it to you."

"I'm not doing this for me. I-I'm doing this for us," he stuttered, "I want this to be something that we agree to try. Let's try to get ourselves right before we go any further."

"Alright," she cringed.

"I mean, this is mutual, right? This is best," he was so consumed with his injuries that he did not notice the pounding of the orb against his ribcage.

"I trust you," she winced.

"I'm sorry," he sighed. "It's just so much right now...it's so intense."

"Don't be sorry...," she sniffled. "Can I still call? Do you not want me to call you?"

"No, of course you can!" his eyes were burning again. "I want you to. I'm not trying to get rid of you....I just....I don't know...."

"OK...," she faked a smile, "I'm going to go...."

"Are you OK?" he said. "I need you to be alright. It's just so I can get things together."

"...I'll be fine," she croaked.

"...I'll talk to you soon...." He couldn't believe the apathy in his own voice. It was uncontrollable. He was not himself.

"Alright," she fought back the tears, "...goodbye."

"...Goodbye," he sighed, but she had already hung up the phone.

Sparking my lighter, I held the red flame up to the tip of the cigarette wedged between my teeth and puffed. Thin clouds of wispy smoke billowed from my mouth and rose, dissipating in the dense night air above the tree line of the boy's backyard. I kept my figure hidden in the quiet shadows of the nearby pines and watched the glowing frame of the boy's bedroom window. The grass was still damp from the rainstorm, and it stuck in soggy strands to my shoes. Inside, the boy lay on his floor and meditated to the white of the ceiling. I took long, patient drags from my cigarette and kept my eyes on the window. Mae collapsed in a heap on her bed and wept until her eyes were swollen and her wearied body surrendered to sleep. As I exhaled the last lungful of my cigarette and flicked the filter to my feet, I saw the light die in the boy's window frame. He had gone to bed; it would not be long.

twenty

They only spoke twice in those first two weeks. Once Mae called the boy and once the boy called Mae. The conversations had been casual and acted as a reflection of their avoidance of their own lives. Fifteen hundred miles apart, they sat isolated in their rooms. The boy fought to gain control over his personal struggle while Mae fought to eradicate the pain that surged beneath her chest. He distracted himself with school and extra hours at the produce market while Mae wept into her pillow and refused meals. He was taking all the steps he could to reconcile his life and return to his love, but his progress was slow. One more week and I believe that he would have felt worthy of restoring his relationship with Mae, but not all fairy tales end as they should. It seems that it is when we are closest to achieving our goals that circumstance swoops in and makes a mess of our teetering, carefully constructed plans. Not everything is happy.

If you have ever lost someone dear to you, you are familiar with the nauseating tingling that starts in the back of your head and pulsates down your spine, spreading to every extremity like lightning bolts discharging from your fingertips. The dizzy swooning, the quiver of reality, and the loss of all control are not sensations but permanent residents in your being as you battle through the never-ending moments of horror. Nothing can prepare you for that avalanche.

"Hello?" the boy said into the phone extending from his mother's outstretched hand.

Her eyes shot waves of terror into his. His body quivered with chills.

"H-h-hello?" even through the stomach-turning sobs, the boy

could recognize Chloe's voice.

"Chloe!" the boy choked. "What's going on?! What is wrong?!"

Every muscle in his body tightened as he braced for impact.

"B-B-Ben was in a car a-a-accident this morning...," every word was murderously torn from the deepest pit of her being. "He's dead!"

Nothing can prepare you.

The phone burst into fragmented shards of plastic as it dropped from his ear and made contact with the floor. The boy collapsed in a mangled heap on his bed and scourged his throat with a heartbroken howl into his pillow. Not one tear dampened his cheeks, but his vocal cords wept uncontrollably. He screamed until his stomach burned. He screamed until the red of his face matched the blood of the innocent and his sorrow matched their terror. He screamed until his palms were scarred with the imprint of his fingers in clenched fists. He screamed until he felt that he might implode. He screamed until he fell asleep. He slept for fourteen hours and then not again for another four days. I read somewhere that after five days, you are legally insane; but who believes in books anymore?

After the first three and a half days without sleep, he was ravenously searching for the assistance of a Remedy. Some bridges you burn, some bridges you keep. Some bridges that you should have burned, you kept; and some that you desperately need are somewhere behind you, smoldering in the hungry flame of Regret. It was at this point in the boy's life that he and I became inseparable comrades.

Sometime wedged between day two and day three of his sleeplessness, his legs moved him to his closet and climbed into a pair of black slacks. His arms pulled a white shirt from a hanger and matched it up with a red paisley tie. A black sports jacket climbed onto his back, and his arms pushed through the sleeves. He did not check the mirror to straighten his hair. He did not decide on matching socks. He could not bear the thought of truly preparing himself for his best friend's funeral. He did not attempt breakfast; it would have ended up half-digested in the bush outside the church anyway. He did not tie his shoes; but he did rummage wildly through his CD collection, making two deliberate selections before wandering out the door and to his car.

August and Everything After guided his vehicle as it cut through the brisk autumn air. The unbuttoned cuff of his sleeve flapped in the current of his window as he took deep, introspective drags of his cigarette. His tie was a loose two inches from his undone collar, and his bloodshot eyes glared into the rearview mirror from beneath disheveled hair. He was a hollow body going through the motions of a human being. It felt absurd to even attempt to allow any real emotions to access his heart. It would be far more than he was capable of managing. Apart from the grief and pain of losing his friend, feelings of guilt, uncertainty, and fear haunted him, and they all surrounded him like wild dogs hungry for the tenderness of his heart. He turned up the music. The most daunting thing for the boy was that he could not cry. He had tried for days, but the release simply would not come. He begged for it; it would have done him good to empty all his misery through his eyes, but he could not force it out. It seems that there is a limit to the amount of times a heart can be crushed before it becomes so calloused that it can hardly feel anything at all.

The church was crowded with people. The boy slid into one of the back rows. Two heavy purple curtains flowed down from the ceiling at the front of the chapel with venerated grace and fanned out onto a sumptuous stage. Skylights overhead channeled natural light down in columns that flickered on the floor and glared against the deep wooden rectangle that sat below a cross at the front of the room. The white trim of the inside of the casket forged a lump in the boy's throat as his eyes scrutinized the room. A light chuckle echoed in the vacant ceiling, and he cringed. People who knew the boy would flash him sympathetic glances or pat his back as they passed, and he would do his best to respond with a nod or the slight lifting of a hand from his lap. Two ushers in black moved down the aisle and waved each row out of their seats, up in a loop past the casket, and back. The boy slid his hands into his silky pockets as he rose and trudged slowly up the aisle. The lights overhead grew distinctly brighter as he moved to the front of the room. Ben's family huddled together in the front row, and his mother rose to her feet at the sight of the boy. Her eyes were quivering puddles of heartbreak as she swallowed him in an affectionate embrace. Robotically, he wrapped his arms around her broken frame. He could feel the jowls of emotion nipping at his heart, but he refused their entry.

"It is so good to see you," she gasped into his ear. "He loved you so much. You were such a dear friend to him."

The boy exhaled slowly. He tried to conjure a gently comforting response.

"…I'm so sorry…," was all that he could formulate.

"Can I go up with you?" she asked, motioning to the casket.

The boy nodded, and she took him by the hand.

Together, they approached the wooden rectangle like two sinners in the presence of an angel. Arm in arm, hand in hand, they stood and gazed upon their loss. He did not look like himself—I think you will find that they rarely do—but his peaceful face possessed the familiarity that they had loved for years. The woman hugged him closer to her side and exhaled through her shivering lips.

"You can let it out…," she sniffled. "You can cry…."

His chest was an ignorant cage of stone and ice. There is nothing more heart-wrenching than watching a mother say goodbye to her son, but even that could not squeeze a single drop from his inflamed eyes. It tore the inside of his stomach into excruciating knots, but it could not dampen his cheeks.

"…I wish I could remember how…," he whispered into the solemn air.

He kept his eyes on Ben's face. His friend looked like a saint, his cheeks glowing in the overhead light, his arms folded, lying faithfully beneath that cross. Somewhere in the recesses of the boy's humanity, a reminiscent smile formed.

The slow murmur of funeral conversation quieted to a hush as the crowd drifted to their seats and the ceremony began. He could hear the sniffled cry of Ben's parents blaring over the deafening silence of the church's remorse, and his eyes singed. Eight rows diagonal from him, Chloe sat with Lynn, a cornflower blue sweater covering her daisy yellow top. She dabbed a tissue to her eyes as she whimpered quietly. A few other mutual acquaintances stood out in the rows of mourners but, other than that, the boy did not recognize anyone. He had been asked to say something at the end of the ceremony, but as he scanned the distant faces, he could not fathom words that would do his friend justice. He knew that if he were to march down the aisle and up to that reverberant microphone, his heart would have exploded in a spew of anger, guilt, and sorrow. He had no happy memories to share; those were locked in a strong box somewhere in the pit of his subconscious, where his self-destructiveness could not destroy them.

The boy rose in instinctive unison with the rest of the crowd and filed out into the parking lot. There were a handful of mutual friends between him and Ben that had been privy to some of their mischief and jokes. Three of those friends were standing outside the church as the boy came out, and he motioned them to his car. They did not say a word; they climbed into the vehicle and sat calmly as the boy fished a cigarette from his pack. Holding it between his lips, he lit it and trails of smoke drifted into his eyes as he fed a disc into his stereo. He leaned back in his seat, twisted up the volume, and cracked his window. The other three passengers followed suit, picking out cigarettes of their own and dropping their windows as the smooth bass announced the introduction to "Another One Bites the Dust." Swirling clouds of white smoke oozed from the cracked windows as the song blared out from the car. The crowd channeled out of the church and past the thumping bass to their vehicles. Some walked slowly, bobbing their pensive heads to the beat. Others shook their heads and smiled knowingly. A few shot perplexed or snobbish looks, but it was not for them. It was for Ben. They did not say a word. They played the entire song from beginning to end, filling their lungs with grating smoke and tapping along with the bass line. When the song faded off into the speakers, the three passengers climbed from the car in glorious clouds of smoke and wandered their separate ways. The boy nodded contently and turned the car's ignition. He had kept his promise to his friend.

A trail of headlights led him to the cemetery where Ben would be buried, but the boy followed the murder of crows that flapped above his open sunroof. With red captivated eyes, he watched them as they swarmed playfully over his car all the way from the church to the cemetery. As he parked his car in the parking lot, they dispersed into a large maple tree that stood in the graveyard. The tree was a brilliant yellow, and the boy kept his eyes on it as he followed the crowd down the pathway. The crowd stopped not far from the tree and circled around his friend's grave. The boy lingered back and stood under the shadow of the maple. He could not hear the final words that the pastor said over Ben, but the boy heard an eloquent eulogy of his own through the rustling of the breeze and the hopping of the crows from branch to branch. It was one of the most beautifully despairing things the boy had ever experienced. He closed his burning eyes and let the wind skim across his face. The crunching of footsteps behind him would have startled the boy had he been fully alive; but instead, he turned slowly to find Chloe inching across the grass.

"Take this...," she gasped once she had been discovered. "Take it...." She extended a small notebook and pen to the boy, who watched her with cautious eyes.

"Take it...," she stepped closer to him and put the items in his hands. "Write us out of here...write us away from all this...write us back...take us back...."

She shook with sobs of horror as the boy enclosed her in his embrace. He held her jolting frame against his chest and rocked her gently as she buried her face into his disheveled clothing. Together, they stood in the shadow of the old maple tree and tried to make sense of the loss of their friend. In the distance, the boy could see the polished wooden box sinking slowly into the ground. The wind whipped harshly into his stinging eyes.

"Some people don't get the chance to rectify their wrong before it is too late," he muttered to himself and hugged Chloe tighter against his chest.

Through his years of friendship with Ben, the boy had become fairly close with Ben's older brother, Vince. Slightly larger and much more aggressive than his younger brother, Vince had spent the first few months tormenting the two. Once the boy had proven that he was capable of taking the abuse, Vince had begun to consider him a friend and treated him like a younger brother. If the boy ever came across more trouble than he could handle, Vince was someone he would call with confidence. After the funeral, the two stood in the parking lot and talked.

"You want to go out for a drink?" Vince asked.

"Right now...?" the boy croaked.

"I can't go home," Vince justified going to the bar. "Plus, it seems like the only logical thing to do."

The boy shrugged, and the two drove to a nearby saloon.

I was seated at the opposite end of the bar with an old friend of mine when the two strolled in, still loosely dressed in funeral garb. I watched carefully as they took two stools close to the door and ordered tall glasses of liquid Remedy. He looked familiar to me at the time, but I could not place his face. It was obvious by their attire where they had come from; and quite frankly, I was offended that I was not invited. They murmured quietly to one another, taking occasional swallows of their drinks, their eyes locked on the wooden bar in front of them. The boy fidgeted a straw wrapper in his fingers, ripping off little bits of paper and dropping them. "A drink" turned into three, and they sat just as quiet and solemn as when they had come in. There is some hurt that liquid simply can not dissolve.

I did not notice the people at the table behind them until the boy lifted his eyes from his drink and glanced over his shoulder. Two girls sat on stools at a tall round table with their boyfriends. It was obvious by their obnoxious laughs and ridiculous conversations that they had consumed an excessive level of liquid Remedy, but that was not what caught the boy's attention. I listened closer.

"How did you not notice it?" the girl's voice was overly dramatic. "There was like a hundred cars driving with their headlights on in the middle of the day!"

"Today?" her slick-haired boyfriend asked.

"Yeah!" she laughed. "It was like three hours ago! It was when we were on our way here!"

"Oh yeah!" the other boyfriend agreed, adjusting his red baseball cap. "It was that kid that died in that car accident the other day!"

Vince and the boy had stopped talking; they were absently watching a television that hung in the corner. The boy poured another swallow of liquid down his throat. He could feel the tension emanating from Vince.

"What car accident?" the girl asked loudly, sloshing her drink.

"It was just a couple days ago," the red-capped boyfriend laughed. "I heard about it...aw man! It was sick! They said that he when his car hit the...."

The boy had declined hearing the explicit details of the incident, but that certainly would not stop others from hearing those

303

details and sharing them in disgusted faces with their friends at the local bar.

"Alright...," Vince said, swiveling around in the stool.

The boy kept his eyes on the television as he nodded and tugged his wallet from his pocket. The red-capped boyfriend was barely through explaining the second unnecessarily graphic detail to his friends when Vince drew back his arm. His thick fist went hurling furiously through the air with sledgehammer force and landed directly against the red-capped boyfriend's face. The boy placed thirty dollars casually on the bar top and waved a "thanks" to the stunned bartender. The girl shrieked as her boyfriend went tumbling backward with his barstool and landed hard against the ground. The other boy shot up quickly, but a glare from Vince lowered him back into the seat. Without a word, Vince straightened his shirt and stormed out the front door. The boy poured the last swallow of his drink down his throat, spun around in his stool, and walked calmly out of the bar.

Stepping out into the cool evening air, the boy pinched a cigarette from his pocket and lit it. Vince stood at the bottom of the bar steps looking out over the horizon, his hand shoved in his pockets, his back to the boy.

"I guess we should get home," the boy puffed smoke into the air.

"Alright," Vince nodded, "I'll talk to you soon."

The two slapped hands, exchanged hugs, and turned separate ways from the parking lot.

I was not looking for him. He was looking for me; he just didn't know it yet. After three and a half days without sleep, you simply cannot make rational decisions. It has been an interesting experience for me to spend this time talking about him the way he used to be, the way he is trying desperately to become again. That is not the way I know him. That is not the way he was when we first became close friends. That is not how we have spent the duration of our companionship. The first time that I truly met him, he was a hopeless ball of destruction. I told you, he is lucky that I was there to pick up the pieces.

It was the beginning of his fourth day without sleep, and he was in dire need of assistance. Remedies have a characteristic unlike nearly every other substance in life. When you are in most desperate need of them, they find you. You can try to resist them for as long as you like, but you can never escape their temptation—not until you truly realize that they are not something that you honestly want. Unfortunately for the boy, not only could he make no such realization, but his self-control was shit. Some bridges that you should have burned, you kept.

I was sitting on a saggy brown sofa with some new friends when Will and the boy came staggering through the front door. It was obvious that they were Remedied, but they were hungry for more. As I passed a synthesized Remedy to my left, I could tell that the thirst in Will's eyes was typical; it had an aged glimmer to it, and my new friends recognized him. The boy, however, they watched with careful eyes. He had more of a desperate glaze over his eyes; it was obvious that he had not slept in days and that he was unfamiliar with our circumstance. I smirked as I flipped a capsuled Remedy to my right. I remembered how I knew him; I remembered why he looked familiar. I had once known his brother, but it was something much more significant than that. I remembered the boy from that day years before when he sat in the tree with the silver heart trinket and thought about the first girl he'd ever tried to love. My smirk grew to a light chuckle but the boy had not seen me yet. I don't think he would have recognized me; he was so young then. Most people are rather apprehensive about their first encounters, but the boy showed a mechanical sense of confidence. He wore faded jeans and a casual tight black jacket with a hood that collected around his neck. I did not catch his name as Will introduced him, but it didn't matter. I didn't need to know his name. As soon as I looked into his eyes, I knew that we would come to know each other well.

The boy lowered himself down into a recliner on the other side of the room. Will sat in a chair beside him and took a pipe from his pocket. As Will thumbed a wad of planted Remedy into the device and offered to him, I watched the boy's eyes glance at me with brief recognition. I smiled and nodded my head as he took it into his hands. Spark. Puff. Spark. It had been years since he had inhaled the thick, sticky smoke. It sank in heavy waves down his windpipe, disseminating into the tiny capillaries and coursing quickly through his veins. Spark. Smoke. Inhale. He could feel the blood tingling beneath his skin. He just wanted to escape the constant pounding of reality. Ben was gone. Spark. Spark. Inhale. He could not change that. Something howled inside his mind. He tried to fight back the salivating jowls of guilt and grief. There was no way to know if he was the rightful bearer of that responsibility. Smoke. Smoke. Spark. His brother was an addict; that certainly was his fault. Spark. Spark. Spark. Not that he had any room to talk. He was the self-defeatist. Aw, Ben! Inhale. Smoke. Inhale. The fluid echo of the wave of Will's hand vibrated off the side of the boy's arm. He extended a pill—the synthesized Remedy—to the boy and mentioned something about the word "escape." With a nod of his head, the boy tossed the pill from the palm of his hand to the back of his throat and swallowed. Fuzzy vibrations shivered across the glaze of his eyes. Will's head swiveled on an elongated neck and tilted in front of the boy. His eyes were black saucers and his ears fluttered. The boy pressed his head back in his chair and the peripheral edges of his vision rushed in blurred streaks. His feet splashed in the tranquil pools of water that collected on the floor below him. The cackle of Will's throat caused the boy to blink and tampered reality. His shoes were solid on the burgundy carpet. The room was slow and quiet and his friend slumped in the chair next to him, chuckling at the backs of his eyelids. It was at this point that I took the opportunity to introduce myself. Rising slowly from the saggy sofa, I approached him cautiously because I could see his fragile state. His eyes were innocent waterfalls of desperation as he turned them to me. I looked down on him with a comforting smile and we shook hands.

"Are you the devil?" he asked me calmly, his eyes vacant of life.

I chuckled and squatted down in the chair next to him. Not exactly.

His eyes flickered again with the distorted pulsations and he gripped the arms of the recliner as the six walls that anchored the room to the house shivered and tore free. He could now distinguish the simple electronic music that popped from the stereo speakers. I inched closer to his seat as the cubic space lifted smoothly into the air. The black velvet of the night quivered with the sound waves that welled out from the detached room. The boy tapped his finger with the droplets of sound from the speakers as the house became a distant image far beneath our space capsule. The higher we sailed, the higher pressure built with silence outside our pod. The music propelled us in soft circles as the boy imagined them into existence. He looked at me with inquiring eyes, and I pointed to the city lights that twinkled under our shoes like stars. One million miles from the civilized ground, we experienced space in a way that no one else ever had. Our connection was something that the billions of people underneath our feet would never comprehend. In complete darkness and solitude, we drifted, entirely disconnected from life and reality. The boy looked peaceful as he sank into the cushion of the chair and repressed his existence. He had found temporary tranquility. Taking him by the hand, I helped him to his feet. His steps were stiff and unnatural as I walked him across the carpet and to the front door. I pushed it open, and his eyes widened at the empty darkness of space that surrounded us. He looked at me with reckless eyes and nodded. Hand in hand, we stepped to the edge of the doorframe, locked our knees, and fell forward. The wind whistled loudly in his ears as it streamed around his face. The music faded in the blackness that echoed behind us. The twinkling city lights expanded as we plummeted toward their bulbs. I turned to see the boy; his eyes were closed and his mouth was curved. It reminded me of the orb, spinning through empty time and space, hurling with premeditated purpose. I wondered if he would ever grasp its significance. He rocketed down the same path that his half of orb had traversed. The lights below were like shattered glass now, rising toward our graceful faces. We sailed toward the eastern rim. We could see the city streets. With a yawn and an overdue stretch, he soared down through his house, landed abruptly in his bed, and finally learned how to sleep. That is how I came to know the boy.

twenty-one

"I like it better how we had it before," the boy scratched his cheek and adjusted his guitar across his lap.

"Alright," Ian tapped his fingers lightly on his bongos. "Let's do it the way we had it."

The two boys had first started playing music together as a casual pastime when they would stumble across instruments at mutual parties. From the beginning, they had unmistakable chemistry and, despite the boy's initial apprehension, he agreed to attempt to meld his bluesy acoustic guitar with Ian's raspy choir voice and tribal drums into a two-man band. The boy could not deny the quality of their sound, and after the first few practice sessions he had grown once again to love the creation of music. Now, the boy and I wrote songs together and they rehearsed them weekly in the concrete basement of his parents' house, while I sat in the corner and watched.

Ian's cell phone rang and he jerked it up from the table.

"Hey!" he answered. "How are you?!" It was his girlfriend.

The boy worked his fingers mindlessly up and down the fretboard and stared at the smooth flooring beneath him.

"Yea," Ian lowered the bongos from his lap and glanced at the boy. "No, I got some time."

The boy propped his guitar up against the wall and walked into his bathroom. Splashing handfuls of water against his cheeks, he scrubbed his eyes and took deep breaths. The picture of Mae taped on his bedroom wall caught his attention in the bathroom mirror as he dried his face. He dropped the towel to his side and stared at it thoughtfully for a moment. My frame in the doorway interrupted his thoughts, and he tossed the towel down into the sink. I walked closely beside him down the hallway and back into the concreted area.

"Let's do this later," the boy said as soon as he was back in the room. "We can come back to this."

Ian still had his phone pressed to his ear and looked at the boy with puzzled eyes.

"Let's practice later," the boy lowered his voice. "Let's go to the bar."

Ian shrugged and smiled willingly.

———— ∞ ————

"So what is the deal with you and Ally?" Ian asked, his fingers drumming on his chest as he stretched out on the carpet.

"What do you mean?" the boy pinched pieces of planted Remedy from a bag and pressed them into a device.

"What's going on with you two?" Ian turned to look at the boy. "You guys have been hanging out a lot!"

"I don't know what you're talking about," the boy fished a lighter from his pocket. "We're friends. We like to hang out."

"Wait," Will shot up from the sofa. "Who is this girl?"

"She's no one," the boy pulled out his lighter. "She is just a friend of mine."

"That girl Ally," Ian responded to Will. "You've met her— blonde chick."

I tapped my foot impatiently from the chair next to the boy.

"Oh yeah," Will chuckled. "She's cute! You should hit that up!"

"Nah," the boy shook his head, "I don't do that."

"Why not?!" Ian sat up. "She is hot!"

"Are you trying to do this or not...?" the boy replied, sparking the lighter. Puff. Smoke. Inhale.

———— ∞ ————

The boy woke up to the taste of liquid Remedy coating his tongue and the jab of Ian's heel in his side. In order to optimize their chances of becoming a successful band, the two had found a small one-bedroom basement apartment—the only kind they could afford. As a result, they shared a bedroom; Ian slept on an old bed and the boy slept beside it on a mattress on the floor.

"Your phone is ringing," Ian croaked.

The smell of smoke and liquor filled the room as the boy threw back his sheets and staggered to the dresser. Rubbing his eyes, he picked up the singing phone.

"Hello?" he grunted.

"Hey...," Chloe giggled. "You alright? Did you just wake up?"

He checked the clock - 12:34. What day was it?

"I'm cool," he coughed. "What's going on?"

"Not much," Chloe sighed. "I saw your old band in the paper today."

The boy cringed.

"Oh, yeah?" he feigned interest.

"Yeah," she said. "They are playing some show tonight at The Shack."

He had played there with them before.

"Cool," the boy replied. "I'm in a new band now. It's just me and one other guy but it's not bad. I'd say it's more of a...."

"Shhhhh!" Ian moaned, waving his hand.

Opening the bedroom door, the boy walked quietly out into the living room.

"That's cool," Chloe shrugged. "There also is something else that I wanted to tell you.... You may have heard it already.... I'm not sure."

"What's up?" the boy flopped down in his leather chair.

"Lynn is pregnant...," Chloe said slowly.

The boy's heart stirred for the first time in months.

"What?! Wait! Hold on!" the boy stammered. "Since when?!"

"We aren't sure...," Chloe hesitated. "...but we don't think it's his."

"What?!" the boy laughed. "It would have to be!"

"Not...necessarily," she replied. "She needs to go to the doctor before she is sure...but she thinks it is someone else's."

The boy was speechless.

"It would have been like...three weeks after...," she continued.

"Three weeks?!" the boy blubbered. "Three weeks?! Are you kidding me?!"

"I know. I know...," Chloe's voice was weary. "We all took it hard...maybe it was her way...."

The boy scratched his head with his fingers.

"Look, I've got to go," she sighed, "but I will let you know when we find out."

"OK," the boy coughed, "let me know."

"Are you alright?" she asked.

"Yeah," he lied, "I'm fine."

"I'm worried about you. You haven't called me in awhile," she said. "Are you holding up OK? Are you taking care of yourself?"

"I'm good," he chuckled. "Don't worry."

I was waiting for him by his car when he came out, his hair still wet from his shower, his face resolved. Flicking my cigarette into the street, I climbed into the passenger seat and we sped toward his parents' house. As we slowed to a stop at the first traffic light, the boy noticed Ben driving the car beside us. Shaking his head, he looked again but the light had turned green and the car had lurched forward. I patted his shoulder and we drove on. A minivan passed us, heading in the opposite direction, and the boy saw Ben's face through the windshield. Rubbing his hand quickly over his head, he tapped the brake but I handed him a cigarette and he puffed it thoughtfully. It was not the first time that had happened, nor the last.

No one was home when he parked his car in his parents' driveway, but he still had his key, so he let us in. Wasting no time, he raced down the steps and into his old bedroom closet. His eyes lingered for a moment on the small carpet square that covered his closet floor and I could tell his mind was drifting backward. A slight nudge of my elbow forced him back to me, and he dug through the clutter of the shelves until he found a thick maroon folder. Snatching it from the closet, he raced out of the house and back to his apartment.

Ian was awake and pouring himself a steaming cup of coffee when the boy burst through the door.

"Good morning...," Ian groaned. "Well, weren't you up and about early this morning."

The boy dropped the folder down on the kitchen table and

looked at his roommate with satisfaction.

"What's that?" he asked, sipping his coffee.

"This...," the boy sat down and flipped it open, sending pages of lyrics sliding across the table, "is everything that I ever wrote for my first band. These...," he picked up some of the pages, "are *my* songs that *I* wrote, that *they* are still playing! These are my first creations. I have these original copies that I wrote. That means that I have rights to these songs!"

"What does that mean?" Ian lifted one of the papers from the table. "Do you want to play them?"

"Yes!" the boy slapped the table. "It means that I'm going to go to their show tonight and take the rights back to these songs! Then we can do whatever we want with them!"

"Alright...," Ian dropped the page back to the table. "Can we get some breakfast first? 'Cause I'm starving."

"Yes!" the boy laughed.

Naturally, I went with him to the show. I rode in the back while he drove with his folder of writings on the passenger seat. We could hear that the concert had already started by the time we pulled into the parking lot and climbed from the car. A man with thick arms and multiple piercings was guarding the front door, collecting money from the latecomers who straggled in. There was some sort of added injury in having to pay to watch the band that you created play, so the boy and I slipped in through a side door that he had recalled from their show there years before. The lights were low and the room was electric. Blue lamps hovered over a long metallic bar; shades of purple and red shot from the spotlights above the stage and shone on the swaying mechanical silhouettes of the spectators. Jack's eye sockets were dark and his frame was thirty pounds lighter as he dipped the microphone in unison with them. His slightly sunken cheeks stretched as his pale lips formed the words to a song the boy could hardly remember writing. From back in the crowd, he was almost unrecognizable, but the boy could not mistake his voice. Staggering backward, Jack took a sweeping bow and slurred a "thank you" at the closing of the song. The boy held the maroon folder tightly in his hand, and the two of us made our way to a pair of barstools and ordered a couple of glasses.

"They play here often?" the boy asked the bartender, pointing to the stage with his thumb.

"Used to...," he replied, wiping the bar top with a rag, "back when they first got signed and their CD came out. Last few months... poor kid can barely make it to shows, and when he does...he is out of his mind." He looked at Jack.

The crowd laughed as the singer stumbled across the stage playing air guitar to the intro of their next song, his shoes tangling in the cord to his microphone. I chuckled, and the boy shot me an angry glare.

"Yep," the bartender continued, "it's a shame. They are good... they've got some good songs."

"Do they just have the one album?" the boy asked.

"Yep," he replied. "They have some new songs that they play sometimes but nothing recorded. I think they just play the old stuff mostly."

The boy nodded.

"I think they've got the CD for sale over there...," the bartender pointed to the merchandise booth in the corner.

"Thanks," the boy waved his hand and scooped his drink up from the bar.

It is sometimes difficult—even for me—to read the boy. Sometimes the smallest of things can be the cause of dynamic change within him. A song can come on the radio or he can drive past an open field at just the right moment and catch the tall grass glistening in the setting sun, and it can completely alter his emotions. Other times seemingly cataclysmic events can occur and cause no change in his untroubled heart. I suppose that only some things have the power to speak to him. By now, I should be accustomed to his sporadic compassion, but I am not.

A few feet from the bar, a tall red-haired boy bobbed his head with the music. Though it had been years since the boy had seen him, he recognized the spiky hair and long, narrow shoulders. Hopping up from his stool, the boy abandoned me at the bar and trotted through the crowd.

"Hank!" he called, squeezing his way between the rows of people. "Hey, Hank!"

He bumped into a man with folded arms and the man thrust back with his elbow, but the boy ignored it. A girl in a rainbow shirt scoffed and scowled as he stumbled, jostling her arm and spilling his drink.

"Hank!" the boy grasped his shoulder, and the spiky redhead spun around.

"Hey!" his dark blue eyes widened at the boy's friendly smile.

"How have you been?" the boy laughed. "How's your band?"

"I'm doing really well!" Hank nodded intently. "The band is OK. We lost a few members due to differences, so that's hard, but we're moving along!"

There was something refreshingly uplifting about seeing the old acquaintance—something about his demeanor was just...full of hope.

"That's how it goes," the boy smiled. "That's the trouble with musicians: We all just want to make music so bad that we just can't get along."

"What about you? Have you been creating any masterpieces lately?"

It is a terrifying thing to realize that faint acquaintances have more faith in you than you have in yourself.

"Masterpieces?" the boy chuckled. "Nah. I am in a new band, but we are just really starting to get off the ground."

"Well, that's a start," Hank clapped his hands together. "As you can see, I still come to shows; I'm still one of the biggest fans of your work."

"You are probably one of the only ones here who knows it's mine," the boy laughed.

Hank nodded sadly.

"Speaking of which," the boy lifted up the folder, "I'm glad I saw you here. I wanted to give you this." He extended the collection of songs to Hank.

"Me?" Hank stared.

He opened up the maroon cover and began thumbing through the pages of the boy's handwriting.

"Those are all originals copies," the boy pointed to the pages. "Some of those we never even had a chance to turn into songs."

"I can't take these!" Hank gawked. "W-what about your new band? Why can't you use these?"

"I'm in a different place," the boy's eyes were on Jack's crumbling physique. "I write different songs now...."

He took a long swallow of his drink.

"Wow," Hank flipped more thoroughly through the papers. "This is awesome! Thank you so much!"

"No problem," the boy smiled. "Take good care of them. They got me through some difficult times. Hopefully I will see you again sometime soon."

"Alright, I will!" Hank closed the folder and stared at its cover. "I will keep an eye out for your new..." he turned to look at the boy, but he was already gone.

Pouring the last droplets of liquid into his throat, the boy slammed the empty glass down onto a passing table and strolled out the front door and into the street.

The boy pulled his wool hat tighter down around his ears and pushed the cigarette back between his lips. Adjusting the guitar across his lap, he plucked a series of notes, paused, and scribbled out some words on the pad of paper that sat on the gravel beside him. Anyone in their right mind would have avoided the chill of that afternoon air but, for the boy, it was the only place that he could find solitude. Even outside the back door, the boy could still hear the clamor of his friends inside the house pillaging through the remnants of the previous night's debauchery. The cloudy haze that swam inside the boy's head told him that they would not find much.

"Are you insane?!" Ally called as she came trotting from the driveway. "It is way too cold! What are you doing?!"

She leaned down over the boy and planted a quick kiss on his lips. She had been doing that the past few months now; the boy supposed it meant that they were dating. He had told her from the beginning that his lifestyle was not conducive to the sort of thing that she was looking for, but that had not deterred her in the least. She was convinced that his neurotic behavior, mysterious beginnings, and sporadic Remedy abuse were tolerable byproducts of his enchanting persona. She was enticed by the notion of becoming intimate with someone who seemed so estranged from the rest of the world. She was a vivacious blonde with a kind heart and an optimistic soul; he was a walking zombie with a detached heart, a shoddy memory, and a calloused soul. They were bound to meet somewhere in the middle.

"Just trying to get some quiet," the boy motioned his head toward the door. "Ian and the guys are a little noisy."

"Oh," Ally craned her neck to look through the window. "What did you all do last night?"

"Not much," the boy yawned, "...just hung out."

Ally cocked her head and arched the corner of her mouth; she thought she knew what that meant.

"We can go in if you're cold," the boy began gathering up his pencil and pad.

"No, I'm fine," Ally waved her hand. "I'm on my way to my mom's for dinner. I'm just stopping by. Plus, I'd rather not deal with those guys if I don't have to." Her eyes were peering through the window again.

"Did you finish another song?" she turned back to him.

"Not yet...," he sighed, "but it's coming along."

"That's like your third one this week!" Ally exclaimed. The boy nodded—fifth. "Is it another sad song?" she asked, and the boy chuckled.

For some reason, any song that was not comprised strictly of major keys and did not contain at least one mention of the word "sunshine," "romance," or "forever" was a "sad song" to Ally. The boy smiled and shrugged.

"It's about change...," he stabbed his cigarette down into the rocks, "and how it can cause you to lose parts of yourself that you may need."

"Cool," she shivered. "Sounds sad. Oh! Speaking of sad...I listened to that Counting Crows CD that you made for me, and I am still not feeling them at all."

"Really??" the boy stared.

If she did not appreciate Counting Crows, there was practically no way that she could appreciate him.

"Yeah," she shook her head, "...too much...whining...."

The boy opened his mouth to erupt in a barrage of rebuttals when Ian came stumbling out the door.

"What's up, Ally?!" Ian hooked an arm around the girl's neck and tugged a cigarette from his pack.

"Hi Ian," she faked a smile, "I'm actually heading out," she pulled her keys from her purse. "Maybe, I'll come by later."

She waited as the boy rose to his feet and dusted his jeans.

"Take it easy on yourself tonight," she said as they hugged. "Don't go crazy. Get some rest."

"I'll try," he laughed, and she shot another knowing look as she hurried back to her car.

"How is that going?" Ian asked.

"What? With her?" the boy replied. "It's whatever...it's good."

"Have you still not done the deed? Made it official?" Ian blew smoke through his nose.

"Nah," the boy shook his head.

"Why not?!" Ian gawked. "What is the deal?!"

"I don't know," the boy shrugged. "It just doesn't feel right. I don't think that it's something we should do unless it is absolutely right."

"I respect that and all," Ian snickered, "...but dude, it's got to be right soon. You guys have been together for a good while." Had they?

"Whatever," the boy waved his hand. "Are you trying to play or what?"

"Hell yes!" Ian pulled two synthesized Remedies from his pocket and handed one to the boy.

"I'll see you after," the boy said, hoisting the Remedy to his friend before tossing it to the back of his throat. Ian did the same and flicked his cigarette hard into the gravel.

"Now, let's practice."

⊸∞⊷

His head felt as if someone had driven a spike into the back of his neck as he rolled across his squeaking mattress and snatched his screaming phone from the nightstand. The trouble with his regular dosing was the condition in which it left him each morning. Not only was his head pounding, but he also had to deal with the harshness of reality until he could pacify his mind again.

"Hello?" he moaned.

"Hey," Chloe had grown accustomed to his new tone, "shouldn't you be awake by now?"

"I'm not sure," the boy tried to swallow the dryness that filled his mouth.

"So, Lynn got her results back...," Chloe sighed.

"...and?" the boy held his breath. He wasn't sure what he was hoping for.

"It's not Ben's baby," she replied. "It's someone else's."

The boy pressed his hand firmly against his forehead. How could it be someone else's? That meant that Lynn had been with someone else only three weeks after Ben's death.

"I know you're angry," Chloe said soothingly, "so am I. But there is nothing we can do about it. I'm going to be supportive of her, because that's what Ben would have wanted me to do. She was upset. She made a mistake. She is trying to deal with it as best she can. Don't let it upset you."

He drew air slowly through his nostrils and tried to steady his temper.

"I've got some good news. Would you like to hear some good news?" she was trying to steady it as well.

"Yes, please...," the boy exhaled.

"I met someone," she smiled. "He is really great. I know that you would like him. We've gone out a few times over the past month and we made it official last night."

"That is good news," the boy croaked.

"I told him about you, so he knows that he needs to meet you and get your approval," she continued. "Hopefully we can get together sometime next week?"

"Yeah, I'd like that," he smiled.

"I know you're upset about Lynn," Chloe said. "Do you want

to talk about it?"

"No," the boy rolled onto his back. "Tell me more about this guy."

The boy could not recall having made the trip back to his hometown since Ben's funeral, but he knew that he must have at least twice. Nevertheless, when Ally insisted on a Sunday drive back to the house where he was raised, the boy was apprehensive.

"It's not much," his hand cut through the wind as he spoke to the blonde-haired girl in the passenger seat. "It's just an old country house."

"That's OK," Ally adjusted the air conditioning vents. "I would still like to see it."

"Alright...," the boy chuckled. "I just don't want you to be disappointed."

"I won't be," she folded her hands in her lap. "I just want to know more about your life."

"What about it?" he asked. "There isn't much to know. It's mostly just cobwebs and bad decisions. I warned you that you didn't want to be inside this crazy head or behind this involuntary wall."

"Don't you think it would help to let those things out?" she asked slowly.

"You would think so," he smirked, "but that's just it! I don't want to be free because I don't deserve to be. I'm self-destructive because it makes me feel some level of atonement."

"But you are just going to end up destroying yourself!" she scoffed.

"You are absolutely right!" he couldn't help but laugh, "I am destroying myself—by smoking and burning the shit out of both ends of my candle. But that's for poetic justice. It's the only control that I can have. All I can hope to do is to one day look in the eyes of that clumsy conductor Fate, the one who broke or destroyed everything I ever loved, and say, 'Now I control you.' "

"Fate doesn't exist...," she sighed.

"You're right," he agreed, "not anymore. Not in my life at

least. I am just trying to feel something. I'm just trying to figure out how to make good things out of bad. There has to be a way to reconcile the decisions we make!"

Ally sat back in her chair and folded her hands quietly. He had tried to warn her that he was not what she was seeking.

As they crossed through the green light of one of the traffic intersections, the boy's eyes glared thoughtfully down the passing road.

"What is it?" Ally noticed his demeanor.

"Nothing," the boy replied, "...that's the road where Ben had his accident."

The boy stared down the windy street as it flashed past. He wondered what his friend had been thinking that day when he turned down that road, what the weather was like. He wondered what his last words had been, what he had last said to his mother. His heart sank at the thought of the woman. It had probably been some time since he had seen her last. He owed her a visit; he missed Ben's parents.

"Who is Ben?" Ally asked, furrowing her eyebrows. The boy cringed at himself.

"My old best friend," he said quietly, and Ally nodded.

Apart from a few minor adjustments, the house was the way they had left it. A tree was missing from the front lawn, a new mailbox marked the driveway, but it was still the same building. The car tires crunched the pebbles against the asphalt as the vehicle came to a stop. A wave of vague childhood memories swept over the boy as he and Ally stepped from the car. It is always interesting to go back to your origins. In the years that you are gone, it becomes this sort of magical place. Things that would hold little value in common places are priceless gems of inception in the abode of your youth. Despite their alterations and your personal memory flaws, those childhood gems cannot be dismantled. They are permanent relics of your youth, and the longer you have been gone, the more powerful they become.

"Wow! What is that over there?" she shielded her eyes and pointed.

The boy turned to see the large flaming red barn that towered in the brilliant light of the diminishing sun. Instantly, he was thrown back to the days of lying on its gnarled floor and tracing his fingers through the grain. He remembered those summers scampering across its beams with his friend and the old blind woman in the rocking chair on the front porch. He supposed she had died by then; perhaps she and her husband were reunited somewhere deep beneath the loving foundation of the symbolic barn. Who was he kidding? Love did not happen that way. It was not some fairy tale. Love was a convenient contract between two people who agreed to look out for the better interest of one another—after their own interests, of course—for as long as mutually beneficial. It was a way for two people to ensure that they would not end up trudging alone through this vile, unmerciful, spinning ball of chaos. It was something that singers sang about and poets ached for but no one truly had because no one understood. It was something that had gotten lost in a sea of prejudice, lust, and prenuptial agreements. It was a pleasant thought for young girls and dreamers.

"Just some old barn," the boy replied dryly.

As they circled around the house and the boy led her through the yard, his memory regurgitated things he had long forgotten. Ally asked as many questions as she could think of, and the boy did his best to answer them. He showed her where he and his brother had buried their dead bird and pointed out which window looked into his old bedroom. Before they climbed back into his car to drive home, the boy stopped at the top of the driveway and peered out over the open field. The sun had almost set, and it sent beautiful dashes of orange across the dying grass.

"What's over there?" she pointed to the trees that lined the other side of the field.

"A neighborhood," the boy laughed.

Ally smiled and shook her head, her blonde curls bouncing against her cheeks in little spirals of confusion.

Choppy brushes of the bongo kept time between blues guitar riffs and Ian's smooth vocals as the two boys worked in the dim lighting of the coffee house stage. The crowd of strangers listened with interest as the boys played their newest creations. It was only their third or fourth show, but their natural synergy gave them the confidence of seasoned musicians. Every eye was on Ian as he slammed the bongos, leaned back in his stool, and belted the words in perfect unison with the boy's guitar. It was their best show yet. With the final note, the crowd rose in applause, and the two boys moved off the stage. Neither Ally nor Ian's girlfriend had much interest in attending their shows, so the boys would spend their time talking to one another, or lingering onlookers, as they packed up their meager equipment.

"Phenomenal job, gentlemen," a man called from in front of the stage. "Really nice work."

"Thanks," Ian waved.

"Cliff," the man introduced himself, shaking their hands. "Do you write all your own songs?"

"Yeah," Ian smiled, "all originals."

"I really like it. It's got a great sound," Cliff said, "zesty and original. Do you have a manager?"

"No," the boy laughed, "we aren't quite that serious."

"Well, you should be!" Cliff exclaimed. "There's no reason why you shouldn't! Listen, my partner and I have a small recording studio. We usually record acoustic artists. If you guys are looking to put something together, I'd be willing to pay you to let us record it for you."

"Why would you do that?" the boy tossed his guitar cable into a box.

"Because it is going to sell," Cliff smiled, "and I want to be the one to sell it for you."

"Really?!" Ian stopped packing and gave the man his full attention.

"Absolutely," Cliff went on. "We could start with something small—just a couple of tracks on a demo and then go from there. No strings attached. As soon as you find a bigger producer that will sign you, you're free to go."

The boy moved closer. "I don't get it. What do you get out of the deal?"

"Publicity," Cliff pulled out his business card. "I get the publicity of your first tracks produced by my studio. People start considering my studio as a good starting point."

The boy looked to Ian; his friend was nodding his head earnestly.

"You want to do this?" the boy asked. "Are we ready?"

"Let's do it," Ian laughed.

"Alright," the boy took the business card between his fingers. "We will call you this week and set up a time."

"Fantastic!" Cliff clapped his hands together. "I can't wait to work with you gentlemen! I look forward to hearing from you."

With that, he turned and walked out of the coffee shop.

"Did that really just happen?" Ian turned to the boy. "Is that guy really going to pay us to record?!"

"Yeah," the boy laughed, "I think so!"

"Does that...mean...that we are, like, an actual signed band?" Ian was tripping over his words.

"I mean, yeah, I guess!" the boy smiled. "It's amateur, but we're going to get paid!"

"That is awesome!" Ian slapped the boy's back and gave him a hug.

"We did it!" the boy laughed. "But we've got a lot of work to do before we go meet that guy."

"Work?!" Ian scoffed. "Who cares about that right now?! We've got to do some celebrating!"

That night, they drank until they fell over. Ian sang their songs loudly from his barstool while the boy played air guitar for their friends. They slipped out around the side of the bar and passed a planted Remedy device around the circle then stumbled back in with smiles twice as big. Their friends bought them injections, the bartenders bought them injections, strangers bought them injections, and they paid for whatever else it took. As they stumbled out to their designated vehicles, Ian hooked his arm around the boy's neck and wobbled beside him.

"I've been meaning to ask you, man...," he slurred, "what is that new song about?"

"Which one?" the boy chuckled and staggered to the left.

"The new one...it goes...'it seems that on that Selfless road is where we came alive...' " he swaggered. "I know it's about a girl obviously, but I'm not sure I get it.... What girl? Not Ally."

The boy's smile dissipated from his mouth. He felt a rumble beneath his chest. He licked his drying lips and stared at the pavement in front of them.

"It's just about a girl I used to know," the boy said dismissively. "Have you got any of the little robots?"

Ian eyed him with suspicion.

"I've got a few, but we've been drinking all night," he dug down into his pocket.

"Yeah," the boy coughed, "but I thought we were celebrating!"

"I can't argue with that!" Ian laughed and pressed a synthesized Remedy into the boy's palm.

The boy threw it to the back of his tongue, swallowed, and vanished.

The only plausible trouble with music is that it comes from musicians, and like most other artists, musicians are capricious. It was the day before they were scheduled to meet with Cliff in his studio. All the arrangements had been made. They had decided which songs to play and had rehearsed them avidly. The boy was sitting at the kitchen table threading a new set of strings through his guitar when Ian called.

"What's up, man?" the boy answered.

"Hey, man, what are you up to?" Ian said.

"Not much," the boy replied. "Just putting on some new strings for tomorrow."

"Yeah, about that...," Ian sighed, "tomorrow is actually not going to work out for me."

"What??" the boy lowered his guitar. "I thought we double-checked our schedules! I think that's the only day he has free this week. I mean, I guess we could ask and see what he has available for next week...."

"I don't think next week is going to work either, man," Ian chuckled nervously.

"...What are you talking about?" the boy rose from his chair.

"Look man...I'm sorry...things are getting pretty serious with my girlfriend, and she doesn't like the idea," Ian tried to explain. "She says the only way that she would feel comfortable with me singing these songs is if we changed all the lyrics so that they were about her."

"No way!" the boy laughed. "Are you kidding me?! So you

aren't going to record...because she told you that you weren't allowed to?!"

"I'm sorry, man. I can't play at all anymore—not if it upsets her," Ian shrugged.

"They are songs, man!" the boy exclaimed. "You didn't even write them! She wants me to write songs about her?! That makes no sense. Are you really going to pass this up? Are you really going to quit because all the songs are not about her?!"

"I've got no choice...," he sighed. "She is more important than any of this."

Closing his eyes, the boy scrubbed the top of his head and clenched his jaw. Once again, his pursuit of music had fallen just short of his goal. He was angry, but he could not blame all that anger on Ian. However irrational his friend's action may have been, he could not be blamed for making sacrifices in the name of love. As I sat down at the kitchen table and looked at the boy, I could see that his mind was working. Somewhere in the faint traces of his memory, the boy could recall a time when he would have willingly done the same.

twenty-two

"Excuse me, sir," a voice called as he strolled along the row of tables.

The boy's faded black shoes pivoted on the paisley carpet as he turned to face the elderly couple seated at the small square table.

"I ordered this steak to be cooked well done and it still has this pink in the center!" she stabbed her fork into the grilled cut of meat and lifted it for the boy to see. "I don't eat bloody meat!"

At the end of the produce season, the boy had been in need of a job and had applied to a nearby fine-dining restaurant. He had friends in the business and they had told him that it was one of the few ways college students could make decent money. It required a certain level of finesse and theatrics that not all people were capable of, but the payoff was well worthwhile.

"I apologize for that, ma'am," with one arm tucked behind his back he swept her plate up from the white tablecloth. "If you just give me one moment, I will take care of that for you and bring it right back out."

"Alright," the woman lowered her voice.

"Sir," the boy turned to the elderly man seated across from her, "would you like me to take your entrée back and keep it hot in the kitchen while we correct our mistake?"

"No," the man coughed and a clump of mashed potatoes caught on his lip. "It will be just fine."

Spinning on his heels, the boy walked briskly back toward the kitchen.

There is a sort of counter-culture that exists in the restaurant industry that only those who have worked in it can understand. It is easy to see how it develops. Most employees of a given establishment are either in high school or college, so their responsibilities and discretions are already limited. Typically, their shifts range from some time late afternoon until some time around midnight, which equates to late-night partying and sleeping till noon. They are paid in cash each night they work, so they always have money on hand, which means instant access to whatever Remedies they please. All of these factors, combined with the fact that they have constant exposure to a fully stocked bar and plenty of idle time to socialize with fellow misfits, have the makings of an entertaining lifestyle.

"Table 421 says her filet is bleeding!" the boy dropped the plate down on the stainless steel table.

"What was the temp on it?" the chef called through the rectangular heating window.

"Well done," the boy passed the plate to the tattooed man.

"That is well done! If I cook it any more, it will be burnt!" the chef picked up the filet with his tongs. "What do you want me to do?"

"Burn it," the boy shrugged.

"Tell that old hag that if she wants shoe leather, she can go somewhere else!" he flung the piece of meat down on the grill.

"Hey, man," a hand tapped his shoulder, "are you ready to take these?"

One of the boy's co-workers stood with a round serving tray of small glasses balanced on the palm of his hand. The boy picked up two of the glasses and passed one through to the chef. Clank. Thump. Swallow.

"I'm going to kill the guy at Table 60," another co-worker burst into the kitchen. "I swear, if he doesn't stop making stupid jokes every time I go to the table, I'm going to reach across and choke him."

"You aren't a difficult person to pick on," the boy teased. "Next time he says something, you should start to cry."

"I think that would only make him laugh more," the co-worker tossed a handful of silverware into a rinse bucket; "I'm dragging tonight. You want one of these?" He passed a small capsuled Remedy to the boy.

"Fifty-three left a half bottle of wine on their table. Who wants in?" a third co-worker asked as he walked through the swinging kitchen doors.

Tossing the capsule in his mouth, the boy grabbed the bottle by the neck and poured a mouthful of the liquid down his throat.

"How long on that steak, chef?" he called out.

"Two minutes," the chef replied. "Hey, what are we getting into tonight?"

"I'm not sure," the boy took another swallow of the bottle. "We'll figure something out."

Wiping the back of his mouth, he pushed through the kitchen doors and strolled gracefully back out into the dining room.

"The chef does apologize for the filet," he said to the woman. "He is correcting that for you and, in just another minute or two, I'll bring that right back out."

"Alright," the woman smiled. "Thank you very much."

The boy nodded politely and walked to the front of the restaurant. The hostess's stomach protruded with an easy seven months of pregnancy as she stood at the entrance, punching buttons on her cell phone.

"What's up, darling?" he kissed her cheek. "How you feeling? How's the little guy?"

"Good," she replied, "...just a couple more months."

"How are you doing, little buddy?" he squatted down to her stomach. "How's it going in there?"

"Say, 'I'd be a whole lot better if you stopped keeping my daddy out till four in the morning,' " the hostess said in her best baby imitation.

"Hey, that's not my fault!" the boy rose back up, "I only make the bad suggestions; he is the one who decides to go along with them."

She rolled her eyes and laughed as the boy moved to the bar.

"What's the plan for tonight?" the bartender said, slapping his hand. "Anything going on after work?"

"I'm sure we will stir something up," the boy leaned against the wooden bar.

"Cool, you trying to catch a smoke?" the bartender asked.

"Yeah, in a minute," the boy replied. "I've got to run this filet back out first."

"Alright, come get me when you're ready."

The woman was sitting patiently at the table when the boy hurried past and back to the kitchen. The chef was positioning the filet in the center of the plate when the boy came through the double doors.

"Here is your hockey puck," he said, spinning the plate into the heating window.

"Thanks," the boy scooped it up and turned back toward the dining room.

"Hey, man," the chef called to the boy, "you want to smoke?"

"In a second," he called over his shoulder as he pushed through the doors.

Despite the slight euphoric tingling that crept up his spine, the boy kept elegant balance as he walked to the table and lowered the plate in front of the woman.

"Do you want to give that a try and make sure that's OK for you?" the boy folded his hands and waited for the woman.

She picked up the knife, cut a sliver of the charcoaled beef, and bit into it.

"This is how it is supposed to be," she said, her wrinkled jaw working the overcooked steak, "...much better."

With a smile and a nod, the boy turned and walked back into the kitchen. Snatching the phone off the wall, he pressed the intercom button and dialed the numbers to the bar.

"Yeah?" the bartender answered.

"Meet me out back," the boy said.

"Will do," he replied. "I'm going to mix up a drink; you want one?"

"But of course," the boy chuckled.

There is some sort of added endurance that comes with working at a restaurant. Perhaps the relentless onslaught of a busy Saturday night builds the stamina to withstand the exhaustion of watching the sun rise with blurred vision.

The boy blinked and scanned the room. Empty bottles and cans stood in hollow rows across his coffee table. Wrappers and plastic bags from some poisonous late-night fast food establishment were scattered on the floor around the table. Ally slept peacefully on the

329

sofa, her keys clenched in her fist. The boy assumed that she had been the one to retrieve the food, but he could not remember. The bartender sat in the chair across the room and dusted little bits of planted Remedy into a device, while the chef sat beside him, licking his lips. I lounged next to the boy on the smaller sofa and he looked at me with weary eyes.

"You coming out?" the bartender pointed to the glass device as he rose to his feet.

The boy shook his head; he had already taken his sleeping pills; he would be fine. Hooking his arm around my neck, I lifted him to his feet. His eyes were sagging and dry as I walked him up the stairs and to his bedroom. He collapsed on the mattress like a desolate tower of emptiness. I tenderly tucked a blanket around him and loomed in his doorway until he fell asleep.

His arms were folded on the desk, cradling his sleeping head, when I came through the front door of the cabin. Something about the past few weeks had been particularly taxing on the boy. I glared at him with disappointment as I marched to his side. It was our most crucial time, and he wasted it with sleep. Now was when I needed him most—when he needed me most—and that was how I found him. We were nearing the final preparations, and he slept. I had no choice but to be angry.

"Get up!" I drew back my fist and planted it firmly into his ribcage.

He grunted and lifted his head up from the desk.

I pulled back my fist again. "We are running out of time!"

I drove it down into his mouth and he tipped backward in his chair and spilled onto the floor. He touched his fingertips to his lips and dabbed the cool blood that dripped from the gash. It was what he needed. I lifted my shoe and drove it down onto his chest.

"Stop taking breaks!" I kicked him forcefully in the side.

He grunted again but maintained his passive defiance. Enraged, I snatched handfuls of the pages from the desk and threw them across the room. A glimpse of sorrow stained his eyes as he watched them soar in crinkled forms to the ground. Gripping the side of the desk, I flipped it over, sending the rest of his work raining to the floor. I then turned my attention back to him. I swung my foot again quickly against his ribcage. His chest cavity moaned, but his face remained unchanged. I brought my heel down hard against his stomach, and he sprayed air and blood from his lungs. I knew that I could get to him. I saw the weakness quivering in his eyes and I pounced upon it. Leaping on top of him, I fired a volley of punches to his ribcage. The faint sizzle of the half of orb grew louder for a moment, then dwindled to a murmur. He lifted his head to attempt escape, but I drove it back against the ground with my fist. A small gash exploded across his forehead. Inhaling steadily, I pounded my punches again against his flexing chest. He drew in a harsh lungful, and the half of orb roared for a moment before fading. With every fraction of strength that I could channel to my muscles, I smashed my fists against his bruising ribs until I thought they might cave in. I almost didn't hear the steady flaring of the ignited half of orb over the heartbroken howl that escaped the boy's throat, but I could feel its fire burning beneath my fists. My shoulders were heaving and my knuckles were bloody wounds as I rolled off the boy and onto my back. He laid, his chest heaving in painful gasps, his lips still spluttering the same blood that oozed from his forehead. Gently stroking his battered chest, he turned to me.

"Thank you," he wheezed, and I nodded with satisfaction.

The boy sat down on the saggy brown sofa and stared at the burgundy carpet.

Mae lowered herself down into her computer chair and stared at the white of her wall.

Something stirred in his chest, and the boy checked his cell phone. Nothing.

Switching on her computer screen, Mae scanned the names of the people online. Nothing. She picked up the framed picture from her desk and contemplated it. It was a photograph of the boy playing the banjo at her cousin's house in Austin. Sighing, she lowered it to the desk and leaned back in her chair.

The boy rubbed his stinging eyes and tried to remember an earlier time, a time before he had sat down. He hadn't always been there, on that couch.

Mae chuckled as she traced her finger along the top of the desk where she had stood to keep her cell phone from cutting the boy off. She stared at the open air and released another heavy sigh.

He turned to me, seated beside him, and I could tell that his eyes were searching for some distant memory. He always looked so pathetic when he made such unattainable attempts. I passed him the smoking device, and he took it reluctantly.

Mae slipped on her flip-flops and grabbed her keys.

I held the flame across the distorted blank space and touched it to the sizzling planted Remedy.

Mae started her van and sped down the dark country road.

He took a deep lungful and returned to us. Will sat on the other side of him, and he was the next to take the device. The boy recognized the melody that drifted from the speakers. He listened closer.

Mae flipped through the radio stations as she cruised toward her friend's apartment.

The boy's eyes distinguished more of their friends seated in the other chairs around the room; most of their faces were familiar. He could now discern the music that came from the stereo. It was some amateur tracks that he and Ian had recorded on his computer. They had composed a small compilation of songs and recorded them onto a CD. The boy had forgotten that Will had a copy.

Mae shifted her van into park and trudged up the metal stairs to the apartment door.

"What the hell are we listening to?" the boy turned to Will. "Turn this crap off."

"It's good stuff," Will laughed. "I like to chill to some nice smooth love ballads."

"Love ballads?!" the boy scoffed. "They aren't love ballads! Are they?"

"Uh," Will increased the volume, "they are definitely love ballads, dude. All of the songs you write are love ballads."

The rest of the room agreed.

The boy assaulted his memory.

"The question is, what is the story?" Will passed the device back to the boy, but he refused it.

The story. The half of orb rattled his ribcage. The boy dug into the darkest recesses of his emotions. The story?

"I'm assuming that they were about Mae?" Will puffed on the pipe.

Saline and water stung the boy's eyes. Mae. He had not heard that name in...he didn't know how long.

"What was the story with that girl? I've never actually heard it," Will continued.

The boy licked his lips and probed his mind. He could feel his heart again behind his chest.

"Is everything alright?" her friend asked as he and Mae sat on his sofa. "How are you feeling?"

"Not so good," Mae replied.

"I can tell," her friend sighed. "We haven't had a late-night visit in a long time."

"I'm sorry," Mae shook her head, "I just couldn't sleep. I don't know what it is. It was so long ago."

"Some things stick with you," her friend said soothingly.

"It's just because it was such an intense thing," Mae tried to explain. "It happened in such a profound way."

"You know," her friend sat back, "I've never heard the whole story of how it happened."

The half of orb shifted inside of her.

"It's a long one...," Mae said cautiously.

"I've got time," her friend smiled.

I inched closer to the boy and listened carefully as he began to tell the story of how he and Mae met. I watched as he forced his struggling memory to recall the details of their relationship. His words grew with conviction as the story progressed. His eyes widened as his mind regurgitated the distant memories. By the time he was halfway through his recollecting, he was no longer telling it to his friends, but he was speaking to himself. They had faded into a distant haze of smoke, but he sat with rising enthusiasm as he remembered Mae.

Mae sat on the edge of her friend's sofa as she told him their story with much less difficulty. She remembered it well. Her friend listened with uncommon interest as she recounted her time with the boy. She could feel the half of orb searing inside her chest as she talked about the passion and dedication that she and the boy had once had. When she had finished, she was wiping the corners of her eyes with her fingers.

"That really is an amazing story," her friend said, watching her with tender eyes.

"I don't really know why we stopped talking," the boy admitted to the smoky room, "...it just happened."

He scanned the faces. They were watching him with glazed eyes. How long had it been since he had spoken to her? How long had we been sitting on that couch? He looked at me and I shrugged. How long had he been out? How long had this daze lasted? Weeks? Months? Years? He sprang up from the couch. Where was Mae? What had he done? How long had he been a zombie? Had he lost Mae? His eyes burned as he fumbled his phone free from his jeans pocket and stumbled out onto the front porch. Little droplets of rain dripped down from the dark clouds overhead and tapped against his skin as he lifted the phone to his ear.

"Hello?" a weak voice answered.

"Chloe!" the boy croaked. "Chloe!"

"Hey!" his friend said quickly. "What's wrong?"

His eyes were stinging pools of pain, prepared to unleash at any moment.

"How long has it been, Chloe?!" he stammered. "How long ago did Ben die?!"

"What?" Chloe's voice was confused. "What are you talking about?"

"How long has it been?!" he tried to steady the trembling.

"...almost two years," she replied.

The boy staggered backward. His throat muscles convulsed, but he could make no sound. His eyelids bulged with thick, salty tears. He spun around to the sound of the front door opening behind him, but my fist landed across his jaw before he could speak. His feet slipped out from underneath him, and he landed on his back in a puddle of wet mud. My shadow blocked the rays from the front porch light as I stood over him. Rain splashed in his eyes and against his cheeks as he stared up at me with acknowledgment. He was finally beginning to understand how this worked.

Scrambling to his feet, he ripped his keys from his pocket with a muddy fist and darted to his car. I was fast on his heels and leaped into the backseat as quickly as he was in the front. I cackled behind him as his soiled hands gripped the steering wheel and he tore like fire down the asphalt. The tires squealed and veered as he clenched his shivering jaw and squinted his leaking eyes. I howled in his ear and sang along with the sad songs that wept from his stereo, but it only made him drive faster. He knew it as much as I did that we had to get out of there.

Back home, Mae switched off her computer screen and flopped down on her bed. There was no sense in looking for someone who had disappeared. Stretching out along her mattress, she put her earphones in her ears and sunk her head into her pillow. Counting Crows played softly through the tangled wires that she fidgeted between her fingers. She stared down at her toes and thought about the boy. Her eye caught the flashing of her cell phone on the bed beside her. Tugging the wire from her ear, she answered it.

"Hello?" she said sleepily.

"...Hey," the boy replied.

"Wow," her heart fluttered, "...how are you?"

"I'm...alright," the boy laughed. "I guess it's been a long time."

"Yeah!" Mae giggled. "It has. What is going on?"

"Nothing really," the boy lied, "I was telling my friends some old stories about you and it made me think that I should call."

"Yeah? I'm glad you did," she tried to keep her voice level; "I haven't talked to you in a long time. It's funny, I was just telling my friend about you and everything that happened and I realized that it really is an amazing story."

"Yeah, it is," the boy laughed.

There was a long pause of silence.

"So, what's new? Any lucky ladies involved in your life?" she hadn't really meant to ask that.

"Me? Nah," he laughed. Ally was hardly lucky, and she had very little to do with the tragedy that was his life. He wanted to scream that there could never be another girl after her. He wanted to scourge his throat with apologies for what he had done. He wanted to tell her that he never had and never would commit to anyone but her, but all that came out was, "What about you?"

"Nope," she sighed, "just can't quite find what I'm looking for."

The orb twirled inside his chest.

They spent the next hour reminiscing on the phone and filling one another in on the previous two years of life. The boy had very little to say about where he had been; it was not something he was quite sure of himself. When he attempted an apology for the way things had come to a close, Mae brushed it off and said that it had been forgiven over time. They agreed that they would do a better job of staying in contact with one another and said heartfelt goodbyes. It seemed to be a nice resolution to a chapter that had gone unresolved, but when they hung up the phone the boy could not get to sleep because his heart was throbbing for a love he had forgotten; and Mae laid with her headphones on, staring at the ceiling with thin tear tracks dribbling down her cheeks.

The squeaking of the wood planks echoed against the narrow walls as the boy climbed the staircase. He was not sure where he was going or why, but he knew it was the way he was supposed to go. He could not recall how he had come to be on the steps or where they led on either side, but he climbed them with determination. There was nothing familiar about them; he had never seen them before, but something drew him upward.

From halfway up, he could see the thick wooden door that stood at the top of the steps. He knew he did not have the key or any plan in opening the door but it was the way he had to go. His steps were solid and sure as he mounted the stairs. Behind him, he could hear coughing and the clanking of glasses, but he kept his eyes on the door ahead. As he ascended the last step, he reached out his hand to the door and it pushed open with ease. The room it opened to was empty except for a bed. From the doorway, the boy could see a figure bundled beneath the bed covers. As he stepped into the room, Mae sat up slowly in the bed. Her skin was pale and sickly, and her eyes were a faded gray. The boy froze at the sight of her diseased disposition.

"Why did you take so long?" her voice groaned. "Why didn't you come? Why didn't you save me? Now, it's too late."

The boy opened his mouth to respond but stumbled backward down the stairs, rolling and tumbling all the way, her words echoing in his mind.

He shot up in his bed with chills and panting breaths. The night was still and quiet. He could hear the gentle tapping of the rain outside. He tried to focus on its monotony to aid him in finding his way back to sleep, but it did not help. He lay in bed on his back, thinking about Mae for the rest of the night.

As soon as it was an appropriate time, he called her.

"Hey!" she said.

"Hey...," he hadn't exactly thought through the reason he was calling. "Sorry to bother you again so soon."

"Oh, please," she dismissed. "You could never bother me."

"I just wanted to call to make sure that you were OK," he explained. "I had a weird dream last night, and it made me think that you might be sick."

"Not that I know of," Mae chuckled, "I'm pretty sure I'm good. Thanks for checking though. I'm actually glad you called. I need to tell you something...."

"What is it?" the boy scratched his head.

"I know I told you before that I was single...," Mae started, "but I actually have been seeing someone for a little while. I'm sorry. I didn't want to tell you because...I didn't want you to know."

The boy tried to swallow the emotions that bubbled up his throat. The half of orb moaned inside him.

"That's OK," he coughed, "I am actually kind of seeing someone as well. I didn't want you to know either."

"Oh...," Mae forced a smile, "well then, there you go."

"Yeah," the boy's voice was flat.

"OK, well," she was flustered; "I guess I will talk to you sometime soon."

"Alright," all he wanted to do was declare that he loved her, but he could not. It wouldn't make any sense. It had been years. There was no way that he could just reappear and expect her to come back to him. He poured himself a glass of water; his chest was on fire.

"Who was that?" his brother asked as he trudged into the kitchen.

Less than a week before, he and Lily had ended their relationship and his brother had been slightly unstable ever since. He had hardly left the house, was barely eating, and spent most of his time in bed. The boy had done his best to be supportive, but his brother was inconsolable.

"Mae," he said, swallowing another mouthful of water.

"Whoa...really?" his brother adjusted his sweatpants and sat down at the kitchen table.

"Yeah," the boy joined him at the table, "...pretty crazy. It's been a long time."

"I know!" he exclaimed. "What did she want?"

"I called her...," the boy admitted.

"How come?!" his brother's eyebrows shot up.

So, the boy sat at the kitchen table with his brother and told him about the dream and about everything leading up to it. His brother asked questions as he tried to fill in the holes of the story and, before long, the boy was telling the entire saga of their romance from start to finish. His brother watched with enchanted eyes and listened intently to the details that had gone previously untold. The boy could tell that his brother was paralleling the story to the one of him and Lily, but it seemed to lift his spirits.

"What are you going to do?" his brother asked.

The boy thought for a moment.

"I think I've got to go see her...," he realized. "I think I need to go to Texas."

"What?!" his brother exclaimed. "Really?!"

"I think so," the boy said more definitively. "You should come with me! You could use a vacation."

His brother scratched his chin.

"Alright!" he said after a moment. "I'll go! I could probably use a few days away."

"Awesome!" the boy drummed his fingers on the table.

Could he actually do that? Could he just pack up and go after her? She said that she was seeing someone, but how could that stop the necessity of true love? He could not let her go that easily.

"Are we really going to do this?" his brother smiled. "When do you want to go?"

"As soon as possible," the boy recalled the words 'too late' from his dream. "Let's go tomorrow."

"Are you serious?" his brother chuckled.

"I'll tell you what," the boy contemplated, "I'm going to go into work tonight and see if it is even possible for me to get the time off. If I can pull it off, then it's a sign, and we leave tomorrow."

"OK," his brother agreed. "Let's see what happens."

The rain was still drumming heavily against the earth that evening, so the boy yanked his black pea coat from the closet and pulled it on before venturing out to the restaurant. He parked his car in the parking lot and raced in through the entrance. With a quick wave hello to his co-workers, he darted up the stairs and into the offices. His manager was sitting behind her desk shuffling papers when he came rushing in.

"Hey!" she said politely. "What's up?"

"I've got somewhat of a crazy request...," he sat down across from her and told the story that he had come to know well.

He spoke with passion and conviction and attempted to capture the significance of the trip. He told it from beginning to end, omitting no detail, because there was power in their saga.

"I have known you for a couple years now," she said when he had finished, "and I have never heard you speak with so much passion about anything. That is the most beautiful, romantic story that I have ever heard. I could not agree more that you should go and rescue your true love. What is it that you need me to do?"

The boy could not believe his ears. No more than six months earlier, his great grandmother had passed away and this same manager had denied him the day off to attend the funeral. He worked every holiday, every weekend, and well over 40 hours every week. There was simply no reason why she should be so accommodating. There was power in their story.

"I need off the next two days. I want to leave tomorrow." He held his breath.

"Done," she said flatly. "Anything else?"

He clapped his hands together.

"That's all," he laughed. "Really? Just like that, I can go?"

"You have to go," she nodded. "You need this girl."

The boy leaped up from the chair and the half of orb leaped up inside of him. Finally people were beginning to understand the necessity and severity of true love. True love is powerful enough that it can allow people to rectify the wrong decisions of their past. True love is devoted enough that it can withstand years and distance. It is blind enough that it can overlook the most horrendous mistakes.

He glided down the stairs and out the front door. The sky had gotten darker and the rain was pouring down in heavy sheets, but that could not diminish the boy's excitement. He relished the storm because it was natural and he appreciated the beauty in all things natural. I told you, everything was different with Mae on his mind. Flipping up his jacket collar, he funneled the rain down his back. Let love rule.

As soon as he arrived back home, he purchased two plane tickets to Texas. He knew it was what he had to do. He knew that he simply could not survive without her. He waited until the tickets were secured and bought before he called her. One way or another, he had to see her.

"Hey!" she said. "How are you?"

"I'm good," his voice was nervous. "What are you up to tonight?"

"Actually...," she replied, "I'm going down to the inlet with some friends. There are some cool bars down there so we are going to go hang out."

"Are you staying the night down there?" the boy asked carefully. "Or will you be back home tonight?"

"Um...I'm not sure," she giggled. "It depends on how much I drink. Why? What's going on?"

"What are you doing tomorrow?" he could not steady his breathing.

"No plans," she laughed.

"Do you want to get some coffee...?" the boy chuckled.

"Wait...what?" she smiled. "How would we do that?"

"I bought a plane ticket...," he held his breath. "I fly in to Texas tomorrow. I have to see you. I can't go another day without seeing you."

"Oh my gosh...," the breath caught in her throat, "...I love you."

"Yeah?" the boy laughed. "You do? Really?"

"Yes!" she exclaimed. "I love you so much! I need to see you, too! Are you serious?! Are you really coming tomorrow?!"

"Yeah!" his shoulders sank with relief. "My brother is coming with me. We fly in tomorrow night at 8:34."

"...and you are coming just to see me?" her voice was full of ecstatic disbelief.

"I'm coming because I have to see you. Is that OK?" he asked. "Can you pick us up from the airport? Will you have time to hang out?"

"Uh, that is absolutely perfect! I will make time!" she exclaimed. "I can't believe this! I am so excited!"

"Me, too!" he laughed. "I can't wait to see you."

"I can't wait to see you! I can't believe I am picking you up tomorrow!" she could not stop laughing.

"Awesome," the boy smiled. "Well, then I will see you tomorrow."

"I am so excited," she said, "I love you so much."

"I love you...," it felt so refreshing to be able to say that again.

From the darkest shadows of the backyard, I watched as he paced along his patio. I was glad to see him happy. I believed I had done well in helping him finding her love again. Everything was once again as it should have been for the boy; but while I watched him treading back and forth in the rain, an uneasy feeling stirred inside of me. As I faded backward into the shadows, something told me that the boy would require my assistance again.

twenty-three

The pinkish-orange glow of the lights below illuminated the small square of the airplane window as they descended into Mae's city. His brother lay awkwardly in the comfortless chair beside him, his mouth drooping, his eyes closed peacefully. The boy had not even considered the thought of sleep. It would have been a convenient way to pass the time, but there was no chance that he could calm his anxious heart enough to settle down into sleep. In just a few moments, he would have the girl of his dreams back where she belonged, in the embrace of his arms. The half of orb was trembling with excitement inside him. He may not have been able to recall every aspect of the previous two years of his life, but he knew that he had never stopped loving Mae. He could not remember what exactly it was that had caused him to push her away, but he realized that it was the most detrimental mistake of his life. He had not been the same since he had lost her or since he had lost Ben. It had something to do with the combination of the two, he vaguely recollected. He had never truly intended to lose Mae. He was just looking for a way to ease the pressures of life. Things were happening too quickly, and he was afraid that he could not keep up with the changes. What if Mae had actually been pregnant? He rubbed the top of his head with his hand. They would have had a three-year-old. The thought actually made him smile, but there was more than that. She had been weeks away from leaving everything behind for him. He was young; he was afraid of that sacrifice. He looked at his sleeping brother. It was his brother's addiction that dealt the first blow to the boy's stability. That is what first sent him spiraling away from Mae. Now, his brother was accompanying him on the quest to make it right. Even in the way his brother slept, the boy could see the gloom that saturated his presence. It must have been nearly four years that he and Lily had been together. They were no strangers to loss. He felt the jerk of the wheels making contact with the tarmac beneath the rumbling body of the airplane. They were two sinners on a journey to salvation.

His brother's eyes opened to the jostling of the chairs, and he looked to the boy with falsified anticipation. The boy could tell by his reminiscent smile that he had been someplace much more desirable. His eyes seemed touched with a lingering tinge of alienation in being rocketed back to reality. The fluorescent lights blipped on and the boy jumped to his feet. His brother rose more slowly, stretching his back and still adjusting to the limitations of actuality. Tugging his bag free from the compartment overhead, the boy slung it across his back and moved quickly down the aisle and out into the terminal.

"Are you sure you are still going to recognize her?" his brother asked once he had caught up.

The boy laughed. Luke had asked the same thing when he and the boy had gone to meet Mae for the first time. Recognizing her back then would not have been difficult either, had they been in the same airport. It wasn't really a matter of recognizing her face or her image. Had she changed her hair color and worn a disguise, he still would have known her. It was the stomach-turning feeling of complete and utter belonging that identified her. It was the excitement that seized his throat and the tranquility that soothed his mind. It was that burning in his chest and that feeling that he was just steps away from being whole again. He squeezed his arms around her waist and lifted her off the ground.

"I've been waiting for you...," she giggled.

"I got a little lost...," he smiled.

Their hotel was not far from the airport, so they loaded into Mae's van and she took them there. The boy could not restrain his eyes from staring at her as she drove. She was like some sort of make-believe dream.

The hotel rooms were small but comfortable. Mae and the boy stretched out together on one bed while his brother reclined on the other, flipping the remote through the shoddy hotel programming.

She kept her head burrowed against his chest, and he hooked his arm around her hip while his brother told her about Lily.

"I just miss her," his brother explained. "It's that simple. I don't know if I am supposed to marry her or not, but I do know that I don't like being without her!"

"You've got to tell her that," the boy traced his finger along Mae's waist.

"I've tried," his brother shrugged. "She doesn't want to talk to me...."

"That's hard," Mae's voice was empathetic. "Give her time. I'm sure she will come around." She rubbed her hand against the boy's stomach.

"Yeah...," his brother sighed, "I'm going to call her."

"Alright, we will give you some privacy," the boy stroked Mae's hair. "You want to go for a walk?"

"Sure!" Mae climbed up from the bed, and the two moved out into the hallway.

Taking her by the hand, the boy walked with her along the thin carpeted passageway.

"I can't believe you actually came," Mae smiled as her flip-flops slapped against her heels.

They stopped at the elevator, and the boy pressed the down arrow.

"I had to," he replied confidently. "I really can't be without you."

"I don't think I can be without you either," she sighed, "but there are some complications...." Mae slowed to a stop and looked at the boy with concerned eyes.

'If this is love,' the boy could hear Adam sing, 'then we're gonna have to think about the consequences.' They sat down on two chairs in the hotel lobby.

"What complications?" the boy asked earnestly.

He would do whatever it took. He would do anything not to lose her again.

"Well, I told you that I'm seeing someone...," her mouth twisted apologetically, "and I know that you are seeing someone...."

Was he? He couldn't remember the last time he had seen or

spoken to Ally; it had been weeks. Their relationship was teetering on the edge of a cliff just waiting for that final push. He could never be what she wanted. She was looking for a committed boyfriend, but the boy's heart would never be committed to anyone but Mae, ever. She could see that fact in his eyes, and she slid her hands over his.

"This is what I want," she said. "I want us to be together. I just need to deal with my situation first."

"I completely understand and respect that," the boy agreed. "My situation has almost eradicated itself, but I still need to do the same."

"But I love you...," she assured. "I always have, and I want to be with you. I just want to go about it the right way."

"Absolutely," he nodded. "Do you want to get some air?"

Mae nodded, and she and the boy walked out of the hotel and into the parking lot. She unlocked her van, and the two climbed into the back seat.

They stayed closed inside there for hours, talking about how much they had missed one another and laughing about the past.

"Do you remember that dog in the bushes?!" Mae clapped her hands together and laughed.

"How could I forget?" the boy chuckled. "That little thing was nuts!"

"He did it like all night!" she laughed again.

Instinctively, the boy leaned in and pressed his lips against hers. It was like heaven. It was like coming home—like going back to who he truly was. He closed his eyes, and the two halves of orb flared with passion. Her eyelids fluttered as he pulled back slowly and collected herself.

"I'm sorry...," the boy whispered, "if that wasn't OK."

"No," Mae licked her lips, "...it was perfect. It's all I want to do...it's just...."

"No, I understand," the boy shook his head. "You're right...."

She jumped toward him and they kissed again, laughing at one another while they held their lips together.

"Stay with me tonight," he tucked her hair behind her ear.

"I wish I could...," she sighed. "I'm sure my mom would love that." She checked the clock. "I've got to go!"

With a quick goodnight, the boy hopped from the back of her van and Mae moved to the driver's seat.

"I will come get you tomorrow!" Mae called from her window as she sped from the parking lot.

The boy waved goodbye and pinched a cigarette from his pocket. Sparking the end, he thought about the way things had happened. He and Mae were right for each other—there was no doubt about that in his mind—but he could not understand why it had taken so much for him to realize that. She had been willing and committed since the beginning. He was the one who had run from it. Fortunately, she had still been willing when he finally crawled from the dark hole inside himself. It seemed impossible, but maybe all the suffering that he had endured would cause him to love her even more. He took a long drag from his cigarette and blew it up into the dense Texas air.

Mae picked the boy and his brother up early the next morning for breakfast. Their flight was not until six that evening, but Mae had to work at one o'clock. She had tried to get someone to cover the shift, but with only one day's notice, it was almost impossible to take off work.

"I'm sorry that you have to sit at the airport for so long," Mae said as she drove. "I wish I could work something out."

"We'll be fine," the boy assured her. "We didn't give you much time to work out your schedule. I'm just glad you had off this morning."

"Me, too," Mae smiled. "So, did you quit wearing seatbelts or something?"

The boy shrugged; the buckle hung loosely behind his shoulder.

"I guess so," he said.

He could not recall when he had stopped. It must have been another byproduct of his reckless haze. Up ahead, he could see the bridge that they had driven across on his first visit. He remembered hearing the story of her friend who had the dream of Mae driving her van over the side of the bridge and he shuddered. As they rumbled onto the overpass, the brake lights flashed on the car in front of them. Mae gasped and her hand shot across the boy's chest as she tapped her brake pedal. The boy smiled; it was the most endearingly protective thing anyone had ever done to him. Mae did not even seem to notice her reaction. The car in from of them let off the brake and accelerated, and Mae casually pivoted her foot to the gas pedal.

"Oh! What do you think of this...?" Mae pressed the "CD" button on her radio.

The boy laughed as the introduction to *Hard Candy* by the Counting Crows played through the speakers. The two had hardly spoken since the CD's release and had never really discussed their feelings toward it.

"I love it," the boy winked. "I think it is fantastic."

"Alright," Mae chuckled, "...me too."

With her now by his side, he sang along again with the lyrics: "She is standing by the water as her smile begins to curl. In this or any other summer, she is something all together different— never just an ordinary girl."

"I still can't believe how much you sound like him...," Mae shook her head as she parked the car outside of the breakfast diner. "How do you do that?"

"Lots of practice," the boy teased.

Breakfast consisted of eggs, bacon, waffles with blueberry topping, orange juice, coffee, and good conversation. They laughed as he and his brother told stories about their youth. Mae talked about her family and her job. She made plans for her next visit to Baltimore, and they all agreed that it had to be as soon as possible. By the time they had finished the meal and paid the check, Mae was nearly running late for work. Jumping up from the table, they raced to the car and Mae sped to the airport. The boy's brother took their bags from the van and walked toward the entrance while the boy said his goodbye. He locked his arms around her waist and held her tightly against his body. The two halves of orbs swam around their chests, basking in the warmth of the other's glow.

"I love you," he said, "...come to me soon."

"I love you, too," she replied, "...I will."

With a final prolonged kiss, they waved goodbye and tore themselves away from one another.

The perpetual proclamations of the overhead speakers kept either of them from finding any sleep. They occupied two rows of chairs that sat back to back. The boy lay on one row with his headphones playing The Shins and Postal Service, while his brother lay on the other with his headphones no doubt oozing some David Gray or Damien Rice ballads. The rest of the time they passed talking about Lily or perusing the trivial shops that lined the terminal. Luckily, their plane was on time; I don't think they could have lasted another minute on those hollow plastic chairs, inhaling the sugary scent of sticky buns.

On the way home, they both slept. He propped himself up against the airplane window, and his brother leaned his head against his shoulder. The boy could finally rest easy in the knowledge that they had made right what he had destroyed.

For the first two weeks, everything was as it should have been. Immediately upon his arrival home, the boy called Ally and told her what she already knew. It was a fairly painless severance; they both had known from the beginning that it was temporary and they hadn't spoken in weeks. That same day, Mae put an end to things with her someone and she called the boy and the two made it official. Everything drifted back to the perfect way that they had remembered it being. They started talking on the phone again every night, they called each other throughout the day just to soak up their love, and they told everyone about their story. The boy's friends laughed at his star-struck dedication and gawked at his refusal of Remedies. He was back on love, and that was the only remedy he required. He spent less time with Will and more time with his co-workers and Joe. His steps were lighter at work because when he got off he knew, if nothing else, there would be a voicemail from Mae wishing him goodnight. It was exactly how they used to be—they never fought, always laughed, and were forever in love. For two weeks.

There are times when I am writing that I realize I have made a mistake. It is at this point that I invert my pencil, trace back to my error, and scratch at it with my eraser until it is extinguished from the clean white of my paper. I have typically found that the harder that I have pressed the lead of the pencil to the page, the darker the markings and the harder I must scratch with my eraser to be rid of them. It does not happen often, but there are times that no matter how fervently I scratch, I can still distinguish gray tracings and smudges amidst my work. I have spent hours working my eraser down to its metal casing and my fingers to their bones and emerged disheveled, my eyes taunted by the faint shading of my mistake. Sometimes the pencil markings are just so dark that they cannot be erased.

The boy swung open the refrigerator and snatched a bottle of water from the shelf. It had been a long night at work and he was going in early the following morning. He had declined all offers to go out that evening and was only waiting on a call from Mae to finish off his night. His cell phone rang in his pocket. There she was, perfect timing as always.

"Hey gorgeous," he answered.

"...hey," she sniffled.

"What's wrong?!" the boy froze.

"Nothing...," she swallowed, "I need to tell you something."

"What is it?" the boy leaned against the counter.

"I-I just can't do it," her voice shook, "...I was at a bar tonight...and I ran into that guy that I told you I was seeing...."

The boy could feel the lump forming in his throat; the half of orb wailed beneath his chest.

"He starting talking to me...," she went on, "and he asked me what it was about you that took me away...he asked if you just knew me better than he did...and I said yes...." The boy took a deep relieved breath. "...but then he started crying...and I just don't know what to do...this distance is so hard for us...."

"Wait," the boy rubbed his head. "What are you saying? What do you mean? We know how to do this. What happened?"

"...I got back together with him," she sighed. "I-I'm sorry."

The boy was speechless.

"...I-I-I don't understand," he choked. "Why? Because he cried?! I thought everything was good."

"It is! It was! I don't know," she stammered. "Yes, because he cried! It's just so difficult. We are just so far apart. I don't know if I could go through all that again."

"Through what?" the boy searched his memory, "...are you worried that it's going to happen again? Is that why you are doing this? You think I'm going to do the same thing?"

"No...I don't know," she said. "I'm sorry. There is nothing else I can do."

She couldn't bear the thought of hurting someone. Unfortunately, the boy had still not rediscovered the ability to cry.

"Alright...," he said with defeat, "...I will let you go."

"OK," she mumbled, "...I still would like to talk...please call me whenever you want...."

"Yeah," the boy chuckled, "...you know what the worst part is? It would be completely different if I lived there."

"You're right...," she sighed. "It would."

Slamming his phone shut, he shoved it into his pocket and rubbed his hands over his face. How could that have just happened? Jerking open the refrigerator door, he tossed the bottled water back onto the shelf and snatched up a six-pack of liquid Remedy. There was simply no way he could let her go again. The half of orb pounded wildly against his ribcage. Twisting the cap off the first bottle, he kicked open his back door and staggered out onto his patio. He poured a swallow down his throat and lit up a cigarette. There was no way he was going to survive. He drained half the bottle in one swallow. She had gone back? That was it? He jerked out his cell phone and began scrolling through the numbers. He was going out somewhere after all. Before he had the chance to make a call, the doorbell rang. He took one long drag before he flicked his cigarette to the ground and emptied the rest of his bottle into his stomach. He twisted the cap off another bottle before tugging open the back door. The doorbell rang again. It was me. I happen to be in the business of heartbreak, and I had a dose of just what he was after. He swung open the door and saw me standing there in my funeral black garb and he knew, right then, that we still had a long road ahead of us.

twenty-four

The crushed rows of tablet Remedy stretched like mountains of unstained snow across the polished top of the boy's wood-framed television. When they were not coddling the fragile demands of high-class diners or draining the taps at local bars, the boy and his co-workers could often be found ingesting the tangy particles of the numbing substance. It ricocheted in streams through the cotton paper and up into the passageway, where it dissolved into the bloodline and coursed throughout the veins. I stood amongst them in their semi-circle as they took turns bowing to their deliverance. Sharp trails of pain shot to the boy's brain as he straightened his back and pinched between his eyes. I handed him his bottle and he sloshed some liquid Remedy into his mouth. He could already feel the tingle of the desensitization warming his fingertips. Soon, he would be securely wrapped in his refuge of apathy. It was only in that haven that he could escape the merciless badgering of his thoughts. His mind still visited her, but something in those tiny tablets detached his weary heart from having any reaction.

Once the television top had been cleared of all antidotes, the five of us pushed open the bedroom door and emerged removed of all feeling. Like tranquilized lions, we prowled civilization, our eyes crazed balls of instability but our disposition as gentle as mice. It was different from the Remedies we were used to. These served strictly as coping mechanisms and aided in the tolerance of weekly sorrow. That is what our lifestyle had become.

Once you have experienced the limitless potential of true love, it is impossible to find happiness in anything else. All other romantic encounters become deficient comparisons to the beauty in what you once had. No matter how hard you may try, you simply cannot shake the vivid devotion to that only true experience. In a way, it has cheapened the significance of any other relationship. Love has become a foolish inkling that instigates poor decisions and false commitments and eventually leads to unnecessary heartache. It is no longer a meaningful contract; instead, it is a trite bargain of distrust and dramatics. Disloyalty is common and arguments are sport, and the only thing that sustains you is the empty promise of change. Time is not a blessing but is often times a chore, and indulgences are tallied favors that are stored in the memory arsenal for altercation ammunition. Perhaps worst of all, you have become a calloused ex-lover with no patience for mediocrity. In his defense, anyone who pursued a relationship with the boy was well aware that the train they were boarding was bound to wreck. He was not secretive with his lifestyle or the condition of his heart. He never claimed to be anything he was not.

"You think you are so smooth," Brooke was standing in the kitchen with her arms folded across her stomach when the boy entered. She had been the first to attempt to tame his impetuous heart.

"What are you talking about?" he sighed. It seemed that she was constantly in the mood for confrontation.

"Do you think I am an idiot?!" she glared into his murky eyes. "I know what you do!" She must have noticed the cloud of apathy that trailed around our heads.

"I'm not hiding anything," he scratched his nose.

By this point, the co-workers and I had made our way out the back door and onto the patio.

"You are better than those guys!" she planted her hands on her hips. "I don't know why you waste your time with their immaturity! You are so much smarter than them! You don't need to be a part of what they do!"

"I'm not better than anyone," the boy said calmly, "and you don't know what I need. I don't know who you think I am, but I think that you're confused."

"I know more about who you are than you think," she argued. "You can try to bury yourself as deep as you want. I can still see who you are, and this is not it. I would not even waste my time with someone like this!" she pressed her pointer finger into his chest.

"This is who I am," the boy shrugged, "I cannot help that. I don't know what it is that you are trying to change or why you think it is possible."

The conversation was migrating to a familiar argument.

"That is what people do!" she shook her hands in the air. "You make changes and sacrifices until you become the person that you should be!"

He and Mae never argued.

"So, I'm not the person that I should be?" he raised an eyebrow.

"No!" she exclaimed. "Not yet! That is why I am trying to tell you that you need to change!"

"Did you honestly get into this relationship thinking that you were going to change who I am?" he asked.

"Eventually!" she said. "I was talking to the girls about it the other night. If you aren't willing to make sacrifices and modify behaviors in relationships, they will never work!"

"Really?" the boy laughed. "What behavioral changes are you making?"

"What would you like me to change?!" her face twisted with confusion.

"Nothing," the boy replied, "because I would never ask you to do that. I think it is a ridiculous request."

"Well, it's my request!" she slapped her hand against her leg.

"I can't help who I am," the boy shrugged.

"And I can't stand another minute with who you are," she threw up her arms. "If you won't change for me, then you must not love me." The boy did not respond. "...Just tell me one thing," she paused, "what is it that makes you so numb? I can tell you weren't always this way. What happened to you that has made you like this? Where did your life go so wrong?"

"...it's a long story," he shoved his tingling fingers into his pocket.

"Well...I hope you can find someone who can straighten it all out for you," she yanked her keys from her pocket, "because it isn't me."

With that, she pressed a compassionate kiss against his cheek and they never spoke again. There was no remorse; there was no animosity. It just was not true love.

Holly hooked her arm around the boy's wrist as they strolled along the laminated floor of the mall. Her bright red hair bounced against her shoulders as she swiveled her head back and forth at the passing stores.

"You are going to buy me a pair of shoes, right?" she tugged at his elbow.

"What?" the boy's head was pounding from the night before. "Why am I going to do that?"

"Because!" she squealed. "I need a new pair!"

"Didn't you just get some last week?" the boy squinted at the blaring fluorescent lights overhead.

"Yeah," Holly giggled, "but I'm sick of them already...."

The boy's eyes caught sight of the jewelry store up ahead and his heart flinched. He had not noticed the shop since his trip years before when he ventured in and picked the ring that he had hoped Mae would wear. He had chosen it with sacred care, but rather than shimmering on her finger, more than likely it sat in a smudged display case, or worse, was wrapped around the skin of another woman. He shuddered at the thought and watched the store entrance with tender caution.

"Oh!" Holly jerked the boy's arm. "Look at those earrings!" She pointed to a set of sparkling diamond studs in the jewelry store window.

"I thought you said shoes!" the boy tried to tug her away from the glass, but her feet were anchored to the floor.

"I wonder how much they are!" she gaped. "Let's go check! Please!"

Before he could respond, she was hauling him through the entrance. A sales clerk pounced on them as soon as their shoes touched the carpet.

"You looking for anything in particular?" the man asked.

The boy did not recognize him.

"How much are those earrings?" Holly pointed into the case.

The keys around the man's wrist rattled as he unlocked the sliding case door and lifted the earrings from the display. The boy probed the store; he did not see the family friend who had taken the deposit on Mae's engagement ring.

"That's not bad...," she looked at the price tag, "birthday present?" She held them up to the boy.

"I don't know if I have any outfits that I could wear them with," the boy teased, but his eyes were flashing around the empty shop.

"I really like them," Holly laughed, "for me!"

"Would you like to try them on?" the clerk smiled.

"No...," the boy cut in, "we aren't going to buy them today. We can come back and look at them."

Holly held the diamonds to her ears.

"Alright," she moaned to the clerk, "I guess I'll have to come back to try them on."

A door in the back of the store swung open. The boy didn't even have to look; he knew who it was. He put his hand on Holly's shoulder and tried to move her toward the exit but the salesman was giving her his final pitch.

"And the good thing is that all of our items in stock right now are anywhere from 50 to 75% off...," his hands waved in swirls in front of her face.

The boy inched closer to the door; he could hear the footsteps approaching from behind them.

"That is a beautiful set," the man said from over his shoulder.

"See," Holly slapped the boy's stomach with the back of her hand, "he likes them!"

"Maybe he will buy them for you!" the boy smiled, turning slowly to face the man.

His glossy head was entirely bald now, and it wrinkled in recognition of the boy.

"Young man!" he extended his hand, "How are you? It's been years!"

"I'm doing well," the boy replied cautiously, shaking his hand. "It's been a long time."

His feet shifted awkwardly on the carpet. He could feel the man's eyes drilling into his.

"Well," the boy cracked through the uneasy silence, "we've got to get out of here before she makes me buy one of everything."

"Alright...," the man waved, "hopefully I will see you in here again sometime soon...." He raised an eyebrow.

"I don't think so...," the boy shook his head as he and Holly walked out of the store, "not again." It doesn't happen twice.

The piercing sting of reliving that memory made his eyes water. It had been so long ago; he would have done anything to go back to that day. It was one of the last days that he ever remembered being truly happy. He would have done whatever it took to change that. He cursed his stupidity in ever having let Mae go. He had pushed her away the first time and had not pulled her close enough the second. Now she was in someone else's arms. The thought made his stomach boil. The piece of orb sizzled between his shoulders. It missed its other half.

"What was that all about?" Holly asked once they were far enough away.

"What?" the boy crashed back to reality. "He is an old friend of my parents'."

"OK," Holly went on, "so, what was with the awkwardness and strange comments?"

"What do you mean?" the boy stared at the ground.

"Forget it," Holly swatted the air with her hand, "I honestly don't care enough. Keep your secrets."

Mae knew everything there was to know about him.

"Oh, before I forget," she switched topics, "tonight is my little brother's birthday. I want you to come over for dinner."

"I can't," the boy sucked air between his teeth. "I'm going out with the guys tonight. I told them last week that I would."

"What?" she stopped in the middle of the walkway. "It is my brother's birthday. Why do you think that you can go out with the guys?"

"Because you never told me it was your brother's birthday and I already have plans," the boy explained. "I'm sorry, but I've been bailing on these guys for the past two weeks. I promised I'd be there tonight."

"Well, call them and tell them you aren't going to make it," she walked quickly away from him.

"I can't do that, Holly," he caught up to her. "I'll see your brother later-"

"You will do it," she interrupted, "because you know how important it is to me, so I have no doubt that you will be there."

Violently adjusting her purse on her shoulder, she spun on her heels and marched away from him down the gallery.

Some days were good. Mae would remain a faded thought that stirred in the back of his mind and only surfaced a handful of times, which he could typically quell with a Remedy before I could blunder him with blows. Other days were bad. Everywhere he turned, he was reminded of her. Texas A&M would be on the morning sports news, it would be raining, Train would be on the radio on his way to work singing some brilliant song that seemed like it was written about Mae and the boy, he would drive past the park where the two of them had gotten caught by the police officer, and he would flip to her number in his cell phone. On those days, she would never escape his mind. She was all he could think about. No matter how hard he would try to relieve his mind of the relentless assault of love, he could not break free from the truth. I was always by his side on those days, and we would coexist with mutual understanding. This had been one of those days. It had started with the jeweler in the mall and had only spiraled from there. He had driven past the elementary school parking lot where they had spent that sunny Saturday afternoon, and he had stumbled across the cologne that Mae had loved in his closet. He had gone to a coffee shop and sat at a small table that lined the wall. A girl sat in the chair behind him and a familiar scent drifted from her table. The half of orb thumped against his ribcage as he recalled the smell of Mae's hair. The girl behind him had the same aroma. More than likely it was some sort of perfume or shampoo that the two girls had in common, but to the boy it was the sweet bouquet of heaven. Pressing his headphones into his ears he tuned in Counting Crows, closed his eyes, and quietly slid down into his chair. It was a lovely form of torture that he practiced on himself. Even though it burned his eyes and tormented his soul, there was something soothing in remembering her existence. It consoled him to know that someone so flawless existed in so foul a world.

He could not change the fact that he loved her and he refused to forget her. I do not believe that he could have, had he wanted to, anyway.

It seemed like something more than just coincidence on the days like this where he could not escape her. I believe that their connection is so great that it binds them across the distance. On those days that he can not pry his mind from her, I believe that he is equally as impressed on her heart. It is on those days when he is most consumed with her memory that she attempts to contact him or remembers their days together. I believe these unmistakable correlations are the doings of the orb. When I first began this story, I told you that the more powerful the orb is, the more glorious and potent is its destruction. I told you that in those quiet moments of stillness, you can hear the orb weeping, that it bellows and howls from its core. I said that this orb lingered much longer than most and that it was different from any other I had seen. I told you that it was mankind's only hope. I told you that this orb almost won. I believe that there are times when people are incapable of realizing their own necessities and the orb is forced to take over. I believe that their seemingly coincidental connection is actually the work of the two halves of the orb, stretching across the distance, in a desperate attempt to become whole again. I believe that their only hope is that the orbs believe in love.

Stretching out along his mattress, he flipped through his stack of pictures. He had stowed them away in a shoebox buried somewhere in the bottom of his closet but the occurrences of the day had caused him to excavate them. There was no real point in attempting to entomb the items; a day such as that would come at least once a week and cause him to uncover the dusty remains. He flipped open the small beige book that she had made and given to him on their first meeting. The small weathered rectangular card sat tucked inside the cover. The boy's eyes stung as he read the curling calligraphy: "This card entitles the bearer to one free kiss from any willing man, woman, or beast." Rolling onto his back, he scooped his phone up from the bed cover and sent Mae a message. "If we weren't meant to be," it said, "what was it all for?" Before he could lower his phone back to the mattress, it rang. Instinctively, he flipped it open.

"Hello?" he croaked.

"Hey, buddy!" Joe replied, "Were you asleep? Are you alright?"

"Yeah," the boy disguised his voice, "I'm good."

"Cool," Joe said. "Are we still on? You ready to meet up?"

"Uh...," the boy skimmed the pictures strewn across his bed.

"Uh oh," Joe snickered. "Is Holly giving you trouble? Does she not want you to come out?"

She wanted him to come to dinner, but he had already made plans. More than likely, he would have canceled them for her, but what they had wasn't true. He was in love with another girl that he could not attain and she had spent all day on his mind; there was no other choice than to go out with his friends and fill his stomach with enough liquid Remedy that his head became a swooning sea of apathy.

"Where are we meeting?" the boy climbed from the bed and snatched up his keys.

As we sped down the asphalt toward the bar, the boy seized his vibrating phone from his pocket. It was a message from Mae in response to his question of what their relationship had been for. He lifted it to his face. "Nostalgia?" it read. I erupted with laughter over his shoulder in the backseat and he jammed his foot down against the gas pedal.

Joe, the boy, three of their friends, and I made light work of squashing the bar. As quickly as the bottles, glasses, and injections tapped the shiny surface, we inhaled them with earnest need. Clank. Clank. Thump. Swallow. Swallow. Swallow. The bartender stood panting and we stood cheering, everyone except the boy. He was propped against the bar with his phone held loosely to his ear.

"Hello?" I heard him say.

"Hey," it was Holly. "Where are you?"

"Out," he replied.

"I know you're out! I can hear the music!" her voice was full of fury. "But you should be at my house for my brother's birthday!"

The boy poured the last generous swallow of liquid into his throat; for some reason, he could still feel.

"Birt-day" he said, chuckling at the memory.

"Don't you laugh!" Holly yelled. "This isn't funny! I am completely serious! This is unacceptable!"

"So, you're mad at me now?" he rattled the ice inside his glass and tipped it to his lips.

359

Holly let out an exasperated sigh. "...I think I'm done with you now...," she said.

"Yeah, OK," the boy laughed through the ice cubes in his drink.

I didn't catch the last thing she said to him; he may not have either. He clamped his phone shut and tossed it onto the bar top. I eyed him and he nodded. Clank. Thump. Swallow. He wobbled in his chair.

"Was that Holly?" one of his friends asked. The boy nodded. "What happened?"

"I guess we just broke up," he shrugged and motioned to the bartender for another.

"What?! Really?!" his friend's eyes widened, "...Are you OK?"

"Right as rain," the boy took the liquid from the bartender and drained some into his stomach.

"He doesn't give a shit!" Joe blurted out. "Never has! Not since Mae!"

The boy's muscles flexed at the name, and he took another quick swallow.

"He's so hooked on that girl...," Joe staggered over to the stool next to him, "it's ridiculous! He wants his relationships to fail! He sabotages them on purpose. He won't give any other girl a chance because he doesn't think that anyone else in this humongous world can measure up to Mae. So, he destroys his relationships on purpose!"

The boy kept his eyes on the glass in front of him. The rest of us moved closer to Joe, who was preaching beside him.

"Did you know," Joe slurred, "that he is so stuck on this girl that he has refused to sleep with any of his girlfriends since?"

The crowd let out a series of "ahhh"s and the boy could feel the widened eyeballs staring at him like some spectacle. He did not reply. Joe was drunk. He just happened to be the target; and he wasn't saying anything that wasn't true.

"I'd say he's done about all he can," Joe threw up his hands. "Now Mae, on the other hand, she is obviously just some ignorant, selfish, broad who needs –"

The boy drew his arm back, spun around in his stool, and drove his clenched fist into Joe's mouth. His friend staggered backward and crashed into a wall. The boy was up from the stool and I had sprung to his side. Everyone else remained in their seats.

"Hey!" the bartender called. "You've got to get out of here!" He was pointing at the boy.

"Don't you talk about her," the boy's voice was shaky as he spoke to his friend.

Joe slouched against the wall and touched his fingertips to his split lip.

"Out! Now!" the bartender called louder, "Or I'm calling the cops!"

Digging a handful of cash out of his pocket, the boy slapped it down on the bar top and we walked out the door.

I drove us home that evening. I tore down the side streets and sailed around the lethal turns while the boy puffed cigarettes and worked his knuckles in the passenger seat. The radio played what I commanded it to and the boy's heart sunk into his stomach as Frou Frou sang "Let Go" and Ray Lamontagne sang "Forever My Friend." I was the reckless tormentor, and he was my defenseless victim. Barely dodging other cars and following only our flickering headlights, I took him on a ride through hell, then parked us safely in his driveway. Staggering in through the front door, we stumbled down the stairs, and I helped him to his room. His eyelids were half closed as I assisted him in gathering up the items and pictures of Mae from his mattress and storing them away in his closet. He kept one particular photograph of her standing in the sand with the ocean behind her from the box and held it up for me to see.

"She is standing by the water as her smile begins to curl. In this or any other summer, she is something all together different—never just an ordinary girl" he sang the Counting Crows lyrics to me and I put the *Hard Candy* CD into the stereo.

As he lay in bed with her picture and listened to the music, the lyrics had a very different impact than they once had on the boy. What he once saw as optimistic had become a dreary depiction of his life. Just a few lines down from the lyrics he had just sung, he noticed the words, "Time expands and then contracts when you are spinning in the grips of someone who is not an ordinary girl" and he thought about the haze that had stolen the two years just after he had lost her.

"You send your lover off to China, then you wait for her to call. You put your girl up on a pedestal, then you wait for her to fall. I put my summers back in a letter and I hide it from the world. All the regrets you can't forget are somehow pressed upon a picture in the face of such an ordinary girl," Adam sang, and the boy agreed. In "American Girls," he sang about the obsessive nature of missing something that you have taken for granted. "Richard Manuel Is Dead" explained how your own inhibitions are the things that make it impossible for you to keep love, or anything significant, in your life. "New Frontier" was about the difficulty in trying to communicate everything that has built up inside of you to someone else; and "Carriage" was about how the most beautifully flawless relationships can come to an end and be looked back on as some insignificant fragment of your past. The boy lay in his bed that night with her photograph and rediscovered the meaning of the album. He fell asleep that night heartbroken and understood.

The heavy mahogany door sent swirls of air back toward the boy as he slowly dragged it open. Long rows of stained glass lined the vaulted hallway that led to the church sanctuary. The boy's flip-flops echoed with cautious distress as he walked slowly onward. There was an eerie sort of discomfort that hung like thick gelatin in the air. He felt underdressed and woefully underprepared. As he inhaled a smooth steady breath, something expanded with his lungs inside his chest. He recalled the orb and pressed forward. Two small wooden doors blocked the entrance to the sanctuary at the end of the hallway. Tugging one open, the boy stepped into a towering chapel with tall arched windows and brilliant golden lights that lowered from the ceiling. Rich red carpet stretched down the aisle past long columns of dark-hued pews. His chest lit ablaze at the sight of Mae smiling, standing at the altar, in a flowing white gown. He looked down at his rubber flip-flops and scowled; they would not do. When he lifted his eyes back to Mae, she was no longer looking at him, but her face was turned to another man who stood, dressed to the throat with fancies, at the altar beside her. He could hear the seared crackling of his ribcage. Two instinctive steps forward sent him spiraling downward.

He landed with his feet hard against the concrete sidewalk in the sultry night air. His flip-flops had been replaced by the restrictive leather of formal shoes. Occasional cars flashed past along the radiant blacktop that paved beside the curbed walkway. Through the pulsations of the sleeting vehicles, the boy could distinguish Mae sitting with her knees together on a slated bench. The white gown had disappeared and she now wore a more casual outfit with flip-flops. The boy smiled with relief as she tucked her hair behind her ear and glanced at him through the traffic. His chest flinched with horror as he noticed the same man from the altar squatted down on one knee beside the bench. A small black box sat open in the palm of his hand, which he extended to Mae. Springing down from the curb, the boy raced out into the street. Mae was sliding the sparkling circular band around her finger and the boy was halfway across the street, when the blaring of the horn announced the blinding headlights of a truck. Mae kept her dazzled eyes locked on her shimmering finger as the half of orb inside the boy's chest roared at the impact of the truck's front end. In lifeless swoops, his body sailed up into the dense crystal air, his limbs flapping with broken despondence. In a shattering thump, he landed square into the paralyzing pavement.

I was beside him when his shoulders jerked up from the mattress and his eyes shot open in red-veined bolts of terror. His forehead glistened and his mouth hung open, sucking in frenzied gulps of oxygen. The muscles in his forearms flexed with twisting tendons and bone as his crazed hands gripped his bunched sheets. A snap of my fingers at the end of his nose brought his attention to me. His eyes were two shivering balls of terror as he looked into my comforting face. "Wake up...," I said, placing my hand gently upon his shoulder, "it is time that I introduced myself."

twenty-five

There is an endless number of song lyrics and old sayings that discuss the closing of something significant. For as long as time can recall, people have been seeking some way to embody that sentimental combination of loss and accomplishment that comes with a conclusion. Belle & Sebastian express their sorrow with the lyrics, "At the final moment, I cried. I always cry at endings." A wise old Englishman is credited with coining the defeated expression, "All good things must come to an end." No matter how gradual or abrupt the finale, there is no way to fully prepare for the outcome. Each new beginning that we launch is done with the knowledge that it will eventually come to an end, and yet, in those final hours of termination, we are frantically trying to reconcile our minds before bracing for the cataclysmic impact. These sayings and songs are attempted manifestations of what it feels like after the dust of completion has settled. I do not claim to be a lyricist and I do not claim to be wise, but I have come to understand that much of the fate of an ending or change falls on individual decisions. Things are often put to rest because people choose to put them there. Usually, good things come to an end because people allow them to. It was like the man and his barn; in completing the final stages, he brought upon himself the consequence of its construction. There is no way to deny the overwhelming nostalgic sense of loss that comes with the closing of anything, but it is a definite series of decisions that bring about that closing. Ultimately, in the end, we are just trying to right the beginnings that we've made wrong.

It took two weeks for the boy to digest his dream. He gave himself two weeks to indulge in the most tantalizing Remedies in an effort to cope with the notion of Mae's engagement. For fourteen days, he bombarded his body and mind with numbing substances. On the sixth day, he pulled the book she had made him from his closet and scribbled out the words, "Utter desperation tastes like whiskey." On the ninth day, he sketched below it, "Love does not expire." On the thirteenth day, he fell asleep with the book under his pillow; on the fourteenth day, he let the Remedies go. They had buried him twice and he knew that a third time might bury him so deep that I could not dig him out. In those two weeks, he used them to battle the knowledge of her engagement; then he abandoned them and called her.

Their conversation was as amusing and lengthy as it had always been. The boy asked questions about work and her life and family. He loved the sound of her voice. He sought to keep her talking for as long as possible just to soak in her essence through the vibrations of her vocal cords.

"There is something that I need to tell you...," she said at the end of their conversation, "it's kind of a big deal."

The orb stirred beneath their chests. He already knew what she was going to say. She was going to tell him that she was engaged, and he was not prepared react. He had poisoned himself for two weeks just to be dull enough to comprehend the possibility. The tone in her voice told him that it had become an actuality. He knew that hearing her say it would have destroyed him.

"I don't know that I am ready for big news right now...," the boy said sheepishly.

"Alright...," she sound relieved. "I'll talk to you about it another time."

Mae and the boy had four more conversations just like that one. They would call one another and laugh until the necessity for sleep dragged them to their beds. At the end of each conversation, Mae would make a halfhearted attempt to tell the boy her news. I would sit with him in his car, parked in his driveway, and listen to him make obvious excuses as to why the information should wait.

"I think I already know what it is," he would say.

"You do?!" she would exclaim.

"Yeah...I think so...," he would reply slowly, "so, I don't think we need to talk about it."

"OK," she would laugh.

It was his way of extending the consecutive days over which they spoke. Right before they hung up, Mae would make a comment about calling him the next day because she still wanted to talk about it eventually. To the boy, the conversations were the only moments of peace that he could find. Otherwise, he spent his time with me, walking the vacant streets or sitting in his room and discussing his unfailing love for Mae. It was on the fifth day that she brought their late-night talks to an end.

"I know that I have been avoiding telling you this," her voice was determined.

"Why?" the boy swallowed hard. "Is it something bad?"

"I don't think so," she replied, "...no, it's not...I'm just worried about how you are going to react...."

The boy clenched his teeth, and the half of orb twisted inside of him.

"I'm just going to say it...," Mae cautioned.

"No, don't!" the boy tried to quell the scorching sensation that inched up his ribcage, but he was too late.

"...I am engaged!" she exhaled, and the half of orb bellowed within him.

He had known it was coming, but there was no way he could have prepared. From behind his chair, I swung my hand across the side of his head. Our decisions bring about these outcomes.

They were still bringing the conversation to a close when we backed from his driveway and fled to the nearby mourner's den. Five tall glasses did nothing for his disposition; it only caused his stool to wobble and his shoulders to slouch. I occupied the chair beside him and each time his liquid ran low, I would order him another and coax it into his stomach. By the time the bartender called the last dosing, the boy's eyes were a misty red. He hooked his arm around my neck and I walked him to the car. Slinging him laboriously into the passenger seat, I climbed behind the wheel and sped off into the night.

His head was spinning and his heart ached when he crawled from bed the following morning. Before staggering into the shower, he checked his phone for a call from Mae, but there was nothing. A steaming cup of coffee seemed to take the throb from his head, so I took him for a ride out into the country and he watched the passing fences as The Killers danced through the stereo speakers.

A large maple tree sprouted in the middle of one of the open fields like a rising mushroom cloud. The boy peered at it with pensive eyes until it faded into the reflection of our rearview mirror. Honeysuckles perfumed the air from small patches that clustered the hillside along the curving pavement like little natural golden trumpets. The boy only lightly inhaled their enticing scent from the wind. It was clear that he had lost some of his appreciation for the naturally beautiful things in life. He perceived them now with sentimental grief. He was defeated. Even in his darkest, most desolate times, somewhere in the core of his heart, he had always known that he and Mae would be together again. The diminishment of that probability meant the diminishment of his outlook on life. There was limited beauty seen in a setting sun because, without the prospect of Mae, there was little reason to look for any at all. Two riders on horseback trotted past, and the boy commented on the clumsiness of their gait. The countryside lilacs were out in full bloom, but he remarked on the superiority of the previous year's blossoms. I jabbed my finger in his ribs and reminded him that he was the only one to blame for the reason it had become this way. He winced at the truth and slumped quietly against the passenger door, the little beauty that there was left in life whizzing by his window unnoticed.

Mae pulled open the ornate glass doors and stepped out across the glossy tile floor. Her flip-flops echoed in the vacancy of the lofty reception hall ceiling. An olive-skinned woman wearing narrow glasses and a grey skirt suit stood in the center of the floor with her hands folded in front of her.

"We are extremely flexible with the setup of the room," the woman explained, "but we do have some recommended layouts depending on what you are looking for."

Mae's eyes scaled the smooth white walls that climbed around white-clothed tables and chairs with ribbons and bows. Tall vases of flowers spouted from the centers of the circular tables and hung in bouquets around the room.

"This is beautiful," Mae smiled.

The boy and I meandered down the city sidewalk with our

hands buried deep in our pockets. The overcast light that leaked through the gathering clouds above amplified the soft gray of the concrete. The boy glared at it as we trampled over its smooth seams and jagged cracks. He was a dead man walking. Each day that we would venture out into the land of the living, I would become more aware of his disintegration. It was as if his legs were still marching against the earth and his heart was still pumping blood to hollow veins, but there was nothing alive inside. He was becoming the things that he despised. A combination of fear and determination had aided him in forfeiting every Remedy except for liquid. As a result, it was becoming increasingly difficult to limit his weekly visits to the neighborhood saloon.

The clamor of the late afternoon crowd spilled from the open door of a passing bar. I tapped his arm and motioned him inside with a nod but he shook his head, denying my request, and continued down the sidewalk. Perhaps he was improving. His hand burrowed deeper into his pocket and he produced a pack of cigarettes, a pen, and a thin notepad. Lighting a stick to his lips, he flipped open the pad and jotted out the words, "My head is surrounded by these haunting addictions of mine. Two of which are in my pocket and one is in your eyes." I smirked over his shoulder.

"There is only one person I know who is dedicated enough to carry a notepad around in case a moment of creativity strikes!" a voice called from up ahead. "What's up, brother?!!"

The boy lifted his eyes from his notes to see Jack strolling eagerly toward us. It had been roughly two years since the boy had seen him stumbling on stage and even longer since they had spoken, but he instantly recognized his old friend. In fact, he looked much more like himself than he had when the boy last saw him. The natural swirls of color had returned to his eyes, lips, and face; he had regained a healthy physique, and he looked genuinely happy.

"Hey!" the boy clasped Jack's hand. "It's been a long time! How are things?"

"Really good, actually!" Jack laughed. "Things are going really well. I got a job working for an insurance company down here...," the boy noticed his oxford shirt and pleated pants, "...I'm renting a pretty nice place around the corner...met a girl...."

"Wow," the boy raised his eyebrows. "What about the band?

You still playing music?"

"Nah. You know...," Jack shrugged his shoulders and shook his head, "it just got to be too much. I, uh...got a little too caught up in it all."

"Yeah," his voice was empathetic, "I heard you were hard up for a little while."

Jack stared into his eyes and nodded, "We hit a rough patch."

"Me, too...," the boy's eyes shifted to the pavement, "but you look like you're doing well! You found a girl...congratulations!"

"Yeah!" Jack smiled. "She's great! You were right! It is worth waiting for. Now I finally understand what you were talking about all that time. Speaking of which, did you ever find that girl—the perfect one you were always looking for?"

A lump caught in the boy's throat; the half of orb shivered in his chest.

"Yeah...I did," he chuckled awkwardly and I sprung to his side.

"Tell him...," I whispered harshly, "tell him that you broke her heart! Tell him that you are still in love with her!" He tried to push me away but I would not budge from his ear. "Tell him!"

"Listen," Jack's face softened, "...I'm sorry for the way things went down between you and me. It wasn't right. I've changed a lot since then...and I just wanted to apologize. You were lucky to get out when you did."

"No big deal," the boy attempted to remain indifferent. "It was a long time ago. We were young."

"Yes, we were," Jack smirked. "I just want to make sure I didn't totally screw you over. But you look alright. You look like you're doing well."

"Doing well?!" I sneered in the boy's ear. "I would hardly say that! Tell him about Mae! Tell him what you did! We'll see how he thinks you look then!"

"Well...," Jack checked his shiny silver watch, "it was good to see you, brother. I've got to get home to meet the girlfriend, but we should definitely get together some time. It would be good to catch up. Is your phone number still the same?"

"Yeah, it is," the boy replied. "Give me a call sometime."

"Alright," Jack shook his hand goodbye. "Take care of yourself."

The boy chuckled; it was not as easy as it sounded. I watched as his old companion strutted away from us and down the sidewalk. As soon as he had rounded the corner, I turned my attention to the boy.

"Why didn't you tell him?!" I shrieked and drove my fist against his ear. "Are you afraid to admit that it was your fault?! Are you afraid to admit that you are the reason you lost the only thing that you've ever loved?!"

Gripping the side of his head, boy staggered away from me, but I stalked his steps. He held up his arm to stop my advance but I clutched his wrist and twisted it behind his back until his muscles pulled and popped.

"There isn't any hope for you," I shoved my knuckles into his back and pushed against him. I followed on his heels as he stumbled forward and caught himself on a nearby lamppost.

"I know!" He spun around and snatched my jacket with both hands; his eyes were red with anger, "I know I lost the only girl I'll ever love! I know it was my fault!"

He thrust me to the side and limped back toward the bar. Straightening my jacket, I chuckled and followed behind him.

The olive-skinned woman in the skirt suit spun a sheet of paper around and slid it across the smooth black desk. Mae and her fiancé sat in two cushioned chairs opposite her, their faces beaming with excitement.

"Thank you so much for everything!" Mae smiled as she touched a pen to the paper and began signing her name, "I know we put you through a lot!"

"That's alright!" the woman laughed, "...it's funny. People are always so grateful to me, but my job really isn't that difficult. It's actually quite nice. I get to spend my time with people who have found true love! It isn't too hard working with soul mates!"

Mae's pen paused at the final swirl of her signature and her eyes stared a hole into the desk. The half of orb fluttered in her chest and her mind drifted backward.

"Congratulations!" the woman tugged the paper from beneath Mae's hand. "This contract reserves our hall for your wedding reception!"

Mae's lips formed a distant smile.

The boy dropped down in his awkward computer chair and flipped on the computer monitor. Running his hand over his head, he scrolled through the names of his contacts that were online. Stretched out along his floor, I watched him with curiosity. It was no longer something that he did voluntarily. It was an instinctive habit. She was never there, but the possibility that she could be required regular reminiscent glances.

The chair squeaked loudly as the boy noticed Mae's name on the list and jumped forward. I shot up from the carpet and peered over his shoulder. Her online status indicated that she was not at her computer, but the boy clicked her name anyway. A small box appeared revealing the contents of her profile. The box was almost entirely empty with white space except for two small words written in thick black – "ichi-go ichi-e." The boy scanned the words again; he had never seen them before. The half of orb rumbled inside of him as he typed the words into his search browser. A list of explanations appeared on his screen. The words were taken from a historic Japanese tea philosophy, loosely translating to mean "each moment, only once." The philosophy stems from the idea that no moment in life will ever be repeated and, as such, should be indulged to the passionate fullest. Things like time and decisions are irrelevant; all that is significant is the potential of that singular moment. I watched the boy's mind working as he processed the enlightenment. There are no mistakes, no repeats, no penance for wrong doings; there is only the capability of what is here and what is now—only the utilization of what is known and what is believed. He reached into his pocket robotically and pulled out his ringing cell phone.

"Hello?" he opened the phone.

"Hey!" Chloe erupted with bubbles. "What are you doing?! Are you sitting down?! Should you sit down or should you stand up?!"

"What?" the boy's mind entered the conversation. "I-I'm sitting down. What's going on?!"

"I've got some big news!" she squealed.

"Oh no...," the boy braced himself, "is it bad?"

"No! It's fantastic!" Chloe laughed. "I'm engaged!"

"What?!" the chair squeaked again as the boy jumped to his

feet. "Are you serious?! That's insane! I-I mean, that's awesome, but insane!"

Chloe could hardly hear his response over her own ecstatic laughter.

"Will you come?!" her voice shook with joy. "Promise you will be at the wedding!"

"Of course!" he chuckled. "Of course I will be there. I wouldn't miss it for the moon!" The world was overrated.

"Alright," Chloe giggled, "I've got to go make some more calls! I just wanted to let you know!"

"Thanks," he smiled, "and congratulations! It's good to see you so happy."

"Thank you!" her voice was a whole octave higher. "I'll call you soon! Love you!"

"Alright," the boy chuckled, but she had already hung up.

Dropping the phone into his pocket, he rubbed the top of his head and thought about how far they had come. His brother was clean—again, Jack was an insurance agent—that made him laugh, Chloe was engaged—so was Mae, and he—he was a desperate mess. Drumming his fingers on the desk, he looked up at me and I smiled down at him.

"I think I like the blues with the yellows," Mae commented as she perused the flower shop aisle.

Three tiered rows of brilliant floral arrangements stretched alongside her, and she stopped at the occasional bouquet for closer examination or to inhale its enchanting fragrance. Her cousin walked beside her, lifting buds from the bunches and showing them to her.

"What are you looking for?" her cousin asked after Mae nonchalantly refused the eighth suggestion.

"...I'm not sure...," Mae sighed, her attention locked on a red rose—its pedals still wrapped tightly into a bud.

There was typically never any good reason to get out of bed before noon. That just meant that the ache of missing Mae began much earlier. Without the glow of her smile, there was little reason to get out of bed at all. The boy was surprised that the sun still rose. It split into narrow beams through the slats of his bedroom window blinds and shone in on his floor. He glanced at the clock — 10:07. The new

Counting Crows CD had been available on display shelves for seven minutes. It was called *Saturday Nights & Sunday Mornings*, and it was the reason that he had gotten out of bed that morning.

Yanking on a pair of jeans, he tugged a T-shirt over his head and slipped on a pair of loose tennis shoes. He tried to sneak out of the house without me but I was standing, waiting by his car, when he walked out into the driveway. There may have been a time when he could have left me behind, but if so, it had been so long that I could hardly recall it. As for the way things were then, we spent nearly every of moment of every day together. He shot me a scornful glare before jerking the keys from his pocket and unlocking the doors.

It was obvious that he was doing his best to ignore my presence in the backseat. He turned up the unique energetic jolts of Modest Mouse, rolled down his windows, and kept his eyes away from the rearview mirror as we cruised to the store. We found a nearby parking space, and the two of us flung open our doors and raced through the entrance. As soon as his feet hit the slim carpeted floor, his head began to swivel with hungry determination. He saw the small black square amid the rows of other plastic wrapped CD cases. Snatching up the disc from the shelf, he studied its cover with awe. It was a two-part concept album. The first half represented the *Saturday Nights* aspect of the title. It was loud and harsh and symbolized the time period in your life where you go out, make bad decisions, and shape an irrevocable catastrophe of your existence. The second half of the album represented the *Sunday Mornings* aspect and was a softer compilation of songs about remorse for the recklessness of all the destruction that occurred in the *Saturday Nights* segment. The boy could hardly comprehend the seamless correlation that the music had to his life as we drove back toward his house. It wept through his speakers and he could feel the emotion in Adam's voice. It was a musical masterpiece—like heaven through hertz. The raw upbeat wit of the singer's self-examination was something the boy had been in dire need of. Fumbling his phone free from his pocket, he dialed Chloe's number.

"It is incredible," he said once she had answered.

"What is?" she asked, her voiced perplexed.

"Don't tell me you haven't gotten it yet...," he replied.

"Gotten what?!" Chloe chuckled with frustration.

"The new Counting Crows," he surrendered. "It came out to-day."

"Oh...," her voice leveled out, "yeah, I've heard most of it.... It's not for me."

"What?!" he exclaimed. "What do you mean?! Why not?!"

"It's just...not for me," she was searching for words. "It's not the music.... It's-it's me. I'm in a different place now than where I used to be, and it just doesn't reach me there."

"What do you mean...you're in a different place? Is it because you're happy? You can no longer relate?" he could not believe his ears.

That was the stuff they had grown up on; it was their lifeline. There was no way to be done. I snickered quietly behind him.

"I'm sorry," she knew that, in his mind, they had just lost a piece of their friendship. "I just can't understand it anymore. It doesn't make me feel the way it used to. Maybe I cannot hear what he is saying anymore or maybe he stopped saying it in a way that could capture me?"

"You went and found happiness...," the boy sighed, "and now you don't get our music anymore."

"I'm sorry...," she replied, "I told you it was me."

"How did you do it?" he asked. "How did you let go of your hurt?"

"Enough became enough," she explained, "and for the first time I truly wanted it gone. So, I turned away and even though it catches up to me on days when the rain is a little more grey or the sun is shining just a little too bright, it stays, for the most part, in the distant rearview."

"I just don't think I'll ever get there," he shifted his car into park.

"Losing Ben did a lot to me," her voice grew more somber, "...it's sad, but sometimes it feels like you have to give up bigger pieces of yourself than you are willing to if you want to let go of the hurt—like you and your writing."

"I couldn't give it up," his eyes burned, "I would die."

"What's the difference?" she replied. He was dead already.

"The fear of the unknown...," he probed his mind, "and the ridiculous hope that there is some sort of light at the end of it all."

"It's not ridiculous," she smiled. "Hold onto it. Take care of yourself. I'll be waiting for you on the other side."

He was glad that Chloe did not find consolation in the new album. That meant that she had truly found her happiness and had let go of her hurt. She deserved that. Enough injuries had plagued her past; she was due. He was happy for her and her emergence, but there was a part of him that could not ignore the wrenching feeling of loss and abandonment. The fact that she had fully arisen from the dark hole that they had dug together meant that he was now alone in it. Leaning back in the driver's seat, he wiped his eyes and exhaled. He had always done his best not to cry at endings.

There was one person he knew would understand. When the rest of the world around him would fall into critical heaps of oppressive debris, she had always been able to salvage him from the wreckage. They spoke the same passionate language. Their two halves of orb were birthed from the same unit. With his phone still clenched in his fist, he sent Mae a message.

"It's heavenly," it read.

I whistled and reclined in the backseat while he anxiously awaited a response.

"Tell me no more," Mae's message replied. "On my way to get it!"

A smile spread across the boy's face; he knew that she would understand. She knew exactly what he was referring to. I watched with ravenous disdain as he popped open his car door and strolled back into the house. Scrambling out to the pavement, I followed him to his bedroom.

He was sprawled out across his mattress when I stalked in behind him. The lights were off, but I could see his grin in the dim glow of his cell phone screen. She had sent him another message.

"I haven't even finished it yet," it read, "but all I can think to say is 'FINALLY.' I've been waiting far too long for this one. I know you have, too."

I scoffed as his smile widened. He shot me a cold glare before replying, "I knew that you would get it. No one else seems to understand this album. Adam is finally coming to terms with the condition of his life and he is learning to appreciate his potential. It's a beautiful album about making some things right as other things are coming to an end."

Shaking my head and chuckling, I walked to the bathroom sink and flipped on the light switch. The boy's eyes were leery as he watched me spin the faucet handle and lift a plastic razor from his medicine cabinet. He was such a desperate fool. Popping the lid from the shaving cream can, I sprayed the thick foam into my palm and spread it across my cheeks. His grinning face lit again in the illumination of his phone.

"It's as wonderful and fascinating and genuine as it ever was with a twist of raw upbeat silliness," she had replied. "I love it. The more I hear, the more I dread the day that he stops. Each album has been a pleasant and necessary surprise."

My mocking smile was even more noticeable surrounded by the heavy white lather. I could feel his angry eyes on me as I scraped the simple razor down the ridges of my throat and watched him in the mirror.

"I couldn't agree more," his message replied. "It's a magnificent parallel of sin and redemption."

I could no longer contain myself. The blades of the razor bounced against my windpipe as it vibrated with laughter.

"Redemption?" I wheezed amidst my cackling. "Redemption? There is no such thing! Not for you, at least!"

He leaped up from the mattress and stormed to the sink.

"What do you want?" he bit his lip and shot furious breaths through his nostrils. "Who are you? What do you want from me?"

Smiling, I tapped the head of the razor against the porcelain sink and let the warm water cascade across its blades.

"It's not a matter of what I want," I pressed the razor again to my neck.

"What is it a matter of then?!" he stepped closer to me. "Why are you here? Why are you in my bathroom?! What are you doing in my life?!"

I consider myself to be fairly patient.

"Relax," I chuckled. "You can use the bathroom in a moment."

"Who are you?!" he shouted. "Why are you tormenting me?

Why won't you just leave me alone?! Why are you hunting me?! What did I do? Why won't you go away?!"

He pushed against my shoulder with his hand. The blade of the razor skipped against my throat, slicing a small flap of my skin. I watched in the reflective glass as the rich dark red dribbled from the slit. I turned to the boy, my black eyes burrowing into him with limitless fury.

"Who is this that questions me?!" I shrieked. "Why won't I leave?! Fool! Do you think that this is where I want to be?! I am as chained to you as you are to me!"

The boy stumbled backward, but I drifted closer to him. His eyes were paralyzed with a fear that I had never seen him possess.

"How dare you accuse me of such things!" I gnashed my teeth. "You think that you have any power against me?! I have existed since the first mistakes of mankind! I am all-encompassing!"

My eyes darkened and I spread out the funeral black fabric of my overcoat. He cowered below me, and I grew above him.

Then I spoke, "I was there with Robert Oppenheimer when he watched his 'little boy' and 'fat man' annihilate 220,000 innocent in a cloud of destruction. I bellowed with laughter when Pope Pius XII decreed his church's noninvolvement in the Second World War. I nurtured, I inspired, I suppressed, I murdered. I held the hand of Geoffroy Therage as he ignited the ignorant flame beneath the innocent soul of Joan of Arc. I peered into his quivering eyes as he questioned his salvation after his deed. I have nourished every bearer of bad decisions and frequented every sinner. I have watched true love die! I was the only one to witness the death of Judas of Iscariot. I tightened the noose around his neck and hummed to his swinging body. I wrapped Pontius Pilate in a blanketing embrace as he wept at the sound of the crucifixion. Don't speak to me about pain! Don't tell me your sorrow! I am pain! I wear sorrow! You want to know who I am?!" The walls of his bedroom trembled. "I will tell you who I am!"

The breath caught in the boy's throat as I thrust my hand inside his chest. My fingers splintered through his ribcage as I worked them toward the radiating center.

"I am whatever you see me as, because I am not a man! I am your remorse!" I screeched with delight as my fingers touched the siz-

377

zling half of orb that pulsated inside him. "I am every sin that anyone has lamented! I am all the wrong outcomes!"

Gripping my fingers around the broken half of orb, I began to squeeze. The boy writhed and groaned in pain.

"I am everything you have ever done wrong! I am your pain in losing your true love! I am the reason thoughts of Ben keep you awake at night!"

The orb flared inside his chest, and I could feel its blue flame charring my fingertips. It seared against my skin and resisted the crushing force of my hand. I squeezed tighter, but the orb burned brighter.

"I am every sense of loss!" I cried. "Do you think it was coincidence that I came into your life when I did?! It was not! Do you know why, at times, I am more distinct to you?! Do you not wonder why I stalk your every action, your every thought?! Is it not suspicious that you have never seen me interact with another human being?!"

His eyes quivered with a beautiful mixture of fear and bewilderment.

"These hands are not my hands!" I cackled. "These are not my eyes! Look at them! This is your depiction of me! This is how you perceive my appearance to be! I have no true physical form! I am abstract! I am your worst nightmare!" It was time that I introduced myself.

"I am Regret!" I howled. "I am your Regret! I am all Regret! And you are to blame for my presence in your life!"

The half of orb sent wailing flames lashing up my arm. Hissing, I released the resilient orb and shrank back from the boy.

"I came to you because you needed me," I snarled.

He was slumped on his back, his chest heaving and intact.

"Do you truly want me gone?" I asked.

The boy nodded, tears streaming down his docile face. The half of orb remained unbroken beneath his unscathed chest, but it now bore the permanent black imprints of my fingertips. He could feel them piercing, five burnt smudges against his deathless love.

"If you want me gone...," I panted, "if you want to fix it...there is only one way. There is no amount of Remedies that can take you back. There is only one way."

Wiping his cheeks with the back of his hands, the boy turned to me.

"You must tell your story," the boy watched my mouth with desperate eyes. "It has always been your rescue. It is what enabled your love. It brought you together the second time. It is your only hope. Write. Tell everyone your story, our story. Remind her—remind Mae— of what it was. Tell it the way that it happened. Alleviate your conscience. Spare no details. Write a book. Remind her of what true love is. Tell the world what true love is. That is the only way that you can truly let go. It is the only way that you can be redeemed. But we must hurry. Write a book. Put it all down. If you can remember what true love was, you can let it go, so that you might find it again. That is the only way." The boy looked at me with aching eyes. "That is the only way to make things right."

It was his suggestion to isolate ourselves up in the cabin. It seemed like the only way that he could escape the distractions and pressures of life. At first, the boy had been reluctant, but within a few weeks, I was able to convince him of the severity of what we were doing. It was the only way that we could achieve our goal in time. So, locked away from the company of civilization, the boy and I began our quest for salvation. We began our journey to right his wrongs.

Mae strolled the cold laminate aisles, her eyes scrutinizing the rows of wedding cake toppers. She traced her finger along the edge of the store shelving and adjusted her purse with her other arm as she walked. The rumbling air-conditioning duct overhead blew chilled swirls down around her as she examined the plastic decorations. As she extended her arm, reaching for one of the toppers, a tingling erupted in the center of her chest. Her hand froze, and her eyes stared through the plastic pair in front of her. A slight flutter of water tickled her eyelids, and her chest expanded as she inhaled a heavy sigh. Her thoughts were of the boy.

———— ∞ ————

The boy's fingers followed along the rugged lettering that was etched into the wooden top of his cabin desk. All his papers were collected in organized stacks except for one, which he stared at with confident resolution. As I moved to his side, I could not remember how long it had been since we had first arrived to my log grave and the boy

379

had carved the words. I read them aloud, "I realize that there may only be one chance that I can change any of this, but it is that one chance that keeps me going. Either way, this is where I leave my hurt. This is where I say goodbye to Regret."

As the final scratches of ink stained the paper, the boy leaned back in his chair and thought about what he had done. He was lucky, he thought. Some people don't get that second chance. He wondered if he would get his.

He scribbled the last words of our story across the final page and placed his cell phone carefully on top of the completed stack. It was finished; it was now up to possibility. If the story repaired the damage done to the orb, he could correct the folly of his life. In recording it all, he could cleanse his conscience of his brother's addiction, pay Ben his due tribute, and alleviate the weight of his own sin. It was the only way that he had any chance of restoring the two halves of the orb, and the only way that he could rid himself of me. He knew that. It was the only way that he could defeat Fate. It was the only thing that could take him back to the beginning. It was the only hope for redemption.

The first signs of spring were oozing through the air by the time we ventured from the cabin. I trailed a few feet behind him as he shuffled down the city sidewalk, his hands buried in his pockets. Every now and then he would glance over his shoulder at me and I would look up nonchalantly at the clouds in the sky and whistle to myself.

He stopped in front of one of the brick row houses and tugged a scrap of paper from his back pocket. Jack had called every week for the previous two months, insisting that the boy attend his weekend cocktail parties. Eventually, the boy had run out of excuses and had succumbed to Jack's persistence. He scanned the address scribbled across the paper before sliding it back into his pocket and trudging up the concrete steps.

Three quick knocks against the thick oak summoned Jack and the boy's old friend threw back the door with a beaming smile.

"Hey! Awesome!" Jack motioned the boy in, "I'm so glad you made it!"

I followed as the boy stepped inside the expansive row home. Smooth bending jazz notes echoed off the brick walls and a handful of well-dressed professionals collected in the center of the shiny hardwood floor.

"Just mixed up some rum & cokes," Jack raised an eyebrow to the boy. "Want one?"

"Yeah, sure" the boy rubbed his hands awkwardly against his jeans.

Two plush white couches lined the brick wall and I lowered myself down onto one as Jack picked a clear glass of brown liquid up from his marble countertop.

"Can't go wrong with the classic," he said, handing the glass to the boy.

I watched the boy with sentimental eyes as he took the first sip of the drink. I had made such a mess of him. Few people ever truly bounce back from that.

"It is so great that you came!" Jack slapped the boy's arm and led him across the wood floor and into his crowd of guests.

"Yeah," the boy smiled and took another quick swallow of his drink. "This is a really nice place."

"Thank you," Jack leaned back and admired the pristine brick and elevated ceilings. "I really like it."

The boy watched me over the rim of his glass while I eyed his friend with sarcastic scrutiny. A smile flashed in the corner of his mouth as he lowered the drink and cleared his throat.

"There is someone I have been wanting to introduce you to!" Jack interrupted our exchange, "Great girl! She is a good friend of mine. She is working on a degree in psychology. She's one of the sweetest people I have ever met. Loves music, the good kind too, like what we used to play."

The boy raised his eyebrows as Jack stepped in amongst the crowd and motioned to the girl's smooth frame. She stood with her back to them, her arms moving gracefully through the air as she talked with a small circle of friends. Her lightly olive-dusted skin gathered the dim light of the room and it clung to her with exclusive consideration.

"Katharine!" Jack called to the girl, "Katharine, I'd like you to meet a friend of mine."

The thin elastic spirals of her hair lifted in the air and bounced gently against her cheeks as she spun to face the boy. Her beautifully soothing eyes shot waves of brilliant forest green into the cold dark centers of the boy's hollow pupils. His eyelids shot open as her glance sent a flurry of lightning to the core of his heart. It leapt inside of him and pounded furiously against his ribcage. Pressing his hand against his chest, he felt the resuscitated muscle dancing inside of him as if it was beating for the first time. Only at that moment did he fully realize how dead he had become. A smile stretched across her mouth as she watched his awe-struck eyes. He inhaled a deep lungful of air as if taking it in for the first time and he exhaled a long shaky breath.

"I'm Katie," she smiled, and the sweet music flooded to his soul. She reached out her hand in that formal way that first encounters require. "It's very nice to meet you."

Each moment happens only once. That was the bitter truth that he battled in his heart. Each moment had happened once for him, and he had let each of them pass him by. But if life had taught him anything, it was to fight—to fight until the bitter end; and that is what he intended to do. He still had some fight left in him. There was still some flame left in that half of orb. He meant to correct his mistakes. He meant to be rid of me. He would succeed. Our journey together had ended within the cold dark walls of that wooden cabin.

I could not help but smirk as I watched their flirtatious dance. I tried to catch the boy's eye as I rose slowly to my feet but there was no way that I could disrupt the captivated stare that he watched her with. It was no bother. I was never much for long goodbyes. She giggled at his devoted charm and he blushed at the glow of her skin.

As for me, I buttoned up my jacket and pulled my last cigarette from its pack. It is only for so long that you can survive with someone like me. Eventually, everyone must make their final attempts to right what they have done wrong. Slinging my things across my back, I ventured out into the city streets. The slushy snow had melted from the warming sidewalks, and the air tasted like the first signs of spring. Inhaling the sweet scent of possibility, I whispered goodbye to the boy and left him to his life.